About the Authors

Clare Connelly was raised in small-town Australia among a family of avid readers. She spent much of her childhood up a tree, Mills & Boon book in hand. She is married to her own real-life hero in a bungalow near the sea with their two children. She is frequently found staring into space – a surefire sign she is in the world of her characters. Writing for Mills & Boon is a long-held dream. Clare can be contacted via clareconnelly.com or on her Facebook page.

USA Today bestselling author **Janice Maynard** loved books and writing even as a child. Now, creating sexy, character-driven romances is her day job! She has written more than seventy-five books and novellas which have sold, collectively, almost three million copies. Janice lives in the shadow of the Great Smoky Mountains with her husband, Charles. They love hiking, travelling, and spending time with family. Connect with Janice at JaniceMaynard.com and on all socials.

Jennie Lucas' parents owned a bookstore, and she grew up surrounded by books, dreaming about faraway lands. At twenty-two she met her future husband and after their marriage, she graduated from university with a degree in English. She started writing books a year later. Jennie won the Romance Writers of America's Golden Heart competition in 2005 and hasn't looked back since. Visit Jennie's website at: jennielucas.com

Christmas Kisses with the Billionaire

CLARE CONNELLY
JANICE MAYNARD
JENNIE LUCAS

MILLS & BOON

First Published in Great Britain 2023
By Mills & Boon, an imprint of HarperCollins*Publishers* Ltd,
1 London Bridge Street, London, SE1 9GF

www.harpercollins.co.uk

HarperCollins*Publishers*
Macken House, 39/40 Mayor Street Upper,
Dublin 1, D01 C9W8, Ireland

Special thanks and acknowledgement are given to Clare Connelly for her contribution to *The Billionaires Club* series.

ISBN: 978-0-263-32115-9

This book is produced from independently certified FSC™ paper to ensure responsible forest management.

For more information visit: www.harpercollins.co.uk/green

Printed and Bound in the UK using 100% Renewable Electricity at CPI Group (UK) Ltd, Croydon, CR0 4YY

THE DEAL

CLARE CONNELLY

For Sharon Villone Doucett, who was one of the first readers to find my books, and who has been such a champion and supporter ever since.

PROLOGUE

Five years earlier, Becksworth Hall,
Wiltshire, England

'You're a Rothsmore, for Christ's sake.'

My father is perhaps the only person more apoplectic than I am.

'She is aware of that.' Surprisingly, my voice comes out clear and calm, even when I feel as if I've run a marathon. I reach for the Scotch on autopilot, topping up my glass. My hand shakes a little. Shock, I suppose.

And I *am* shocked.

'This isn't like Saffron.' My mother wrings her gloved hands in front of her pale peach suit, the wedding corsage still crisp and fragrant. I reach for my own in the buttonhole of my jet-black tuxedo jacket, and dislodge it roughly, pleased when the pearl-tipped pin snags on my finger. A perfect circle of burgundy blood stains the white rose at the decoration's centre.

'How do you know, Mother?'

I don't mean to sound so derisive, but in the four hours since my cousin received a text from my bride's best friend explaining that the love of my life wasn't going to be showing up to our wedding, I've had to endure more platitudes and Saffron-defending than I can stand.

'Well, she's…' Antoinette Rothsmore struggles to describe Saffron. There are any number of words I could offer. *Suitable. Wealthy. Privileged. Appropriate. Beautiful. Cultured.* Words that describe why my parents introduced us and cheered from the sidelines as we hooked up. But the reason we got engaged is simple.

I love her. And she's left me.

'Nice,' my mother finishes, lamely.

Saffron *is* nice.

Too nice for me?

Perhaps.

I haven't seen her in three days, but when I did, she was in full preparation mode for our wedding, reminding me that the photographer from *OK!* magazine would be coming to take pictures of the party so not to let my groomsmen get too messed up on Scotch before the ceremony.

I throw back the single malt and grip the glass tightly. How many have I had? Not enough to make this feel like a distant dream.

'Nobody does this to a Rothsmore.' My father's face has turned a deep shade of puce. I'd think it's sweet that he cares so much except I don't for a second imagine he cares about the fact I just had my heart handed to me in tatters in front of five hundred of Europe's elite. Princes, dukes, CEOs—everyone.

Not that I care about the embarrassment. I care about Saffy. I care about the fact we were supposed to be married and she's sent me a 'Dear John' text via a friend and my cousin.

'What would you like to do, Father? Sue her?'

'If only,' he snaps, then shakes his head. 'Though the last thing this family wants is a scandal. Damn it, Nicholas. What did you do to her?'

I blink, his question something I haven't considered.

What did I do to her?

Is it possible I said or did something to turn her away?

No.

This isn't about me.

This is pure Saffron. Passionate, affectionate, changeable.

I grimace, rubbing a hand over my jaw, neatly trimmed just the way Saffron likes.

I fix Gerald with a firm stare. 'I did nothing, Father, except agree to marry the woman you chose for me.' I don't say the rest. That I fell head over heels in love with her as well.

We used to laugh about the nature of our relationship—how we both knew it was a heavy-handed set-up from our parents. How their interference was like something out of a nursery rhyme. Except we were going to have the last laugh, because we were in love.

We were in love.

When had I started believing in love? What kind of goddamned idiot fool have I become to worship at the altar of something so childish?

I snap the Scotch glass down against the table, a little louder and harder than I intend, and I see my mother jump in my peripheral vision.

I've been an idiot.

There's no such thing as love. No such thing as 'happily ever after'. No such thing as 'meant for each other'.

And suddenly, all I want is to get away from this. From my parents and their expectations, from this life I've been groomed all my life to lead. I want to get away from Saffy, from our wedding, from my damned broken heart.

I want to get drunk, and then I want to get laid—one way or another I'm going to forget Saffy ever existed.

I stumble a little as I head for the door. 'Where are you going?' My mother, behind me, is anxious-sounding.

'Get Alf to fire up the jet.' I hear my own words, slightly slurred.

'But why? You can't leave. What if Saffron comes looking for you?'

I prop an arm on the doorjamb for support, blinking at my mother for several long seconds. 'Then I won't fucking be here.'

CHAPTER ONE

Five years later, Sydney, Australia

Oh, my God. Oh, my God, Oh, my God. There's an ancient grandfather clock against the far wall and it ticks loudly, but I can barely hear it over the desperate rushing of blood in my ears. Am I really going to do this?

The intimate rooms are perfectly climate controlled—it's cool in here but that's not why my skin is marked with delicate goose bumps. I run my hands over my naked legs, waxed and oiled so they're smooth and soft in honour of this assignation.

It's not too late to change your mind, my brain shouts at me.

But I don't really want to change my mind. I made the decision to do this months ago, meticulously planning every detail in order to give myself one night of passion. To give myself a life—even just for one night. It's been too long since I've had anything even remotely resembling a life. Too long since I've let go and enjoyed myself.

I still have too much to do, too much to achieve and, despite the tremendous growth and success of the charity, I want more. I need more. Faster, bigger. My charity is my all, and I'm happy with that.

But my body. Oh, my body. Lately, something seems to have awoken in me, a curiosity, a need I no longer seem able to deny. I want to get laid. No, I want to have sex. Really fantastic sex, and then I want to change back into my signature gown, swan out of this room and become, once more, the woman the world expects me to be.

I flick my gaze to the clock across the room. There are three minutes to go. Three minutes until Nicholas Rothsmore the Third arrives to seduce me.

My heart bounces against my ribs. I swallow. I need more champagne. No. No more champagne. I only had two sips at the party—I know better than to get drunk at something like this.

It's work for me, not play—though I have perfected the art of looking as if I'm playing when I'm not.

But this? Being here in Room Six, the sumptuous décor the last word in elegance and sophistication, dressed only in lingerie, waiting for a man I know solely through the club's exclusive, private online forum?

My pulse notches up a gear.

I'm waiting to have sex with a stranger.

Not just a stranger.

I lie back against the bed, my eyes sweeping shut

as I picture the man in question. Nicholas Rothsmore the Third isn't just a man. He's unbelievably sexy, all tousled hair and rock-hard abs, and a firmly committed playboy. Who better to have one delicious sexual encounter with, no questions asked, before going back to my real life?

I lift a hand to check the bright pink wig is firmly in place, tucked all around the hairline as my stylist showed me, so there's no risk of movement. It's soft and silky, the hair falling in waves to my shoulders. My mask is bright silver and covers not just my eyes, but lower on my face as well, stopping just above my lips, in keeping with the masquerade ball theme downstairs. Of course, I have a separate mask stashed in the wardrobe across the room, as well as my distinctive couture gown, to avoid any likelihood that Nicholas recognises me, after.

After.

Such a delicious word loaded with promise. After this. After sex.

My heart is hammering so hard now I'm surprised it hasn't beaten a hole through the wall of my chest.

I can't have anyone know I'm doing this.

I *never* get involved with clients, and Nicholas is one of the club's most prominent members. The last thing I want is to do anything to undermine the club or my charity. Chance is the reason for all of this.

I doubt anyone has any idea how hard I work behind the scenes. On the surface, I'm Imogen Carmichael, entrepreneur and socialite—my mother's daughter. But behind closed doors, when other people my age are falling in love, getting married, having babies, or even just getting wasted and falling in and out of God knows whose bed, I'm working. I'm working on Chance, I'm working on it, for it, every waking minute, and there's still so much more to do. We're nationwide now, but I want more—there are children all over the world who need what we offer. I've been toying with the idea of opening a London branch for over six months now but I know it's going to take a lot of my time and spread me kind of thin.

That's my focus. That's my life.

It's why this night is perfect for me. It's one night, and with a guy I know to be as interested in serious relationships as I am. Which is to say, not at all. He's perfect one-night stand material, and excitement is shifting through me.

How long has it been since I was with a guy, anyway?

My lips tug downward as I consider that. At least three years. No! Nearly four. Jackson and I broke up just before Christmas.

Yes, it's been a long time and, at nearly thirty, if I don't take control of this, I'm going to grow my virginity back. That's a thing, right? I'm sure I read it in one of those glossy magazines at the airport lounge a while ago. Okay, maybe nothing that drastic, but I am in danger of forgetting what it's like to be touched, kissed, driven wild with pleasure.

And I miss sex. I don't want a relationship, though God knows there are times when I wish I had someone I could talk to, someone I could bounce ideas off. But I don't have the headspace for a boyfriend. Where would I even fit a relationship into my life? And what would that do to Chance?

One day, maybe. When the charity is big enough to run without me, when we're fully established—and not just in America, around the world—maybe then I'll open myself up to something more. But I'm a long way from that, and I'm not going to do anything that might risk what I've spent my life building. I owe it to Abbey to keep my focus, to make this a true success.

The quietest noise sounds, but it might as well have been the tolling of a bell. I'm hyperaware of everything in that moment and I sit up, then push to standing, the stilettos I kicked off by the bed waiting for me. I slip them on and catch my reflection in the mirror across the room.

Holy crap.

I look…like sex on legs. I look like someone who does this all the time. The corset is firm at my back and pushes my breasts up, like two pale orbs, and my legs are curvy and slim. The wig completes the look and the mask adds an element of decadence that is just perfect for The Billionaires' Club.

'Knock, knock.' His cultured British tone would be haughty if it weren't for the permanent husk that thickens his words. 'Is there a Miss Anonymous in there?' My tummy squeezes at his sexy, teasing voice.

'Yeah.' My own voice comes out high-pitched. I suck in a deep breath, cross the plush carpet to the door and grip the handle. It's cold beneath my touch. I count to ten slowly, a trick I learned in school, when my nerves used to get away from me.

Slowly, I draw the door inward, my heart unbearably loud and urgent now.

And at the sight of him, it skids to a stop.

A bead of anxiety runs through me. We planned this secretly on the forum, and my only condition was anonymity. He isn't to know who I am—in fact, I went out of my way to create the impression that I'm some bored housewife just looking to get my rocks off. Naturally, he had no objections to that—if I know one thing for certain about Nicholas it's that he doesn't do commitment or serious.

Which makes him perfect for this. For tonight.

'Come in,' I invite, waving my hand towards the room. These Intimate Rooms were designed with seduction in mind and they have everything a couple could need for a sensual encounter. The bed is bigger than a king, laid with thousand-thread-count sheets. There's a fridge stocked with the finest French champagne money can't buy, a luxurious en suite bathroom with a spa bath and fragrant oils, and members are invited to request a bespoke 'toy chest' if their tastes run in that direction.

Nicholas requested handcuffs and seeing that on

the booking sheet two days earlier made my body break out in a sweat. A good sweat. I haven't been able to stop thinking about it since.

He swaggers into the room, his navy-blue suit slim-fitting and flattering to his trim and toned frame. His eyes take in the room, though I'm sure he's been here before. He crosses to the window—the thick black velvet blinds are drawn for privacy. He flicks the blinds open a little, showing a slice of Sydney Harbour, the unique Opera House right outside the window.

I'm nervous.

Beyond nervous.

I'm full of doubts and desire in equal measure.

I have literally never done anything like this in my entire life.

My tummy loops into a billion knots.

'So.' He turns to face me, his lips flicking in the sexiest smile I've ever seen. My insides burst a little. 'What shall I call you?'

'Miss Anonymous is fine.' My voice sounds so prudish and disapproving. I force a smile.

'Anon for short?' he quips, moving to the fridge as he discards his jacket over the back of the black velvet armchair.

I nod quickly. 'Whatever.' My name doesn't matter.

'You seem nervous.'

Crap. So much for seeming cool and in control. My lips curve into a small smile; his eyes drop to them. My throat goes dry. 'I am, a little.' When all else is lost, go for honesty.

'Why?'

He lifts the top off the champagne expertly and pours two generous glasses. He turns to me, his eyes dragging down from the tip of my head and performing the slowest, most sensual inspection I can imagine. As his eyes shift over my body, I feel as though he's touching me even when he's on the other side of the room.

Slowly, so slowly, he lingers on the generous curves of my breasts, my nipped-in, corseted waist, my hips and lower, so heat flushes my cheeks and I'm grateful for the face mask I wear.

Lower, lower, over my legs, until, at my ankles, he grins. 'Nice shoes.'

I lift a foot, to dislodge one, but he shakes his head, his eyes flying to mine. 'Leave them on. For now.'

My pulse races. Anyone who knows me—who knows me as I really am—knows I'm not one to be told what to do. But for some reason, the idea of momentarily relinquishing control is kind of empowering and very appealing. I do as he says, leaving the shoes in place. He lifts a finger and bends it, signalling silently for me to join him.

I walk across to him with what I hope passes for a seductive stroll, a feline smile on my lips the closer I get. Here, just a foot or so away from him, I breathe in and taste the masculine fragrance he wears—

woody and alpine and intoxicatingly sensual. His shirt is crisp white and at the cuffs he wears shining black cufflinks, which I have every reason to suspect are diamonds.

When someone applies to join The Billionaires' Club, we run a detailed background check to maintain our exclusivity and privacy. I mean, membership comes with an annual fee of a million dollars, plus the buy-in, so I know the members can get their hands on serious cash, but we need to know more than that. Criminal records, credit history, scandals, *everything.*

So I know Nicholas Rothsmore's background, probably better than most who just presume he's a playboy bachelor living off his family's considerable wealth. Sure, he was born with the proverbial silver spoon but he's also smart as all get out and a crazy hard worker. Five years ago he arrived in New York to take over his family's American branch of the Rothsmore Group and in that time he's trebled their revenue and expanded beyond a blue-chip investment portfolio to a remarkable presence in the tech world.

Even without his family, he's a formidable and impressive entrepreneur. Then again, his silver-spoon start in life probably didn't hurt.

'Your eyes,' he murmurs, scanning my face thoughtfully, and my heart rate kicks up a gear, so that I doubt my veins are going to be able to hold the blood in place. 'They're so…'

Instinctively, I blink, shuttering my eyes from him. They're a very dark blue, the colour of the sky at dusk, and I know it's unusual. I don't want him to recognise me. 'No cheating,' I say, taking the champagne flute he offers, lifting it to my lips. 'This is secret.'

'Right.' His grin is pure devilish heat and his expression is one of amusement. 'Well, Miss Anonymous, what's your thing?'

'My thing?'

'Yeah. What are you into?'

I think about it for a moment. 'I don't have a lot of spare time. I guess, reading…'

'Fascinating.' His laugh is a slow vibration that travels around the room before landing at the base of my spine, sending little shards of awareness through my nerve endings. 'But I meant, in bed.' He takes a step forward, closing the distance between us, his fingers lifting to curl the edges of the wig, teasing the flossy pink strands between his thumb and forefinger.

'Right.' I slap my forehead exaggeratedly and my smile holds a silent apology. So much for acting as if I do this all the time. 'I'm…a little out of practice.'

'Are you?' His gaze flicks to my cleavage again, lingering there for so long a faint murmur escapes my lips. Heat travels along my body as though he's touched me.

All I can do is nod.

'Why is that?'

We'd agreed not to discuss anything personal. I think of how to answer in a way that won't give me away. 'I've been single awhile.'

His smile is just a lazy flicker of those sculpted lips, framed by a squared jaw and a brush of stubble. I like the stubble. I itch to feel it and rather than denying myself that impulse, I surrender to it, lifting my hand to his face so I can run my fingertips over his jaw.

It shouldn't be so sensual, but just the act of touching him like this is so illicit and sinful that I make a low, husky sound, my body trembling with the first flush of desire.

'So you *are* nervous?' He comes closer, so our bodies brush, and then he moves behind me, so close I can feel his nearness, his warmth, even though he doesn't quite touch me.

He dips his head forward, something I only realise when I feel his breath on my shoulder, warm and smelling of champagne.

My knees tremble.

'Look.' He lifts his hands to my shoulders and angles me slightly so I can see us in the mirror. The sight of myself in this costume—so different from my usual appearance—and Nicholas Rothsmore at my back, his long, tanned fingers curved over my pale shoulders, fills me with a need that demands indulgence.

'Tonight, we're just two people.' He speaks slowly,

the words buzzing right against my ear. 'Who came here to fuck.'

I swallow, my throat moving convulsively. His coarse description sends a *frisson* of awareness down my back, because he's right. This is physical, primal, animalistic. 'Right.' I went into the forum looking for this. I don't know why I'm panicking at the eleventh hour. I draw in a deep breath and smile slowly, calming my nerves.

'That's what you want?'

'Count on it.'

His hands move to my back, where a delicate lace ribbon holds the corset together. He loops a finger beneath the bow, watching me with a hint of mockery as he pulls on one loop, loosening it appreciably.

'You can stop this at any time, if you change your mind,' he murmurs, pulling on the other loop.

My breath snags in my throat. I shake my head slowly from side to side. No way on earth am I going to put a stop to this.

'Good,' he growls, easing the corset down so my breasts spill over the top. He stops moving and stares at me in the mirror, his eyes hot and possessive, glued to my body as though I'm the first woman he's ever seen.

Strangely, I don't feel at all self-conscious now, despite the fact I haven't been naked in front of anyone in a really long time. I'm someone who wears underwear even at the gym or the spa; when other women seem perfectly happy to strip down completely in the sauna or whatever, I'm buttoned up in the corner, sweating into my cotton.

I just don't really do the naked thing.

But here, in the privacy of this intimate room, wearing a mask, with a prearranged lover loosening my lingerie, I have no reluctance; not even a hint of hesitation. This is what we're here for. It's just a transaction.

Convenient, satisfying sex.

At least, I hope it's satisfying. His reputation sure as heck precedes him, but then, sometimes the myth is bigger than the man.

I don't chase that thought down; I don't have *time* to think about that. His hands are running up my sides, his eyes on mine in the mirror as he brings his hands around front to cup my breasts, his fingers finding my nipples and tweaking them so I let out a low growl, the pleasure from such a simple touch totally overwhelming.

'I don't want to stop it.' The words are squeezed from my throat, breathing and speaking almost completely beyond me.

'Good.' Another husky admission before his fingers are sliding into the corset, pushing it even lower until it hits my hips and then falls apart completely, leaving me standing in just a scrap of elastic and lace. His eyes hold mine as he slips a finger into the waistband of my thong and then flicks it. I jump a little, and laugh, the sting unexpected, and unexpectedly sensual. Especially when his hands caress the area almost instantly, soothing the flesh.

My pulse is trembling like a fire in my veins and heat is rushing my insides. He moves his hands around my hips; still watching me intently in the mirror, he slides one hand into the front of my thong. I'm so glad I waxed there too.

His fingers brush my flesh, finding my clit with expert precision, moving over it slowly at first, so I gasp because the touch is unfamiliar and for a second I fight an urge to ask him to stop, because I haven't been touched here in a really, really long time. And *never* like this. He is some kind of maestro because the very idea of objecting disappears from my mind almost instantly as I succumb to the blinding heat of this pleasure, this possession. It's just the lightest touch but flame explodes to molten lava and I'm burning up, heat in every cell of my body, every nerve ending.

His mouth drops to my shoulder, kissing my flesh there, moving closer to the nape of my neck. His breath is cool, his kiss warm, his touch perfect and suddenly pleasure is like a lightning rod, forking through me, so I have to bite down on my lip to stop from crying out.

'Don't be quiet,' he urges, and I blink, finding his eyes in the mirror. He's watching me with an intensity that robs me of breath, his steady grey gaze fascinating and intelligent and somehow all-seeing, so I feel as if beyond my arousal he must be comprehending so much more about me right now. As if he might be seeing into my buttoned-up soul, might be seeing all of my usual tensions and removing them from me.

And I don't care.

'Look,' he prompts, lifting one hand to my breast and cupping it, while his fingers work faster until I'm tumbling so close to the edge of a ravine that I can only exhale in short, shallow rasps. There's nothing to grab onto; nothing to save me from falling.

'Watch yourself,' he says more insistently, though it takes me several seconds to process his words because my brain is no longer firing on all cylinders. All of my blood is busy being pleasured inside my body, being lit on fire by his intensely skilled ministrations.

'Oh, my God.' The words tumble from my lips and then I'm groaning, tilting my head back but doing exactly as he said—watching me, us, this. Watching as he moves his hand and pleasure makes me blush and my nipples hard and then I can't watch any longer because I'm scrunching my face up and giving myself over completely to the total subjugation of sense and reason in place of white-hot desire.

I am falling, I am falling too fast to stop, and yet somehow I'm also flying, all the way to heaven.

I dig my nails into my palms and, because I am secret and he is not, I cry his name as I tumble over the edge. 'Nicholas,' I moan into the glamorous bedroom. 'Oh, God, Nicholas.'

It is a wave that won't stop, as if the last four years of celibacy have left me with a hyper-charged sex drive. How did I not realise that until now?

'Oh, this is going to be fun,' he drawls, his British so very sexy, so husky, so hot, and I laugh, because I've already had more pleasure than I bargained for. I can't imagine what else he can do with those clever, clever hands. And that mouth…my eyes drop to it in the mirror and it lifts into a knowing smirk.

'Oh, yes, that'll be fun too.'

My eyes jerk to his. He's watching me with what I think is amusement.

Normally, I might feel embarrassed at having been so completely lost to that amazing feeling, but I'm not. Because firstly, there's nothing wrong with sexual pleasure—and this is the man to know that. And secondly, he has no idea who I am! This is totally anonymous, totally secret, totally no-consequences, no-holds-barred sex.

That knowledge is empowering, so I spin where I'm standing and look up at him. Even though I'm tall, there's a height differential between us that means I have to look up.

'How come you're wearing clothes?' I murmur.

His shrug is pure indolent heat. 'I'm not sure.'

'Let's do something about that, shall we?'

His nostrils flare at the challenge in my words. My fingertips tremble a little as I begin to undo his buttons, concentrating hard on the task so afterwards I think I probably could have moved a little more seductively. Not that I can muster much energy to care, because now I'm eye height with his naked chest and it is a sight to behold.

The first thing I notice is a tattoo that runs above his left pec, near his heart. It reads, in a strong cursive script, *I am my own*. I trace it with my eyes, imagining what would lead someone to have that written over their heart. I don't ask. We're not here for that kind of inquisition.

'Holy crap.' It's just a whisper, so soft and hoarse in the silence of the room, with only the grandfather clock's metronomic beat for company, but he hears and he grins.

'Yeah?'

'Oh, yeah.' Now it's my turn to look a little mocking when I turn to face him. 'Like you don't already know.'

Because how could he not? While he's slim, he's also insanely toned, a buff chest loaded with muscles, eight firmly defined ridges calling out to be touched. I lift my fingers and trace over the pectoral definition, lingering on his own hair-roughened nipples, surprising myself when I flick one, just as he did with the elastic in my underpants, and he lets out a growl.

'Retaliation,' I simper, grinning as I move to the other.

His hand catches my wrist, his eyes flaring. 'Careful, Miss Anonymous.'

'Oh?' My fingertips tingle. With his hand clamped

around my wrist, his eyes watching me, I blink—a study in wide-eyed innocence. 'Why is that?'

'You're baiting me,' he points out.

'Yep.' And I flick his other nipple, so he tilts his head back, staring at the ceiling, his Adam's apple moving beneath his stubble. More than that, through the confines of his trousers, I feel his cock jerk and power rushes my veins. Power, desire and a surge of sheer, desperate attraction.

I drag my fingertips lower over his body, moving them in teasing circles over his washboard abs then out to his hips, up a little, and lower, to the soft leather belt that's threaded through his trousers.

Now my lack of speed is deliberate. I can tell it's driving him crazy and, hell, I love that. I loosen the clasp and pull on the edge of the belt, watching him as I slide it out of his belt loops. I drop it to the ground beside us then concentrate on the button and zipper, easing it down, pushing the sides apart.

Suddenly, and out of nowhere, I'm uncertain. He understands and takes over, kicking his shoes off and stepping out of his trousers at the same time. Only his dark grey boxer briefs remain.

'My turn,' he murmurs, and I don't understand what he means until he kneels at my feet, looking up at me as he slides my lace thong lower. I watch, the pink wig swishing against my shoulders as he uses my techniques against me, moving too, too slowly. Frustration gnaws at me. I don't want slow. I want to be naked and possessed by him.

I go to step out of my thong but his hands are firm around my thighs, holding me where I am. He makes a tsking noise in response to my silent expression of inquiry, and then he's slowly pushing the lace lower, so I have to stand there and wait until finally my thong is at my ankles and I can kick out of it.

I keep the shoes on and he makes no effort to remove them.

I can't think about my shoes though. He's kneeling before me and now his mouth is moving to my clit, and the pleasure I've been surfing since he walked in the room is dragging me away again, swallowing me into its midst, so I'm dropping off the edge of the earth, just pure sensation and feeling.

I can't believe I'm doing this, but the last thing I think before I come—this time against his mouth—is that wild, anonymous sex might be the hottest thing ever.

CHAPTER TWO

JESUS CHRIST, SHE is unbelievably responsive. I lift her up easily, carrying her across to the bed. Her breasts are soft against my chest and I'm searching for her lips, kissing her, tasting her sweetness as I bring her to the edge of the bed and drop her onto it.

She laughs, a sound so sexy that I swear it writes itself into my mind as though it were chiselled from stone. There's something about it, husky, sweet, laced with promise and heat. I don't give her a second to recover; my mouth chases hers and pushes her backwards, my body coming to lie over hers even as she scrambles higher up the bed so she's lying fully on it.

I trap her wrists with one of my hands, pinning them above her head so her beautiful round breasts are high and firm and then I bring my mouth down to one, sucking on a nipple, rolling it with my tongue, flipping it, my body weight holding her still as she writhes with pleasure. I smile against her pale skin and then move to her other breast, my spare hand plucking the nipple I just released, and I grind my hips so my rock-hard dick—that is giving me no end of grief right now, desperately needing to bury itself deep inside her—throbs and begs for release.

Soon.

We agreed to fuck, once. She was very specific about this. She wanted to get laid.

I can't be away from the party for long. It has to be efficient.

A quickie? It feels as if it should have been outlawed, given how damned sexy she is. This is not a woman who should ever be made love to quickly, unless it is a desperate preamble to a long, slow seduction.

She deserves to be explored and tasted and delighted until she is hoarse from crying out in pleasure.

As if my thoughts have conjured her voice, she spills my name into the air over and over, arching her back, begging me to take her.

I don't want to, though. I want to prolong this; I want to lose myself in her.

These rooms were built for privacy—not even a hint of the party downstairs reaches us, and I'm glad. I kind of hope she's forgotten that a thousand of the world's most well-heeled individuals are just a hundred or so metres away.

'Please,' she whimpers, but in a way that makes it clear it has nothing to do with her desire to re-join the party, or her worry that she might be missed. It's more than that. She needs me.

I push up on my elbows, staring down at her, but

I want to see more. I want to watch her come. More than just her expressive eyes and pouting lips, I want to see her whole face. I move my hand to the mask and begin to shift it but she jerks away and, from what I can see, her expression sobers instantly.

'No.' The word is deadly serious. 'It stays on.'

Shit. I forgot. Anonymity is part of the deal.

'Sorry.' I grimace. 'I just wanted to see you.'

Her smile is laced with pleasure. 'You can see enough.'

I arch a brow but inwardly I disagree. Still, it's better than nothing, and sure as hell better than I expected when I agreed to this.

I'm no stranger to random hook-ups, but something about this woman's approach fascinated me. Her desire for anonymity, and the fact she is new to the club—I haven't seen her profile on any of the forums before and thanks to networking I'm pretty familiar with most of the members.

So she is new. Someone who has just come into money?

No. I can't say how, but I can tell she's old money. Cultured. She has a certain air about her, a way of speaking that's instinctively familiar.

'You do realise we're here to sleep together?' she prompts, her brows lifting above the edge of the mask.

My laugh is immediate. 'Are you complaining?'

'Nope.' She digs her white teeth into the pillow of her lower lip and need rushes through me. Fuck, she's hot. So hot. I drop my head and pull her lower lip between my teeth, my whole body mashed to hers, her nakedness its own kind of torture, so close to me, so close and yet there's still a scrap of cotton between my cock and her sweet warmth and suddenly I'm done being patient and I'm done with the idea of making this last.

Sex is sex. She wants a wild time, and that's what I'm going to give her.

I push up onto my elbows. 'Stay here.'

There's a box of condoms in the bedside table. I pull it out and cross back to the bed. She's watching me in a way that fills me with a torrent of needs and I intend to indulge each and every one of them.

There's something about not knowing who she is that makes this even sexier. Except…

Ridiculously, for the first time, I wonder about her life outside this, outside this room and our agreement. 'You're not married?' I prompt, staring down at her as my lungs work overtime trying to suck in enough air to keep me alive.

'Married? I told you, I haven't done this in a long time.'

My smirk is to hide my cynicism. It doesn't work. 'I don't think celibacy and marriage are necessarily oxymoronic.'

She grins, and I hold my breath, needing her to tell me she's single. I like sex. I fucking love it, unapologetically, but there are some lines I will never cross, and fucking someone else's wife is one of them.

I like my women to be completely mine, even if it is just for one night.

'No, Nicholas.' The words are soft, sweet, and they run over my skin like oil. 'I'm not married.'

Good. But I don't feel a burst of relief—yet. 'Engaged? Seeing someone? I'm not getting in the middle of anything?'

Her teeth are gnawing at that perfect, full lower lip again. She pushes up to kneel and moves across the bed, somehow managing to look elegant and coordinated. Her hands connect with my chest and my breath hisses out of me.

'I am definitely not in a relationship with anyone. Except my remote control. And my MacBook.' She grins, and I feel a kick of curiosity about who she is outside this.

I ignore it.

Tonight isn't a prelude to anything except sex.

And I'm more than optimistic that this will prove satisfying.

In the back of my mind is my father's edict.

'Five years, Nicholas, and each year I expect you to come home wiser and ready to make me proud. And each year you disappoint me.'

I slide a finger into the box of condoms and pull a foil square out. Miss Anonymous takes it from my fingers, lifting it to her lips and tearing the top off. I watch with a racing heart as she pushes my boxers down, just low enough to release my cock, then her hand is cupping my length, her fingertips brushing my tip, delighting in the drop of cum she finds there.

'I'm so glad your reputation isn't exaggerated,' she teases, sliding the condom over me and easing it down my length. My breath hisses out of me as she snaps it at the base, then squeezes me in her palm, my cock jerking against her hand, my whole body standing to attention.

'I've had enough. Reading about you on that idiot gossip blog, seeing you with a different woman every goddamned night. If you'd married Saffron you'd have three kids by now.'

Everyone seems to have forgotten Saffy left me—for a firefighter from Bristol, as it turns out.

'If you're not married by the time you're thirty then you can forget about becoming Lord Rothsmore. You can forget about the whole damned thing.'

It has been distinctly tempting to tell him to go to hell with his bloody title and inheritance. As if I give a damn.

Except I do. I care about my mother, and I care about my father, I even care about the legacy into which I've been born. But more than that, I'm becoming a little bored of this lifestyle. What started off as rebellion has become an unbreakable habit and it's all just a bit too easy.

Miss Anonymous is right. My reputation precedes me. Women fall at my feet, doors open because of my name and the title I'm due to hold.

I'm ready for a challenge. I'm ready for something different and unexpected.

I've decided I'll go home soon—before I turn thirty—and show my parents that, heirs or not, I am someone they can be proud of. I am someone who can think with more than his dick.

But for now, for tonight, I'm going to enjoy being the man my reputation has made me.

'Exactly how long has it been?' I prompt as I find her lips, tangling my tongue with hers, pushing her head back, so she falls flat against the mattress once more.

Her eyes, expressive and somehow familiar, swirl with uncertainty and then they zip closed a little, hiding herself from me. 'A while.'

'A month?'

She laughs, a skittish sound. 'Longer.'

'Six weeks?'

She shakes her head.

'Jesus. Two months?'

Pink spreads across her décolletage. 'A bit more.'

I frown, hating the thought of that, and hating it for her—because she's so sensual, so responsive, so completely driven by desire. I can't imagine how she could go even a night without sex, let alone months.

I nudge her thighs apart with my knees, and push my tip to her entrance, running my fingers over the bright pink of her wig. 'Let's see what we can do about that, huh?'

She nods, no smile on her lips, but I feel her anticipation and I recognise it because it one hundred per cent matches my own. Her breath is held; the room is quiet except for the incessant ticking of the clock against the wall. Outside, Sydney sparkles, beautiful, old, subtropical.

My hands press against the bed on either side of her and I watch as I slide inside her, slowly at first, but her muscles are so freaking tight that I lose my control for a second. Instinct takes over and I thrust deep inside her, grunting as I drop my head and kiss her hard, mimicking the thrust of my body, the tease of our flesh, the taste of her.

She lifts her hips, rolling them, and I have to fight to stop myself from going faster and harder and losing this.

This is sublime.

'Fuck me,' she whispers, her hands in my hair, driving through it urgently, and I grind my teeth together and do what we both want, thrusting into her hard, quickly, until she's moaning over and over and then she's pushing at my chest, trying to roll me over.

She's not strong enough but I flip anyway, turning onto my back and dragging her with me, so I get to look up and see her full, round breasts moving with every thrust, as she lifts up and down my length, taking me deep inside her.

She moves fast, running her hands over her own body, and I am totally transfixed by the sight of this, of her. She is stunning, fascinating, wanton, sexy. She is everything in that moment.

I dig my fingers into her hips, holding her down low on my shaft, and then I buck, taking control once more, driving into her until her cries are louder and hoarser and she's falling apart again, and I'm so close to coming, but I don't. I can't. I won't.

I hold on, I keep myself on edge, steadying myself with monumental discipline and effort, and then I push up to sitting so I can run my tongue over her delightful breasts once more, chasing circles around her nipples, teasing her flesh, sucking her deep into my mouth and teasing her until her hips are jerking frantically and I can feel how close she is.

But so am I and I don't want it to end. Yet.

I hold her still, pressing a light kiss to her lips before rolling us once more, so I'm on top, staring down at her eyes, running my gaze over the mask and trying to imagine what she looks like beneath it.

I make do with tracing the outline of her mouth with my tongue and she whimpers beneath me. I run my tongue lower, over the divot in her chin then lower to her décolletage, and the valley between her breasts, and then I push my cock deeper inside her, thrilling in the power of this possession, in how well we fit together, in how maddeningly mind-blowing this is.

It has to be the anonymity and the sheer directness of this. While I never take a woman to bed who wants more than one night, there's still a bit of dancing around to do. Dinner, flirtation, conversation. This, boiling down an encounter to the truth of sex, is rare.

And I like it. I could become addicted to the idea

of walking into a private room and finding a gorgeous woman dressed in lingerie waiting for me to drive her wild.

Yeah, this is fucking near perfect.

She cries my name and it drags me back to the present, back to what we're doing. The clock is ticking across the room and it matches my internal chronometer, the one that's telling me it's time to go home and face the music, to pick up the mantle my father wishes to pass on.

It's time to stop enjoying nights like this, time to stop fucking around and settle down.

But for now, for this night, I have a beautiful woman in my arms, I'm buried deep inside her and I am going to enjoy the rush of power as I drown in pleasure. There is only this, right now.

I watch him from across the crowded party. The wig and mask have been disposed of. I'm myself again: Imogen Carmichael, founder of The Billionaires' Club, founder of the Chance charity—strait-laced, professional, no-nonsense. I'm the woman everyone wants to talk to and I only have eyes for him.

He looks the same as always. Disastrously handsome, confident, cocky, hot, and, now that I've felt his body up close to mine, I can't look at him without feeling a rush of desire, a slick of heat between my legs.

He's talking to Minette Gray, the daughter of a Mexican mining magnate who's launched a successful Hollywood career for herself. She's stunning, with a mane of long, silky black hair and skin like crushed onyx, eyes that glisten and bright red lipstick. I look at them and for a second I'm transfixed by what a striking pair they make. In the background, beyond the floor-to-ceiling windows, the lights of Sydney sparkle like something out of a movie. I shift my gaze to them, refusing to acknowledge the sharp stab of jealousy that hits me out of nowhere.

Nicholas Rothsmore is a Player with a capital 'P'. Isn't that why I chose him to be my very casual, very temporary lover?

I needed someone who'd be good in bed, discreet and wouldn't particularly care about my 'no questions asked' demand for hot, anonymous sex.

Check, check, check.

Her laugh reaches me across the room and I jerk my eyes back to them on autopilot. He's leaning closer, whispering in her ear.

Shit.

I spin away, pushing down the unwelcome sense of possessiveness that steals through me, focussing on business. That's what I'm good at. It's who I am.

My eyes skate across the room. There are Hollywood A-listers, Grammy-Award-winning singers and musicians, Tony-Award-winning stage actors, royalty, sultans, billionaires, media tycoons. Anyone who's anyone is here, and a tingle of pride shimmies through me because this is all because of me—and all for Abbey.

I think of my best friend, as I often do, of the way

she died, the pain she felt, and I square my shoulders. I might have sacrificed a personal life but it's been worth it.

Nicholas Rothsmore was fun, but that's over now.

I pull my phone from my clutch and load up The Billionaires' Club app that runs the forums. Miss Anonymous has a profile with a picture of a stiletto—I have a predilection for heels. She's served her purpose now. I'm done with Miss Anonymous, done with the future Lord Rothsmore.

I click into the brief bio and scroll to the bottom, where a red button invites me to 'delete profile'.

I click and she's gone. Miss Anonymous has had her fun and now it's time to get on with my life.

If cities were animals, New York would be a gazelle. Fast, nimble, elegant, stunning. I stare down at this adopted city of mine, contemplating the first solo Saturday night I've had in…for ever.

It's been a week since Sydney, and I've been flat out closing the Hewitson merger, but that's done now. Usually, I mark my business triumphs with the kind of partying that would make my grandparents roll over in their graves.

Champagne, women, music.

I frown, surveying the empty penthouse. Only the kitchen lights are on, so it looks somehow more cavernous than normal.

I won.

This deal has been in the works for three years.

Three years of meetings, negotiations, hard slog and now it's with the lawyers and I can relax. And celebrate.

Out of nowhere, I close my eyes and remember what I was doing this time last week. I remember her pale body splayed against the dark sheets of the Intimate Rooms in the Sydney base of The Billionaires' Club and my body is tighter than granite, aching, not just for sex but for *her*.

Miss Anonymous.

I was right that not knowing her name was part of the appeal, but now the not knowing is driving me crazy. Because I want to see her again.

I want to fuck her again.

A smile lifts my lips, because I don't just want to fuck her, I want to have her every which way until she's incoherent with pleasure.

In one month, I turn thirty and England beckons. Lord Rothsmore awaits. In one month, I'll become the man my parents want me to be—or something more like him, anyway. But for the next four weeks I'm still a free agent, and I know just how I want to spend it.

Determination fires my step. I stride indoors, the temperature change marked. My cell phone is across the room. I lift it, loading up the app and selecting our private message conversation.

Except it's no longer a conversation with an exchange of words. My comments remain but hers are gone. Italics proclaim *These messages have been deleted.*

I hadn't expected that. Why?

Okay, that's weird. But it doesn't change how I feel and what I want.

'Fancy round two, Miss Anonymous?'

I figure her American accent makes it likely she lives here in the States. I can get my helicopter to my jet and travel *anywhere*. The minute I think it, I realise how desperate I am to see her again.

Even though I've spent the last five years fucking my way around the world, I freely admit last weekend was the best sex I've ever had. There was something so illicit and hot about it.

Her mask, her hair, her body…

I groan into the night air, looking back at the screen.

Message undeliverable

What?

With a frown, I click out of our message chat and surf to her profile instead. It doesn't come up when I type 'Miss Anonymous'. Adrenalin shifts in my gut.

I go to the list of members using the app and scroll through it slowly, my eyes looking for the stiletto she used as a profile picture. Which makes me think of the sky-high shoes she wore as I ran my hands over her clit, feeling her pulsing beneath me as she exploded with pleasure, and I'm so close to coming at just that memory.

I have to find her.

But where the hell is she?

She can't have left the club. It's not like that. The entry process is gruelling and elaborate. No one signs up and leaves.

So?

Her profile might have been anonymous but it must have been created by a legitimate member of the club. Even the online avatars are vetted. So who the hell is she? And where did she go?

CHAPTER THREE

'IMOGEN? THERE'S A Mr Rothsmore here to see you.'

Oh, my God. In the midst of studying the floor plans for a new school Chance will be funding in a couple of years, I jump so hard I bang my knee against the edge of my desk. Pain radiates through me. I ignore it, scrambling for the receiver of my desk phone.

'What did you say?' My voice comes out completely different.

'A Mr Nicholas Rothsmore,' says my loyal assistant—a woman to whom I offered a job after we met in a shelter for battered women that Chance was involved in supporting; she speaks slowly, as if I might have misunderstood. 'He has a membership enquiry.'

Oh, my God.

'I'm in the middle of something,' I demur, wincing, because The Billionaires' Club is founded on three tenets: exclusivity, privacy and exceptional customer service. My door is always open to members. 'I only have a few minutes.'

'I'll send him in.' She disconnects the call and I stand up quickly, my mind spinning. I have about ten seconds to get my thoughts in order.

I'm wearing a cream suit made up of a pencil skirt and a fitted blazer, with a lemon-yellow silk camisole beneath. No bra and my traitorous nipples are already straining against the soft fabric in anticipation of the fact he's about to be here in my office, my sanctuary. I look around quickly for anything that could give me away.

I've had a manicure since the ball—the nails that were bright pink are now a muted beige. I took great care that night to remove any identifying jewellery. My lips were painted bright red whereas now they bear just a hint of gloss, and my long hair tumbles in waves over one shoulder. I pull on it and then remember my eyes…that he remarked on.

Crapola.

I swing around behind my desk and grab my handbag, lifting my oversized Jackie O–style black sunglasses out and pushing them onto my face right as Emily opens the door.

'Mr Rothsmore,' she announces, a slightly bemused look crossing her face as she sees me in my disguise.

My voice! Oh, crap. He's heard me talk. No, he's heard me scream, over and over. Argh!

'Thank you, Emily.' I spent a lot of time with my grandparents, just outside St Louis, so the southern drawl isn't much of a stretch.

Her bemusement increases. 'Would you like anything to drink?' she prompts.

'We won't have time for that,' I say, still in a voice that hums with the Deep South. 'I've only got a few minutes.'

Emily's trying not to laugh. Crap.

At least Nicholas doesn't look any the wiser.

'Well, if *y'all* change your mind,' she says, with a wink at me right before she pulls the door shut behind her, leaving me alone with sex god Nicholas Rothsmore in the middle of my Manhattan office. I'm grateful the lenses of my glasses are darkly reflective, so I can stare at him without him having any idea.

He's wearing jeans today, low-slung and faded, with a long-sleeved black T-shirt. It's snowing out, so I imagine he's left a jacket somewhere, and I imagine it to be distressed leather, something that goes with this billionaire-bad-boy-about-town look.

I manage not to drool, but my tummy is clenching with serious lust.

'Imogen.' His voice is crisp, professional, but that doesn't matter, I hear it filtered through lips that have kissed me all over, sucked my nipples until pleasure exploded through me, and I find myself unable to push those memories away. My breasts ache now and heat fires low in my abdomen.

He crosses the room, extending a hand for me to shake, and my pulse shoots up a thousand notches; my body temperature skyrockets.

Act natural. Act natural.

I skirt around my desk, holding my own hand out, and I realise my fingers are trembling, just a little but enough for me to feel incredibly self-conscious. He doesn't appear to notice as he shakes my hand.

'Ignore the glasses,' I explain a little stiltedly. 'I had an operation.'

An operation? On what? My corneas?

If he thinks it's a weird excuse, he doesn't say anything. Maybe he presumes I had a big weekend and am wearing sunnies to cope with the hangover.

'I need your help.'

Straight to it, then.

'Sure, have a seat.'

'I'm fine.' He ranges to the windows, his stride long and lean, his body powerful. I mean, he looks powerful and sexy and yet I imagine him naked and my knees almost buckle beneath me.

He stares out at the city, snow falling fast beyond my window, the buildings lit up despite the fact it's mid-afternoon.

'Well, Mr Rothsmore, how can I help you?'

'I was at the masquerade last weekend,' he murmurs, still not looking at me. And I'm glad, because it means I get to look at him. And keep looking. At his broad shoulders, his narrow hips, his firm ass, his long legs. Legs that have straddled me, legs that have pressed hard against mine.

He turns around and again I'm glad for the glasses. He's waiting for me to speak. I swallow, bringing much-needed moisture to my mouth. 'Yes?'

A single word, husky and dry.

'I met a woman there. I didn't get her name but I'd like to speak to her. Can you put me in touch?'

My heart hammers like nobody's business. I'm dying inside. 'I…'

My pulse is thready in my veins.

'You know privacy is one of the member guarantees,' I hear myself saying, moving to the bar across the room and pouring myself a mineral water. I take a sip to buy time.

'Yes,' he agrees, his eyes narrowing slightly.

'That guarantee benefits everybody.' I move to my desk, propping my hip against it with what I hope passes for nonchalance.

'Nonetheless, the club is about networking and I have a *proposition* I'd like to make her.'

I swallow, desire flushing through me. This isn't how it's supposed to be! One night, no strings, no more. But, God, I want to push him to the floor and kiss him, hard, and beg him to make love to me. I sweep my eyes shut for a second.

Safe in the knowledge I've deleted Miss Anonymous from our forums, I shrug. 'Have you checked the app?'

'She's not there, despite the fact we exchanged messages. I'd appreciate it if you could have someone from IT locate her and give me the details.'

I'm floored. And kind of flattered. 'That would definitely be against membership rules.'

'And you don't break the rules, ever?' he prompts, lifting a brow, and he's just so perfectly rakish that my heart does a funny little tremble. I definitely broke the rules last weekend, even if they're just rules of my own creation.

'Rarely,' I say with a small smile, which I quickly flatten. I smiled a *lot* that night. I can't give myself away. In fact, I really need to wrap this up. As much as I don't want him to go, he has to.

That night was an aberration. An itch I needed to scratch, and I scratched it. A lot.

'Then perhaps this will be one of the occasions you will?'

I am instantly reminded that he is from a very wealthy, very ancient British family, a member of the aristocracy. He speaks with an authority and arrogance that would usually piss me off, but coming from Nicholas it is incredibly hot.

'I'm afraid not.'

His eyes narrow. I suspect he doesn't often get told 'no'.

'Not even if I make it worth your while?'

My heart turns over in my chest. 'What are you suggesting?'

'A million-dollar donation to Chance. For a name.'

My sharp intake of breath is involuntary. It takes me several seconds to process this. My fingers tremble. I curve them around the water glass and sip, needing to process this.

'A million dollars.' He's found his way to my Achilles heel and I'm sure he knows it.

Because I make it a policy of taking whatever I can for the charity. Even my parents' donations, when I have mostly wanted to tell them to go to hell and take their 'too little, too late' conscience-pricking gifts with them.

I take everything that's offered because I know the charity is now the wall that stands between life and death for so many helpless, impoverished children out there.

'For a name,' he murmurs, his hands in his pockets as he watches me intently.

'Who is she?'

'I only know that she's single,' he says with a grimace that signals frustration.

'That probably accounts for seventy-five per cent of our female membership.'

He scowls at me. It shouldn't be hot but it is.

'We exchanged messages. She's deleted them, and disappeared off the forums.'

I can't tell him the truth. But that doesn't stop me from asking, 'Why do you want to find her?'

He stares at me for several long seconds, a muscle twisting in the base of his jaw. 'It's personal.'

I dip my head forward, trying to slow my breathing, hoping my cheeks won't be too pink. 'So is the member's information. If you want me to look into our records and find out who she is, then I'll need more to go on.'

His eyes stick to me for a long time and I want to rip off my glasses so I can look him right in the eyes. I want to rip his clothes off. I want to fuck him right here.

Oh, my God.

What's happening to me? I've been single for four years and it never bothered me, but now I can't be in the same room with a man without wanting to leap into bed. Not bed. Desk. Floor. Window. And not *a* man. *This* man.

'Fine,' he grunts. 'We spent time together in the Intimate Rooms.'

There's a part of me that deeply appreciates his discretion, even though he doesn't know I'm Miss Anonymous. I'm glad he's not going into all the sordid details of what we shared. I appreciate that he's respecting our privacy.

'That's what the rooms are for.'

'I'd like to see her again.'

The room is suddenly a void, as if a black hole has opened up and swallowed us. The atmosphere grows thick, the air is heavy in my chest. Everything's different.

'Why?'

His eyes explode with strength. 'That is also personal.'

I swallow, desire unfurling in my gut like a slow-slithering snake. I want him. I want him so badly.

But that's crazy. I don't do relationships, and I particularly don't do relationships with men like this. Entitled, wealthy, spoiled, arrogant.

Even when they're savant-like in bed.

I clench my hand into a fist to ball up my own temptations.

I have to get rid of him before I do something really stupid. Like giving in to this.

One night. That was all it was meant to be.

'If she's deleted her profile, it suggests she doesn't want to be found, Mr Rothsmore.' His name in my mouth is so sexy. I want to kiss it against his skin.

I watched him get dressed on Saturday night. I lay in bed sated and so full of pleasure, and I watched as he pulled on his shorts, his trousers, donning the tuxedo he'd had on earlier. Even after sleeping together, that simple act of voyeurism felt strangely intimate.

'Perhaps.' His eyes narrow.

'In which case, I can't help you.'

'For a million dollars, you're not willing to discover who she is?'

I wait a moment.

He pulls a card from his pocket. It's jet black, matte, thick, with gold writing across the front. As he brings it closer I make out his name and, beneath it, a series of numbers.

'I'll tell you what, Imogen. You find her and ask her to call me. Whether she does or doesn't, the million dollars is yours regardless.'

I stare at the card, the trap he's unknowingly set one I refuse to enter. Because it's dishonest. I can't take his money under these circumstances. I mean, the woman he's looking for is standing right in front of him.

'A million dollars? You must have shared something pretty special.'

Damn it! Why the heck did I ask that? I jackknife off the edge of the desk, leaving his card where he's placed it.

'You could say that.'

Oh, God. I didn't need to hear that. Temptation is slicing through me.

And yet, he's loaded. Seriously loaded. A million dollars isn't even small change to him. It's the lint in his pocket after he's got rid of his small change.

And Chance is my life's purpose.

I toy with the morality of this, mentally tossing it back and forth.

'I'll try to find her,' I say, quietly.

It seems to placate him. He nods, moving towards the door. 'Then I won't take up more of your time. You'll let me know, one way or another?'

His hand curves around the handle. He's leaving. I swallow back an urge to shout the truth at him.

'Count on it.'

Count on it.

Her words jam against me, hard, holding me completely still. I'm back in Sydney, in the Intimate Rooms.

'That's what you want?' I asked her.

'Count on it.'

Count on it. Common enough, I guess, but no.

I spin around, catching her staring at me. Except it's impossible to tell because of those damned glasses she's been wearing.

Suspicion moves quickly to certainty.

I shut the door and stride across the room, and it's so unexpected that she doesn't even have time to react. I stand before her for a second, and now I look at her lips and I kick myself for not realising sooner.

I lift a hand to the glasses and pull them from her face before she can comprehend what I'm doing.

Those eyes, eyes that have stared into mine as pleasure made her wild with insanity and desire, look back at me, heavy with surprise now. Those lips that I have tasted and dragged between my teeth form a perfect 'O'.

'Miss Anonymous,' I drawl, and before she can answer I lift my hand around to the base of her skull and pull her head forward. I'm kissing her, kissing her first with exploration to test my theory, even when I know I'm right. And as I feel her familiar mouth, taste her sweetness, my kiss turns hard and heavy with censure for trying to hide from me, for lying to me, for being about to let me walk away.

She makes a strangled noise into my mouth and I swallow it; my body, denied the pleasure of hers for nine long nights, throbs with a need that will not be suppressed.

And whatever impulse had prompted her to try to get rid of me, it's gone now, as her hands lift urgently, pushing at my shirt, running it up my body, so her palms connect with my naked chest, her fingertips finding their way back to paths she explored last weekend.

'You were going to fucking hide from me.' I curve my hands around her ass, lifting her onto the edge of her table, spreading her legs. The skirt she's wearing splits with an almighty sound and she laughs, that husky sound having been imprinted on my memory in some strange way.

'It was meant to be one night, we agreed,' she says, tilting her head back so I can run my mouth down her throat, my teeth lightly nipping at the flesh on her collarbone. I feel her tremble beneath me and I have no time for the sensual seduction I thought I'd be engaging in. It's been nine nights and I don't think I've gone that long without sex since—

Well, since ever.

I reach into my back pocket, pulling my wallet out and flicking it open to find a condom without breaking our kiss. I move higher between her legs; the skirt splits more. I don't fucking care.

I undo the button of my jeans and slide the zip down, freeing my rock-hard, aching cock. I shift for a second, just long enough to rip the packet open and push the condom down my length, and then I lift my head to stare at her for a long second, my eyes laced with a thousand and one feelings—anger, annoyance, heat, need, mockery, impatience.

'You were going to fucking let me walk away just now?'

She bites down on her lip and in response moves forward, her hands against my chest, her face tilted, her lips seeking mine. I deny her that kiss, instead lifting her off the edge of the desk, using my hands to push the scrap of lace at her core aside, and sliding her onto my cock, stifling a moan as her muscles squeeze me so tight I convulse a little.

I take one step across her office and push her back against the thick, cold glass, bracing her there as I push into her hard. The eyes that meet mine are the same—exactly the same. And she knew it! Those fucking glasses.

Anger that she wanted to hide from me crests in my gut and I kiss her, pressing her head against the glass as my body takes command of hers. She is crying my name into my mouth, over and over, her nails digging into my shoulders, her heels pressed to my back.

Her muscles tighten, her whole body vibrates and her cries get louder and faster. At the moment she comes I let go of my own control, I stop fighting this, exploding with a guttural roar, pushing myself hard against her as I come buried deep inside her; finally feeling this release and giving myself over to it completely.

It is fast. It is animalistic. It is bliss.

I hold her, locked between the glass window and my frame, my body weight keeping her where she is, unwilling to put distance between us yet.

I push my head up, my cock still inside her, and fix her with an assessing gaze. 'What game are you playing, Imogen?'

Her throat moves as she swallows. 'Game?' It's husky, the southern accent forgotten, and her voice just as I remember it from Sydney.

'Does fucking members without their knowledge give you a thrill?'

Her spectacular, memorable eyes widen. 'No!' Her denial is sharp and fierce. 'I've never done that before. You were the first. And the last.'

Given my own attitudes to sex, it feels faintly chauvinistic that I'm relieved at that, but I am. I don't like the idea that she uses her position to find her way into bed with members.

'Why did you lie to me?'

'I didn't.' She drops her eyes. I shift my hips, my dick already growing hard again, surprising her so she jerks her attention back to me quickly.

'We agreed to a night. That's the deal we had. It's all I wanted.'

My laugh is spontaneous and deep, a sound of disbelief. 'You didn't want this?'

I have the satisfaction of seeing her cheeks flush pink. 'I…shouldn't have.'

'Why not?'

She shakes her head, and slowly she shifts before

me, her expression going from sexy deer in the headlights to the force of nature I know her to be—the woman who set all this up off her own back, who's created an unbelievable empire.

'Because I meant what I said in our messages. I just needed to have sex.' More heat in her cheeks but she doesn't blink away from me now. 'I hadn't been with anyone in ages and I felt like I'd forgotten what intimacy is like.' She lifts her shoulders. 'I wanted to get laid. And let's face it, you're somewhat of an expert in the meaningless sex department.'

She's right. I've made one-night stands an art form and my reputation makes sure everyone knows it. So why does it piss me off royally that she says it so casually?

I make no apologies for the way I live my life. This is who I am. I've tried to fit myself into a different mould before, to be Lord Rothsmore In Waiting, and it was an abject failure.

At least when I get back to England this time I'll have a better idea of who I really am.

'You weren't supposed to come looking for me,' she says.

I roll my hips once more, enjoying the look of heat that shifts over her features. Desire flares between us, a flame too bright and searing to ignore.

'Why did you come looking for me?'

That's a great question. The thing about one-night stands is that they're *always* one night. That was what we'd agreed. I'm the one who wants to shift the goalposts, to make this something else.

Except, it's not as if I'd be changing the terms of our deal substantially. She wanted casual, no-strings sex. We obviously still have chemistry. So why not have fun until I leave? It's exactly the kind of relationship I do. Never commitment, never serious, never more than great sex, and lots of it. I am the king of casual fun, and suddenly it feels like a month of that with Imogen would be a lot like bliss.

'You know who I am,' I murmur, and with her back propped against the glass, her legs wrapped around my waist, I separate the lapels of her blazer so I can see the skimpy yellow singlet top thing she's got on underneath. It's soft like silk. I slide my hands under it; her skin is warm to the touch. She's not wearing a bra. My dick is hard again. Rock hard, as if I didn't have sex just minutes ago. My palms curve over her breasts, tormenting her nipples just how she likes it.

It was only one night but I learned a lot about her and I'm not ashamed of using it to get my way.

Her eyes hook to mine, powerful and yet powerless, lost as well as found.

'You know who I am,' I say again, and drop my head to take one of her nipples into my mouth through the flimsy fabric. It adds an extra layer of eroticism to something that's already pretty damned hot. I press my teeth to her nipple, just enough to make her draw in a sharp breath of pleasure.

'Yes.'

It's not clear what she's saying 'yes' to.

'You know I am due to inherit my father's title, the estate, the whole thing.'

She groans, nodding.

'In one month, I'm due back in England to take up my place in that life.' I'm surprised how flat the words sound—the usual derision not in evidence. 'I have only weeks left in Manhattan.'

Another gurgling noise as I transfer my mouth to her other breast and give it the same little bite. Her insides squeeze my cock so tight. I need more of her. All of her.

Impatiently, I push at her blazer and she pulls her arms from it, understanding that I need all of her, all of this. The camisole follows, the wet patches from my mouth visible as it scrunches to the ground at our feet. I have to put her down to get the tattered skirt from her body and I drag it off her with the lace thong, leaving both on the floor before spinning her around so her back is to me.

I push her forward at the hips, so her arms are braced against the windows, and I take the briefest second to imprint this memory on my mind—the sight of her naked ass, how hot she looks from behind. I spread her legs with my knee, and bring one hand around to her breasts, keeping it clamped there as my other holds her hips steady. I take her from behind quickly, thrusting into her, our voices mingling at the total possession of this, the rightness of my being buried deep inside her. The hand on her hip travels lightly to her clit, and I run it over her cluster of nerves as I move deeper and harder inside her.

My voice is music, deep and throaty, taking over the room. There's no clock here ticking as a background accompaniment to this passion, but the desire is just as intense and just as overwhelming.

I forget that we're in her office, I forget there's a secretary just down the hallway. I forget everything except how this feels, how badly I need her, how it's been nine nights of tormenting, snatched memories, of how I didn't even want to go out and hook up with someone else because I didn't think it could live up to this.

I am angry at that—angry at my dependence on being with her—but I am also thrilled because I've found Miss Anonymous and I have four weeks in which to enjoy her.

So long as she agrees…

CHAPTER FOUR

WHAT THE HECK just happened?

I press my overheated forehead to the glass, staring down—way down—at Manhattan. My office is on the ninety-second floor of this glass and steel monolith. Believe me, I'd have preferred to cut costs and rent something cheaper, but my parents own two floors of this building and gave me a great deal on rent—besides which, my clients expect a certain air of wealth and prestige. The whole Billionaires' Club is predicated on the idea of unattainable wealth and prestige, so I can't exactly have my office headquarters in some three-storey brick walk-up in Brooklyn.

His breathing is ragged, just like my own. I stay right where I am, pleasure like fireworks just beneath my skin, exploding fast at my pulse points. I stare down at the snow-covered city, thinking of the time I went to visit Meemaw and Pa. I'd heard about them, but had barely spent more than an hour in their company. My mother worked hard to distance herself from her working-class roots. She'd married Hollywood royalty, she was a theatre queen and she wasn't going to have the fact that she came from an ordinary family in the south do anything to harm her carefully cultivated image. I didn't have those hang-ups, and right after Abbey died, I just felt as if I needed to see my grandparents, to spend time with them. I wanted the authenticity their life offered; I wanted to be as far from my parents and their set as possible.

So I went to Meemaw's, and only a day or two after I arrived, a tornado crossed town. It was loud and fierce and so fast. It must have lasted only two or three minutes before it moved away again and the most surreal, unnatural silence followed.

That's what's happening now.

Silence, but weird and unnatural and, contrasted with our earlier passion, it is freakishly quiet in my office.

And I have no idea what to say, which makes me even more freaked out because I pride myself on being able to fill difficult silences and cover awkwardness with a quip or a joke.

Now, I've got nothing.

I'm just a tangle of nerves and excitement. My whole body feels as if it's been stretched in a thousand directions, stretched by the speed with which my blood has terrorised it.

His hands on my back are gentle now, inquisitive, returning me to the here and now with a slow, sweet touch. He curves his palms over my shoulders and turns me around to face him.

It makes it so much harder to kick my brain into gear because one look at his face and I'm melting. What the heck is wrong with me? I don't *do* rich guys. I find all that money off-putting and there's no mistaking Nicholas Rothsmore's background of privilege and wealth. It is in the strength of his spine, the confident tilt of his chin, the sophistication of his eyes, the dimple of his chin that for some reason screams aristocracy.

But there's also something hard-worn about him, something broken and devil-may-care. Something that tells me he's a risk-taker and an adventurer, that he might have been born to fit the mould of a privileged aristocrat but that he's worked hard to fight his way free of it.

That alone keeps me rooted to the spot, unable to look away from a face that I have been seeing in my dreams since we snatched an hour together in Sydney.

'I'm…'

He lifts a finger and presses it to my lips, his dark brows knitting together as if I'm a puzzle he's trying to solve.

'I didn't expect to see you again,' I say against his finger. When he doesn't move it, I dart my tongue out and flick it. His eyes flare wide and power rushes through my body.

This is bigger than me, bigger than him.

'You made pretty sure of that.'

'Not quite.' I bite the soft flesh of his finger now,

and he presses it to my lips, so I roll my tongue over it and feel his cock jerk against me.

He's like the Energizer Bunny of sex. Then again, apparently I am too, because desire ignites inside me, and I wish we were anywhere but my office.

My office!

'Oh, crap.' I press my hand to his chest and push him back, everything forgotten except the fact Emily and I have an extremely casual relationship and she walks in whenever she needs anything. Not to mention I've just been screaming like a banshee at the top of my lungs.

I sidestep him and move away as if he's explosive dynamite and I'm right in its trajectory. I need space. Space to think and I definitely absolutely need to get dressed.

'That was…completely unprofessional.' I lift a hand and smooth my hair over one shoulder, my fingers grazing my nipples by accident, so I have to spin away or risk him seeing my instant physical reaction to the simple touch.

'It was also completely fucking great.'

A smile curves my lips. There's a bathroom across my office—I work long hours and frequently have to attend Billionaires' Club events, which I go to directly from here. Fortunately for me, there's also a wardrobe and it's always stocked with an array of outfits. I pull out a black pantsuit and a silk camisole, trying not to think about what Emily will say when she notices the obvious change of clothes, pulling the silk top on quickly to dispense with the whole nakedness thing.

I spin around to find him watching me with an expression I can only describe as indolent. He's like some kind of crack cocaine to me—I'm high on him and already craving my next fix.

I stare across at him—he's pulled his boxers back on but there's still an expanse of toned abs and tanned skin—and my mouth goes dry, my stomach loops and my fingers tingle.

'I don't do this.'

He lifts a thick, dark brow, his expression quirking with curiosity. 'Do what?'

'This.' I gesture from him to me. 'Sleep with clients. Sleep with *anyone*.'

He laughs, the sound bouncing around my office. My pulse trembles. 'You weren't a virgin.'

I jerk my head. 'Yeah, but…'

He begins to prowl towards me.

'It had been a while.'

I told him that in Sydney. There's no point in denying it.

'What's "a while"?'

I swallow, my throat bone dry. I wave my hand in the air in what I hope passes as some kind of descriptor of time. He catches it in his, lacing our fingers together and holding it at my side.

Up close, I look at him—really look at him—in a way I haven't had the luxury of doing yet. I notice things that previously passed me by. Not because they didn't warrant notice, but because there's so much of him that demands attention: his square jaw; his perfectly sculpted lips; the little indent above his mouth, forming a bridge to his nose; a nose that is straight and strong—patrician, appropriately, given his pedigree—but that has a bump halfway down, as if it's been broken at some point. His lashes are thick and dark and clumpy, and close up it almost looks as if he's wearing eyeliner. He's not, but that's the effect the weight of his lashes combines to create. He has a silvery scar near his hairline—a single, trembling line about an inch long, very faint and, going by the shimmery paleness of it, earned long ago, perhaps even as a boy.

My tummy swoops. 'Oh, you know, years.'

'Years?' The word is like a curse, and his brow dips as if he can't even comprehend this concept. I can't really blame him—standing here in a post-orgasm glow, I have no idea why I've denied myself this for as long as I have.

I go to pull away but his hand squeezes mine. 'Years?' Softer, gentler, less shocked, more wondering.

'Yeah.' I don't meet his eyes. I hate feeling like this. Most people look at me with awe and it's pushed my vulnerabilities deep inside me. But suddenly, I feel gauche and insecure; I feel like the gangly, solitary teen I was after Abbey died and I realised I had no one who really knew me.

I make an effort to straighten and transform into Imogen Carmichael, entrepreneur, philanthropist.

'It's not a big deal, okay?'

'I beg to differ. Are you some kind of masochist? Or nun?'

'Clearly not the latter.'

'So why the hell have you been single so long?'

I square my shoulders but make no effort to pull my hand away from his. I like touching him. That should set alarm bells off inside my brain. Maybe it does. I ignore them, though, staying right where I am, his naked torso with that cursive script tattoo inked over his heart calling to me.

'I've been busy,' I point out, waving my free hand around the office.

'But sex is…'

'Yeah, yeah.' I roll my eyes. 'To *you*, sex is like breathing. I get it.'

'I was going to say,' he interrupts, a little gruffly, 'that it's an instinct. And it's more than sex, it's companionship. It's falling asleep in someone's arms, it's having someone to laugh with.'

'Says you, Mr Manhattan Playboy?'

He lifts his defined shoulders. 'So? A varied sex life doesn't mean I don't still enjoy those perks.'

It's an admission I didn't expect. Our eyes connect and something electrifies my pulse. 'With a different woman every night, right?'

His eyes hold mine unflinchingly and I admire him for his lack of apology. Why should he apologise? He's a renowned bachelor; he lives as he preaches. Everyone who sleeps with him knows what they're getting.

Great sex.

Lots of it.

But just for a night or so.

I knew that—it's why I approached him, specifically, in the forums. I didn't want the complication of a guy who might want more from me.

Which somewhat begs the question as to why he's here.

And why I don't feel more annoyed about it.

'You like sex,' he says, as if I'm a puzzle he wants to work out.

My cheeks flush. Because up until a week ago, I didn't know how *much* I like sex. I've only been with two guys. My college boyfriend, who it turns out was using me to access my mother's production company connections, and Jackson, who was 'great on paper' but a complete dud in real life. It's a shame it took me six months to work that one out.

In any event, the sex with both was…nice. At best.

'Apparently,' I murmur, scanning his face.

I had no idea it could be so completely mind-blowing. I mean, I've read my fair share of romance novels and watched movies where the women just have to be kissed on the nose to go into a full-blown orgasm, and I've always thought it was a stupid fantasy.

Not so much now.

'You came looking for sex,' he prompts, and I get a glimpse of the determination that's made Nicholas Rothsmore such a success in business, away from his family's prestigious standing in society. He has a needle-sharp focus and he's using it to sift through my soul.

'Yes.' I jut my chin out unapologetically.

'Why?'

I open my mouth to answer and then shake my head. 'I told you, it's been a while.'

'So why now?' he persists.

My eyes drop away from his, skimming the walls of my office. This place is my home away from home and yet it's nothing like the real me. Elegant Scandinavian furniture, obvious signs of wealth and success. It's what my clients expect.

'I guess…' I search for an answer. The truth is, it wasn't one thing or another. People in the club have been pairing off lately. There've been engagements and rumoured weddings, and I guess it's made me realise how far I am from that. It's the knowledge that I'm approaching thirty and that happy couple life is nowhere near being on my horizon. But mostly, it was desire. Curiosity. Loneliness—the kind that permeates me on a cellular level, so I could no longer ignore it.

He squeezes my hand so I jerk my attention back to his face.

'I just wanted to get laid.' The admission is bare-faced, if only a fraction of the complex knot of emotions that led me into the Intimate Room. 'And then get on with my life.'

'Ah.' He grins, just a flash, but I have the strangest—and most unpleasant—sensation that he's laughing at me. 'Sex isn't a part of your real life?'

I shake my head. 'This is…' I wave around the office. 'My business. The club. The charity. That takes pretty much all my time and energy. It's hard to meet anyone, but—'

'But?' he prompts, when I don't finish the sentence.

My teeth press into my lower lip as I think that through. 'But, I'm twenty-nine and I have barely been in a relationship. I mean, a couple of guys but nothing serious, nothing that could ever go anywhere.'

He's quiet, listening attentively.

'And suddenly, everyone seems to be pairing off, like the club has become its own kind of Noah's Ark or something.'

He laughs gruffly.

'I'm almost thirty and I have no social life to speak of.' I grimace. 'I haven't dated in four years. The guy I have the most frequent conversations with is my doorman, Mr Silverstein, and he's seventy-five years old and very happily married. My parents won't get off my back about being single. It doesn't matter that I've built all this, they really only care about me getting married and having babies—not so many that I ruin my figure, mind you.' I pause to roll my eyes, making the mental excuses for my mother that I always bring to the fore when I'm frustrated with her. How she's an aging Hollywood starlet who sees youth and beauty as her greatest assets—and both are shifting away from how she wants them to be. 'But more than that, I'm…getting used to being alone.' I swallow, the raw truth of the confession surprising me.

'It's not that I want a relationship.' The very idea fills me with panic. 'There's no way I could fit one in. I barely have time to workout in the day. I have to get a manicurist to come to the office if I need my nails done.' I shake my head, hating how entitled that sounds, resisting an urge to explain it's part of the whole image thing my clients expect me to project.

'So our night in Sydney was…what? Your sexual equivalent to an in-office manicure?' he teases.

Heat blooms in my cheeks.

'Dial-a-Fuck?' he pushes, and I laugh, shaking my head.

'Honestly? I was seriously starting to worry I might have forgotten how to even do sex.' I laugh, and am relieved when he does too.

'So… Dial-a-Fuck meets sex refresher course?'

'Sex for Beginners,' I agree with a wink.

'Well, Miss Carmichael, I'm delighted to say you passed, with flying colours.'

'Thank you, sir.'

Silence hums around us, buzzing like paparazzi at fashion week. I hold my breath and wait, though I have no idea what I'm waiting for.

'Why did you come here?'

His brows lift, just a little. 'I was looking for you.'

Heat spreads through my body.

'Why?'

His hands lift to my hair, flicking it between his fingers. 'You suit blonde.' His smile is somehow self-deprecating. 'Then again, you also suit pink.'

I laugh. 'Did you come here to discuss my hair?'

'No.' His eyes pierce mine. 'I came here to find Miss Anonymous.'

'Why?'

'Because last week was the best sex I've ever had, and I haven't been able to stop thinking about you. I want more. More of her, you, this. And I think you do too.'

My jaw drops, my heart stops, my pulse cracks like a frozen river.

'Nicholas—'

His name rushes from my lips, too much air, too much feeling. It's too much. If sex were a college degree, this guy would hold several PhDs. He really thinks I'm the best? The best he's ever had? Pride soars in my chest, and, more than that, the addiction centres of my brain are going into overdrive because he's damned right. I do want more of this.

But… 'We agreed it would just be one night.'

'That was before.' He shrugs away the objection, as though it doesn't matter.

'But you're not… Neither of us wants… I mean, what are you saying?'

'I'm glad you asked,' he says teasingly, pulling me closer, wrapping his arms behind my back so our bodies are cleaved together in a way that is both sexy and intimate. 'I came here wanting to fuck Miss Anonymous again, and I did. And still I want more. And now, I think I can see a way for both of us to get what we want.'

'What's that?' I sound as if I've run a marathon.

'Go out with me.'

Panic spirals through me and I shake my head on instinct. 'I don't date, Nicholas. I didn't mean to imply that I want that…'

'Relax.' He grins, and something fizzes in my gut. 'I don't mean for real.'

'What do you mean?'

'You haven't dated in a long time, and that seems like a waste. So date me. Play with me. Fuck me.' He says the last in a voice that is so deep it rumbles right through my bones. 'I'm moving home in a month and, suddenly, I can't think of any way I'd rather spend what remains of my time in New York than with you.'

His voice whips against me, seductive and intense. But I hold onto Chance, to what I owe Abbey, to the single-minded focus this business takes to run. 'I can't.' My tone is clipped, strange-sounding in the midst of our conversation and what we've just done. 'I don't have time to date.'

'That's a cop-out.' His words are a little mocking.

'I'm sorry you feel that way, but it's the truth. I work really hard, and I can't spare the time to fill your last few weeks here in New York.'

'You're saying you'd rather work than do more of this?' He lifts a brow and, damn it, he is so hot, and I want him, and he knows it. He knows what he's doing to me. I swallow, frustration biting into my belly.

'Look, Nicholas, I appreciate the offer.' I wince, knowing it sounds like some kind of real-estate merger. 'But this was only meant to be one night. I hadn't—'

'Had sex in a really long time,' he supplies, a smile on his lips, as if he's teasing me, and a smile twitches on my own lips in response.

'I haven't had a *life* in a really long time. No friends, no boyfriend, I barely see my family—though I can't say that's a bad thing, actually—but I got… I know it's kind of sad to admit this, I got lonely, okay? I just wanted one night to be like a regular woman in her twenties. And it was great. *You* were great. But that's all it can be between us. I can't afford to get distracted.'

'Great. I don't want to distract you.' He wiggles his brows. 'At least, not beyond this month.'

'Nicholas,' I groan, lifting my hands to my face

and covering my eyes. 'I can't do it. This all means too much to me—'

'I get it.' I remove my hands to find him watching me. 'Your work is important to you. But you just said you haven't had a life in a really long time. So why not give yourself one? Just for a few weeks.'

His words catch in my chest. I frown.

'I'm not talking about a relationship, and I'm not talking about long-term. I'm literally talking about you and me, doing more of this.' He gestures towards my desk and the window that still bears my handprints. 'Dating for a few weeks, having fun, all kinds of fun, until it's time for me to leave.'

'And then what?'

'Then, I go back to my life, and you can go back to working twenty-two hours a day and pretending you're not a red-blooded woman.'

It's crazy. But what's craziest of all is that it makes sense. It's everything I wanted and never thought I could have. A relationship with clear boundaries, limits on what we get from one another and a stop point that would make it impossible for this to overshadow my real life in any way. It's exactly the kind of relationship I would create, if I thought there was any likelihood I'd find a guy to go along with it.

It feels almost too good to be true. 'You want to date me?'

'Well, I want to fuck you,' he says with a devilish

grin that takes any impertinence out of his correction. 'But you *should* be dated. And I'm pretty good at the whole dating thing.'

My heart kicks up a notch. 'And not at all arrogant with it, right?'

'It's not arrogant if it's true.'

I roll my eyes again but stifle a laugh. 'I suppose you have a point.'

'So? Four weeks of debauched fun. What say you, Miss Carmichael?'

My body unequivocally and enthusiastically says 'yes'. A thousand times over, yes. But I have to think this through. I'm not someone who jumps off the deep end without looking at every angle first. 'I don't date clients.'

'Ever?' Then, before I can answer, 'Right, you're a date virgin.'

'I am not!' I splutter, laughing. 'I have dated.'

'A millennium ago.'

'Shut up.' I punch his shoulder playfully but his eyes flare in a way that promises it could very quickly go from playful to something else entirely if I'm not careful.

'No one has to know about this.'

'Yeah, right.' Could we actually keep this a secret? Is that remotely feasible?

'What? You're planning on taking out a full-page ad?'

'No, but, you're kind of recognisable, and so am I.' Temptation is dragging me towards the line of acceptance, though. 'Why don't we just, you know, sleep together? My apartment has a basement garage, you can come and go and no one needs to know…'

'No.' He lifts a hand, curving it around my cheek, his eyes flaring with mine. 'It's obvious you're a total novice and need a first-rate education. I'm going to take you out.'

'Wine and dine me?'

'Yes.'

Heat soars in my chest.

'It wouldn't work. I can't have people talking. This matters too much to me.' Once more, I wave my hand around my office, indicating the club.

'I respect that.' He studies me for a beat. 'I promise I won't do anything that could damage your reputation in the club. Scout's honour.'

I laugh, because he is far from a Scout. 'Dating you would do that though.' And it would. Not just because I'm me, but because he's Nicholas Rothsmore and his reputation would be enough to drag me towards scandal—just the kind of scandal I promise my members the club will help them avoid.

'So we'll keep it secret.' He says it as if it's simple.

Before I can ask him exactly how he proposes to do that, he pulls me closer, tighter, so our bodies meld and thought becomes a little harder.

'I saw something on the forums about the Christmas gala,' he murmurs, his eyes sweeping my face.

'That we're looking for donations of time?'

He nods, then drops his head so his lips buzz mine

so lightly it's a form of torture. I push up on my tip-toes without meaning to, so my face is closer, wanting an actual kiss.

He pulls back, just a little, teasing me, tempting me. Frustration kicks in my abdomen.

'So?'

'So,' he murmurs, buzzing my lips again, then sliding a hand between my legs so I sway forward and exhale softly. 'If anyone runs into us, we'll tell them I'm helping with the Christmas gala.' His fingers brush my clit and I dig my fingers into his shoulder, holding on for dear life as he stirs my body to a new fever pitch.

It's so plausible. Members with certain expertise often volunteer their time or resources when it comes to organising events. Ellie Little recently provided a heap of supercars for a member event. This isn't unprecedented.

People would believe it.

Probably.

He slides a single finger inside my core and my knees threaten to buckle. His arm clamps around my back as if he *knows* somehow.

'Think about it,' he murmurs in my ear before sucking my lobe into his mouth, teasing it between his teeth. 'How else will you know what really…' he moves his finger deeper, brushing his thumb over my clit; my breath hurts '…really…' he bites his teeth down on my earlobe and I make a sound of total surrender '…great dating feels like?'

I hold him as he moves faster and pleasure is like a tidal wave swirling around me. I'm not sure I care about dating so much as sex, and sex specifically with Nicholas, but at the same time I'm completely intrigued.

Pleasure is making thought almost impossible, so I ask the first thing that occurs to me before I lose myself utterly in this moment. 'Why would you do this?'

'Beyond the fact the sex with you is fucking fantastic?'

I nod, tilting my head back, staring at my ceiling as everything explodes in my chest.

'Because in a month I will become the man who's going to be Lord Rothsmore and any kind of social life will be a distant memory.' I cling on tighter as my eyes fill with stars. 'This month with you will be like my very own goodbye party to my real life.'

If I weren't cresting over a wave of sublime release, I might almost have felt sorry for him, I might have paid more attention to the heaviness in his voice. But I cannot think properly, I cannot act as I normally would. I cry out his name and tip over the edge, my eyes blinking open to find him watching me with an intensity that takes my breath away.

'Say yes,' he prompts, a smile flickering across his lips, as though he knows I'll agree—how can I not?

My throat is parched, my body awash with a

shock of feelings, but I nod, jerkily. In that moment, I would have agreed to give him my soul; I would have agreed to anything he asked of me. We have thirty days, not one thousand and one, and yet sex, I think, has become my Scheherazade's tale, and he is the master storyteller, intriguing me more and more with each and every encounter…

CHAPTER FIVE

WELL... THAT WAS UNEXPECTED.

I settle into the luxurious leather of my limo, staring out at Manhattan as I cut across town. I can still smell her on my skin, on my hands, taste her in my mouth. Desire slides across me like warm water, and I throw my head back, squeeze my eyes shut and exhale.

Miss Anonymous is Miss Imogen Carmichael.

I've met her before, but only briefly, and while I thought she was attractive, I haven't really given her a second thought. I focus on that memory now, remembering the way she was with me, the same way she is with everyone in the exclusive club. Friendly, but in a way I instinctively understood to be guarded. She is exceptional at seeming warm without giving much of herself away.

She's calm and measured, and the club is a testament to that. It's a behemoth of an organisation and she oversees all aspects of it, an impressive tribute to her hard work.

What is unexpected is the heat that runs just beneath her surface. The passion that makes her lose herself in the moment just as completely as I do—if not more so. She's driven by instincts, and her instincts are fire and flame.

It isn't that I haven't had good sex. I have. But she's on a whole other level. There's nothing practised about her, there's nothing overthought or contrived. She does as she feels, and she feels as she needs, and her body answers mine in every way.

It's utterly surreal.

It must have been, for me to suggest we date.

Date! What the actual fuck?

I don't date. I screw. I screw beautiful, available, temporary lovers then move on. A week here and there, sometimes longer, but always on my terms, and always only if my lovers understand my ballgame. I don't do promises, I don't do hearts and candles, love, promises of a future. If I date a woman, it's because she knows how temporary and superficial it will be.

One day, I'll marry, someone like Saffy, except I'll never make the mistake of falling in love with them again. The pain of Saffy's desertion has been muted by the passage of time but it's still there, a pressure in my solar plexus whenever I remember it. When I think of how it felt to stand in front of the church and realise that she simply wasn't going to show. It's a pain that only grew when, a month later, I learned she'd fallen in love with someone else. While I was preparing for our wedding, she was working out how to leave me for some new guy.

I feel my tattoo restlessly. *I am my own.*

I'd forgotten that for a while. I'd let the union my parents had pushed me into, had championed and supported, become something else in my mind, so I'd actually let myself fall *in love* with Saffron. So much so that I was devastated when we broke up. Devastated, humiliated, burned to a crisp.

Never again.

When I get married, it will be to someone who wants the title I can give her and the money at my disposal, who understands that, beyond polite companionship, I'm not offering anything more and that, beyond a need for a couple of heirs, I'm not looking for anything further.

It makes me see my parents' marriage through a new light. I used to think their lovelessness was kind of sad—the way they wasp their way through life. Now, I get it. It's a practical marriage. They married because it made sense, they had their son and heir to carry on the family name and probably never touched each other again.

Yeah, it's a well-worn blueprint for marriage in their circles, in my circle, and I have no doubt my own will be just like it.

But until then, for one month, I'm going to enjoy Imogen Carmichael, and I'm going to make it one of the best months of her life. I'm going to take dating to the next level, set the bar so fucking high for the poor next guy that he has to spend the rest of his life working to make her as happy and fulfilled as I have in these four weeks.

Why? Because I'm Nicholas Rothsmore and I'm always, without fail, the best at everything I do, and now that includes dating Imogen.

A box arrives the following afternoon. It's gunmetal-grey with white cursive script embossed across the top, proclaiming the name of an exclusive Manhattan lingerie boutique. My breath immediately speeds up. I ignore Emily's curious glance as I take it from her, moving to my desk and placing it carefully on the corner.

'RSVPs are coming thick and fast,' I say. 'Ticket payments are way ahead of where we were at this time last year.'

But, curious or not, Emily is all professionalism. She consults her clipboard for a moment. 'And donations are great too. Sir Bennet Alwin has donated a guided tour of Australia's Great Barrier Reef on his own personal submersible.'

'I wouldn't mind winning that,' I say with a smile. He's one of the leading naturalists of our time, and the Great Barrier Reef is regrettably a dying wonder of the world.

'You can bid,' she points out.

It's true, there's nothing to preclude me from entering the auction bidding, but, much like dating members, I have my own little set of rules that stands me apart from the other club members. In the past, I've matched donations for items that can be replicated, so the charity wins twice.

'I might. What else?'

'There's the private performance by the London Philharmonic, the flight over the Baltic in Yuri Ostromonov's helicopter, the private cruise of the Antarctic and the custom diamond choker from Alec Minton.'

'Wow. That's quite a haul.'

'That's just in the last week.'

I shake my head, floored by people's generosity, even when I know half of it is about advertising and the kudos that comes from being visibly associated with The Billionaires' Club.

'Seriously, you should see my inbox. It's overflowing with offers.'

'Great. Well, let me know if you need me to wade in.'

'Nope, I've got this. The caterer asked you to go by some time this week to review the menu. You're free Friday afternoon.'

My heart notches up a bit. Before Nicholas left, he turned and said, 'Friday night. I'll be in touch with details.'

But the afternoon is a separate matter. I nod, turning away in case the heat in my blood has converted to pink cheeks. 'Sounds good. Send me a meeting invite once it's confirmed.'

'Done.'

As soon as I'm alone, I cross the room and lift the box, running my finger over the embossed text with a small smile. My fingers shake as I pull on the satin ribbon. It loosens then drops to the floor, just a spool of white against the carpet.

I lift the lid slowly, placing it on the desk. There's a gold sticker joining two sides of tissue paper together. I slide my finger under it, easing it up, deliberately moving slowly to counteract my body's impatience, needing to control my instincts—which shout at me to rip the damned paper and see what's inside.

The paper lifts and a delicate cream silk fabric sits inside, perfectly nestled, so I have to lift it out to see what it is. My breath hitches not at the beauty of the lingerie, though it is stunning, so much as at the idea that he, Nicholas Rothsmore, bought it for me.

I hold it up a little higher, skimming my eyes over the delicate spaghetti straps, which lead to a low V of lace. I can tell that when I wear it, my breasts will be visible through the frothy, twisting swirls. Silk kisses lace and it falls in soft folds down to what I guess will be my hips when I finally put on the exquisite piece. I spin, looking back to the box, and smile, because there are matching briefs, silk and lace, with ribbons at the side, so they can be undone with no more than a slight tug.

Anticipation supercharges my blood. I'm about to lay the lingerie back in the box and stuff the lid on when I catch sight of an envelope in the bottom.

Intrigued, I reach for it, opening the back and lifting out a single piece of thick card.

It bears his name at the top, and a coat of arms, which, I imagine, belong to his ancient family. I stare at it for a moment, making out a lion, a spiky-looking flower and a bird with a full and impressive plume of feathers.

Aristocratic guys I generally avoid like the plague. And with good reason. All my experience has made me wary of people with too much money, but at least people who've had to work to earn it or fight to keep it have some appreciation for the value of it and an understanding for what life is like for those who don't; the liberties and choices many are deprived of because of a lack of financial viability.

But it's the lords and the sirs, the counts and the barons who are, by far, the most…wankery. In fact, the only member I've expelled from the club was a lord with an impeccable reputation, but we discovered he'd drugged a waitress at a club event—one of our members had found them in the Intimate Rooms just in time—but, God, it could have been so much worse.

Not that all the guys with titles are bad. They're just definitely not my type.

I have no idea what my type is, but it's not Nicholas.

That gives me a sense of relief because I don't want to get involved with anyone right now, and so the only way I can really date him is because I know it will go nowhere.

Miss Anonymous—
I'll pick you up at eight o'clock.
Wear this.
N

It's so simple, so completely to the point, but my heart stammers as though he's breathed the words into my ear, and I need to sit down for a second to regroup. His handwriting is bold and confident, just like him, and he uses—what else?—a fountain pen. I lift it to my lips without thinking and breathe deeply, as though I might somehow catch a lingering hint of *him* on the card.

Friday is still three nights away and suddenly the wait feels excruciating.

Fortunately, I'm flat out too busy to pine or anticipate…*much.* Wednesday will be spent doing membership interviews and vetting, Thursday will be planning out next year's events and schedules, making sure we have something seriously incredible planned for each month. Right now, The Billionaires' Club is the hottest ticket in the world—my waiting list is a mile long.

It's a great position to be in but it's also dangerous territory—someone else could set up and start taking my business if I don't make sure our offering is consistently *better.* Extra is my middle name.

We've got Egypt on the calendar next year, including the kind of money-can't-buy access to the Pyramids of Giza followed by a starlit dinner right beneath the Sphinx, with delicacies from all over the world being flown in for members. Imagine a carpet of stars, a thousand candles lighting the way and one of the world's best jazz musicians crooning some beautiful music all evening long. Followed by a night in a tent that, once you're inside, is more like a six-star hotel.

It's taken a huge amount of work to organise—dealing with the authorities and making sure we're not violating any local customs or laws—but this is what people pay their million dollars a year for. Oh, the ticket price itself is extra on top, but without being a member, you don't get a look-in.

On Friday, I meet with the gala caterers to do a small tasting of the menu, as well as the wines, and go over the running of the night, explaining when we'll serve which courses and why.

It's a busy day, and I'm glad for that, glad that by the time six o'clock rolls around I've barely had time to stop, let alone think about Nicholas.

Okay, that's a lie. I've barely stopped thinking about him but in a 'back of my mind' kind of way. But as I lather myself in the shower then towel off before smoothing oil over my hairless legs, all I can think about is the next few hours and the certainty that soon his hands will be where my hands are.

My pulse fires at just the thought. When I slip on the lingerie he sent me, my body is already a field of live wires so my breasts tingle and my stomach twists.

I stare at myself in the mirror, still nowhere near ready, but wanting to stay just like this. Not to go out so much as to stay in. I wish I hadn't agreed to date him, only to sleep with him. Except I'm actually a little excited to see what a guy like Nicholas has planned.

And sex is happening.

I just have to wait a few more hours.

Is this completely crazy? I don't get involved with members. Even though The Billionaires' Club is my creation, my baby, and I'm prominent in the community, there's a distance between me and everyone else. I have to oversee things, to make sure it goes smoothly. I have to run the business side of things and manage membership difficulties.

I can't be seen fooling around with someone in the club.

This *has* to stay private. And it has to be brief. He said he's going back to England in a month, but that's no real impediment to us seeing each other. I mean, the club has rooms all over the world; we host events everywhere. He attends most of them, like all of the members. So I'm bound to see him again, often enough that we could keep this going on a semi-permanent basis.

And then what?

I see him slinking off to the Intimate Rooms with someone else? I hear along the grapevine he's getting married to Lady Asher Cumber-something-or-other?

Because that's how this plays out.

And if I don't retain a bit of control here, I'll get hurt. I might seem, on the outside, as if I have everything ordered in my life, but loneliness is pervasive and powerful, and the temptation of being one half of a pair might lead me to forget the sense in all this.

I'll have to be clear with him from the outset, and clear with myself too. With a small smile curving my lips, I think of the tattoo above his heart and reach for a pen. *I am my own.* I write the words hastily on the back of a store receipt and stick it to my dressing table mirror.

It's a good incantation. I'm going to say it often. Just in case.

It's snowing again and cold out. With no idea what we're doing or where we're going, I dress with versatility in mind. A pair of slim-fitting black leather trousers paired with a silk shirt with long, bell sleeves that falls off one shoulder and is a dirty gold in colour. I like it because the colour flatters my skin, the softness of the fabric hugs my curves and makes it pretty obvious I'm not wearing a bra, and when the sleeve drops over one shoulder, you can see the hint of lace from the camisole he sent me.

I take a few minutes to style my hair, curling it with my wand so it falls in big loose waves over one shoulder. Make-up is simple—as always—just a slick of mascara and the bright red lipstick I wore the night we fucked in Sydney.

My heart is pounding like a bird trapped in a too-small cage.

There are still twenty minutes to go. Waiting is killing me.

I pace through to the kitchen and pour a Chardonnay, press play on my phone so soft piano music connects to the speakers that are wired through my apartment, filling the space with beautiful, calming jazz. It helps, but I'm still looking at the clock every ten seconds.

'This is ridiculous,' I groan, pacing across the lounge for my handbag. On a whim, I swap it for a small gold clutch that matches my shirt and opt for my faux fur coat, wrapping it around my shoulders as I pace back to the kitchen.

Shoes! I need shoes.

Damn it.

I can only laugh at myself and my state of nervousness as I survey my extensive collection of stilettos. Again, with no idea what we're doing, I should probably choose a shoe for all occasions.

But as I remember the way he looked at my stilettos that night in Sydney, a wild impulse has me pulling out one of my favourite pairs. Supple leather, a pointed toe, and a heel so high and spindly it's a wonder they don't snap in two, gives me a few extra inches in height and a mega-boost in confidence.

I add a couple of bangles on a whim, and have three big gulps of wine then stand perfectly still and wait. I breathe in, I breathe out, I empty my mind, I still my trembling—all the tricks the psychologist taught me right after Abbey died, after I'd started having panic attacks.

I don't have the attacks any more but I still get flushes of anxiety, especially when I have to speak at an event. No one would ever know—I pride myself on presenting the image of a calm and collected entrepreneur, but in no small part my success at faking a confidence I don't feel comes from this arsenal of stress-management techniques.

My buzzer rings.

My heart leaps to my throat.

I spin and stalk across the lounge, adrenalin pumping through me as I lift the phone off the cradle. 'Hello?' Just a husk.

'Miss Anonymous?'

My smile is broad and instinctive. 'I'll be right down.'

I hang up, take one last look at myself and exhale slowly—it does nothing to quell the butterflies rampaging my stomach. They chase me as I exit the apartment and descend in the lift.

'Good night, Mr Silverstein.' I smile as I approach the door. He pulls it inward, a kind smile cracking the lines that form his face.

He lets out a low whistle. 'You look mighty pretty, Miss Carmichael.'

He has a southern drawl a lot like my pa's. It softens my heart whenever I speak to him.

'Thanks.'

'Got a club function?'

I nod, because it's easier than admitting the truth—that I have a sort of date.

'Have fun, be safe.'

He says the same thing every time I go out at night. I like it. Even though I'm long past the point of needing protecting, it's still nice to feel as if someone cares.

Nicholas is waiting just outside, standing on the kerb, the back door of his low-set black car open. A driver sits behind the wheel. I don't know what I'd expected. A motorbike, maybe? Not necessarily this. But most people I know are chauffeured around. In fact, I'm probably an anomaly for the fact I use cabs or the subway.

As I step onto the kerb, his eyes trail their way over me, slowly, dragging heat and electricity wherever he looks. My heart stutters, my stomach dives.

Anxiety is back, pulsing through my veins. I refuse to show it.

He takes a step towards me, and another, and my pulse races, my heart twists.

'You look good enough to eat,' he murmurs, holding a hand out to me. I place mine in it; sparks dance the length of my limbs, and my eyes widen in recognition of the strength of this attraction and connection.

'I'll hold you to that.'

His eyes show amusement, but he doesn't laugh.

Heat explodes between us. I stay where I am; he doesn't move either. We're separated by several feet, but holding hands, just staring at each other.

He's wearing beige trousers, a white shirt and a dark blue jacket, with brown shoes. He looks handsome, sexy, stylish and wealthy.

I wish he weren't wearing anything.

'What are we doing tonight?' I hear myself ask, my lips shifting into a slight smile.

'Ah. It's a surprise.' He jerks on my hand a little, pulling me towards him, and he kisses me on the cheek. It's so chaste and weirdly sweet that a different kind of heat, a warmth, flows through me. And then, a whisper in my ear, just low enough for me to catch, 'But I promise it's going to end in my bed.'

CHAPTER SIX

La Chambre is one of Manhattan's chicest, hardest-to-get-into clubs. But I went to school with one of the owners, so my entry is guaranteed, any time.

I chose to start our night here for a few reasons. Obviously, because it's exclusive, we can relax in privacy. It's also named the French word for *bedroom* because its central design feature is that it feels like an extremely sumptuous and classy series of bedrooms. Each private booth is filled with velvet cushions, soft seats that recline fully, and privacy curtains for intimate moments.

The food and wine are second to none, and the lighting is dim. But more than that, I've done my research. The head chef of La Chambre consults for Est Il Est, the company that has a long history of catering Billionaires' Club events. Meaning we can totally pass this off as research if anyone from the club sees us.

'It's like a grand bedroom.' She looks at me with those huge dark blue eyes, and I can't tell if she's laughing at or judging me. A little of both, I think.

For someone who's so wildly abandoned in bed, she's incredibly strait-laced when out of it. Yes, I see a hint of disapproval curve her lips and I ache to reach around and kiss it away.

And I will, later. For now, we're in the dating portion of our night.

Besides, I've found myself wondering about Imogen this week, about more than just what makes her tick in the bedroom. She's young to be so incredibly successful, and while I know she has the backing of her parents' wealth behind her, she also has the work ethic of someone determined to make it on their own. I should know—I share that trait.

'Ah, Mr Rothsmore.' The maître d' bows as he approaches us, a gesture of servitude I can't stand but know I'll have to learn to live with. 'Welcome back. I've reserved your usual table.'

I nod. 'Thank you, Jake.'

He leads us through the restaurant and the hand I place in the small of Imogen's back is purely friendly, even when I want to dip my palm a little lower, trailing my fingers over the delicate curve of her rear in those—God help me—leather trousers. As if she needed to get any hotter.

My 'usual' table is at the back of the restaurant, a booth that's set away from the others. The chairs are actually a wrap-around banquette, comfortable and soft. I watch as Imogen shrugs out of her coat and hands it to Jake, then wish I hadn't watched because the delicate shrug of her shoulders—one bare from where her silk shirt has slipped down—is enough to make my cock hard against my pants in a way that's almost painful. Then, I see just a few millimetres of lace and know she's wearing the twin set I bought for her and I'm pretty much done for.

'Everything okay?' she murmurs, batting her eyelids at me as she sits down. I order a bottle of champagne—my friend's private vineyard supplies a Legacy collection for special clients—and a soda for myself, then give her the full force of my attention.

'That depends. How do you define okay?'

'You look pale, suddenly,' she murmurs, her delicious lips quirking at the edges.

'Funny, that, given the fact my blood has rushed south all of a sudden.'

She dips her head forward, her blonde hair forming a curtain that blocks me from seeing her face. Impatience has me reaching down and pushing it behind her ear so I can see her properly. Her eyes lift to mine, meeting them with a mix of emotions I can't fathom.

'You come here often?' she queries and something shifts in my gut. A doubt? Does she not like the restaurant?

'From time to time. Have you ever been?'

She looks around, her expression impossible to decipher. 'Nope.'

I sit beside her rather than across the table. It's not my usual play but I don't really want to be separated from her. Once Jake brings our drinks, I'll have him draw the curtains. Our knees brush beneath the table. She jumps a little. I smile.

'You're nervous again.'

Her eyes flex to mine. 'A little.'

'Why?' I lift my finger to her perfectly painted, beautifully shaped lips. 'Don't tell me. Because you haven't done this in a really long time.' Her eyelashes are incredibly long, like wings hovering just above her eyes. They flutter as a bird might flap and I stare at her, transfixed, until Jake reappears with the drinks. He places them on the table and, without looking at him, I say, 'Close the curtains.'

'Yes, sir.'

Imogen's eyes flare, anticipation in their depths. I shouldn't play with her—she's too sweet and way too inexperienced—but I pull away from her a little. 'We don't want anyone to see us.'

Her lips part a little. 'See us doing what?'

It's just a question but it might as well be an invitation to lift her up and fuck her right here on this table.

I'm seriously tempted. But I've got the night planned and, for a reason I can't really fathom, I care about showing her what her social life should be like. Maybe it's like passing a baton, enlisting an apprentice right before I hang up my New York shoes and go back to England?

'Dating, of course.' I grin.

'Right.' She swallows, her delicate, pale throat

tensing with the gesture. 'I've been thinking about that.'

Something switches inside her, and the nerves are gone. She sits a little straighter, reaching for the champagne glass without sipping it in what I now recognise is a prop technique. She likes to hold something. To stop herself fidgeting?

Her fingers curve around the stem. 'Go on,' I prompt, matching her gesture, pulling my own soda tumbler towards me.

'This whole dating thing.' She pauses, a furrow on her brow. 'We need to discuss it further.'

My lips quirk but I take a drink to hide the smile. I don't think she'd like to feel as if I'm laughing at her. And I'm not, really, more just thinking how cute she is like this—trying to bring her impressive business mind to a social agreement.

'Okay, so discuss it.'

'I'm serious,' she murmurs, her eyes forcing mine to hold hers.

'What is it?'

'I was thinking, earlier, about how crazy this is and I think we need to have some more rules in place.'

'Rules?' I jerk my brows without meaning to. 'Out of nowhere, I'm thinking of a headmistress and I've got to tell you, Imogen, it's very hot.'

She grins, leaning forward and pressing her hand to my shoulder. 'Maybe later, Mr Rothsmore.'

Oh, crap. Role play. With her? Suddenly, she has about a thousand upper hands as I start to imagine her in all sorts of costumes and can barely think straight.

'My business means everything to me,' she says, her smile slowly falling from her face. 'It's not just… It isn't just something I've worked really hard to build. It means a lot. To a lot of people. And part of that is my image. I really can't have anyone find out about us.'

'We've already dealt with this.'

'I know.' She nods a little jerkily. 'But what we didn't talk about is what happens after.'

After? 'In a month?' I never think more than a day ahead. Even planning to see her until I leave was somewhat paradigm-shifting for my mentality. Planning beyond that is not something I have the skillset for.

She nods. 'We'll see each other again. It's inevitable.'

'So?' I lift a brow. 'That's kind of fun.'

'No.' It's like a whip, cracking across me. 'I don't want this to be something that goes on, where we see each other in Monaco and decide to pick up where we left off.' A *moue* of disapproval shifts over her lips. 'That's messy and inelegant and definitely leaves room for discovery.'

Her summation is adamant, but she has a very good point. I could see me spying her from across the room at an event and finding an excuse to drag her into a hallway to have some fun, only to be seen by a passing member. It's risky.

'We need a line in the sand,' she goes on carefully, as though she's thinking on the fly. 'The Christmas gala should be our last night together. After that, we're civil, polite strangers. If you see me at an event, you say "hi", and keep moving.'

There's nothing in her suggestion that worries me. I know what my future holds and it is far away from Imogen Carmichael and this wonderful world she's created.

'Fine.' It's easy to agree to that.

Seeing her obvious relief dents my pride a little.

'Okay.' Her smile is bright. 'So privacy and a hard stop point.' She nods. 'Good.'

'You forgot the third rule,' I say, unable to explain why something is firing in my chest that feels a lot like impatience.

'Did I? What's that?' She's businesslike again, focussed on me and what she could have missed.

'A whole lotta fun in between.' I swoop my head down and kiss her, swallowing her surprise and laughing deep in my throat. Yeah, this is going to be fun all right.

He kisses as if it's a sport and he holds all the world records in it. He kisses as if his sole purpose for being is getting me off. He kisses as if he were meant to be doing this.

I surrender to him, lifting a hand and curling it in his shirt, clutching onto him in case he gets it into his head to stop what he's doing. I don't want him to stop. Beneath the table, I lift one leg a little, onto his knee, and his hand curves around the leather, keeping it hooked there, his tongue duelling with mine as he kisses me harder, his other hand lifting to the back of my head and pushing through my hair, holding me right where I am.

I have no intention of going anywhere.

My head spins, afterwards, when he lifts away from me. He really is the quintessential English nobleman, so handsome, so swarthy and fancy yet masculine all at once. There's something cultured and inaccessible about him that even someone like me, who grew up with Hollywood royalty and can generally move in all circles, finds intimidating yet fascinating.

'Are you hungry?'

Am I? 'I think I was when I was at home but, I've gotta say, Nicholas, you have a habit of pushing such considerations way down my list.'

He laughs. 'I'm glad.'

I reach for his hand, putting mine over it without really thinking about it—funny how such a gesture can become natural so quickly.

'So England, huh?'

Something sharp crosses his expression. Something very un-Nicholas that makes me feel concern for him, or worried for him. Something.

'Yes.'

Okay, there's definitely something here. Curiosity shifts inside me. 'You're not looking forward to going home?'

He lifts his shoulders. 'It's home,' he says after a moment. 'I always knew I'd move back, eventually.'

'How long have you been in New York?'

'Five years.'

'That's right.' I remember reading this in his file. 'You came here after—' I stop what I'm saying, but not in time. His eyes zip to mine, his expression dark.

'After my fiancée left me at the altar?'

I grimace. 'Sorry.'

He flips his hand over and squeezes mine, then reaches for his drink. 'It was for the best.'

It's a comment designed to move conversation on, to shut down worry and any further line of enquiry. I don't succumb to it. 'Why?'

He takes a drink. 'We weren't well suited.'

I don't know much about his fiancée. I can't even remember her name.

'Saffron,' he supplies and I realise I've spoken my thoughts aloud.

'She's not in the club?' Though our membership has grown, I know every member by name and sight and there are no Saffrons. We have a Pearl and a Cinnamon, though.

'No. It's not her thing.' His smile is indulgent.

'No?'

'No.'

Hmm. Another closed door. I don't really like closed doors. 'Why not?'

'Apart from the fact she ditched me in front of five hundred of our nearest and dearest?'

'But why? Why did she dump you?'

'That's the billion-pound question,' he drawls, and for a second, his face is in the shadow of an almighty rain cloud and I want to draw the sun back out.

'You never found out?'

'Why she left me?' He shakes his head. 'But I can guess.'

'Why, then?'

'She was like a bird in an aviary,' he says, after a moment. 'Beautiful, smart, funny, but completely defined by who she was, who her parents were, by what was expected of her.'

'And that's marrying someone like you?'

'Yes.' He dips his head forward. 'She hated it. I didn't realise how much until she left me.'

'Hate it or not, it's still a pretty shitty thing to do.' I wince. 'Sorry.'

'No, you're right. I think she knows that. The problem is, she did love me, but she hated what marrying me would mean more.'

Something makes my voice a little high-pitched. 'And you loved her?'

His eyes are swirling with emotion when they meet mine. 'I did, or I thought I did. I don't know. I have to tell you, the whole thing turned me off love and marriage for life.' His laugh is husky.

'So you're a dedicated bachelor?'

'I wish.' He rolls his eyes and he's Nicholas

Rothsmore, playboy, careless sex god, once more, so I relax, relieved I haven't sent him into some kind of grief spin by making him talk about his ex. 'I have been recalled to the manor.' He grins, showing me he's joking, only there's an edge to his words.

'Rothsmore Manor?' I tease.

He shakes his head. 'Actually, our country seat is Becksworth Hall.'

Somewhere I remember reading that. 'It sounds very grand,' I tease.

'Oh, it is.'

'Like something out of *Pride and Prejudice*?'

'Pemberley has nothing on Becksworth.'

I laugh. 'Tell me about it.'

'Not much to tell. If you've seen one grand country home, you've seen them all. Ancient, huge, imposing, miles of windows, stables, a lake for trout fishing, strawberry patches for summer picnics.'

I can't help my sigh. 'That sounds idyllic.'

'In some ways.'

'Not in others?'

But he's done being questioned.

'What about you?'

'What about me?' My turn to sip my champagne and buy time. It's delicious. Crisp and fruity all at once, with enthusiastic bubbles that tickle my mouth as I swirl it around.

'You're from New York?'

'God, no, I wish.' I laugh. 'I'm a Cali Girl. Can't you tell?'

His eyes sweep my face, my hair, my golden skin and he grins. 'Now that you mention it…'

Heat fires in my veins, as hot as any day on a Malibu beach.

'So why New York?'

'I like it here.'

He reaches forward and tucks my hair behind my ear. 'It seems a little unfair for you to demand me to open the wounds of my past and you not tell me about something as simple as a geographical shift?' He says it in a way that's light-hearted but I feel his will of iron beneath the words.

Only he doesn't know. He doesn't understand that my move to New York was bound up in the wounds of my own past. How linked it all is to Abbey and a need to flee LA.

I don't realise I'm frowning until he reaches over and rubs his finger across my lips.

'It made sense, for the business,' I obfuscate. And I think he knows I'm not being completely honest, but he lets it go.

'Where'd you get the idea from?'

'For The Billionaires' Club?'

He dips his head once in a sign of encouragement.

'From a friend of mine—an actress, who was complaining about even the best bars being paparazzi haunts, and wanting to just get away. To have somewhere to let her hair down without having it splashed over the papers the next day.'

'I would imagine a lot of actresses live for the attention of the paparazzi.'

'You're wrong,' I say quickly. 'That attention can be used to build an image, sure, but it's a double-edged sword. And not being able to escape that hounding, it's horrifying. Everyone deserves to be able to switch off their "persona" and just be themselves for a while.'

He's watching me in a way that gives me goose bumps and makes my head feel light, because he's looking at me as though he sees the real me, deep inside who I am, beyond my own 'persona'.

'You're speaking from experience?'

'Sort of. Not really. I like to fly beneath the radar as much as possible, but my parents, on the other hand…'

He waits, encouragingly, as if he doesn't know about them. And maybe he doesn't. I forget sometimes that I'm out of the East Coast bubble.

'My mother's an actress. Or was. Now I guess she's a socialite. She never met a camera she didn't like.'

Wow. I sound so bitter. So serious. And I am—God knows I carry a lot of resentments but I usually do a much better job of hiding them. It's hard to hide things from Nicholas.

I force a smile to my face. 'The club was only meant to be for a few people, but it just took off.

I started with a single venue here in Manhattan but…'

'You found a gap in the market, and the market rose to meet it.'

It sounds so cynical when, actually, it wasn't at all. 'I studied business at college—I thought I'd get a job out this way but, once I got here, I found I didn't really want to spend my time working hard to make rich people even richer.' I smile to take the sting out of the statement. 'Then, the club took on a life all of its own.'

'And you have your charity too, right?'

My smile now is natural. 'Chance, yeah.'

'It does something for kids?'

'Excuse me, sir?' a voice calls from beyond the curtains.

'Yes?' Impatience curves Nicholas's expression.

The curtains open and the waiter reappears, placing a platter on the table top. 'Compliments of the chef.'

Oysters—one of my favourites—with a variety of toppings, and caviar atop thinly sliced cucumber. It breaks the serious mood that had descended on us, and I'm glad. Glad for the reprieve. We promised each other a whole lot of fun and talking about broken engagements and my parents is hardly fun.

Beneath the table, I brush my hand over his knee. He turns to look at me slowly, but that doesn't stop the slash of heat that steals across my body.

Dating was his idea and I really liked it but now

all I want is to be back in bed with him, exploring the desire that fogs the air around us.

I am hungry only for Nicholas Rothsmore.

CHAPTER SEVEN

I'M NOT SURE if it's the champagne I've been drinking, or the incredibly decadent Belgian mousse we shared after dinner, or the fact we're walking hand in hand through New York with the lights of the Brooklyn Bridge twinkling in the background, snow dusting down from an inky black sky, and Christmas lights twinkling overhead, but suddenly I feel as if I'm floating.

'So, is this a normal first date, Nicholas?'

His fingers squeeze mine. I love how he does that, as if it's his way of agreeing with me or something. 'I mean, we've already had sex on two separate occasions, so I'm not sure we can classify this as a first date?'

'No, no, no,' I demur with a grin. 'Those weren't dates. It was fucking.' Champagne has taken away any of my usual tendencies to hesitate. 'And you told me fucking is different from dating.'

His laugh is like a caress. I close my eyes and let it wash over me.

'It is.'

'But you don't really date.'

It's not a question; I know the answer.

'I date,' he corrects, pausing before leading us across the street.

'Oh, yeah?'

'Sure. I date like this—when I know it's just for fun, with no chance of becoming more than what it is.' His eyes meet mine for the briefest second. 'But not a lot of women are interested in that.'

'Really?' I pull a face. 'Because you're such a catch they insist on a wedding ring on the first night?'

He laughs. 'Something like that.'

'I can actually kind of believe it.'

'I wasn't serious.' He drops my hand so he can put his in the small of my back, guiding me further down the street. It's a perfect, perfect New York winter's night. Bundled up in my jacket, with Nicholas at my side, I feel warm, safe and as if I just don't want the night to end. 'It's just hard to meet someone who understands that I really, truly don't want to get involved.'

'Beyond sex.' I am definitely emboldened by champagne.

'Yeah.'

I look up at him thoughtfully. 'Is that what the tattoo means?' I blink and see those words *I am my own* written over his heart.

He doesn't pretend to misunderstand me. 'The tattoo means a lot of things.'

'Yeah?' Curiosity barbs in my chest.

His smile is self-deprecating. 'About a year after the wedding—the wedding that never happened—' he laughs '—my dad came to New York and he was livid. I don't think I've ever seen him like that. We argued—which we don't do. It's very un-British.' He grins, so sexy, so full of passion that I think Nicholas flies in the face of any stereotype regarding stiff, unfeeling upper lips.

'What did you fight about?'

'My lifestyle, which he hated. The nickname "Playboy of Manhattan", which people delighted in calling me.' He expels a sigh. 'He did everything he could to get me to go home, but at the same time I think he knew the business here needed me. So in the end, he issued an ultimatum. Sow my wild oats, get the partying out of my system. Then, at thirty, get married and come home to settle down.'

'And you're nearly thirty?'

He nods. 'It's time to face the music.'

'So, what, you go home and get married, sometime next year?'

For a second, something like fire flashes in his eyes, and then he shrugs. 'That's the deal we made.'

'Wow. So, what, like a dynastic marriage?' I'm kind of joking; the whole idea sounds so preposterous and so unlike Nicholas that it *has* to be a joke.

But his look sparks with something like muted anger. 'Yes.'

I stop walking. 'You can't be serious.'

He lifts his shoulders, staring down at me with eyes that seem to hold an entire universe in their depths.

'"You have been born to privilege, Nicholas. It is not for you to abandon this family's legacy on a whim."'

He is impersonating someone, putting on an even toffier accent.

'But surely you can carry on a family legacy while marrying who you choose…?'

'I would choose to stay single,' he corrects, turning again so we're shoulder to shoulder, taking a step forward. I move with him.

'Why?'

'Because I like being single. I like working hard. Playing harder. I don't want to get married. I don't want to have children. These are things my parents expect of me, but they don't reflect my wishes.'

My heart shifts a little inside my chest. 'Have you explained that to them?'

'My parents?'

'No, your secretary.'

He laughs. 'Has anyone ever told you that you have a smart mouth?'

I gape, because I don't. I really, actually don't. I'm very careful with what I say, moderating my language, aware that I am the representative of Chance and The Billionaires' Club everywhere I go. But there's something about Nicholas that makes me feel completely at ease, as if I can relax completely.

'Did I offend you?'

His laugh is uproarious. 'Do I look like I'm made of glass?'

I smile, relieved. 'I don't know why, but I feel like I can say anything to you,' I explain, simply.

His gaze hooks to mine again, probing. 'It's because of the stop point. We both know this is an aberration. Not real. Out of step with the lives we're both going to lead. So we can let go and have fun without worrying about any kind of consequences or future.'

That makes sense.

'I have told my parents, on several occasions, what I think of their expectations and their title, and even their fortunes.'

'Really?'

He's quiet, deep in thought. 'Except I do care,' he says, after a moment. To our right, a ferry boat passes under the bridge, bleating its low, thundering horn as it goes. The snow falls a little thicker now, landing on the bridge of my nose. I dash it away. 'Not about the money—I have made more than enough on my own. But the title is something that matters.'

We've slowed right down without meaning to. We put one foot in front of the other, but slowly. 'I was raised to care about it, and I do. There's so much history wrapped up in it, so much of my family's past. And there's a responsibility there to shepherd the title, the estate, the fortune on to a new recipient.'

It rankles my American sensibilities. I can't understand any of that old British aristocracy stuff. 'That's the way these things work, I guess.'

'Yes. I didn't much care for it when I was younger but now, at nearly thirty, I feel the weight of it in a new way. I don't want to be where my family's claim on the title ends.'

'Naturally.'

'You really think so? Sometimes I can't believe I actually give a shit.'

I laugh. 'I can. I can see that. Legacies are important. They should be protected.'

'And you? Is there some family tradition your parents are desperate for you to carry on?'

I bite down on my lip, thinking about that for a second before shaking my head. 'Not really.'

'They must be proud of you?'

'You think?'

'Sure. Why not?'

I wrinkle my nose. 'They're not easy to please.' I don't feel like talking about them. As much as I've come to a place in my life where I accept the limitations of my relationship with Mom and Dad, it still hurts. It hurts in a way I'll probably never get over.

After Abbey died, I needed them in a different way. I needed them to be there for me, to make things better, and they weren't. They just couldn't.

They've never really been there for me since—they just don't get me.

'Even when you're running a global empire, trading in luxury and world-class networking events?'

'Even then,' I quip, shutting down his line of questioning with a tight-lipped smile. 'Where, exactly, are we going?'

'We're nearly there.'

'Nearly where?'

'Don't like surprises?'

'I like some surprises.'

'Speaking of which,' he murmurs, surprising me by bundling me into his arms and pushing me against a wall. My breath catches in my throat, my face tilting towards him. 'Did you get the box I sent you?'

A smile lifts the corners of my lips. 'Which box would that be?' I feign ignorance.

'A little box of silk and lace, and a rather delightfully placed ribbon, if memory serves…'

'Ah.' I can't stop the smile that spreads over my face. 'You're just going to have to wait and see.'

'Haven't I been waiting a decade already?' he groans, dropping his head forward and brushing his lips over mine. Desire sets up camp in my belly.

'Did you choose the lingerie yourself?' I can't help asking.

His face is serious. 'Of course. Did you think I had my assistant do it?'

'Or your driver,' I tease.

'Edward can cross town in fifteen minutes flat but I don't think he and I share the same taste in women's apparel.'

'I'm glad to hear it.'

'You don't like Edward's taste either?'

I laugh. 'I don't think I've even clapped eyes on the man. I just meant I like the idea of you going into a boutique and picking something out. For me.'

'Ah.' He nods, sagely, his own mouth quirking into a delicious smile. 'I did.' He drops his head a little closer, so his breath teases my cheek. 'You know what else I did?'

My heart rate accelerates. 'What?'

'I ran my fingers over it.'

Heat pools between my legs.

'I imagined you in it.'

God. I feel weak-kneed.

'And then...'

I hold my breath, waiting. Desire is like a moth inside me, my blood the flame to which it's drawn. I feel the wings beating through my veins, hollowing me out from under my skin.

'Yeah?' My voice is just a croak.

'I went home and jacked off, imagining you in it.'

'Oh, God.' It's a tremulous acknowledgement of one of the sexiest images I've ever had planted in my brain.

He's smiling; I'm not. I'm burning up. I can no longer wait to be with him. I look around us—we are practically alone, save for the cars hurtling past and the occasional jogger out for a late-night run.

'I want to go home with you.'

He nods.

'Now.'

He laughs. 'I'm glad to hear it.'

'Wherever you were taking me, scrap it. I just want to get in a cab and go back to yours.'

'I'm taking you there now.'

I push away from the wall, my expression showing him I mean business. 'Good, then let's go.'

A few minutes later, he leads me across the street and towards the Hudson.

'You live on the water?'

I wrack my brain, trying to remember his address details from the paperwork, and come up empty. Someone better at this than I am might have taken the time to pull his file out for review, to re-familiarise themselves with his bio. But it never occurred to me and, actually, I'm kind of glad, because it's nice learning about Nicholas straight from the horse's mouth, rather than having a heap of his life story stored in my memory banks.

'I don't.'

'Then why are we going down here?'

'Just a second.' He grins, and I know he likes this—knowing something I don't. His hand curves around mine. He must feel the way my pulse is rabbiting in my wrist.

We pass a big building with a sign that proclaims MANHATTAN HELICOPTER RIDES in shining red letters.

But the office is boarded up. Further along there are a couple of security guys, and several sleek black helicopters. Nicholas holds something up and one of the security guys waves us through.

'Good evening, Mr Rothsmore.'

He dips his head in silent acknowledgement, shepherding me past more of the helicopters before changing course and weaving us between two. We approach one, larger than the rest, with *Rothsmore Group* emblazoned across the tail.

'What is this?'

'A helicopter.'

I roll my eyes. 'No kidding.'

'I thought it'd be the fastest way back to my place.'

I laugh, a little unsteadily. 'You're going to pilot the thing?'

He leans closer, so I smell his intoxicating fragrance, and my gut rolls in a way that I am learning to get used to. 'It's not my first time.'

He holds the door open for me, then supports my hand as I step up into the helicopter. Inside, it's like a cross between a private jet and a spaceship. The interior is all beige leather with shining wood panelling. I take the co-pilot's seat, but behind us there's a cabin with four deep armchairs facing towards a central table. Each has a thick black seat belt coming from both shoulders into a latch between the legs.

I reach for the clip and hook it in place, the pressure between my legs exacerbating an already fraught central nervous system.

Despite all of the events I've organised for the club, this is actually my first time in a helicopter.

I have to say I'm a little afraid of the whole idea. I mean, they're so un-aerodynamic…how can a helicopter possibly hope to survive if something goes wrong with it? They're like a dead weight on the atmosphere, pure drag. At least a plane *looks* as if it should glide, even if the rational part of me knows that an aeroplane is also a dead weight.

My point being, I thought I'd be afraid, climbing into this thing, but the second Nicholas takes the seat beside me, I relax. I smile. More than that, my insides buzz and hum with excitement.

This is going to be fun—and that's what we're all about.

New York glitters beneath us. The world-famous bridge cuts over the darkness of the Hudson, the only void of light in what appears to be a sparkler as we get higher over the city.

I am torn between looking at the view and looking at Nicholas, who flies the helicopter as though he does so every day. And perhaps he does.

I note the strength and capability of his hands as he manages the controls, pushing levers while he manoeuvres the navigation stick. Perhaps he feels me watching him because he shifts to look at me, his eyes pinning me to the spot, and his smile, though slow to spread, is as if it's poured from hot lava, pure sex appeal and dynamism.

I swallow and look away, butterflies now rampant in my stomach. He begins to bring the helicopter in lower, over the city proper, and another void looms before us. Central Park, I recognise from the surrounding buildings. I'm on the Upper East Side, a little further north, but he lowers the helicopter down gently, onto the roof of a high rise that must be just south of the park. Billionaires' Row—that figures.

A cursory look from my window shows three other helicopters on the roof. He unhooks his seat belt then reaches across; before I realise what he's doing, his hand is between my legs. My face jerks towards him, and a low, soft breath escapes me as desire floods my system.

I might have expected him to look teasingly but he doesn't. His face is serious, tense. There is an air of urgency in his movements now. The seat belt slides loose but his hand stays between my legs, and, with his eyes latched to mine, he begins to move his fingers, so that, through the leather of my trousers and the silk of the underwear he bought with me in mind, I feel a surge of pleasure forming, building, like a wave rushing to shore.

'These pants are seriously fucking sexy, but, God, how I wish you were wearing a skirt,' he mutters in his inimitable accent, his voice deep, like a growl.

I can't respond. I bite down on my lip and tilt my head back, my legs moving a little wider apart.

He makes a sound of impatience and his hand shifts up so he can slide it inside the leather and silk and touch my flesh, my hot, wet flesh, his fingers finding their way easily, constrained by the tightness of my trousers but in no way hampered in their effectiveness.

'Fuck.' The word bites out from my mouth; desperation is swirling through me. Intensity fires in my soul and before I realise what I'm doing, I push up from the seat, dislodging his hand, straddling him in his seat. His cock is hard between my legs and, despite the layers of clothing separating us, I grind myself down on him, groaning at the waves of pleasure that fill me.

I kiss him, hard; his hands tangle in my hair, pulling at it, pulling me down so our lips are entwined, and I grind harder, the power of this something I'll never forget. Pleasure is shifting, building, running like sand through fingers, I am tipping over the edge and I can't stop. I whimper as I feel the release starting, tingling low in my gut, and I move faster, more desperately.

He's speaking, words that are so low I don't catch them, but the tone of his voice adds an extra layer to my needs. His hand curves around to my arse, holding me down as he pushes up, thrusting as if we're having sex, and we sort of are, despite the regrettable lack of penetration.

Pleasure bursts like a sunray, slicing me with heat. I moan, low in my throat, as I tip right over the edge, my nails digging into his shoulder, my body shivering.

My breath is ragged. I lift up, blinking, bringing him into focus. His expression is like a mask of concentration, his skin flushed, his pupils dilated. My own release was intense but now I crave something else, something more. I want to make him feel like I do. I move quickly, back to my seat.

The cockpit isn't huge and as I climb back into place, my shoe flicks something.

'Shoot. Sorry.'

He angles his face to mine, his lips lifting at the corners.

'Imogen, you could smash the windscreen right now and I wouldn't give a shit.'

I don't answer. Instead, I reach across and undo his trousers, my eyes flicking to his, checking for his reaction. As though he might stop what I'm about to do. I free his cock, wrapping my hand around it and pulling it from his boxers, drawing my hand up and down a few times, pumping him until I feel a hint of his cum leak out.

He's watching me with an intensity that makes my blood simmer all over again and I want him properly, not in a cockpit, somewhere I can relish and savour every damned move.

That will come.

But first, this.

I bend forward but, before I do, I catch the glint of speculation in his eyes and smile to myself. I've surprised him. He wasn't expecting this. I like that, so much.

I start slow, flicking his tip with my tongue, chasing a bead of cum, tasting its salt, letting a small sigh escape before I run my tongue over him a little more, his hard tip smooth beneath my exploration. He groans and my name is somewhere in that groan, almost indiscernible. I open my mouth and move down his shaft, slowly at first, exploring him with my tongue, lifting up and looking at him, so I see the tortured look on his features. I take him deep this time, faster, and bring my hand to his base, moving in time with my mouth, fast.

'Imogen, fuck, do you have any idea what you're doing to me?'

I don't stop.

'I'm so fucking close,' he groans, moving down in the seat a little further.

I move my hand down a little, cupping his balls, and then I take his cock into my mouth completely, so I taste him right at the back of my throat.

His hand comes to my head, his fingers there light, no pressure, more as though he just needs to hold onto something. To me.

My stomach does a funny little dive.

I move faster, and now his hand on my hair is almost pulling me away.

'I'm going to come,' he says, warning in his voice.

I flicker my eyes to his, a smile on my lips.

His eyes narrow. 'You're sure?'

In response, I take him inside me with a fevered intensity so I feel the beginning of his spasm, the urgency of his movements as his hips lift a little so he thrusts into my open mouth, his hand on my arse, his fingers digging into my flesh as he begins to spill his seed. I keep him deep, I take him all, I hold him while he loses his control, and he holds me, his hands on my body as if he can't possibly take them off.

It is the hottest thing I've ever done—and it's just the beginning.

CHAPTER EIGHT

'THE ORVILLE-GREENS ARE coming, and the Weiss-inghams too.'

My father lists two families who have daughters a few years younger than I am. 'The Sinclairs, Mo-rialtos, Lyons.'

I grip the phone more tightly, telling myself not to react.

I've been expecting this.

'It's going to be a New Year to remember. A new beginning.'

I expel a harsh breath, reaching for my coffee. It's a bleak, grey day, and I have more to do than I can put into words.

'Anyway, we can go over the details at Christ-mas. You're still planning to be home for Christmas?'

I hear the apprehension in his voice and a fissure of sympathy opens up inside my impatient chest. Be-cause at the root of all his bluster, my dad is worried. He's worried about the family's future, he's worried about the fact they're getting older and have no grand-children, and he's worried about me—that I'm going to waste my life with a string of different women, never doing the 'responsible' thing and taking up the reins of the Rothsmore estate.

'Great.' It's too curt. I soften it slightly. 'Yeah, I'll be there. How's Mother?'

'Planning the party, you know.' My father's tone is a little weary. 'In her element.'

It's true. My mother is never happier than when she has a social event looming, particularly in the grounds of Becksworth Hall. I can just picture it, strung with fairy lights, marquees set up with braziers of fire to keep guests warm; an orchestra serenading people as they arrive; a field given over to cars and helicopters; the guest rooms full to the brim.

And this time, a bevy of eligible women for me to choose a bride.

The thought bothers me more than it should. I've known this was coming. I'm almost thirty—how long did I expect I could put this off for?

Out of nowhere, I think of Saffron, of how against our union I was at the start, how much I resented being set up and pushed into a relationship by my parents. It had felt wrong at the start, but we'd been well matched. They'd been right.

Well, half-right.

Saffy hadn't seen the appeal, evidently.

That was five years ago and I'm different now. I have no intention of getting involved with anyone I don't feel I'm compatible with. I'm not looking for love this time. That's where I went wrong with Saffron; I see it clearly now. I bought into a fairy tale, a myth, where I should have simply seen it as a dynastic union, just as Imogen said.

Imogen.

Out of nowhere, my storm clouds lift and I'm smiling, my eyes sweeping shut so all I can see is her pale blonde head descending on my cock, feel the sweeping warmth of her mouth around my flesh, the flicker of her tongue, impatient and hungry, teasing me to a desperate release.

'Dad, I have to go.'

'But—'

'Later.'

I disconnect the call and surrender to the memory, pushing back in my leather chair, staring at the ceiling of my office, my body harder than black diamonds. Imogen is everywhere—my memory, my mind, my senses, my soul.

The blow job in the cockpit was just the beginning. Neither of us was sated by that release, as fucking amazing as it was. I reach for my phone on autopilot, flicking open our chat window.

I can't stop thinking about you and your extraordinarily talented mouth.

I smile as I send the message.

A minute later, she responds.

My mouth and I are glad to hear it.

My smile stretches. I drink my coffee, but half an hour later I send her another message on the spur of the moment.

Busy later?

I see three little dots appear as she starts to type, then they disappear.

It's a few hours before she messages back.

What do you have in mind?

My gut kicks. Dating. We're dating. Not just fucking, though that's a given.

I'll pick you up at seven?

Another surprise?

Great question. What shall we do? I look towards the windows, which frame a panoramic view of Wall Street. The sky is woolly. It's freezing too. I can think of one surefire way to stave off coldness.

Dating, idiot. Dating.

I open up a browser and type in a few questions. Five entries down, the search engine has provided the perfect solution for me. I type a message.

Yes. Bring a bikini.

;) Have you looked outside?

Trust me.

She doesn't reply.

I click on the link and open the booking form,

then place my phone down, thoughts of Imogen and the night ahead already making the idea of an afternoon's work damned near impossible.

Seven o'clock can't come soon enough.

I love to swim. I was on my college team, and it's one of the few activities I regularly make time for. There's something about it I find meditative and calming, and I find being underwater, away from noise and other people, is also an excellent opportunity for deep thinking. I have at least three quarters of my ideas while submerged in my apartment complex's huge swimming pool.

Usually, I wear a one-piece, a habit that's a hangover from my college team days.

But for tonight, I've chosen a barely there string bikini, bright red. It felt bizarre pulling it out of the drawer given the weather—we're in the midst of a cold snap that feels as if it'll never end.

But his premise has intrigued me.

More than I wanted it to. I had a huge afternoon with some investors in the charity and I had to concentrate—almost impossible with my phone buzzing in my pocket and the memories of a few nights ago shifting against me.

I'm wearing the bikini beneath a black jersey dress and a floor-length trench coat, with a pair of gold stilettos. My hair is pinned into a bun high on my head, loose and casual.

The buzzer sounds and I move towards it. 'I'll be right down.'

'Okay.' Even that single word made up of two

syllables, spoken through telephone cabling at a distance of forty odd floors of concrete, has the power to double the speed of my pulse.

I grab my bag and sling it over my shoulder, moving quickly to the elevator.

Mr Silverstein looks at me thoughtfully as I click my way across the marbled lobby.

'Good evening, Miss Carmichael.'

'Hi, Mr Silverstein. Keeping warm?' I nod to the inclement weather—it's dark now, but the glass has a frost to it showing that the temperature is arctic.

'As warm as can be, ma'am. Out again?'

I nod, my eyes darting to the revolving door. I see his dark car parked right outside. My heart soars. 'Yeah.'

'Take care, miss.'

I smile, because for the first time in years, I'm doing exactly that. Taking care of myself. My needs. My wants. Things I hadn't even realised I felt or needed to tend to. And, sure, in three weeks there'll be the Christmas gala ball and this will end, and my time with Nicholas Rothsmore will be like an island in my life, girt by water and isolation on all sides, but it will still be there—a month of hazy, heady sex, of total indulgence and hedonism, a secret, joyous letting down of my hair.

'Goodnight.'

He opens the door for me and I don't look back.

Nicholas steps out of the car as soon as I appear on the pavement, his eyes crinkling at the corners with the force of his smile. 'Did you bring your swimming costume?'

'Did you expect me to be wearing only a swimsuit?' I tease. 'It's kind of cold, or hadn't you noticed?'

He pulls me to him abruptly, suddenly, jerking my body to his and wrapping his arms around my midsection so I'm tight to his hardness, contoured perfectly. 'Is it?'

Heat belies my statement. I feel it as surely as if the sun had burst out from the other side of the earth, channelling the heat of a few weeks ago, in Sydney.

He releases me just as abruptly, but not before he's placed a quick kiss on my forehead—just enough to send need lurching through me.

'You look beautiful.'

'Thank you.'

He opens the back door to his limo and I step in, noting there's a small box of my favourite champagne truffles on the back seat.

Once we're in and the car is moving, he hands them over.

'For me?'

He grins. 'Second date.'

'Ah.' I take them, dipping my head forward with a smile. 'Perfect.'

'Never date a guy who doesn't bring you truffles.'

'Duly noted.'

'How are you?'

His question, so simple—just a basic function of civility and etiquette—etches through me because of the way in which he asks it. As if he really cares about the answer.

'Good. Busy day. You?'

'Less busy than it should have been, thanks to some very distracting fantasies I struggled to ignore.'

My ego bursts, higher than an eagle. 'Lovely.'

'Yes, just what I was thinking.'

'Are you wearing trunks as well?'

He nods.

'So we're going swimming?'

'Later.'

'Seriously?'

'Yep.'

I laugh. 'International Man of Mystery?'

'Something like that.'

Curiosity grows. Even when the car slows to a stop, I have no idea where we are or where we're going. The door is opened by a driver, Edward, I think Nicholas had said his name was.

'Thanks.' I look around for any kind of clue. There's nothing.

'This way.' Nicholas puts a hand in the small of my back and leads me to a black door in a brick wall.

'I feel like you're taking me to some kind of Mafia hideout.'

His laugh dances across my spine like tiny little needles. 'More fun, less chance of death.'

'Glad to hear it.'

The door opens as we approach; presumably there's a security camera monitoring activity.

A woman wearing a sleek black dress greets us. 'Mr Rothsmore?'

He nods.

'Welcome to Uden Syn.' She pronounces the name with an accent, but even if she hadn't, the words would still have meant nothing to me.

'Miss Carmichael?' She holds a hand out for my coat. Nicholas's hands are at my shoulders, helping me out of it. A frisson of anticipation warms my belly.

In fact, I'm warm all over, and while that might have something to do with Nicholas, it's also this place. We're in a small corridor, dimly lit, but very, very warm. The heating must be switched to full.

'Do you have your phone?'

Nicholas offers his and she waves it over a device in her pocket. 'Your phone will now open the door to your room. Take your clothes off and leave them in the locker provided, then head in.'

Alarm has me jolting my eyes to Nicholas's. I did give him a blow job in the cockpit of the helicopter, and we did sleep together in the Intimate Rooms of the Sydney club, but that's a far cry from engaging in some kind of public orgy.

'Is this some kind of sex club?' I demand in a low whisper as he guides me down the corridor.

When we reach a door with the number eleven on it, he shoots me a look before swiping his phone.

'I'm serious, Nicholas,' I whisper despite the fact we're now alone in an elegant if somewhat utilitarian room. It's big enough for a chair, a wardrobe, and, as with the corridor, it's dimly lit and super warm.

'Do you think I'd bring you to a sex club?' he prompts with a lifted brow, shifting out of his shirt. The subtle lighting casts his handsome face in shadow, highlighting the planes and angles there.

'I don't know.'

He kicks out of his shoes. 'Public sex isn't really my thing.'

'It isn't?'

'Well, public sex with *you* could be,' he says with a slow wink. 'But not sharing you with other people. This isn't an orgy.'

I'm relieved, though, ultimately, not surprised. He wouldn't bring me somewhere like that. Not without talking to me first. I don't know what came over me.

I smile, relaxing and surrendering to this once more.

It takes us a minute to get undressed. His trunks are black briefs that perfectly cup and display his impressive cock, his tight ass. I can't help but stare, and he clearly notices, if his grin is anything to go by.

'Let's go.' He takes my hand in his and I fight an urge to tell him I'd rather stay. Right here. The chair looks sturdy enough to take us both.

When we push into the next room, it takes my eyes a second to adjust, and then to compute what they're seeing. We're not alone, but it's not some weird sex club thing—put your keys in the bowl. There's low, throbbing music surrounding us, and about twelve other people are dotted through the room, paired off, and painting each other. The only light in here is a black light, and the paint comes up as neon, glow-in-the-dark, on their bodies. And they're painted *all over.*

I'm bowled over. This looks *fun.* And different.

'Welcome, Mr Rothsmore. Here's your station, this way.' Someone appears wearing a bright outfit so they're visible, their teeth gleaming bright blue. He guides us across the room to a table with a shining line around it to delineate it is set up with paints. Each has an iridescent dot for accessibility.

'This is seriously cool,' I say appreciatively, after the waiter has gone through the rules and explained how it all works. A minute later, a bright bottle of wine is brought and two glasses, etched with paint so we can see them clearly in the room.

'Who first?' Nicholas teases.

'You.' I smile, and he returns it—I can tell because his teeth almost blind me.

I reach for one of the brushes and some paint, staring slowly, putting some paint on his cheek.

'How does it feel?' My eyes dart to his.

'Cold and mushy.'

I grin. 'It was your idea.'

'I may need to rethink it.'

'No, don't. I like it.' I smile again, dotting some paint over his shoulder. In just my bikini, my breasts are tingling, straining against the insufficient material. I work my way across his back, swirling paint—

different colours throw different lights in here—and then lower, to the expanse of flesh just above the waistband of his bathers. I feel his breath grow shallow, and I can't resist curving my hand around to his front, feeling his cock, secure in the anonymity the darkness of the room affords.

He's hard, and I'm not surprised. Being this close, touching without touching, is seriously hot. There's even something about the paint, its wetness, the sound of it against his body, the gentle persistence of colouring his skin, that has me aching for him.

I slip my hand inside his trunks and I feel his breath snag. 'I thought you weren't into public sex,' he observes, *sotto voce*.

'So did I.' But I pull my hand out of his pants, snaking it over his chest, to a just-painted nipple. I tweak it and then pull away, laughing softly at the paint on my fingertips.

'Caught, red-handed,' I quip.

He grabs my hand in his and holds it towards my chest, running my fingers down my abdomen, towards my own bikini briefs. At the elastic, he steps closer, and drops his head so he can whisper in my ear, 'Later tonight, I want to watch you get yourself off.'

Pleasure vibrates through my gut.

'I… I haven't ever done that before.' I'm glad he can't see the mad flush in my cheeks. 'In front of someone else, I mean.'

'Don't worry, I'll be there to lend you a hand if

you need it,' he promises, and I want to go, I want to have him, now.

But he's intent on torturing me, clearly, because when he starts to paint my body, he's so much better, slower, more devastatingly sensual than I was with him. He drags the paintbrush but with a feather-light touch, so I want to beg him to press harder. He trails a hint of colour over my shoulders, my arms, then back up to under my arms and the flesh at the side of my breast, so I make a soft whimpering sound. I see his smile, but it's just a flash, then he's back to concentrating.

I reach for a glass of wine while he works, needing to do something to steady my fluttering nerves.

He kneels at my feet, his mouth so close to my clit that I ache to push forward, to feel him there, his lips against me—knowing that it will come tonight. Later. Soon.

He drags the brush higher, lightly, over my calves, to my knees, the backs of my knees, my inner thighs, and as he paints with one hand, in the cover of the room's darkness, he uses his other to push aside the Lycra of my briefs and slide a finger inside my wet, pulsing heat. I gasp, loudly, so he freezes, looking up at me.

'Not. A. Sound.'

The words ring with a quiet authority I don't think of ignoring. I don't want to. I nod, gripping the wine glass and taking another fortifying sip before assuming a position that I hope seems normal.

As he moves the paintbrush over my legs, he moves his finger inside me, and I resist an urge—just—to buck back and forth. This isn't designed to get me off. He's teasing me—again. Torturing me. He knows how close I am to exploding and yet he's pulling away, his touch too light, too brief.

'Nicholas…' His name comes from my lips like a snatch of need. I hear my desperation and am unable to care.

'Yes, Imogen?' His smile shifts over his face.

'Please.' Just a simple word, but it means everything because I need him in a way that had bowled me over. I thought one night would be enough. I thought *once* would be enough, but it wasn't. It couldn't be.

'You want this?' he murmurs, moving his finger back inside me. No, two fingers now, and it's instantly more fulfilling, more promising, but still…

I nod, running my hands through his hair. He draws the brush around my back, kneeling higher now, blocking me more from sight, so I do what I'd wanted earlier and move my hips to get greater purchase, to feel more of him.

'You have to be patient,' he teases, except I can hear his own urgency and I get it. He wants me as badly as I want him.

'That's physically impossible.'

His laugh is low and husky. 'Then I probably shouldn't tell you that I plan to take you home and fuck you until your voice is hoarse?'

'Oh, God.' The promise is so erotic. 'What else?'

'How I'm going to run my tongue along here…' he draws his fingers out and in '…to taste you as you come? How I'm going to make you come again and again and I'm going to watch you, listen to you begging me for more, begging me until you can't think straight.'

'I'm already there,' I promise throatily.

His laugh is a dismissal. 'You only think you are, Imogen. Believe me, it gets worse.'

He is right.

We stay for another hour, and by the time we leave, my body is in a state of sensual torture. There's no helicopter waiting for us tonight. We take his car, and I don't sit too close because I feel as if one touch, now we're alone, will result in a complete explosion, and a short car ride isn't the place to satisfy that. I sit on the edge of my seat, staring out of the window at New York, the invisible paint we'd used in the black-lit room dry now and any hint of it concealed by the clothes we've put back on.

But not being able to see something doesn't remove the evidence of it and I feel every brush stroke in the fibres of my soul.

The driver brings the car into a basement garage and I expel a sigh of relief that Nicholas clearly hears, if his soft laugh is anything to go by.

But I'm not amused.

I'm alive with feelings that are new to me and seriously intense.

I am fuelled by a hunger that I insist on owning.

Edward opens the doors and we step out, my smile polite, my mind elsewhere.

We reach the elevator and the doors open after only a second. I contemplate jumping him but for the same reason I resisted in the car, I keep my distance now, aware that he's watching me, trying to decode me.

He has no idea what he's unleashed.

But he's about to find out.

The doors ping open into his apartment and the details I recall from last time flitter in my mind once more—the triple-height ceilings, a wall of pure glass, a balcony overlooking Central Park with a swimming pool and a hot tub. I know from the tour he gave me last time that there's an indoor squash court down the corridor, a yoga studio he's converted into a gym, four bedrooms, five bathrooms and two separate staff rooms, which he has vacant.

'I don't like living with other people, even if they're at the end of the corridor.'

I get his point. I hate it too. I have a cleaner who comes once a fortnight and that suits me just fine.

As soon as the front door clicks shut, I turn around to face him, my breath dragged from my lungs, the rasping sound filling the elegant Jeffersonian lobby.

'Didn't you say you were going to fuck me so hard I couldn't speak?' I demand, crossing my arms over my chest.

His expression shows surprise but only for a moment, then he's sweeping across the tiles, scooping me up over one shoulder as if I weigh nothing and carrying me to my heaven, my desperation, the sweetest torture I've ever known—his bedroom.

CHAPTER NINE

'OH, MY GOD.'

I must have fallen asleep. I push up onto my elbows to find Nicholas watching me, that unbearably sexy grin on his too-handsome face, and my heart does a painful little catapult against my ribs.

'What time is it?' I reach across the bed for his wrist and the platinum gold watch he always wears. 'It's seven o'clock? Why didn't you wake me?'

I push the sheet back, looking around for my underpants before remembering I only have paint-smeared bikini bottoms to put on. And they're in the lounge.

'Because it was more fun to watch you sleep,' he says, his voice frustratingly relaxed despite my obvious panic.

And I'm panicking, for no reason I can easily pinpoint. Yes, I need to get to work, yes, I have meetings in an hour. But it's more than that.

For some reason, spending the night feels like crossing a line that mentally I wasn't willing to cross. It is a bigger surrendering of myself than I intended. Another line in the sand, one I hadn't realised I wanted to abide by.

'I'm serious, Nic.' The diminutive of his name slips out, but not for the first time. As soon as I say it I have a vivid recollection of crying the shortened version of his name over and over again, as pleasure racked my body in a way I almost couldn't process.

'You got somewhere you have to be?'

I pull a face. 'It's seven o'clock on a Wednesday morning. What do you think?'

'I think you should cancel it and come back to bed,' he murmurs, patting the matte black sheets. As a further enticement, he pushes the sheet back, revealing his rock-hard, naked body.

Predictably, my insides squeeze. And despite my panic, a smile spreads over my face. 'I can't,' I say, in an almost whining tone. 'Help me find my bikini.'

His laugh is low, a rumble. 'Oh, no, Miss Anonymous. I have no intention of aiding your escape. In fact, if I had my way, you'd be tied to this bed so I could have my very evil way with you some more.'

Okay.

I have meetings. But there's also this. I stop looking for my bathers and give Nicholas the full force of my attention. At his mention of tying me up, I remember something from our night in Sydney.

'You ordered handcuffs.'

He lifts a brow, his expression teasing, silently prompting me to continue.

'In Sydney.' Heat blooms in my face. 'You had

handcuffs put in the toy chest,' I remind him. 'But we didn't...'

He stands up, his dick at a ninety-degree angle to the rest of him, his haunches so strong and capable. 'Yes?'

He likes teasing me. I get it. I suck in a breath and assume my very best kickass CEO expression. 'We didn't use handcuffs.'

'No.' He shrugs nonchalantly, his naked body next to mine now.

'Why not?' It's breathy—all of me is consumed by his closeness.

'I wasn't sure you were ready.'

Indignation flares inside me. 'Oh, really?'

'Hmm,' he agrees, and then he's lifting me up, wrapping my legs around his waist and carrying me easily through his bedroom to the tiled adjoining bathroom.

'What are you doing?' Though it's self-explanatory when he flicks on the shower taps and steps past the wide glass wall.

'Helping you get ready for work.' He grins, and when he eases me onto his cock, I give up pretending I want to be anywhere but here.

'I thought we were talking about handcuffs,' I murmur as water douses me from overhead, plastering my hair to my face.

'Let's see.' His eyes probe mine and then he takes another step so my back connects with the tiled wall and one of his hands captures both of my wrists, pinning them over my head. It's just him, and yet his grip is vice-like. I couldn't easily wriggle free, even if I wanted to.

There's a challenge on his features as he thrusts inside me and there's something almost painfully erotic about not being able to touch him. I surrender to the strength of this feeling as he thrusts hard and deep, filling me, awakening barely rested needs.

My ankles dig into his back and I hold on as though my life depends on it until I'm coming around him. I go to pull my hands free but he shakes his head, dropping his mouth to my breasts and pulling one of my tight, sensitive nipples between his teeth. I shake all over, the pleasure doing funny things to me.

My orgasm is intense, and even as I come he continues to torment my breasts and hold my arms high above my head so there is no reprieve from the pleasure, no relief from this insanity.

I drop my head to his shoulder as my tortured breath ravages my body and then he's easing my feet to the floor, pulling out of me gently, letting my arms go all at once. It's a strange desertion. He's still rock hard.

'You didn't…finish,' I murmur, hating that I can still feel so embarrassed after all we've shared.

'Mmm…' he murmurs, biting my earlobe. 'As much as my parents are desperate for me to get married and have kids, I don't think they have a New York–based heir in mind.'

'Oh, my God.' It is a shocking wake-up call. 'I didn't even think...'

'I did. A bit too late,' he says with a self-deprecating shake of his head.

'I'm on the pill,' I say, to reassure myself as much as him.

'And I'm clean.' He shrugs. 'Still, I'd rather not take the risk.'

Why does that make my gut clench—and not in a good way?

I paste a smile on my face and reach for the body wash. 'And now, I really do have to get ready for work.'

He runs his mouth over my cheek, capturing my lips, his smile sweet and slow. 'Coffee?'

My heart lurches. 'Thanks.'

I lather myself all over, my body so completely raw and tender that everywhere I touch is like an erotic shadow of last night. My breasts are pink from the brush of his stubble, my inner thighs too, and I have a row of hickeys across my hip, leading towards my buttocks.

He was right to pull out, not to come. He's sure as hell right to protect us from any unwanted consequences.

But just the mention of that has made me think about a future that I would have said, two weeks ago, I don't actually want. A future filled with the laugh of a small person, the dependence of a child, the love of a little one.

I'm not maternal—I have no idea what being maternal even looks like, since my mother wasn't and I suspect I'm even less so. I don't have anything to go on. And yet, at the mention of little Rothsmore heirs, something very close to my ovaries fired to life in a way that has taken my breath away.

Thank God we agreed this was just going to last a month. I can't imagine much worse than being with Nicholas Rothsmore for real, allowing myself to do something really stupid and fall in love with him.

And there is such a risk there, because he's too good at this. He's charming and funny, sophisticated and smart, so damned thoughtful and, as for his bedroom prowess, there's no need to wonder why he's earned the nickname 'the Playboy of Manhattan'.

But only a fool would fall in love with Nicholas Rothsmore, and I'm no fool. Reassured, I step out of the shower and towel myself down. When I step into his bedroom, my eyes are transfixed firstly by the stunning view of Central Park, and then by a bag on the foot of the bed. I recognise the distinctive thick black paper with the embossed white logo. Curious, I reach in and pull out a lingerie twin set. My smile hurts my cheeks.

Pale cream and the most delicate lace, it antagonises my already sensitive body, the lace so raw on my nipples that I gasp as I move, every single shift of my flesh reminding me of his possession of my body.

I suspect this is something he foresaw.

When I slip into the kitchen a few minutes later, his knowing smile confirms my suspicions.

'Thank you for this.' I wave a hand over my flesh.

He shrugged. 'It seemed like a wise precaution, given the whole paint-on-body situation.'

'I didn't mean to fall asleep,' I say, reaching for the coffee. He's made it black, which is strange, because that's just how I have it. I sip it and let out a small moan of appreciation.

'Good?' he prompts over the rim of his own mug.

'Shh,' I tease. 'Let me drink this, then we'll talk.'

We drink our coffee in silence, my little ritual one I'm glad to observe, even side by side with Nicholas.

'I didn't mean to stay over,' I reiterate, a few minutes later, placing the empty coffee cup in the sink.

'Why?'

'I just didn't plan on it.' I shrug.

'We were up *late*.' He says the word with emphasis.

I think it was about two when I last saw the time. 'I remember.'

'It would have been kind of dumb to slink home at that hour.'

'Nonetheless,' I murmur, my voice a little icy, 'I prefer to sleep in my own bed.'

His face shifts with something like amusement and then he shrugs. 'Sure, if you'd like.'

I'm slightly mollified, but not completely. Our conversation from earlier sits inside me like the sharp edge of a blade and I can't really say why.

'Do you have much on today?'

'Yeah.' I nod, looking around for my clothes. They're arranged on the edge of a chair. I stride to them, pulling the dress on over my head only to find him watching me with a small smile on his face. My blood pounds through me. 'You?'

'Sure.' He shrugs. 'But I'd like to see you tonight.'

Tonight. Pleasure sounds in my head, pleasure so intense it almost drowns out the warning bells. Because he is ever so slightly too much for me to handle. Because I would fully believe it if a doctor told me he had the addictive properties of a drug and that I was already way over quota.

'Not tonight,' I say, shifting into my coat, then looking around for my handbag. It's on the kitchen bench. I lift it over my shoulder, checking I have everything.

'Tomorrow night?'

My heart is hammering. I keep my head bent so he doesn't see the way I'm shaking. 'I'll message you.'

He nods, a frown on his face that he quickly erases.

'I don't have my bikini,' I say, when I reach the door.

'Leave them. Next time, we'll use the hot tub.'

It conjures images that are too hot to forget.

I smile and nod, pushing down on my doubts as to the wisdom of this. 'Sounds fun.' I lift up and press a kiss to his lips then turn and walk away, needing a bit of space and a bit of time.

And maybe he gets that, because I don't hear from him at all that day. Nor the next. By Friday afternoon I'm starting to worry I've done something stupid and ruined this.

And it is truly the best sex I've ever had, but, more than that, I'm having fun.

Why did I get so bogged down in worrying about the future when we've both been clear about what we do and don't want?

Because I'm a worrier. It's what I do. If it were a job, I'd be supremely qualified.

Before I can regret it, I pull my phone out of my handbag and pull up our message chat.

Is it my turn to plan a date?

I have a pounding in my throat as I send it, and a nervousness that seems somewhat ridiculous. But when he hasn't replied an hour later, I'm having to fight not to send another text.

It's six o'clock when finally a message buzzes in.

What a day. Hot tub? Beer? Takeout?

My smile is so huge I feel as if it's splitting my face in two.

Perfect. See you soon?

His answer is immediate.

The sooner the better.

I breathe out, relief rushing through me. Everything's fine; nothing to worry about, whatsoever.

CHAPTER TEN

THREE DAYS AND I feel as though I haven't seen her in three years. It's just like that first godawful week, after Sydney, when I had no idea who the fuck Miss Anonymous really was and I worried I might never learn. That I might never see her again, nor know the pleasure of her beautiful, sensual body.

I am beyond impatient.

I have had to fight hard not to message her, but I had the feeling when she left on Wednesday morning that she needed a bit of space, and the last thing I want is to pressure her. This is all about fun—for her and for me.

Fortunately, things exploded at work, which kept me busy. Still, I must have checked my phone eleven billion times. My bed smells like her, sweet and lightly fragranced, so I have lain awake at night and remembered *everything* we shared.

She arrives a little after seven and I prowl to the door, buzzing her up and waiting impatiently.

When she walks in, I groan and pull her into my arms, smiling as I kiss her, holding her tight to my body, breathing her in, tasting her, feeling her, needing her, wanting her, loving this.

'Hey.' My greeting, minutes later, is gruff.

'Hey yourself.' Hers is breathless.

I want to drag her to bed and never leave, but already the sex thing is taking over from what was meant to be a casual flirtation, some harmless dating fun.

I have to slow that down a bit, as much as that idea is akin to scrubbing my skin with acid.

'What do you feel like?'

Her cheeks rush with pink in that way she has.

'For dinner,' I clarify, grinning, anticipation tightening my gut, and in all parts of me, as I look forward to how I know this night will end.

'Oh.' She bites down on her lower lip; I brush my thumb over her flesh, so she parts her mouth and bites the pad of my thumb instead. 'Pizza?'

'A girl after my own heart.'

'There's a great place just a few blocks away.'

'I'll get delivery.' I move towards the kitchen bench, lifting my phone and loading the app. I place an order for a few different ones. When I turn around, she's stripped down to her underwear, her eyes locked to mine with an intensity that almost bowls me over.

'Hot tub?'

Hell to the yeah. I nod, affecting an air of calm nonchalance. 'Go ahead. It's warm. I'll grab some beers.'

I hear her squawk as she steps out onto the balcony—it's just below zero out there. I turn around just in time to see her running across the tiles and up the one step before sliding in over the edge, so just her head bobs up. The relief on her face takes my breath away.

So does the fact she's here, in my penthouse, her smile, her eyes, her body, her laugh.

I spin away and yank out some beers, cracking the tops of them as I walk, placing hers on the edge of the hot tub.

'Oh, thank God, it's real beer.'

'What did you expect?'

'Tepid lager?' she says with an impish grin.

I laugh, stripping out of my clothes, down to my jocks, and stepping over the edge of the spa. She's watching me with undisguised hunger and my dick reacts accordingly.

'It did take me a while but it turns out I've developed a taste for your beer.'

She sips from her bottle, moving to one of the seats on the edge of the tub. Manhattan sparkles beneath us, an array of little tiny lights that make up a thriving island metropolis.

'Do you think you'll miss it?'

'American beer?'

'New York,' she corrects, smiling.

'Yeah.' I'm surprised by how deep the word comes out, and troubled seeming.

'I can't imagine not living here,' she says, simply.

'You don't miss home?'

'LA?' Her face is one of disgust. 'I miss it during the winter,' she says after a second. 'And I miss some people. And I guess there's always a nostalgia for where you grew up, so that on certain days I find myself thinking about the way the light would hit my bedroom wall, and I long to go back. Not to LA but to when I was a teenager and everything was so much simpler.'

It's a fascinating statement.

'In what way is your life no longer simple?'

'Are you kidding? My life is a study in clean simplicity,' she says with a self-deprecating smile. 'No mess, no fuss, no complications. I mean that people aren't simple. Life is messy and complicated, no matter how hard you try to fight that. I can control only so much, you know?'

'You sound like someone who's been hurt,' I prompt with curiosity, swimming across to her and taking the seat right beside her, careful not to touch because touching Imogen invariably leads to much, much more.

'Not really.' But she's lying.

'Imogen?'

Her eyes fix to mine, her pupils huge, swallowing up almost all of her icy blue. 'I'm just speaking generally,' she says unconvincingly, after a lengthy pause.

There's more to it, I'm sure of it. 'As you get older,' I say, sipping my beer, 'things do get more complex.'

'Yes.' She smiles, a little uneasily. 'You come to understand people and their motivations better.'

We're quiet a moment, reflective.

'So what happens when you go home?' It's a clunky attempt to change the topic but I let it go. My wheels are turning, wondering what she was thinking about a minute ago, and we'll come back to it later, when she's a little more relaxed, less guarded.

'What do you mean?'

'I mean, do you become the Playboy of London?'

Frustration nips at my heels, a frustration that's hard to fathom. 'No, I expect not.'

'I can't really see you hanging up your bachelor shoes.'

'It's been five years since what would have been my wedding day,' I say with a shrug. 'Five years of the kind of pace of life that would wear anyone down.'

'You're over it?'

I shake my head, surprised to realise that I'm speaking the truth. 'I'm ready for the next phase of my life.'

Her eyes skim my face, perhaps trying to see if I'm being honest.

'I wouldn't necessarily be going home,' I continue, 'if it weren't for my father's demands.'

'Demands?' she prompts, moving to close the space between us. 'You don't seem like someone *anyone* could make demands of.'

'His insistence, then.'

'Same deal.' She laughs softly.

'He's my father,' I point out. 'He holds a certain power.'

'I can understand that,' she says, her forehead crinkling with her frown. 'Even when I'm someone who's turned disobedience into an art form.' It's said lightly, with a curve of her lips, but I feel there's more to it.

'You? Miss Strait-Laced?'

'Do I really seem that strait-laced to you?' she points out with a slow, tempting wink.

'Not in bed,' I assure her. 'But everywhere else.'

She opens her mouth but closes it again, grimacing slightly.

'That wasn't a criticism.'

'I know. And you're right. This…' she waves from her chest to mine, inadvertently drawing my gaze downwards '…is the craziest thing I've done in years—probably since I put as much of my trust fund as I could get my hands on into the charity.'

So many questions fire in my mind. 'So how have you disobeyed your parents?' I ask the question in a voice that rings with amusement because I think she's probably, at twenty-nine, beyond the point of giving too much of a shit what her mom and dad think of her. And yet, look at me. A grown man, the same age, about to leap the Atlantic to placate my father's expectations of me.

'In every way,' she says simply. 'My life is a study in parental disappointment.'

'Surely not.' I'm not joking now. 'Look at what you've achieved. They must be proud of you?'

'Proud?' She shakes her head on a small laugh. 'Proud is what they would have been if I'd married the CEO of Alpine Moor TV at twenty-three, like they wanted. Proud is what they'd be if I'd pursued the modelling career my mom desperately tried to line up for me. Proud is what they'd be if I'd stayed home in LA and troubled myself with my mom's hospital benefits.'

'But you're doing something so much bigger,' I point out. 'Look at the business you've built, and the charity you're funding.'

'Yes, but I deal with underprivileged kids, which is definitely not the kind of charity my mom thinks I should be championing.'

'No?'

'Oh, no. My mom would much rather I raise money to help embattled hedge-fund managers maintain their country club memberships.'

She's being sarcastic but I feel her resentment burning from her in waves, her hatred for wealth and society, her derision for its constructs evident.

'A charity's a charity,' I say simply.

'I used to think that too.' Her smile is wistful. 'I used to be so proud of my mom and dad and the work they did. Or the work I *thought* they did. My mom was forever organising benefits, fundraising, sponsoring events.' She shakes her head mournfully.

'Ironically, I probably got some of my philanthropic aspirations from Mom.'

'Why is that ironic?'

'Because, as I got older, I realised that my mom and dad really only cared about supporting the causes that *sounded* good. They wouldn't go near domestic violence or women's shelters, nothing to do with providing homeless women with sanitary items. My mom was *mortified* when I suggested any such thing.'

Her words zing with anger, despite the fact we're talking about events that transpired a long time ago.

'Then there was the time I tried to fundraise for a charity that buys groceries for families on food stamps. My mom honestly threatened to disown me.' Her smile is just a tight imitation.

'I'd like to say I'm surprised,' I say, eventually. 'But that kind of attitude is pretty prevalent.'

'Yeah, only amongst the very, very wealthy.'

'Not everyone feels that way.'

'A lot do.' She shrugs. 'And I hate it.'

'I can tell.'

She looks at me appraisingly for several beats. 'Can I tell you something? In confidence?'

It annoys me that she even needs to check. 'Of course.'

'When I first built The Billionaires' Club, I used to get a perverse kind of pleasure from taking money from the super rich and funnelling it to support a cause most of them would be embarrassed to be associated with.'

'So the club was spite?' I murmur, a smile on my lips because it's so ridiculously badass I can't help loving that.

'No.' She shakes her head. 'It was five per cent spite.' And then she laughs, such a contrast to the mood of a moment ago that my insides glow with warmth.

'I think most of our membership is actually pretty cool. Sure, there are a few people who wouldn't know a social conscience if it grew legs and bit them on their jewelled rears,' she says with a flick of her brow. 'But I've been bowled over by some really amazing offers from some club members over the years. Chance wouldn't be what it is without the club. I can never resent the members for that.'

'Tell me about the charity.'

'What do you want to know?'

I don't really want to admit how little I know about it. I gather it's something to do with children, underprivileged children, but that's about it.

'Why start your own charity rather than working for one that's already up and running?'

'Control,' she answers, simply and passionately. 'And contacts. I have access to what the charity needs and I can cut out a lot of middlemen. Plus, I like to know that there's no top-heavy administrative board or whatever. I run everything. It's my baby, my project.'

Her passion is overwhelming.

'Why children?' I prompt conversationally, but her face tightens, her eyes flashing away from me. She reaches for her beer, and I know she's using it to buy time. I wait with the appearance of patience as she sips her drink. But I'm not letting her move on.

'Imogen?'

She's upset. Her features are strained, her eyes showing a depth of emotion that I didn't expect.

Still, I don't let it go.

'You must care a great deal to have poured so much energy into it.'

'Yes.' A whisper, barely.

There's more here. A story she's not telling me and, for some reason, it feels vitally important that I know it.

'Why?'

'It's important,' she says quietly, simply, turning to face me once more, her eyes showing a profound pain.

'Lots of things are important. Why this?'

'There are almost sixteen million kids in America living in abject poverty, and that's with an incredibly low poverty line. I founded Chance for them. Because everyone deserves a chance and it's by no means guaranteed that everyone will get one. Our luck in life is predetermined at birth. Not just by wealth, by lots of factors, but financial security is a cornerstone of success. And there are sixteen million kids here, in the States, who struggle to get enough food to survive. Forget about books and sports, holidays, the safety of a good home and the comfort of parents who aren't worried about how they're going to keep the lights on.'

Her voice cracks and the passion she feels overwhelms me and makes me feel like a selfish git, all at once.

'This is a developed country, the envy of the world, and we have this vulnerable subset of society doing it so tough. I met a girl at an event last month who cried because I gave her a double pass to see a movie. She's never been to the cinema before.' She swallows, her eyes filling with tears. I feel as if a cement block has been dropped right onto my heart. I didn't expect this. And I *hate* seeing her upset. I hate even more that I've done this to her.

'I'm sorry,' she mumbles, beating me to the apology I want to offer. 'I just get so frustrated. The Billionaires' Club enables me to pour a fortune into the charity every year, but it still never feels like enough.'

'I bet you're making a huge difference,' I contradict gently.

'Maybe. I just want more, and I want it now.'

I pull her closer, into my arms, and press a kiss to her eyelid, tasting her salty tears, wishing them gone.

'I had this friend,' she says quietly against my chest. 'Abbey.'

I'm still, waiting for her to go on. It's started to snow, lightly, so the contrast in temperatures out of the spa and in is marked.

'She died, when I was a teenager.'

'I'm sorry.'

I feel her expression shift and I suspect it's a grimace. 'We were really tight, growing up. She lived just a block away and we spent almost every weekend together.' Her voice is grim, despite what sounds like happy memories. 'And then, when I was fifteen, the news broke that her dad had been charged with a federal crime—embezzlement. He'd set up a Ponzi scheme and taken people for billions. It wasn't Abbey's fault, but her whole life went down the drain. Her mom left, hooked up with some Swiss athlete and moved to Europe, her dad was locked up.'

'Shit. The poor thing.'

'I did what I could.' She lifts her face to mine, and I can tell she's back in the past, more than a decade ago, but the pain is just as real as if it were happening now. 'I had a credit card I maxed to cover what I could. I snuck her into our pool house to live. We did that for three months and no one ever knew. Then my dad found her.' Fury lashes her face, her look one of utter rage. 'And called social services. I was forbidden to see Abbey ever again. My credit card was cut up.'

Her tears are back; my heart breaks for her, and her friend.

'She was like a sister to me, I thought she was like a daughter to them, but when she needed help, they wouldn't do a damned thing because they were so ashamed of what Abbey's dad had done.'

'Jesus.'

'She ended up in foster care, but it wasn't pretty.' She swallows, turning away from me, focussing on a high rise across the street. It glows like a candle on this black New York night. 'In fact, it was downright awful. Her first foster father turned out to be a victim of her dad's scheme. He used to hit her.'

My stomach drops. 'I hope she pressed charges.'

'No.' It's a pained sound. 'She died.'

'He killed her?' My own fury is intense.

'He might as well have. She was miserable. She drank a big bottle of his vodka then went to watch the sunrise over Malibu. She was found at the bottom of the cliffs a day later.' A small sob escapes her and she covers it by reaching for her beer. My heart is breaking for Abbey, but also for Imogen, who comes across as so incredibly cool and professional but is, actually, very soft-hearted.

'My parents didn't let me go to the funeral. I think they were actually glad she was dead. They'd been worried about what kind of scandal she might drag me into.' The fury is back and I infinitely prefer it to her grief. 'I hated them after that. I mean, they're my parents, so I love them too, but I don't respect them, and I don't like them, and I hate what they stand for—or, rather, what they were too afraid to stand for.'

'I can understand why you feel that way.'

'Three years after founding Chance, *The New York Times* ran a profile about me. It was very flattering, full of praise for what I was doing. That was the first time my parents publicly acknowledged my work. After that, they started to donate, and even got their hoity-toity friends—the same ones who helped ruin Abbey's life—to hold benefits to raise money. You have no idea how it stung to take that cash.'

'Why did you?'

She fixes me with a look that is simple and sad, a surrender to pragmatism. 'Because that money could stop twenty kids from doing what Abbey did. We fund counsellors for at-risk kids—not just in-person sessions and drop-in clinics, but twenty-four-hour phone banks. The charity needs every penny it can get—I will never not accept donations, even from people who are so hypocritical it makes me sick.'

I lift a hand, running a finger over her cheek, studying her, somehow committing her and this to memory, because in the back of my mind I'm aware of the ticking of a time bomb, counting down to my future, our lives beyond this.

'I'm sorry about your friend.'

Her expression shifts to one of sadness, and then wistfulness. 'Me too.' She sighs, sips her beer. 'I wish I could have done more.'

'It sounds like you tried.'

'Yeah.'

'And you're doing so much for other kids like her.'

She nods, and pushes a smile to her face. 'Wow. I really tanked the mood, huh?'

'I'm glad you told me.'

'I don't know why I did. I don't really talk about Chance to members of the club.'

And despite the seriousness of our conversation, I can't help smiling. 'Is that what I am?'

'Uh huh.' She pushes up onto my lap, straddling me in the spa. I like her like this. Close and pliant in my arms; her body fits so perfectly with mine.

'One of the first kids I funded, in the first year of Chance, has just graduated medical school.' Her smile is bright. 'She was on the brink of dropping out of school when I met her. In fact, she kind of gave me the idea. I wanted to help her—not a little bit. A lot. I wanted to make it easy for her to study. She was so bright, so bright, and she just couldn't get a leg-up. That's what Chance does. You have to bring the attitude and the hope, but we will make it possible for dreams to come true.'

'I think you're amazing.' The words come from me before I can stop them, and I wish I hadn't said it, because it's the kind of compliment I usually avoid giving women, for the sense it creates of things meaning more to me than they do. I'm usually more careful.

Fortunately, Imogen doesn't really react. She makes a little face, an expression of mock coyness, and then pulls away from me, kicking across the hot tub to the other side.

'This is a nice touch, Lord Rothsmore.' Her smile

is back, and my heart relaxes—I hadn't realised how much I wanted to see her smile again.

'What's that?' My voice is deep and gruff.

'The hot tub, the lights, the snow.'

'I'll take credit for the hot tub but the rest is just this city.'

'It's quite the bachelor pad.' She looks over her shoulder to the cavernous living space. 'I can see how you got the reputation for being the Playboy of Manhattan.'

She wiggles her brows, flirty and teasing, light-hearted, except I feel something decidedly heavy flick through me.

'I'm really not so bad.'

'No judgement.' She lifts her hands in front of her. 'I don't care.'

There it is again. What do I want? For her to be jealous? That's kind of petty.

And stupid, given that I'm moving home in a few weeks with every intention of turning my lifestyle on its head completely, meeting someone who I can see a future with. A future that will look nothing like this. I'm not looking for someone I can laugh with and make love to all night long.

'Do you ever think how different your life would have been if your fiancée hadn't…?'

'Left me at the altar in front of our nearest and dearest?'

She winces. 'That must have sucked.'

I laugh, just a short, sharp noise of agreement. 'That's one word for it.'

'I'm serious. You must have been livid.'

'I was many things.' I drain my beer and place it on the edge of the hot tub.

'Like?'

'Livid, sure. Hurt. Heartbroken.' I catch the speculation that sweeps across her expression. 'That surprises you?'

'No, of course not.'

'You don't think I have a heart?' I can't resist probing, my voice light.

'Why would you say that?'

'When I said I was heartbroken you looked surprised.'

She shakes her head. 'You were getting married. It goes without saying you were in love with her.'

I give Manhattan my full focus for a minute, studying the beautiful, sparkling high-rises. Something inside me pulls tight—the thought of leaving this behind is not something I relish, even though I know the time has come.

'I wasn't really.' The admission isn't one I've ever made, even to myself. 'I wanted to love her. I suppose I thought that loving her would mean my parents hadn't masterminded the marriage. That it would have come down to Saffy and me being right for each other.' I grimace. 'At least she figured it out before we made it official.'

Imogen sits up a little higher, so her beautiful

breasts in that lace bra float on the surface of the water.

'Do you think you'd still be married, if she hadn't?'

'Probably. I didn't love her but I liked her a lot, and I respected her. We enjoyed one another's company. Our marriage made sense.'

'Do you ever speak to her?'

'No. Not for any reason—but I bear her no animosity.'

'You're far kinder than I would be. I mean, to leave someone on their wedding day—'

Her indignation is palpable.

'You think she should have married me just to avoid creating a scene?'

'Well, no. I guess ideally she should have realised how she felt before it was your wedding day.'

'It was a hard decision to make. She thought the wedding day would come and she'd feel okay about it. She didn't. She didn't know until she was living it.'

'Still.' Imogen's lips twist with disapproval and I want to bottle this part of her—her indignation and spark are so uniquely her, she is incredibly fiery. 'She deserves for you to hate her.'

I grin. 'To what end?'

'Because she embarrassed you?'

'I'm not so easily embarrassed,' I say with a lift of my shoulders. 'It sucked at the time. It was pretty shitty. So I went and got hammered. I got laid. And then I got on with my life.'

Imogen's eyes flare wide and I feel as if she wants to say something, but then she lets out a small sigh. 'Selfishly, I'm very glad she didn't marry you. It's been very nice having you as my sex toy for a while.'

It's so completely not what I expect that I burst out laughing. I'm still laughing when she crosses the hot tub and sits in my lap, and I laugh right up until she kisses me. I stop laughing, and I kiss her right back.

CHAPTER ELEVEN

SEVEN DATES. WE'VE had seven dates and more soul-bursting orgasms than I can possibly keep track of. I shift in the bed and look at Nicholas with a feeling that is a lot like dread.

He's sleeping, lightly, and I can't really blame him. It's some time before dawn, the night wrapping around New York even as the city insists on twinkling with its sparkly lights. We went to a Broadway show last night and I teased him beforehand, that it was a bit predictable.

He insisted it was a quintessential New York date and that I hadn't really lived until I'd been taken to a Broadway show. I prepared to tease him all night, that it was cheesy or schmaltzy or something, but then he went and made it all 'next level' and I got caught up in the fairy tale of the whole thing.

When he came to pick me up from my place, he brought a single red rose and a box of chocolate truffles—he's very cleverly discovered how much I love them. We rode in his limousine with classical music playing, and, on arrival at the theatre, we were escorted to a private box where champagne and sushi were brought to us. We had our own butler for the duration. Afterwards, we walked back to his place, talking and laughing the whole way.

He was right.

It was a new experience, a different experience, and one I'm so glad to have shared with him. I mean, I've been to shows before, obviously, but never like that. It was…lovely.

No, that's so bland. It was perfection. It was heart-stopping.

As was what happened after. My body hums and sings with the pleasures I experienced. Pleasures he gave me like gifts, beautiful little explosions of delight that have weaved their way into my soul.

The Christmas gala is one week away. I'm looking down the barrel of workplace mayhem as I make sure everything is organised for our biggest event of the year. While every Billionaires' Club party is a big deal, this is the one that draws almost the entire membership. It is our biggest fundraiser, a night not to be missed, and every year there's an expectation that it will get bigger and better.

And I think this year will be pretty epic—but I can't risk anything going wrong. Ordinarily, I wouldn't let anything rob me of my focus. And yet, Nicholas definitely does that, and I wouldn't, for all the stars in the sky, put a premature end to this.

I'm already dreading the gala purely for the fact it's our line in the sand, the end to what we're doing. I know how fast this week's going to go.

I contemplate reaching for him, running my hand over his taut stomach, and lower still, waking him with my hands or my mouth, drawing him none-too-gently from his sleep. But he's so peaceful and despite the fact tomorrow—no, today—is Sunday, I have to go down to one of the Chance facilities to give a talk. As tempted as I am for round two hundred, I know where my duties lie.

I push the sheet back with serious regrets and tiptoe out of his bed, out of his room, and I tell myself not to look back.

I sleep until midday then dress quickly—jeans and a sweater, a simple black coat and flats for today. I don't dress up for Chance sessions. The whole thing is to be relatable to these guys. They have enough adults in their lives that don't get them. I want them to see me as a friend, someone they can trust.

One of the things that's become harder as the charity's grown is that I get to do way less of this hands-on stuff than I'd like. I don't get to talk to as many of our kids, I don't get to meet them all. I've hired amazing staff, though, and I check in with them with enough regularity to know when things are working, and when they're not.

Where'd you go?

The text message from Nicholas comes through as I arrive at our Brooklyn Chance headquarters. I smile.

I didn't want to wake you, Sleeping Beauty.

I add an emoji with its tongue poking out.

Why didn't you stay?

But we've talked about that. I feel better not actually sleeping the night—which is a silly distinction, but one that somehow makes sense. Boundaries will be my saviour when all of him is a sink hole, drawing me closer, making me want him, making me need him in a way I definitely didn't expect.

I have a thing today.

A thing?

Alicia Waterman, the manager of this Chance facility, walks towards me, her no-nonsense air instantly reassuring. I only have time to dash out a quick reply.

I'm giving a talk to some Chance kids in Brooklyn. I'll call you later.

'Alicia.' I stuff my phone into the back pocket of my jeans. 'All good to go?'

'All ready.' She nods crisply, falling into step beside me. 'There's a huge turnout. Over two hundred.'

I let out a low whistle. 'That's great.'

'Will you have time afterwards for a quick sit-down? I need to talk to you about some of our vocational partners.'

'Uh oh. That doesn't sound good.'

Her smile is tight. 'I'm sure it will be fine; just a hiccough. I just need to go through some options.'

A presentiment of concern moves down my spine. 'You're sure?'

She grimaces. 'It'll wait.'

'Okay, fine. After.'

'You need anything?'

I survey the disused warehouse we've converted into a loft space. The high ceilings give it a feeling of freedom, and the office partitions are all on wheels, meaning for events like today we can move them around to open it right up.

My heart bursts as I step into the building.

Pride, unmistakable, is like a firefly dancing through my system. I did this. All these people are here because of me, and all of them have a chance because of me. And because of Abbey. I close my eyes and picture Abbey, and the ever-present sense of purpose has me pushing up towards the stage at the front of the room.

There's a lot of chatter but as I take the steps it quietens down a little. I stand at the lectern, push my phone onto silent, sip the water and begin to talk.

I love this—speaking to these kids. I used to get nervous but very quickly I realised that it's not about me, it's about them. I'm here to tell them what they need to hear, to give them what has been missing in their lives.

I speak from the heart, and close everything else out.

I didn't plan to come here, but when Imogen messaged to say she was speaking at a Chance function, curiosity got the better of me. Before I knew it, I'd done a quick search and was flying my helicopter towards Brooklyn.

It doesn't occur to me until I'm almost inside the warehouse that she might not have wanted me to come. I contemplate waiting outside, but that's just dumb. She won't care.

Besides, I want to see this. I want to see what she does when she's not facilitating a club where the world's super-rich elite blow off steam.

The room is completely silent, despite the fact it's full of kids. They're older kids, teens, mostly. I move to the back of the room.

An efficient-looking woman with a clipboard and short black hair regards me with a look of curiosity and scepticism. I nod at her, as if I belong, and stand against the wall.

My eyes fall on Imogen and something locks inside me.

'My meemaw used to have a saying.' She smiles, naturally, comfortably, her eyes skimming the room, and I can tell that she has a gift with this, with making every single person in the space feel as though she's talking only to them. 'You can't see a dolphin when the water's choppy but that don't mean it's not there.' She does a perfect southern accent, as she did the day I came looking for Miss Anonymous. It makes me grin.

'I know you're all here today because the waters around you are choppy.' She takes a minute to let that sink in, her expression shifting so it's serious, sympathetic. I feel compassion bursting from her every pore. 'Maybe it's worse than choppy. Maybe you feel like you have a tsunami bearing down on you with nowhere to go. But that's not the case. Chance is your port in the storm, your anchor, your home and your family. You belong here with us, you're one of us, and we will do everything we can to help you.' Her eyes scan the room once more, and this time, they pass over me then skid back, surprise showing on her face for the briefest of moments so I feel a wedge of guilt, as if maybe I've driven her off course.

But she smiles, right at me, and my stomach soars, then she continues seamlessly. 'Just because the water's choppy doesn't mean there isn't a dolphin—you have a dolphin inside you, your future is out there, bright and waiting for you to grab it with both hands. I'm so proud of you all, and I'm thrilled you're a part of the Chance family. You belong here. Merry Christmas.'

The audience erupts, a huge applause that is almost deafening in this cavernous space. When she smiles, she looks so sweet and young, not at all like the founder of The Billionaires' Club.

She waves a hand and steps off the stage, and my pride in her catches me completely by surprise. I can't take credit for how good she is at this; it has nothing to do with me. And yet I feel an immense wave of warmth.

The woman with the clipboard takes the stage. She speaks for a few minutes, directing everyone to a table set up against the wall, loaded with pastries and hot chocolates. A better look shows there's a second table, which looks to be overflowing with coats and jumpers, all neatly folded, ready for new owners to take them home.

'What are you doing here?' She comes up from behind me, her smile bright and perfect.

I can't help it. I dip my head down and kiss her, so overwhelmed by how great she did, by the words she spoke, by the power she wields to make a true difference.

But she pulls away quickly, her eyes skittering around the room. 'Nicholas.' She shakes her head. 'Not here. There are people here who know me.'

Shit.

We're dating *secretly.* And I completely forgot. I forgot this is all kind of pretend. Not real. It's not my place to act like the doting boyfriend, which I'm definitely not.

I forgot myself for a second.

'Sorry,' I say, sincerely. 'I was just so proud of you.'

Her smile is back, her eyes twinkling. 'Seriously?'

'Yeah.' *Pull it together, you soppy bastard.* 'Christ, you were amazing up there.'

She blinks quickly, as if she's trying to combat tears or something. 'I have to talk to Alicia. Can you wait?'

'Yeah.' My voice is hoarse. 'I can wait.'

She squeezes my hand discreetly. 'Mingle.' Her smile is pure sensual promise. 'Eat something yummy.'

I lean a little closer. 'Oh, I intend to.'

Her cheeks glow and I laugh as she walks away, before doing just as she instructed, and find myself talking to a sixteen-year-old called Isaac, whose parents kicked him out of home when he came out to them as gay. He's smart and polite, and, when he tells me he was living on the streets until three months ago when someone told him about Chance, I feel like finding out where his parents are so I can go and give them some hard truths.

He introduces me to one of his friends, a girl called Bryony, whose parents died when she was thirteen. She was taken in by her aunt, but they fought non-stop. She ran away from home and ended up in Brooklyn, working as a prostitute until she found Chance.

My gut tightens.

These poor kids.

And their guardian angel, Imogen.

It's hard to fathom the effect this has on me—seeing for myself what she's doing, how hard she's worked to make a difference. I feel immediately impotent and completely selfish. I've worked my arse off these past five years but for what? To make myself richer? To make my family's already considerable fortune greater?

When this is how people live?

'Hey.' She appears at my side, and her smile is a little tighter now, her eyes less sparkly.

'Is everything okay?'

'Yeah.' Her eyes run over the room and before she can say anything else, a young teenager, maybe thirteen, comes bounding up to her.

'Imogen!' She puts her arms around Imogen's waist and Imogen dips down lower to wrap the girl in a proper hug.

'Sasha. I was hoping I'd see you today. How are you, sweetheart?'

'Good. I got something for you.'

'You did?' Imogen frowns. 'I'm pretty sure that's against the rules.'

'I know. But I saw it and I thought of you. Hang on. I'll be right back.'

'I'll be here.'

Imogen slides a glance at me. 'She's twelve. She became a part of Chance four years ago, when her parents were going through a divorce. Her mom was living in a car at the time. Sasha was stealing stuff from *bodegas* to get by.' She shakes her head wistfully.

Sasha appears a second later. 'Here.' She hands a small bag over. Imogen opens it and laughs, pulling out some saltwater taffy. 'I remember you saying you love it.' Sasha grins and Imogen nods.

'I do. So much. You've spoiled me.'

Sasha beams. I'm completely transfixed by Imogen's look of gratitude and surprise—that someone who does so much for so many should be genuinely chuffed by such a token gift. It's…charming. And… beautiful. No. Lovely.

She's lovely.

She quizzes Sasha. 'Did you get something to eat?'

'Uh-huh.'

'And a jacket?'

'No.'

'Go pick one out, honey.' Imogen waves towards the table. 'The forecast is for more snow this week.'

'I know. Merry Christmas.'

Another hug, and as Sasha disappears into the crowd again Imogen's eyes are moist. 'You ready to go?' she asks, looking up at me.

'Sure. You can leave already?'

'Yeah.' Her smile is dented. I wait until we're outside before I ask her what's going on.

I like that she doesn't try to fob me off. She could have, but, then again, I've come to know her pretty well and I don't think I'd be convinced by a lie.

Something's bothering her, something other than the sight of so many kids in need of Chance's support.

'It's our intern programme,' she says thoughtfully. 'We have a partnership with Eckerman Walsh for kids who want to move into finance. They take five Chance high school seniors a year on internships and help fund college for some. But they're going through a significant restructure and they've asked to put a pause on it for two years, while they right the ship.' She looks up at me, apology on her features. 'Sorry. I don't mean to bore you with that.'

'You're not,' I demur, instantly.

'I'll work it out. It's just that this year's kids were due to start in September and now they have nowhere to go. It'll be crushing.'

I don't even think about it. 'They can come to me.'

'What?' She's startled. 'What do you mean?'

'My office here. I run three hedge funds within my umbrella of companies. Let them come to Rothsmore Group for their internships. We'll take up the same terms as Eckerman Walsh, including college tuition. In fact, I could offer the same for each of the cities my fund has a presence. London, Rome, Sydney…'

'Nic…' She shakes her head from side to side so her blonde hair fluffs against her beautiful face. 'I can't let you do that.'

'Why not?'

'Because…' Her voice trails into the ether.

'Because?'

'Because, I feel like you're only offering because we're sleeping together.'

'I'm offering because I've just spent an hour of my life seeing that I've been a useless, selfish git, that there are incredible kids out there who deserve a better chance in life and you're giving it to them. I'm offering because I want to help in some small way that I can.'

Her mouth drops open. I look around quickly and steal a kiss, a kiss that makes me ache for her, a kiss that makes me feel things I can't compute.

'You said you never turn down donations to the charity,' I remind her.

'I know. But you're…you. I don't want you to think I'm taking advantage of you…'

'Oh, you're welcome to take advantage of me any time,' I tease, wiggling my eyebrows dramatically.

But she shakes her head, lifts a hand to my chest. 'It's so generous.'

'I can afford it.' I smile. 'And I insist. I *want* to do this.'

And I really, really do.

'So, your grandmother sounds pretty wise.' Imogen blinks up at me from the book she's reading. She likes to read. And I like watching her read. About five dates ago, she found her way to my library upstairs and has been working her way through the classics, just for fun.

'She was.' Imogen's smile is full of affection.

'Did she really used to say that? About the dolphin?'

'Yeah! Why? You thought I made it up?'

'I just haven't heard it before.'

'Oh, she had all these really neat sayings. Like, *"It don't matter how scratched up you are, you get back on the bike."*'

I laugh. 'I could have used that advice.'

'Why?'

'Oh, I came off my bike a long time ago and never rode again.'

She looks surprised. 'That doesn't sound like you. Quitting?'

'I wasn't afraid to ride again,' I clarify. 'I just didn't particularly like the feeling of crashing off it.'

'I can't say I blame you. Still, Meemaw would have insisted you keep riding.'

I smile. 'What else would she say?'

'Hmm… *"If you're careful, you only have to light a fire once."* Lots of them didn't make much sense, but she'd say them and Pa would look at me and roll his eyes. I miss them.'

'They're both gone?'

'Yeah.' She blinks away the memories.

'You were close?'

'Yeah.' Her eyes shift, as if she's running over memories. 'I started spending a fair bit of time with them, once I was a teenager. I used to go down there most summers. It was nice to get away from my parents, from Hollywood.' She lifts her shoulders. 'It was Meemaw who gave me the idea for Chance.

She used to say to me, *"There's a lot of bridges need building in this world—someone's always gotta place the first stone."*'

I smile. 'Meemaw sounds pretty smart.'

Imogen nods. 'The smartest. And you? Do you have grandparents?'

'No. My parents were in their forties when they had me. My father's parents were both gone, and my mother's only lived until I was maybe four or five. I never really knew them.'

'Was it a second marriage?'

I frown, not following.

'It seems kind of late in life to start a family?'

'Right. Actually, on the contrary, they were married quite young.' I reach over and brush some of her hair back, as if I can't help myself. 'They had fertility problems. A lot of miscarriages. A stillbirth. Then years of not being able to conceive. I think that's got a lot to do with why they're so damned keen for me to settle down and start a family of my own.' I wiggle my brows to downplay my frustrations. I do understand why my parents feel the way they do but that doesn't mean they don't drive me crazy.

'God, they must have doted on you,' she murmurs, watching me from narrowed eyes.

It's such an amusing observation that I laugh. 'Not at all. I mean, yes, my mother often describes my birth as some kind of miracle, but they're both by-products of their environment. They were glad to have me, grateful to have been able to produce an heir at last, but doting wasn't really in their vocabulary. I went to boarding school when I was seven years old. I only saw my mother and father on holidays, and, even then, they were frequently abroad.' I frown, because I don't often think back on that time. 'I liked school, though.'

Imogen's eyes crease with the sympathy that comes so quickly to her. She puts the book down and crosses the room, her eyes huge in her delicate face.

'You were too young to be sent away.'

I stare down at her, something moving in my gut. 'Was I?'

'Yes.'

I don't say anything; she's probably right.

'Promise me something.'

I nod slowly. I know that I would promise her just about anything.

'When you get married and have your little lords and ladies, don't send them away.'

I wonder why that thought fills me with a strange sense of acidity.

'I see it again and again in the kids I work with at Chance—all they really want is parents who are there, who love them.'

I imagine she's right about that. It seems to me that children have a universal set of needs and yet a lot of parents probably fail to meet them.

'Promise me,' she insists.

And I nod, because Imogen is asking something

of me and it's within my power to give it to her. 'I promise.'

She smiles, and it's as though the world is catching fire. My lungs snatch air deep inside them. Everything is frozen still inside me. She's the most beautiful person I've ever known, inside and out.

And in a matter of days I'll leave her for ever.

CHAPTER TWELVE

December 21st, the Christmas Gala,
Billionaires' Clubrooms, Manhattan

IT'S FINALLY TIME.

I stand in the middle of the ballroom and look around, taking it all in. The formalities are over, the auction concluded—we've raised twice what I'd hoped. The millions of dollars from ticket sales added to the auction revenue means I'll be able to fast-track the shelter I've had designed in Phoenix.

A lump forms in my throat, pride in what I've done, hope for the future of children making me feel, understandably, a little emotional. But it's more than that. It's the knowledge that this is my last night with Nicholas. That come what may, at the end of this evening, it will be the end for us.

A month ago, that made sense, but now, it feels a thousand shades of wrong. Everything inside me rails against the idea. I don't want tonight to be the last time I see him, but what other option is there? He has to go back to England. And if it were just a matter of work, maybe we could try a long-distance thing. I've been wanting to expand Chance to Europe—a London base would be a good start. Maybe I could get over my worries about what the membership will think if news breaks that I'm dating someone from within its ranks. Maybe I could make it work. But Nicholas is going home to find some aristocratic heiress and make a suitable match. There were a dozen reasons we gave our dating deal a time limit of one month, and none of those reasons has gone away.

Except I don't want it to end.

'Hey.' His voice behind me is the cherry on top.

I try my hardest to school my face into a mask of professional inquiry, but the second I turn around and see Nicholas Rothsmore in a tuxedo, my pulse shoots into overdrive and I feel as though I'm being driven at high speed around a hairpin bend.

I don't want this to end.

I want…what? What do I want?

'Nic…' I breathe his name into the room, needing nothing more than to crush my body to his and kiss him, hard, kiss him slow, kiss him all over.

'Quite the shindig.' His eyes probe mine and I have a feeling he's fighting a similar urge to mine; that he wants to pull me to him and kiss me.

My eyes drift to his watch. It will be at least an hour before I can leave. Emily, my assistant, will take care of everything after that; she is amazing.

'You having fun?' I murmur.

'I'll have more fun if you dance with me.'

I shake my head a little. 'I feel like that could be a giveaway.'

'I've seen you dance with at least five guys tonight.'

My heart turns over in my chest. 'Jealous, my lord?' I'm teasing him, a light-hearted joke, but his eyes narrow and he nods.

'Beyond belief.'

Blood fills my heart too fast; my chest hurts. What do I want from him? How can this night be the last one we spend together? 'That's work.'

'So? I'm work too. I'm your new internship partner, remember?'

Remember? I've thought of very little else since our lawyers rushed through the paperwork so this year's ballot of kids wouldn't miss their selections.

'You raise an excellent point.' And temptation makes me foolish. 'One dance.'

He holds his hands out, and I step into them, taking a position that would pass, if anyone cared to look carefully, as purely businesslike.

'I have been watching you,' he says slowly, the words brushing low against my ear, so no one else can hear. 'And trying to work out if this dress has a zip hidden somewhere.'

'Pre-emptive planning?' I prompt, my eyes running over his face.

'Yes. I intend to remove it from you just as soon as we get back to my apartment.'

My pulse races faster; my chest still hurts, as if it's being cracked wide apart. I don't want this to end.

Ever.

The realisation slices through me like the sharpest blade of a knife.

'I want to strip the dress from you and carry you to the hot tub, pull you into the water and onto my cock. I want to fuck you there, first.'

I swallow, his imagery insanely erotic, but even that isn't enough to push my realisation from my mind.

I don't want Nicholas to go. I don't want 'us' to be over. And there *is* an 'us'. Despite our insistence that this is pretend dating, like an education for me and nothing more, I have done perhaps the most stupid thing in my life.

I've fallen in love with him.

I fell in love with a man. It was a trap. When we started this, I thought he was the opposite of everything I wanted. He's rich—he's going to be a *lord*, for Christ's sake—and he's shallow. He's meant to be, anyway, but he isn't. He's caring and sweet and compassionate and intelligent and fascinating and—

Oh, my God.

I stop dancing for a second.

His eyes are skipping over my face. He's going to work out something's wrong.

'What else?' I start to dance again, lifting my lips into an approximation of a smile.

'There's a lid for every pot. You can't fight it when you find what fits.'

Meemaw used to say it about Pa, when she was frustrated by him, but always with a smile. As if he drove her crazy but she loved him completely.

'I want to spend some time saying goodbye to your beautiful breasts,' he groans, his voice a whisper that sends darts down my spine. But the words cause my heart to splinter into a billion pieces, because he's talking about saying goodbye as though he's totally fine with this.

My eyes sweep shut, and I know, in that moment, if anyone cared to look they'd see the face of a woman whose heart is being completely shattered.

'And this arse of yours.'

I have no idea how I hold it together. His words are making my body tremble with anticipation, but in the middle of my chest a cavity is being scraped out. I am hollow.

I am in love with a man who is wrong for me in every way. He's moving to another country. He's going to marry someone else and, even then, against his will—he would rather be single and continue to do what he's been doing these last five years.

What kind of an idiot falls in love with an unavailable playboy?

I look at him—I can't help it—and see a frown on his face. 'Are you okay?'

Shit. I don't even feel as if I can lie properly. 'I'm

fine. Just emotional. This event is the culmination of a lot of work.'

He visibly relaxes. 'I can see that.'

I love Nicholas Rothsmore. I don't know when I first started to love him, but somewhere along the way, I fell and I fell hard. It's like being struck by lightning; how does he not feel it?

Does he feel it?

His hand at my back shifts, just a little, closer towards my arse. I blink up at him and drop his hand, stepping backwards.

He doesn't feel it. He does this kind of thing all the time, and, even if he didn't, he learned his lesson from the first and last woman he let himself love.

He's built a wall around his heart that I don't think I can chip through.

'Imogen.' Orla, one of the club's Australian members, who I really like, catches me as she passes, oblivious to the explosions that are detonating inside my soul. 'You've outdone yourself.'

I zipper over my heart and take a breath, resuming my usual calm, unflappable exterior. 'You're having fun?'

'Oh, yes.' It's slightly breathy. Her eyes shift over me for a second and her cheeks flush. 'Definitely.' She puts a manicured hand on my wrist, her eyes shining. 'I've got some ideas for the next Sydney gala. I'll email you.'

I smile. Life goes on. Things move forward.

With or without Nicholas, the club will continue, the membership will grow, the charity will survive. But my heart won't recover. I have never been in love before, but I don't think you need to have first-hand experience to know that love has transformative powers.

I love Nicholas, and my life will never be the same after he leaves.

I have to tell him.

Orla slinks off, her beautiful dress caressing her frame. I watch her for a second and then turn back to Nicholas. His grin is pure, devilish playboy.

He doesn't love me, and all telling him will achieve is a premature end to this.

He won't take me home tonight; it will be over and I need that not to be the case.

One more night, one more night of fun and sex and pretending this is casual when I know it isn't. At least, not for me.

'I have to circulate,' I say softly.

'I expected as much.' But then, leaning even closer, 'You're sure you don't want to try out an Intimate Room? I can get some handcuffs…'

And despite my breaking heart, heat blooms through my body. 'Later.'

He laughs. 'Count on it.'

His use of the phrase I utter so often pulls at me, because it is this phrase that led him to discover I was Miss Anonymous. Would I take it back if I could? Would I make it so this never happened?

No. Not in a million years. Even as I feel my heart breaking, I know I would never wish we hadn't shared this. Nicholas has changed me, and I think for the better.

I continue to circulate, brushing past the billionaire property developers Ash Evans and Sebastian Dumont just in time to catch them shaking hands, Ash laughing at something Sebastian's muttered.

This is what the club promises its members. It's a safe place to do business, to network and to relax. It's a safe place but not, as it turns out, for me.

I run my tongue over his tattoo, hating it in that moment, because I don't want Nicholas to be his own. I want him to be mine. I flick his hair-roughened nipple, enjoying the feeling of his chest lifting, his breath snagging in his lungs as I move lower. His naked body is tanned against the matte black of his sheets. I kiss my way down his body, tasting his flesh, remembering everything I can about this, taking his hard cock into my mouth, absorbing the guttural oath he spills into the room as I move my mouth up and down, my nipples tingling, heat pooling between my legs.

I will never get sick of this. Him, me, naked. I want this to last for ever.

But it is already approaching dawn, and I hate that. Never have I wanted a night to last longer than I do this night.

I taste a hint of his salty pre-cum and then his hands are under my arms, pulling me up his body, his mouth seeking mine, his frame rolling me, so I'm on my back, his arousal hard between my legs. I arch my back and spread my legs wide, wordlessly begging him to take me, to make love to me, needing his body to console mine in the only way he can.

But he breaks the kiss and reaches across me. I hear a drawer and then something metallic. His hands curve around my wrists; he pulls them to the bedframe and then cold metal surrounds me. I pull on my hands. They're cuffed to the bed.

I stare up at him, my eyes wide, lips parted.

'Do you trust me?'

My stomach swirls with acid. 'With all my heart.'

His smile is sensual. A second later, his hands are trailing over my flesh, so light, barely touching me, and I'm crying his name out over and over. His mouth follows them, his tongue flicking my nipples, as he moves lower with his hands, spreading my legs to make way for his mouth.

His tongue is gentle at first, running over my seam, exploring me, rediscovering me. I thrash from side to side, my handcuffed wrists a new form of torture as I ache to touch him or touch myself, to do something to relieve this tidal wave of sensation.

'Please,' I groan, incapable of saying anything else. He keeps my legs pinned wide as he sucks my clit into his mouth and flicks it with his tongue. I am on fire; I am burning up. 'Please,' I whimper, needing him, needing more, needing everything.

He pulls away, up my body, his mouth finding my nipples, his hands roaming my skin freely, inquiringly, and I'm so hungry for him I can barely cope. I need to feel him inside me.

'I want you,' I beg.

'I know.' His smile is tighter now, tension on his face. He pauses, rolling a condom over his length, and hope is a beast inside me.

His eyes hold mine as he pushes his rock-hard arousal into my wet core; my muscles spasm around him and I jerk against the handcuffs, wanting to touch him now, to feel his muscles bunch beneath me as I run my hands over his skin.

His laugh is soft, a caress against my skin. He moves inside me, deeper, and I groan, surrendering to this completely. My body is an instrument and he plays me with perfection.

Dawn is coming. Even in winter, when the sun rises later, nothing staves off morning's eventual appearance. I watch him sleep, my own eyes heavy, my mind heavier, my heart a dead weight.

I love him, and I have no hope that he loves me back. For me, this has been completely unprecedented. For Nicholas, this is his life, his norm. I have no reason to think anything has changed for him since we started up with this, whereas all the boundaries of my world have shifted.

My eyes run over his beautiful face, disbelief curdling my insides.

This is so much harder than I thought it would be.

I shift in the bed.

A coffee will help.

I step out quietly, drawing one of his shirts from the wardrobe and pulling it over my nakedness as I prowl through to the kitchen.

It's snowed overnight. When I look down from the windows, I see the pavement is white like chalk, cars covered in a pale, sparkling blanket. I press a button on the coffee machine, cursing as it stirs to life. Even though it's quiet, it's not silent, and I look towards his bedroom door in time to see Nicholas shifting in bed. He looks for me and my heart groans, because I'm his first thought on waking.

How can this be the end?

He disappears from view and a second later steps into the lounge area, a pair of grey boxer shorts low on his hips. My eyes find his tattoo on autopilot; acid coats the inside of my mouth.

'Is it even morning?' he asks groggily, his face showing bemusement.

'I have to get going,' I say, my own voice tight like a wire that's been pulled too taut.

His eyes focus blearily on his watch. 'It's five o'clock.'

'I know.' I pull the coffee from the machine and cup it in my hands. I keep my back propped against the kitchen bench. I hope it looks nonchalant. I hope I seem better than I feel.

'Come back to bed.'

My heart groans. 'I can't.'

'Why?'

I swallow, focussing on the black liquid inside my cup. 'Because we said this would be the end. And I have to go.'

I don't think the stilted statements make much sense, and this is confirmed when I lift my attention to his face. 'Stay.'

'A few more hours?'

'No.' He frowns. 'I don't have to be in England until New Year's Eve. Spend Christmas with me.'

I feel as if I'm being stretched on the rack. 'What?'

'A week's extension on our original deal?' His tone is teasing.

Something shifts in my chest, something painful. 'Why?'

He shrugs his shoulders casually. 'Why not?'

My knees tremble. Fire spits through my veins. It's so close to what I want, but, now that I understand how I feel, being with Nicholas for another night—let alone seven—would just be too hard.

'Because, I can't.'

His expression is sceptical. I draw in a deep breath. 'I have to get back to my normal life,' I say emphatically—my normal life is my lifeline. It's the talisman for who I used to be. 'I have the Christmas drive for Chance, and the Christmas lunch I do every year.' I bite down on my lip, looking away from him because I can't bear to look into his eyes for another moment. 'I can't.'

The last word wobbles a little. I sip the coffee to stave off some kind of emotional scene.

'One more week.'

'No.' I am emphatic. I speak as if my life depends on it, and in many ways it does.

He's quiet a moment. 'I don't understand. Last night was…amazing. You're saying you don't want more of this?'

'We said a month,' I murmur. 'We were clear about this. The Christmas benefit was to be the end.'

'And that's what you want?'

I open my mouth to say something, but what can I say? That yes, I want more. I want too much more. How did this happen? The club and Chance have been my total priority for so long and I would have sworn they always would be, but now there's something—someone—else who matters just as much, and despite the fact I swore this would be fun and casual and no-strings, despite the fact I initially loved the boundaries we put in place, I want to push against them now. I'm in love with him, and I know he doesn't love me back, but, God, I can't ignore how I feel.

'Damn it, Imogen, it was an arbitrary line in the sand you decided on. Why can't we shift it by one fucking week?'

His anger sparks my own. I can no longer control my feelings, my rawness. 'Because a week isn't nearly enough, Nicholas. I don't want just one more week with you. I want a lifetime, okay?'

CHAPTER THIRTEEN

HER STATEMENT HANGS between us like a thousand and one daggers. I stare at her; nothing makes sense. I must have misunderstood.

'What are you talking about?'

She sips her coffee, her face pale, her features drawn.

She's so quiet and impatience is slicing through me.

'For God's sake, Imogen, that doesn't make sense. What do you mean?'

Her eyes are huge and hollow, emotions rushing through her that I can't comprehend. All I want is to keep this fun going—and it is fun. This last month has been one of the best of my life. I love spending time with Imogen. I love hanging out with her. God knows, I love fucking her.

'I'm in love with you.' Her eyes pierce me, accusation in them, anger too. I am silent, grappling with the words as though maybe I've misunderstood, as though I've magicked them up out of my deepest fears.

'What?'

Her smile is laced with self-condemnation. 'I fell in love with you. It was the last thing I thought would happen, and honestly I have no idea how it *did* happen. Without meaning to and without me even realising, somehow you've become a part of me. And I can't just pretend I don't love you, and go back to sleeping with you and dating you and getting to know you when inside my heart is breaking.'

I'm silent. I'm completely floored.

'It's fine.' She smiles but her eyes look moist. 'I know you're not in love with me. I'm not telling you this because I'm hoping you'll get down on one knee and propose marriage.'

She swallows; I still can't speak.

'But I can't spend another week with you, sharing my life—my body—with you, knowing that you'll never be able to give me the one thing I really want.' She pauses for a second, her cheeks growing pink. 'I'm sorry to deprive you of a week of sex, but I have no doubt you can find someone else to fill your bed until you leave.'

My ears are filled with a screeching noise and everything in the room is too white, too bright, as if it's been overexposed or something.

'What?'

Fuck. That's not right. Focus. Concentrate. Say something better.

She shakes her head sadly and panic surges in my

chest. 'Imogen, you know…' I groan, drag a hand through my hair. 'It's not you.'

'But it is me. And it's the fact I fell in love with you, and you don't love me, and if I stay with you another night, I'm going to feel… I'm going to feel…a thousand things, and none of them good.'

'Love was never on my radar.' It's a stupid thing to say but I'm grappling with her statement, desperately trying to make sense of it.

Her eyes spit fire. 'Do you think it was on mine?'

'No.' My own frustration comes through in the word.

'Damn straight. I love that we had rules and boundaries and that this was—in theory—simple fun. But it's different now, everything's different, and I would hate myself if I didn't admit that. To myself, and to you.'

Her eyes close for a moment and I feel as if the ground has just swallowed me up. I'm falling and beneath me are the very fires of hell.

I hate hurting her. The realisation is like a punch in my gut. I'm hurting Imogen and this was always about helping her. About pleasuring her. And now I've hurt her and I can't believe that.

I need to make it better. I have to make her understand.

'You are incredible. Some guy, some day, is going to win the lottery when you fall for him.'

'But not you,' she murmurs, her eyes huge in her face. My chest kicks.

'Not me.'

She nods, but, God, her lip is trembling and I feel like a monster.

'Once, I believed in love, and it was a disaster.' I move closer, needing her to feel the sincerity of my words. 'I honestly believed I loved Saffy and when we broke up, it was like being woken from a dream I'll never find my way back to again. I don't *want* to find my way back there. I don't want to feel like that. I don't want to think I love someone. I don't want to give anyone else that power over me.' I lift a hand to her cheek and almost swear when she flinches out of my reach, as if I've shocked her with raw electricity.

'You are your own,' she says, but archly, with a hint of anger that I'm ridiculously glad about—I much prefer anger to the brokenness that confronted me a minute ago.

'Yes.' I am relieved. 'I'm my own, I belong only to myself, and that's the way I like it. I'm sorry, Imogen. I'm sorry if I did anything to make you hope for a future here. I thought I was clear—'

'Oh, you were.' The words are weary. 'Which just shows what an idiot I am.'

'No, Imogen…' But what can I say? She's right. Any woman who would fall in love with me needs her head examined. I try again. 'I think we should forget I suggested this.' I clench my jaw. 'I'll go back to England, as planned. I'm sorry. I didn't want this—I didn't have any idea you were developing feelings for me or I would have ended it sooner. I'm sorry,' I say again. Though it's manifestly insufficient, I have no idea what else I can say.

Silence wraps around us, a prickly, angry silence like the icy morning after a winter's storm.

'You are a goddamned coward, Lord Rothsmore.' She bites my future title out with disgust. Her statement crashes around me and I don't speak, because she needs to get this off her chest and I'm okay with that. I have to be—I'm breaking her heart. She finishes her coffee, placing the cup down hard on the bench top.

'You're too scared to let yourself feel this.' Her eyes lance me. 'You think you're the only person to be hurt? You think that means you need to put yourself in emotional stasis for the rest of your life? How is that even going to work? You're going to go home and make a sensible marriage and what? Feel nothing for your wife?'

I don't want to talk to Imogen about my future. Suddenly, the plans I've set in place chasm before me like an awful void. I grind my teeth together, trying to focus, trying to work out what I can say that will make this better.

I have to fix this.

'That's how it works,' I say quietly, calmly, even when I'm not calm.

'And that's what you want?'

I stare at her for several long seconds, pulling myself back mentally. 'I have accepted what is required of me,' I correct. 'And nothing is going to change that.'

She is so pale.

'I feel like we were clear about this from the start,' I say softly, and tears sparkle on her lashes.

'Hasn't anything changed for you since then?'

My gut churns hard. I shake my head. It can't. I can't do this. 'No.'

No. The word is emphatic. I look at him, my heart no longer in my chest. I have no idea what happened to it. Maybe it withered and died completely?

He doesn't love me. He doesn't want me—or at least, only for another week. I think about that, and wonder if I can shelve my own feelings, purely to squeeze every moment out of this that we possibly can. But there's no way.

I can't do it.

I move away from him, towards my ball gown that is discarded in the lounge, where he removed it last night. It's beautiful, but all I can think of is that it's what I wore on our last night together.

My throat feels as though it's been scraped with sandpaper.

'Imogen, listen to me.' His voice is gravelled. I don't stop what I'm doing. In fact, I move faster, pulling the dress up over my hips, discarding his shirt with my back to him. It's ridiculous to want to shield my nakedness, given what we've shared, and yet I do.

'I care about you, okay?' His voice is so deep, so

rough. 'If things had been different, maybe this could have worked out, but I'm not the guy you want me to be. I don't even believe in love, I don't believe in happy endings. I believe in *this*.'

When I look around, he's gesturing from his chest, towards me.

'I believe in the power of a resounding physical chemistry, and I believe in respect and civility. I believe in fun.'

'You have turned partying into an art form all so you can avoid feeling any kind of emotional connection with someone. You're living with your head in the sand and you don't even realise it.'

'And what exactly are you doing, Imogen? You haven't had sex or even dated a guy in four years and you tell me *I'm* the one who has my head in the sand?'

'I put my life on hold to run Chance,' I fire back, anger sharp in my mind. 'I don't have much of a social life but that's because I want to make the world better. You spend all your time having frivolous, meaningless affairs because you're shit scared of *feeling* anything for anyone. All because you loved someone once and she didn't want to marry you.'

'Jesus Christ,' he curses, his eyes sharp with fierce determination and frustration. 'This is spectacularly unreasonable.'

I suck in an indignant breath.

'Do you think you have any right to lecture me? You're the one who's moved the goalposts. You're shitty at me because I don't love you, when love wasn't even on the cards. Ever.'

I drop my head forward a second, his words like ice cubes, but ones I need to feel.

'I never expected you to love me. I'm just telling you why I can't spend another week with you.'

He holds my gaze even as I feel regret shift inside him.

'I told you to forget I suggested that. I'm sorry.'

I stiffen my spine, fixing him with my best Imogen Carmichael expression. I am the founder of The Billionaires' Club, founder of Chance, and I will not let him see how badly this is hurting me. Even as tears fill my throat, my eyes, my soul, I stare him down.

'So this is really what you want?'

A muscle jerks in his jaw and I sense his indecision, but I also sense his stubborn determination and I know what his answer will be, even before he says it. 'It has to be.'

'Don't. That's a cop-out.'

'Damn it.' He drags a hand through his hair. 'What do you want me to say? That I want you to go? That I'm sorry I hurt you and that I wish we hadn't got involved? That if I'd known we'd be having this conversation I would have left it with one perfect, sublime night in Sydney?'

His words are like knives, sailing through the air, each one slamming into me. He softens his voice but it's no less empathic. 'Do you want me to say that I don't love you? That I wish you didn't love me? That I don't believe in love, that I don't want it? That you and this has been great but it's not my real life any more than I am yours?'

A sob wells in my throat. I stare at him, unable to speak.

'This was never about love,' he adds for good measure. 'We both know that.'

I nod, slowly. I can feel a ticking time bomb in my chest; I have to get out of there before I cry.

But he's not prepared to let this go.

'I don't want it to end like this.'

Nor do I. I don't want it to end at all.

I steel myself to face him one last time and my heart almost gallops away from me. 'What difference does it make how it ends? It's over.'

I scoop up my bag and walk to the door with as much dignity as I can muster. I pull it open, holding my breath, wondering if he'll stop me, wondering if he'll say anything else. I'm still holding my breath at the elevator. The doors slide open and I step inside. The doors begin to slide shut and right as they're about to latch shut in the middle, his hand slides between them.

'Don't fucking go like this,' he groans, pulling me towards him, and, damn it, the tears I've been fighting are sliding down my cheeks. He pushes his hands into my hair, holding my face steady so he can look at me. 'Please don't cry.'

He is shocked. He didn't expect any of this.

So much of this is hard to understand, impossible to fathom, but there's one thing that always, without fail, makes sense. He kisses me and everything slides into place. Our kiss tastes of my tears. My body, my treacherous, traitorous, opportunistic body, melds to his, my hands lifting to encircle his neck, and he lifts me off the ground for a moment, holding me tight to him.

This is so perfect. I love him.

But he doesn't love me and there's no fix to that. This kiss is just delaying the inevitable.

A sob forms in my mouth and I break the kiss, pushing at his chest and wriggling to the floor.

'Don't.' The word is tremulous and soft, but it holds a mighty warning. 'Don't mess with me. You know how I feel and what I want. Don't look at me as though this is hard for you when it's all *because* of you.'

He takes a step back, his mouth open, shock on his features, and I take advantage of his response to reach across and press the button to close the elevator doors.

This time, he doesn't stop me.

'Lara Postlethwaite graduated with a first in philosophy. Did I tell you that?'

I look at my mother through a fog of Scotch and disbelief. The early evening light catches the books that line my parents' ancient library, making them appear to shimmer in gold, and all I can think of is

Imogen and the joy she took in my Manhattan library. The way she devoured book after book after book.

'I happen to know she thinks you're fascinating.' My mother's smile beams with maternal pride. A vulnerable ache forms in my chest.

My mother is growing older. I don't know why I haven't noticed before, but sitting by her and looking at her, I see not just a meddling society matron, but a woman who'll soon be seventy, who wants to know her son is married, that grandchildren are on their way. It's been easy to put all this matchmaking and expectation down to their concern for the title and the lineage. But what if there's more to it?

What if this is largely a case of a mother simply wanting to know her son is happy? Wanting to see that Saffy didn't ruin me for all other women?

'And I presume she'll be at the New Year's Eve ball?' my father chips in from across the room, his eyes meeting mine over the top of the broadsheet newspaper he's been reading for the better part of an hour.

'Oh, yes, m'dear.'

Perhaps my mother senses my lack of interest. Undeterred, she shifts in a slightly modified direction. 'Of course, Cynthia MacDougall is flying in and so looking forward to catching up with you.'

Cynthia I like. We have had a low-key flirtation going on for years. She's pretty and smart and doesn't really go in for all the aristocratic bullshit. She's personally wealthy enough that I know she's not a gold-digger, and I know she wants kids.

She'd be a good match for me; she definitely ticks the boxes of what I'm looking for.

So why does that very idea make me feel as though I'm being buried beneath a tennis court's worth of just-poured cement?

I recline in the seat, closing my eyes a moment, wishing it were so easy to drone out my mother's wittering about potential brides.

'I think a June wedding would be perfect, if you can make that timing work, darling.'

My gut is being squeezed in a vice.

I've been back in England three days and I feel as if I'm withering away into nothing. I stand abruptly and move to the windows, which perfectly frame a view over the east lawn towards the Kyoto garden and then the nearby stables.

I love this place. I have always felt at home here.

But not now. Right at this minute, I would do almost anything to be back in Manhattan, in the penthouse that was my bolthole when things turned bad with Saffy.

But I don't want to be there alone.

I press my hand to the glass, then drop my head forward, the cooling glass against my forehead bringing some kind of sharp sanity.

I want Imogen.

My insides groan.

I want her but I can't have her. I tried. I tried to

extend what we were and she didn't want that. I will never forget the sight of her face when she pushed me out of the elevator. Her tears—because of me.

Oh, God. I'd do anything to have her not cry. I'd do anything to fix this.

'I'm sorry to deprive you of a week of sex, but I have no doubt you can find someone else to fill your bed until you leave.'

As though what we were could be boiled down to a simple equation. Sex.

It was so much more than that. Because she was right, I could easily have found someone else to seduce for a night, if I'd just wanted to fuck some warm, willing body.

But I haven't wanted that. Not since Sydney. Not since I met Miss Anonymous and lost a part of myself to her.

I spent over a week on tenterhooks, as though my very survival depended on my ability to find her once more. I found her, and I held on as tight as I could for as long as I could. Even at the end, on that last morning, I offered what I could to prolong our farewell, because I wasn't ready to walk away from her.

Would I have been ready a week later? Would New Year's Eve have rolled around, and might I have hopped onto my jet and come here to England, to my parents' party, to meet the potential brides my parents had yet again selected?

'The Greenville on Strand could host it,' my

mother continues, a little hopefully, as though booking a suitable venue is of more concern than finding someone to marry. 'The ballroom there has been redecorated and is quite perfect.'

Fuck. Fuckety-fuckety-fuck. The idea is anathema to me.

Sleeping with someone else. Marrying someone else. I only want Imogen.

I want her in a way that is filling me with boiling lava; I need her. I need her and I need her to know that.

My face hurts from stretching this smile across it. I look out on the sea of kids eating their Christmas lunches, their faces happy, the mood ebullient. I alone am suffering. I stand in the background, watching the festivity as it overtakes the hall, knowing that there are eighty-seven of these lunches being held around the country for all the kids we support, that Christmas is alive for the Chance community.

And usually this is my favourite day of the year. I feel as if this is what Christmas is truly about—the ability to give and make better the lives of those who owe you nothing.

I know how important this day is but my heart is too heavy to appreciate it. I find it almost impossible to enter into the spirit, so I keep my head down, busying myself with the logistics I don't really need to worry about. I clear tables and disappear into the kitchen, filling the sink with warm sudsy water and losing myself in the anonymity and pure, physical labour of washing dishes.

I take my time, the feeling of warm water on my gloved hands at least a little soothing. Staff move around me, chatting amongst themselves. I keep my back turned. I try to cheer myself, thinking about the incredible donation of gifts we received this year, gifts that made sure every child was spoiled with something truly lovely.

Ordinarily, I'd be walking on the clouds. But not today.

Not since he left.

I pause in my dishwashing, my eyes filling with tears once more. I'm such an idiot. What did I think? That I'd tell him I'd fallen in love and he'd leap into the air and exclaim, *Me too, darling!* Nicholas Rothsmore wasn't the 'fall in love' type—he showed me that again and again. All the love was coming from me, and it just proved what a fool I am.

'Bins are overflowing, Amy!' one of the wait staff calls to another.

'I'll do it.' I shuck the rubber gloves off and walk away from the sink, keeping my head dipped so no one speaks to me. I have to get it together. I have no interest in causing people to speculate on what's going on in my life.

I grab one of the bags out of the bin and tie it, carrying it carefully through the kitchen and banging out of the doors and onto the street. It's Christmas Day and it's deserted out here. Everyone's at home with their families, enjoying this perfect snowy Christmas.

I open the lid on the bin and drop the bag in it, then lift my head when I hear the closing of a car door.

And everything comes into a strange kind of focus, too bright, shaky, weirdly discordant. As though I'm looking through those old-fashioned 3D movie glasses.

Striding towards me dressed in jeans and a leather jacket is Nicholas Rothsmore, and damn if my heart doesn't rejoice even as I know I have to protect myself somehow.

Confusion sears me. Did he stay in New York? Is he here till New Year's, just as he said? Is this some Hail Mary, 'one last night' kind of booty call?

Nicholas Rothsmore is the love of my life but I swore I'd never see him again. So what the hell is he doing here now?

CHAPTER FOURTEEN

'HI.'

He has this incredibly sexy, raspy quality to his voice, like a radio commentator or something. It makes my blood pound even as my stomach is dropping to my feet.

I find it hard to meet his eyes. 'What are you doing here?'

My throat is so dry. I swallow but it barely helps.

It's some consolation that he looks uncertain. Nervous? Apprehensive?

My stomach loops some more.

'I came to see you.'

I turn back to the building. Things are slowing down in there. I don't have to rush back—I'm superfluous now, here because I have nowhere else to be, no one else I want to spend this day with.

'What for?' The words are soft, showing my hurt, and I hate that. I hate how much he's hurt me. I hate that I let him.

He moves closer and I startle a little, wariness at

war with a deep-seated physical need. I shoot him what I hope passes for a warning glare.

His expression shifts.

'What do you want, Nicholas?'

A muscle jerks low at the base of his jaw. 'I have spent the last ten hours working out what the hell I would say to you and now I find I have no fucking idea where to start.'

'Tell me why you're here, on Christmas Day,' I demand, looking inside again.

'I came to see you,' he says, as if it's simple.

'Yeah, but why?'

'That's harder to explain.'

I grab hold of my anger, glad to feel it, glad to have some line of defence against the desire and wants that are ruining me from the inside out.

'Forget about it.' I spin away from him. 'It doesn't matter. You shouldn't have come.'

No. His response, when I told him I loved him, is burned into my consciousness. I will never forget it. I will never forget how that felt.

'Wait a moment.' He catches me, turns me around to face him, and my body jerks with recognition of this, of what he means to me. I wrench my hand free, glaring at him, wishing he could understand how much he's hurting me. 'Just let me get this out.'

But I'm done waiting. 'I don't think there's anything left to say, Nicholas. Unless you've had some kind of miraculous heart transplant?'

His jaw shifts, and I glare at him, waiting, but he says nothing for so long that I actually wonder if he's just here to hit me up for one last night before he leaves. My skin crawls. What started out as 'just sex' is now so much more that it would be an insult to even pretend we're not. Except that's what he did. It's galling and frustrating and hurtful and enraging, all at the same time.

'Please.' The single word brings me to a stop. I look at him with a growing sense of desperation. Doesn't he realise how hard this is for me? Doesn't he realise how much I hate this?

He must take my silence for consent, because a moment later he speaks, his voice thickened with concentration.

'My mother is in full planning mode, first for a New Year's Eve ball, which I gather is going to be a little more like the casting room of *The Bachelor*, with me as the prize.' He winces self-consciously. 'She's already got the wedding planned, now we just need to find someone for me to marry.'

Does he have any idea it's like being scratched all over? His words are vile. I hate them. I hate that he is here telling me this.

'We've discussed your obligations.' My voice simmers with contempt.

His own is gently placating. 'And six weeks ago, I was happy to go along with them. What did I care who I ended up married to? My only criterion was that it be someone I could stand spending time with.

In many ways, the less I had in common with her, the better. This was to be a straightforward arrangement. No muss, no fuss. Simple, right?'

'Undoubtedly.' I can't do this. I spin away from him again, needing to be alone, or at least away from him, breathing in frigid, ice-filled air. My lungs stutter.

He reaches for my elbow, spinning me around gently, insistently.

'And then I met you and, somehow, everything changed.'

I draw in a sharp breath.

'I don't know when it happened, but what I wanted when we started this has shifted and now I need so much more. From you, from my life, from my marriage. Everything's different, Imogen. Everything.'

The world stops spinning. This doesn't make sense.

'What?' I blink, wishing I didn't sound so completely non-comprehending. 'Wait.' I hold a hand up. 'This doesn't make sense. You left three days ago. After telling me you didn't love me, that you'd never love me.'

'I know that.' He runs a hand through his hair, his frustration and confusion barrelling towards me.

'I…' He draws in a breath, his eyes scanning my face, then he shakes his head, as if it's not quite what he meant, and starts again. 'When I was twelve, I came off my bike and I never rode again. I refused. I didn't like the way it felt to fall, so I gave up the pleasure of riding, which I had, up until then, loved very much.' He closes the distance and cups my face.

'You've told me that.'

His eyes gaze into mine. 'I hated the way Saffy made me feel. I hated being let down, hurt, burned, stripped raw in front of so many people. I felt worthless, Imogen. Worthless and unwanted. So I promised myself I would never fall in love again. That I would never be so gullible as to believe in love—what a stupid construct! But, Imogen, I left New York and I nearly turned my back on a whole lifetime of experiences and joy—a lifetime with you—because I was too scared to get hurt again.'

I can't get enough air in. His eyes drop to my lips, and there's a frown on his face, as if he has no idea where he stands with me.

'I fell in love with you, anyway, and I have been fighting it the whole time we've been together. I have not been able to put you out of my head for even a day. Not one single day, not an hour, in fact, since we met. I love you. I am obsessed with you, and I should have known that when you told me how you felt. I should have understood, but I have spent five years running from even the idea of love and I didn't know how to turn my back on that.'

His thumb pad brushes over my lips and I shudder. In a good way, I think. Or maybe just in an emotionally drained way because, despite the fact it's only been three days, I feel as if I have been strapped over a pile of burning coal and I'm so spent.

'It has been an agony and a form of torture to think of you going home to marry someone else,'

I mutter, my heart still so sore, so hurt, that I find forgiveness and understanding hard to muster, even in the face of what he's just said.

'I know.' He drops his forehead to mine, his warm breath fanning my face. 'I hate that. I am so sorry. The sight of you in the elevator, pushing me away, has replayed on my mind like some godawful ten-second clip since I left.'

'Left? You went home?'

He nods.

'And now you're back?'

'I couldn't stay there. I had to see you. I needed you to know, as soon as I realised, that I am head over heels in love with you. And not in a way I've ever felt before. This is so different. I feel as though if I don't spend the rest of my life with you, a part of me will die. I can't explain it. You're in my blood and my breath; you're a part of me.'

And for the first time in days, I exhale slowly and I smile. I smile in a natural way because I feel the first flicker of true happiness. In a very, very long time.

He drops a hand and laces his fingers through mine. 'I'm sorry I was so stupid.'

I laugh then, and shake my head. 'You were stupid.'

'Completely.'

'But you're done?'

'Being stupid? I can't promise that.' He grins and my heart stitches together a bit. 'But I will never hurt you again, Imogen. You are everything to me, and

I plan on spending the rest of my life showing you that. If you'll let me.'

Stars shift in my field of vision. 'I…don't…' I frown, and lick my lower lip. 'Are you…?'

'Asking you to become Lady Rothsmore and all that entails? Yes. Though not very well, evidently.'

I don't know what to say. I never thought I'd get married and not to someone with more money than Croesus, but here I am, head over heels in love with this man, and nothing matters beyond that. Not his title, his wealth, nothing. There is an imperative in me to agree to this—an imperative of my own making. My happiness is built on this conversation.

'I know I hurt you,' he says, mistaking my pause for doubt. 'I know I screwed up, monumentally, by letting you think, even for a second, that we were ever just about sex. When you told me I could find someone else to fuck for my last week in America, my God, Imogen, I wish you could have seen inside me and know how that made me feel.'

I shake my head urgently. 'Don't.' I lift a finger to his lips. 'I don't want to talk about that morning. We were both hurting.' I smile at him then, a smile that I think is laced with all my hopes for our future. 'There's no sense discussing the past when our future is waiting.'

His face shifts as comprehension dawns. 'Do you mean…is that a "yes"?'

I laugh and push up on my tiptoes so I can kiss my acceptance into his mouth. 'It's a hell yes.'

* * *

'They can't wait to meet you.' His expression is slightly sardonic.

I stand up, walking across the lounge. 'It's mutual.'

'I have, however, told them in no uncertain terms to cancel the booking for the wedding venue in June.' His expression is laced with affectionate exasperation.

I grimace. 'How did they take that?'

'They're thrilled to hear there is going to be a wedding of any kind.' He pulls me into his arms, moving his hips a little, dancing in time to the New Year's Eve broadcast that's on in the background.

'I can't believe this is happening,' I say, despite the fact we've spent the last week living like hermits in his penthouse, pretty much in bed the whole time, except when hunger called.

'It's happening.' He pulls me closer. Fireworks dance just beneath my skin. 'How do you feel about watching the fireworks from the hot tub?'

'I think that would be pretty perfect.'

It's perfect out—a bright night, filled with stars and light, too cold even for snow, but the hot tub is warm and luxurious. I sink into it, naked, sighing.

'I do love this city,' I say with a smile, catching his eye as he steps into the water.

'We can stay here, you know.'

It's about the hundredth time he's made that offer.

I smile. 'I know.'

'I mean it, Imogen. I came back here fully expecting that if I was lucky enough for you to accept my proposal it would mean that we spent our life right here, in America.'

'I know. But I don't want that.'

'Seriously?'

'I love New York, but I'm ready for a change.' I move towards him so I can sit on his lap. 'I can run The Billionaires' Club from there, and I've been wanting to build a Chance presence in Europe for a long time. I've seriously been thinking about opening a Chance location in London. I don't know what's been holding me back but I do know nothing will stop me now.' I smile at him, my happiness pouring out of me. 'This is exciting for me, in lots of ways.'

'Yeah.' He grins and my heart flips over. I love how truly pumped he is for me—how proud he is. How much he wants me to pursue my dreams and see my future continue to revolve around helping others. 'And New York's only a quick flight away.'

'Perfect for weekends,' I agree, our life suddenly looking pretty damned blessed. And the thing is, having decided what I want most in life, I don't really feel like waiting. I've never been one to overthink or delay, anyway. 'You know, if your parents aren't expecting us for another week, maybe we could take a little detour on the way.'

'Yeah? Sydney?' he teases with an arched brow.

I smile. 'I was meaning more like Vegas.'

'Vegas?' He frowns and then, as comprehension

dawns, he smiles. 'You're thinking, what? The Little White Chapel?'

'Why not?'

'Why not in-fucking-deed?'

'Then we'd arrive in England already married. Unless you think your folks would hate to miss…'

'Oh, they'd be livid.' He grins. 'But only until they realise I'm finally married and "settled down". Besides, nothing will stop my mother from throwing you a "welcome to the family" party to end all parties.'

I expel a soft sigh, contentment bursting through me. I lift my hand out of the water, staring at the beautiful solitaire diamond Nicholas presented me with the day after Christmas. It's round, at least ten carats and fits me like a glove. Just like him.

'Then let's do it.' I smile, flipping over so I'm straddling him.

'Say no more, Lady Rothsmore.' He kisses me, slowly, sensually, and then pulls away. 'It's really what you want?'

I laugh, moving myself over him, taking him deep inside. 'Count on it.'

We arrive in England, man and wife, partners in every way. Despite the fact I've only been here a handful of times, with Nicholas by my side, I know that I've come home.

* * * * *

A BILLIONAIRE FOR CHRISTMAS

JANICE MAYNARD

For my mother, Pat Scott, who loved Christmas as much as anyone I have ever known.

One

Leo Cavallo had a headache. In fact, his whole body hurt. The drive from Atlanta to the Great Smoky Mountains in East Tennessee hadn't seemed all that onerous on the map, but he'd gravely miscalculated the reality of negotiating winding rural roads after dark. And given that the calendar had flipped only a handful of days into December, he'd lost daylight a long time ago.

He glanced at the clock on the dashboard and groaned as he registered the glowing readout. It was after nine. He still had no idea if he was even close to his destination. The GPS had given up on him ten miles back. The car thermometer read thirty-five degrees, which meant that any moment now the driving rain hammering his windshield might change over to snow, and he'd really be screwed. Jags were not meant to be driven in bad weather.

Sweating beneath his thin cotton sweater, he reached into the console for an antacid. Without warning, his brother's voice popped into his head, loud and clear.

"I'm serious, Leo. You have to make some changes. You had a heart attack, for God's sake."

Leo scowled. "A mild cardiac event. Don't be so dramatic. I'm in excellent physical shape. You heard the doctor."

"Yes, I did. He said your stress levels are off the charts. And he preached heredity. Our father died before he hit forty-two. You keep this up, and I'll be putting you in the ground right beside him..."

Leo chewed the chalky tablet and cursed when the road suddenly changed from ragged pavement to loose gravel. The wheels of his vehicle spun for purchase on the uneven surface. He crept along, straining his eyes for any signs of life up ahead.

On either side, steep hillsides boxed him in. The headlights on his car picked out dense thickets of rhododendron lining the way. Claustrophobic gloom swathed the vehicle in a cloying blanket. He was accustomed to living amidst the bright lights of Atlanta. His penthouse condo offered an amazing view of the city. Neon and energy and people were his daily fuel. So why had he agreed to voluntary exile in a state whose remote corners seemed unwelcoming at best?

Five minutes later, when he was almost ready to turn around and admit defeat, he saw a light shining in the darkness. The relief he felt was staggering. By the time he finally pulled up in front of the blessedly illuminated house, every muscle in his body ached with tension. He hoped the porch light indicated some level of available hospitality.

Pulling his plush-lined leather jacket from the backseat, he stepped out of the car and shivered. The rain had slacked off...finally. But a heavy, fog-wrapped drizzle accompanied by bone-numbing chill greeted him. For the moment, he would leave his bags in the trunk. He didn't know exactly where his cabin was located. Hopefully, he'd be able to park closer before he unloaded.

Mud caked the soles of his expensive leather shoes as he made his way to the door of the modern log structure. It looked as if it had been assembled from one of those kits that well-heeled couples bought to set up getaway homes in the mountains. Certainly not old, but neatly put together.

From what he could tell, it was built on a single level with a porch that wrapped around at least two sides of the house.

There was no doorbell that he could see, so he took hold of the bronze bear-head knocker and rapped it three times, hard enough to express his growing frustration. Additional lights went on inside the house. As he shifted from one foot to the other impatiently, the curtain beside the door twitched and a wide-eyed female face appeared briefly before disappearing as quickly as it had come.

From inside he heard a muffled voice. “Who is it?”

“Leo. Leo Cavallo,” he shouted at the door. Grinding his teeth, he reached for a more conciliatory tone. “May I come in?”

Phoebe opened her front door with some trepidation. Not because she had anything to fear from the man on the porch. She’d been expecting him for the past several hours. What she dreaded was telling him the truth.

Backing up to let him enter, she winced as he crossed the threshold and sucked all the air out of the room. He was a big man, built like a lumberjack, broad through the shoulders, and tall, topping her five-foot-nine stature by at least four more inches. His thick, wavy chestnut hair gleamed with health. The glow from the fire that crackled in the hearth picked out strands of dark gold.

When he removed his jacket, running a hand through his disheveled hair, she saw that he wore a deep blue sweater along with dark dress pants. The faint whiff of his aftershave mixed with the unmistakable scent of the outdoors. He filled the room with his presence.

Reaching around him gingerly, she flipped on the overhead light, sighing inwardly in relief when the intimacy of firelight gave way to a less cozy atmosphere. Glancing down at his feet, she bit her lip. “Will you please take off your shoes? I cleaned the floors this morning.”

Though he frowned, he complied. Before she could say another word, he gave her home a cursory glance, then settled his sharp gaze on her face. His übermasculine features were put together in a pleasing fashion, but the overall impression was intensely male. Strong nose, noble forehead, chiseled jaw and lips made for kissing a woman. His scowl grew deeper. "I'm tired as hell, and I'm starving. If you could point me to my cabin, I'd like to get settled for the night, Ms....?"

"Kemper. Phoebe Kemper. You can call me Phoebe." Oh, wow. His voice, low and gravelly, stroked over her frazzled nerves like a lover's caress. The faint Georgia drawl did nothing to disguise the hint of command. This was a man accustomed to calling the shots.

She swallowed, rubbing damp palms unobtrusively on her thighs. "I have a pot of vegetable beef stew still warm on the stove. Dinner was late tonight." And every night, it seemed. "You're welcome to have some. There's corn bread, as well."

The aura of disgruntlement he wore faded a bit, replaced by a rueful smile. "That sounds wonderful."

She waved a hand. "Bathroom's down the hall, first door on the right. I'll get everything on the table."

"And afterward you'll show me my lodgings?"

Gulp. "Of course." Perhaps she shouldn't have insisted that he remove his shoes. There was something about a man in his sock feet that hinted at a level of familiarity. The last thing she needed at this juncture in time was to feel drawn to someone who was most likely going to be furious with her no matter how she tried to spin the facts in a positive light.

He was gone a very short time, but Phoebe had everything ready when he returned. A single place mat, some silverware and a steaming bowl of stew flanked by corn bread and a cheerful yellow gingham napkin. "I didn't know what you wanted to drink," she said. "I have decaf iced tea, but the weather's awfully cold tonight."

"Decaf coffee would be great…if you have it."

"Of course." While he sat down and dug into his meal, she brewed a fresh pot of Colombian roast and poured him a cup. He struck her as the kind of man who wouldn't appreciate his java laced with caramel or anything fancy. Though she offered the appropriate add-ons, Leo Cavallo took his coffee black and unsweetened. No fuss. No nonsense.

Phoebe puttered around, putting things away and loading the dishwasher. Her guest ate with every indication that his previous statement was true. Apparently, he *was* starving. Two large bowls of stew, three slabs of corn bread and a handful of the snickerdoodles she had made that morning vanished in short order.

As he was finishing his dessert, she excused herself. "I'll be back in just a moment." She set the pot on the table. "Help yourself to more coffee."

Leo's mood improved dramatically as he ate. He hadn't been looking forward to going back down that road to seek out dinner, and though his cabin was supposed to be stocked with groceries, he was not much of a cook. Everything he needed, foodwise, was close at hand in Atlanta. He was spoiled probably. If he wanted sushi at three in the morning or a full breakfast at dawn, he didn't have to look far.

When he finished the last crumb of the moist, delicious cookies, he wiped his mouth with his napkin and stood up to stretch. After the long drive, his body felt kinked and cramped from sitting in one position for too many hours. Guiltily, he remembered the doctor's admonition not to push himself. Truthfully, it was the only setting Leo had. Full steam ahead. Don't look back.

And yet now he was supposed to turn himself into somebody new. Even though he'd been irritated by the many people hovering over him—work colleagues, medical professionals and his family—in his heart, he knew the level of their concern was a testament to how much he had scared them all. One moment he had been standing at the head of a large conference table giving an impassioned pitch to a group of global investors, and the next, he'd been on the floor.

None of the subsequent few minutes were clear in his memory. He recalled not being able to breathe. And an enormous pressure in his chest. But not much more than that. Shaken and disturbed by the recollection of that day, he paced the confines of the open floor plan that incorporated the kitchen and living area into a pleasing whole.

As he walked back and forth, he realized that Phoebe Kemper had created a cozy nest out here in the middle of nowhere. Colorful area rugs cushioned his feet. The floor consisted of wide, honey-colored hardwood planks polished to a high sheen.

Two comfortable groupings of furniture beckoned visitors to sit and enjoy the ambience. Overhead, a three-tiered elk antler chandelier shed a large, warm circle of light. On the far wall, built-in bookshelves flanked the stacked stone fireplace. As he scanned Phoebe's collection of novels and nonfiction, he realized with a little kick of pleasure that he was actually going to have time to read for a change.

A tiny noise signaled his hostess's return. Whirling around, he stared at her, finally acknowledging, if only to himself, that his landlady was a knockout. Jet-black hair long enough to reach below her breasts had been tamed into a single thick, smooth braid that hung forward over her shoulder. Tall and slender and long-limbed, there was nothing frail or helpless about Phoebe Kemper. Yet he could imagine many men rushing to her aid, simply to coax a smile from those lush unpainted lips that were the color of pale pink roses.

She wore faded jeans and a silky coral blouse that brought out the warm tones in her skin. With eyes so dark they were almost black, she made him wonder if she claimed Cherokee blood. Some resourceful members of that tribe had hidden deep in these mountains to escape the Trail of Tears.

Her smile was teasing. "Feel better now? At least you don't look like you want to commit murder anymore."

He shrugged sheepishly. "Sorry. It was a hell of a day."

Phoebe's eyes widened and her smile faded. "And it's about to get worse, I'm afraid. There's a problem with your reservation."

"Impossible," he said firmly. "My sister-in-law handled all the details. And I have the confirmation info."

"I've been trying to call her all day, but she hasn't answered. And no one gave me your cell number."

"Sorry about that. My niece found my sister-in-law's phone and dropped it into the bathtub. They've been scrambling to get it replaced. That's why you couldn't reach her. But no worries. I'm here now. And it doesn't look like you're overbooked," he joked.

Phoebe ignored his levity and frowned. "We had heavy rains and high winds last night. Your cabin was damaged."

His mood lightened instantly. "Don't worry about a thing, Ms. Phoebe. I'm not that picky. I'm sure it will be fine."

She shook her head in disgust. "I guess I'll have to show you to convince you. Follow me, please."

"Should I move my car closer to the cabin?" he asked as he put on his shoes and tied them. The bottoms were a mess.

Phoebe scooped up something that looked like a small digital camera and tucked it into her pocket. "No need," she said. She shrugged into a jacket that could have been a twin to his. "Let's go." Out on the porch, she picked up a large, heavy-duty flashlight and turned it on. The intense beam sliced through the darkness.

The weather hadn't improved. He was glad that Luc and Hattie had insisted on packing for him. They had undoubtedly covered every eventuality if he knew his sister-in-law. Come rain, sleet, snow or hail, he'd be prepared. But for now, everything he'd brought with him was stashed in the trunk of his car. Sighing for the lost opportunity to carry a load, he followed Phoebe.

Though he would never have found it on his own in the inky, fog-blinding night, the path from Phoebe's cabin to the next closest one was easy to pick out with the flashlight. Far more than a foot trail, the route they followed was clearly an extension of the gravel road.

His impatience grew as he realized they could have driven the few hundred feet. Finally, he dug in his heels. "I should move the car," he said. "I'm sure I'll be fine."

At that very moment, Phoebe stopped so abruptly he nearly plowed into her. "We're here," she said bluntly. "And *that* is what's left of your two-month rental."

The industrial-strength flashlight was more than strong enough to reveal the carnage from the previous night's storm. An enormous tree lay across the midline of the house at a forty-five-degree angle. The force of the falling trunk had crushed the roof. Even from this vantage point, it was clear that the structure was open to the elements.

"Good Lord." He glanced behind him instinctively, realizing with sick dismay that Phoebe's home could have suffered a similar fate. "You must have been scared to death."

She grimaced. "I've had better nights. It happened about 3:00 a.m. The boom woke me up. I didn't try to go out then, of course. So it was daylight before I realized how bad it was."

"You haven't tried to cover the roof?"

She chuckled. "Do I look like Superwoman? I know

my own limitations, Mr. Cavallo. I've called my insurance company, but needless to say, they've been inundated with claims from the storm. Supposedly, an agent will be here tomorrow afternoon, but I'm not holding my breath. Everything inside the house got soaked when the tree fell, because it was raining so hard. The damage was already done. It's not like I could have helped matters."

He supposed she had a point. But that still left the issue of where he was expected to stay. Despite his grumblings to Luc and Hattie, now that he was finally here, the idea of kicking back for a while wasn't entirely unpleasant. Perhaps he could find himself in the great outdoors. Maybe even discover a new appreciation for life, which as he so recently had found out, was both fragile and precious.

Phoebe touched his arm. "If you've seen enough, let's go back. I'm not going to send you out on the road again in this miserable weather. You're welcome to stay the night with me."

They reversed their steps as Leo allowed Phoebe to take the lead. The steady beam of light led them without incident back to his car. The porch light was still on, adding to a feeling of welcome. Phoebe waved a hand at the cabin. "Why don't you go inside and warm up? Your sister-in-law told me you've been in the hospital. I'd be happy to bring in your luggage if you tell me what you'll need."

Leo's neck heated with embarrassment and frustration. Damn Hattie and her mother-hen instincts. "I can get my own bags," he said curtly. "But thank you." He added that last bit grudgingly. Poor Phoebe had no reason to know that his recent illness was a hot-button issue for him. He was a young man. Being treated like an invalid made him nuts. And for whatever reason, it was especially important to him that the lovely Phoebe see him as a competent, capable male, and not someone she had to babysit.

His mental meanderings must not have lasted as long

as he thought, because Phoebe was still at his side when he heard—very distinctly—the cry of a baby. He whirled around, expecting to see that another car had made its way up the narrow road. But he and Phoebe were alone in the night.

A second, less palatable possibility occurred to him. He'd read that a bobcat's cry could emulate that of an upset infant's. And the Smoky Mountains were home to any number of those nocturnal animals. Before he could speculate further, the sound came again.

Phoebe shoved the flashlight toward him. "Here. Keep this. I've got to go inside."

He took it automatically, and grinned. "So you're leaving me out here alone with a scary animal stalking us?"

She shook her head. "I don't know what you're talking about."

"The bobcat. Isn't that what we're hearing?"

Phoebe laughed softly, a pleasing sensual sound that made the hair on his arms stand up even more than the odd noise had. "Despite your interesting imagination," she said with a chuckle, "no." She reached in her pocket and removed the small electronic device he had noticed earlier. Not a camera, but a monitor. "The noise you hear that sounds like a crying baby is *actually* a baby. And I'd better get in there fast before all heck breaks loose."

Two

Leo stood there gaping at her even after the front door slammed shut. It was only the realization his hands were in danger of frostbite that galvanized him into motion. In short order he found the smaller of the two suitcases he had brought. Slinging the strap across one shoulder, he then reached for his computer briefcase and a small garment bag.

Locking the car against any intruders, human or otherwise, he walked up the steps, let himself in and stopped dead in his tracks when he saw Phoebe standing by the fire, a small infant whimpering on her shoulder as she rubbed its back. Leo couldn't quite sort out his emotions. The scene by the hearth was beautiful. His sister-in-law, Hattie, wore that same look on her face when she cuddled her two little ones.

But a baby meant there was a daddy in the picture somewhere, and though Leo had only met this particular Madonna and child today, he knew the feeling in the pit of his stomach was disappointment. Phoebe didn't wear a wedding ring, but he could see a resemblance between mother and child. Their noses were identical.

Leo would simply have to ignore this inconvenient attraction, because Phoebe was clearly not available. And though he adored his niece and nephew, he was not the kind of man who went around bouncing kids on his knee and playing patty-cake.

Phoebe looked up and smiled. "This is Teddy. His full name is Theodore, but at almost six months, he hasn't quite grown into it yet."

Leo kicked off his shoes for the second time that night and set down his luggage. Padding toward the fire, he mustered a smile. "He's cute."

"Not nearly as cute at three in the morning." Phoebe's expression as she looked down at the baby was anything but aggravated. She glowed.

"Not a good sleeper?"

She bristled at what she must have heard as implied criticism. "He does wonderfully for his age. Don't you, my love?" The baby had settled and was sucking his fist. Phoebe nuzzled his neck. "Most evenings he's out for the count from ten at night until six or seven in the morning. But I think he may be cutting a tooth."

"Not fun, I'm sure."

Phoebe switched the baby to her left arm, holding him against her side. "Let me show you the guest room. I don't think we'll disturb you even if I have to get up with him during the night."

He followed her down a short hallway past what was obviously Phoebe's suite all the way to the back right corner of the house. A chill hit him as soon as they entered the bedroom.

"Sorry," she said. "The vents have been closed off, but it will warm up quickly."

He looked around curiously. "This is nice." A massive king-size bed made of rough timbers dominated the room. Hunter-green draperies covered what might have been a large picture window. The attached bathroom, decorated in shades of sand and beige, included a Jacuzzi tub and a roomy shower stall. Except for the tiled floor in the bathroom, the rest of the space boasted the same attractive hardwood he'd seen in the remainder of the house, covered here and there by colorful rugs.

Phoebe hovered, the baby now asleep. "Make yourself at home. If you're interested in staying in the area, I can help you make some calls in the morning."

Leo frowned. "I paid a hefty deposit. I'm not interested in staying anywhere else."

A trace of pique flitted across Phoebe's face, but she answered him calmly. "I'll refund your money, of course. You saw the cabin. It's unlivable. Even with a speedy insurance settlement, finding people to do the work will probably be difficult. I can't even guesstimate how long it will be before everything is fixed."

Leo thought about the long drive from Atlanta. He hadn't wanted to come here at all. And yesterday's storm damage was his ticket out. All he had to do was tell Luc and Hattie, and his doctor, that circumstances had conspired against him. He could be back in Atlanta by tomorrow night.

But something—stubbornness maybe—made him contrary. "Where is Mr. Kemper in all this? Shouldn't he be the one worrying about repairing the other cabin?"

Phoebe's face went blank. "Mr. Kemper?" Suddenly, she laughed. "I'm not married, Mr. Cavallo."

"And the baby?"

A small frown line appeared between her brows. "Are you a traditionalist, then? You don't think a single female can raise a child on her own?"

Leo shrugged. "I think kids deserve two parents. But having said that, I do believe women can do anything they like. I can't, however, imagine a woman like you needing to embrace single parenthood."

He'd pegged Phoebe as calm and cool, but her eyes flashed. "A woman like me? What does that mean?"

Leaning his back against one of the massive bedposts,

he folded his arms and stared at her. Now that he knew she wasn't married, all bets were off. "You're stunning. Are all the men in Tennessee blind?"

Her lips twitched. "I'm pretty sure that's the most clichéd line I've ever heard."

"I stand by my question. You're living out here in the middle of nowhere. Your little son has no daddy anywhere in sight. A man has to wonder."

Phoebe stared at him, long and hard. He bore her scrutiny patiently, realizing how little they knew of each other. But for yesterday's storm, he and Phoebe would likely have exchanged no more than pleasantries when she handed over his keys. In the weeks to come, they might occasionally have seen each other outside on pleasant days, perhaps waved in passing.

But fate had intervened. Leo came from a long line of Italian ancestors who believed in the power of *destino* and *amore.* Since he was momentarily banned from the job that usually filled most of his waking hours, he was willing to explore his fascination with Phoebe Kemper.

He watched as she deposited the sleeping baby carefully in the center of the bed. The little boy rolled to his side and continued to snooze undisturbed. Phoebe straightened and matched her pose to Leo's. Only instead of using the bed for support, she chose to lean against the massive wardrobe that likely held a very modern home entertainment center.

She eyed him warily, her teeth nibbling her bottom lip. Finally she sighed. "First of all, we're not in the middle of nowhere, though it must seem that way to you since you had to drive up here on such a nasty night. Gatlinburg is less than ten miles away. Pigeon Forge closer than that. We have grocery stores and gas stations and all the modern conveniences, I promise. I like it here at the foot of the mountains. It's peaceful."

"I'll take your word for it."

"And Teddy is my nephew, not my son."

Leo straightened, wondering what it said about him that he was glad the woman facing him was a free agent. "Why is he here?"

"My sister and her husband are in Portugal for six weeks settling his father's estate. They decided the trip would be too hard on Teddy, and that cleaning out the house would be much easier without him. So I volunteered to let him stay with me until they get home."

"You must like kids a lot."

A shadow crossed her face. "I love my nephew." She shook off whatever mood had momentarily stolen the light. "But we're avoiding the important topic. I can't rent you a demolished cabin. You have to go."

He smiled at her with every bit of charm he could muster. "You can rent me *this* room."

Phoebe had to give Leo Cavallo points for persistence. His deep brown eyes were deceptive. Though a woman could sink into their warmth, she might miss entirely the fact that he was a man who got what he wanted. If he had been ill recently, she could find no sign of it in his appearance. His naturally golden skin, along with his name, told her that he possessed Mediterranean genes. And in Leo's case, that genetic material had been spun into a ruggedly handsome man.

"This isn't a B and B," she said. "I have an investment property that I rent out to strangers. That property is currently unavailable, so you're out of luck."

"Don't make a hasty decision," he drawled. "I'm housebroken. And I'm handy when it comes to changing lightbulbs and killing creepy-crawlies."

"I'm tall for a woman, and I have monthly pest control service."

"Taking care of a baby is a lot of work. You might enjoy having help."

"You don't strike me as the type to change diapers."

"Touché."

Were they at an impasse? Would he give up?

She glanced at Teddy, sleeping so peacefully. Babies were an important part of life, but it was a sad day when a grown woman's life was so devoid of male companionship that a nonverbal infant was stimulating company. "I'll make a deal with you," she said slowly, wondering if she were crazy. "You tell me why you really want to stay, and I'll consider your request."

For the first time, she saw discomfort on Leo's face. He was one of those consummately confident men who strode through life like a captain on the bridge of his ship, everyone in his life bowing and scraping in his wake. But at the moment, a mask slipped and she caught a glimpse of vulnerability. "What did my sister-in-law tell you when she made the reservation?"

A standard ploy. Answering a question with a question. "She said you'd been ill. Nothing more than that. But in all honesty, you hardly look like a man at death's door."

Leo's smile held a note of self-mockery. "Thank God for that."

Curiouser and curiouser. "Now that I think about it," she said, trying to solve the puzzle as she went along, "you don't seem like the kind of man who takes a two-month sabbatical in the mountains for any reason. Unless, of course, you're an artist or a songwriter. Maybe a novelist? Am I getting warm?"

Leo grimaced, not quite meeting her gaze. "I needed a break," he said. "Isn't that reason enough?"

Something in his voice touched her...some note of discouragement or distress. And in that moment, she felt a kinship with Leo Cavallo. Hadn't she embraced this land

and built these two cabins for that very reason? She'd been disillusioned with her job and heartbroken over the demise of her personal life. The mountains had offered healing.

"Okay," she said, capitulating without further ado. "You can stay. But if you get on my nerves or drive me crazy, I am well within my rights to kick you out."

He grinned, his expression lightening. "Sounds fair."

"And I charge a thousand dollars a week more if you expect to share meals with me."

It was a reckless barb, an attempt to get a rise out of him. But Leo merely nodded his head, eyes dancing. "Whatever you say." Then he sobered. "Thank you, Phoebe. I appreciate your hospitality."

The baby stirred, breaking the odd bubble of intimacy that had enclosed the room. Phoebe scooped up little Teddy and held him to her chest, suddenly feeling the need for a barrier between herself and the charismatic Leo Cavallo. "We'll say good night, then."

Her houseguest nodded, eyes hooded as he stared at the baby. "Sleep well. And if you hear me up in the night, don't be alarmed. I've had a bit of insomnia recently."

"I could fix you some warm milk," she said, moving toward the door.

"I'll be fine. See you in the morning."

Leo watched her leave and felt a pinch of remorse for having pressured her into letting him invade her home. But not so much that he was willing to leave. In Atlanta everyone had walked on eggshells around him, acting as if the slightest raised voice or cross word would send him into a relapse. Though his brother, Luc, tried to hide his concern, it was clear that he and Hattie were worried about Leo. And as dear as they both were to him, Leo needed a little space to come to terms with what had happened.

His first instinct was to dive back into work. But the

doctor had flatly refused to release him. This mountain getaway was a compromise. Not an idea Leo would have embraced voluntarily, but given the options, his only real choice.

When he exited the interstate earlier that evening, Leo had called his brother to say he was almost at his destination. Though he needed to escape the suffocating but well-meaning attention, he would never *ever* cause Luc and Hattie to worry unnecessarily. He would do anything for his younger brother, and he knew Luc would return the favor. They were closer than most siblings, having survived their late teen and early-adult years in a foreign land under the thumb of their autocratic Italian grandfather.

Leo yawned and stretched, suddenly exhausted. Perhaps he was paying for years of burning the candle at both ends. His medical team *and* his family had insisted that for a full recovery, Leo needed to stay away from work and stress. Maybe the recent hospital stay had affected him more than he realized. But whatever the reason, he was bone tired and ready to climb into that large rustic bed.

Too bad he'd be sleeping alone. It was oddly comforting when his body reacted predictably to thoughts of Phoebe. Something about her slow, steady smile and her understated sexuality really did it for him. Though his doctor had cleared Leo for exercise and sexual activity, the latter was a moot point. Trying to ignore the erection that wouldn't be seeing any action tonight, he reached for his suitcase, extracted his shaving kit and headed for the shower.

To Phoebe's relief, the baby didn't stir when she laid him in his crib. She stood over him for long moments watching the almost imperceptible movements of his small body as he breathed. She knew her sister was missing Teddy like crazy, but selfishly, Phoebe herself was looking forward to having someone to share Christmas with.

Her stomach did a little flip as she realized that Leo might be here, as well. But no. Surely he would go home at the holidays and come back to finish out his stay in January.

When she received the initial reservation request, she had researched Leo and the Cavallo family on Google. She knew he was single, rich and the CFO of a worldwide textile company started by his grandfather in Italy. She also knew that he supported several charities, not only with money, but with his service. He didn't need to work. The Cavallo vaults, metaphorically speaking, held more money than any one person could spend in a lifetime. But she understood men like Leo all too well. They thrived on challenge, pitting themselves repeatedly against adversaries, both in business and in life.

Taking Leo into her home was not a physical risk. He was a gentleman, and she knew far more about him than she did about many men she had dated. The only thing that gave her pause was an instinct that told her he needed help in some way. She didn't need another responsibility. And besides, if the cabin hadn't been demolished, Leo would have been on his own for two months anyway.

There was no reason for her to be concerned. Nevertheless, she sensed pain in him, and confusion. Given her own experience with being knocked flat on her butt for a long, long time, she wouldn't wish that experience on anyone. Maybe she could probe gently and see why this big mountain of a man, who could probably bench-press more than his body weight, seemed lost.

As she prepared for bed, she couldn't get him out of her mind. And when she climbed beneath her flannel sheets and closed her eyes, his face was the image that stayed with her through the night.

Three

Leo awoke when sunlight shining through a crack in the drapes hit his face. He yawned and scrubbed his hands over his stubbly chin, realizing with pleased surprise that he had slept through the night. Perhaps there was something to this mountain retreat thing after all.

Most of his stuff was still in the car, so he dug out a pair of faded jeans from his overnight case and threw on his favorite warm cashmere sweater. It was a Cavallo product… of course. The cabin had an efficient heat system, but Leo was itching to get outside and see his surroundings in the light of day.

Tiptoeing down the hall in case the baby was sleeping, he paused unconsciously at Phoebe's door, which stood ajar. Through the narrow crack he could see a lump under the covers of a very disheveled bed. Poor woman. The baby must have kept her up during the night.

Resisting the urge to linger, he made his way to the kitchen and quietly located the coffeepot. Phoebe was an organized sort, so it was no problem to find what he needed in the cabinet above. When he had a steaming cup brewed, strong and black, he grabbed a banana off the counter and went to stand at the living room window.

Supposedly, one of his challenges was to acquire the habit of eating breakfast in the morning. Normally, he had neither the time nor the inclination to eat. As a rule, he'd be at the gym by six-thirty and at the office before eight. After that, his day was nonstop until seven or later at night.

He'd never really thought much about his schedule in the past. It suited him, and it got the job done. For a man in his prime, *stopping to smell the roses* was a metaphor for growing old. Now that he had been admonished to do just that, he was disgruntled and frustrated. He was thirty-six, for God's sake. Was it really time to throw in the towel?

Pulling back the chintz curtains decorated with gamboling black bears, he stared out at a world that glistened like diamonds in the sharp winter sun. Every branch and leaf was coated with ice. Evidently, the temperatures had dropped as promised, and now the narrow valley where Phoebe made her home was a frozen wonderland.

So much for his desire to explore. Anyone foolish enough to go out at this moment would end up flat on his or her back after the first step. *Patience, Leo. Patience.* His doctor, who also happened to be his racquetball partner on the weekends, had counseled him repeatedly to take it easy, but Leo wasn't sure he could adapt. Already, he felt itchy, needing a project to tackle, a problem to solve.

"You're up early."

Phoebe's voice startled him so badly he spun around and managed to slosh hot coffee over the fingers of his right hand. "Ouch, damn it."

He saw her wince as he crossed to the sink and ran cold water over his stinging skin.

"Sorry," she said. "I thought you heard me."

Leo had been lost in thought, but he was plenty alert now. Phoebe wore simple knit pj's that clung to her body in all the right places. The opaque, waffle-weave fabric was pale pink with darker pink rosebuds. It faithfully outlined firm high breasts, a rounded ass and long, long legs.

Despite his single-minded libido, he realized in an instant that she looked somewhat the worse for wear. Her long braid had frayed into wispy tendrils and dark smudges underscored her eyes.

"Tough night with the baby?" he asked.

She shook her head, yawning and reaching for a mug in the cabinet. When she did, her top rode up, exposing an inch or two of smooth golden skin. He looked away, feeling like a voyeur, though the image was impossible to erase from his brain.

After pouring herself coffee and taking a long sip, Phoebe sank into a leather-covered recliner and pulled an afghan over her lap. "It wasn't the baby this time," she muttered. "It was me. I couldn't sleep for thinking about what a headache this reconstruction is going to be, especially keeping track of all the subcontractors."

"I could pitch in with that," he said. The words popped out of his mouth, uncensored. Apparently old habits were hard to break. But after all, wasn't helping out a fellow human being at least as important as inhaling the scent of some imaginary rose that surely wouldn't bloom in the dead of winter anyway? Fortunately, his sister-in-law wasn't around to chastise him for his impertinence. She had, in her sweet way, given him a very earnest lecture about the importance of not making work his entire life.

Of course, Hattie was married to Luc, who had miraculously managed to find a balance between enjoying his wife and his growing family and at the same time carrying his weight overseeing the R & D department. Luc's innovations, both in fabric content and in design, had kept their company competitive in the changing world of the twenty-first century. Worldwide designers wanted Cavallo textiles for their best and most expensive lines.

Leo was happy to oblige them. For a price.

Phoebe sighed loudly, her expression glum. "I couldn't ask that of you. It's my problem, and besides, you're on vacation."

"Not a vacation exactly," he clarified. "More like an involuntary time-out."

She grinned. "Has Leo been a naughty boy?"

Heat pooled in his groin and he felt his cheeks redden. He really had to get a handle on this urge to kiss her senseless. Since he was fairly sure that her taunt was nothing more than fun repartee, he refrained from saying what he really thought. "Not naughty," he clarified. "More like too much work and not enough play."

Phoebe swung her legs over the arm of the chair, her coffee mug resting on her stomach. For the first time he noticed that she wore large, pink Hello Kitty slippers on her feet. A less seductive female ensemble would be difficult to find. And yet Leo was fascinated.

She pursed her lips. "I'm guessing executive-level burnout?"

Her perspicacity was spot-on. "You could say that." Although it wasn't the whole story. "I'm doing penance here in the woods, so I can see the error of my ways."

"And who talked you into this getaway? You don't seem like a man who lets other people dictate his schedule."

He refilled his cup and sat down across from her. "True enough," he conceded. "But my baby brother, who happens to be part of a disgustingly happy married couple, thinks I need a break."

"And you listened?"

"Reluctantly."

She studied his face as though trying to sift through his half-truths. "What did you think you would do for two months?"

"That remains to be seen. I have a large collection of

detective novels packed in the backseat of my car, a year of *New York Times* crossword puzzles on my iPad and a brand-new digital camera not even out of the box yet."

"I'm impressed."

"But you'll concede that I surely have time to interview prospective handymen."

"Why would you want to?"

"I like keeping busy."

"Isn't that why you're here? To be *not* busy? I'd hate to think I was causing you to fall off the wagon in the first week."

"Believe me, Phoebe. Juggling schedules and workmen for your cabin repair is something I could do in my sleep. And since it's not my cabin, there's no stress involved."

Still not convinced, she frowned. "If it weren't for the baby, I'd never consider this."

"Understood."

"And if you get tired of dealing with it, you'll be honest."

He held up two fingers. "Scout's honor."

"In that case," she sighed, "how can I say no?"

Leo experienced a rush of jubilation far exceeding the appropriate response to Phoebe's consent. Only at that moment did he realize how much he had been dreading the long parade of unstructured days. With the cabin renovation to give him focus each morning, perhaps this rehabilitative exile wouldn't be so bad.

Guiltily, he wondered what his brother would say about this new turn of events. Leo was pretty sure Luc pictured him sitting by a fire in a flannel robe and slippers reading a John Grisham novel. While Leo enjoyed fiction on occasion, and though Grisham was a phenomenal author, a man could only read so many hours of the day without going bonkers.

Already, the idleness enforced by his recent illness had

made the days and nights far too long. The doctor had cleared him for his usual exercise routine, but with no gym nearby, and sporting equipment that was useless in this environment, it was going to require ingenuity on his part to stay fit and active, especially given that it was winter.

Suddenly, from down the hall echoed the distinct sound of a baby who was awake and unhappy.

Phoebe jumped to her feet, nearly spilling her coffee in the process. "Oh, shoot. I forgot to bring the monitor in here." She clunked her mug in the sink and disappeared in a flash of pink fur.

Leo had barely drained his first cup and gone to the coffeepot for a refill when Phoebe reappeared, this time with baby Teddy on her hip. The little one was red-faced from crying. Phoebe smoothed his hair from his forehead. "Poor thing must be so confused not seeing his mom and dad every morning when he wakes up."

"But he knows you, right?"

Phoebe sighed. "He does. Still, I worry about him day and night. I've never been the sole caregiver for a baby, and it's scary as heck."

"I'd say you're doing an excellent job. He looks healthy and happy."

Phoebe grimaced, though the little worried frown between her eyes disappeared. "I hope you're right."

She held Teddy out at arm's length. "Do you mind giving him his bottle while I shower and get dressed?"

Leo backed up half a step before he caught himself. It was his turn to frown. "I don't think either Teddy or I would like that. I'm too big. I scare children."

Phoebe gaped. Then her eyes flashed. "That's absurd. Wasn't it you, just last night, who was volunteering to help with the baby in return for your keep?"

Leo shrugged, feeling guilty but determined not to show it. "I was thinking more in terms of carrying dirty diapers out to the trash. Or if you're talking on the phone, listening to the monitor to let you know when he wakes up. My hands are too large and clumsy to do little baby things."

"You've never been around an infant?"

"My brother has two small children, a boy and a girl. I see them several times a month, but those visits are more about kissing cheeks and spouting kudos as to how much they've grown. I might even bounce one on my knee if necessary, but not often. Not everyone is good with babies."

Little Teddy still dangled in midair, his chubby legs kicking restlessly. Phoebe closed the distance between herself and Leo and forced the wiggly child to Leo's chest. "Well, you're going to learn, because we had a deal."

Leo's arms came up reflexively, enclosing Teddy in a firm grip. The wee body was warm and solid. The kid smelled of baby lotion and some indefinable nursery scent that was endemic to babies everywhere. "I thought becoming your renovation overseer got me off the hook with Teddy."

Phoebe crossed her arms over her chest, managing to emphasize the fullness of her apparently unconfined breasts. "*It. Did. Not.* A deal is a deal. Or do I need a written contract?"

Leo knew when he was beaten. He'd pegged Phoebe as an easygoing, Earth Mother type, but suddenly he was confronted with a steely-eyed negotiator who would as soon kick him to the curb as look at him. "I'd raise my hands in surrender if I were able," he said, smiling, "But I doubt your nephew would like it."

Phoebe's nonverbal response sounded a lot like *humph.* As Leo watched, grinning inwardly, she quickly prepared a serving of formula and brought it to the sofa where Leo sat with Teddy. She handed over the bottle. "He likes it sitting up. Burp him halfway through."

"Yes, ma'am."

Phoebe put her hands on her hips. "Don't mock me. You're walking on thin ice, mister."

Leo tried to look penitent, and also tried not to take note of the fact that her pert nipples were at eye level. He cleared his throat. "Go take your shower," he said. "I've got this under control. You can trust me."

Phoebe nibbled her bottom lip. "Yell at my bedroom door if you need me."

Something about the juxtaposition of *yell* and *bedroom door* and *need* rekindled Leo's simmering libido. About the only thing that could have slowed him down was the reality of a third person in the cabin. Teddy. Little innocent, about-to-get-really-hungry Teddy.

"Go," Leo said, taking the bottle and offering it to the child in his lap. "We're fine."

As Phoebe left the room, Leo scooted Teddy to a more comfortable position, tucking the baby in his left arm so he could offer the bottle with his right hand. It was clear that the kid was almost capable of feeding himself. But if he dropped the bottle, he would be helpless.

Leo leaned back on the comfy couch and put his feet on the matching ottoman, feeling the warmth and weight of the child, who rested so comfortably in his embrace. Teddy seemed content to hang out with a stranger. Presumably as long as the food kept coming, the tyke would be happy. He did not, however, approve when Leo withdrew the bottle for a few moments and put him on his shoulder to burp him.

Despite Teddy's pique, the new position coaxed the desired result. Afterward, Leo managed to help the kid finish the last of his breakfast. When Teddy sucked on nothing but air, Leo set aside the bottle and picked up a small, round teething ring from the end table flanking the sofa. Teddy chomped down on it with alacrity, giving Leo the opportunity to examine his surroundings in detail.

He liked the way Phoebe had furnished the place. The

cabin had a cozy feel that still managed to seem sophisticated and modern. The appliances and furniture were top-of-the-line, built to last for many years, and no doubt expensive because of that. The flooring was high-end, as well.

The pale amber granite countertops showcased what looked to be handcrafted cabinetry done in honey maple. He saw touches of Phoebe's personality in the beautiful green-and-gold glazed canister set and in the picture of Phoebe, her sister and Teddy tacked to the front of the fridge with a magnet.

Leo looked down at Teddy. The boy's big blue eyes stared up at him gravely as if to say, *What's your game?* Leo chuckled. "Your auntie Phoebe is one beautiful woman, my little man. Don't get me in trouble with her and you and I will get along just fine."

Teddy's gaze shifted back to his tiny hands covered in drool.

Leo was not so easily entertained. He felt the pull of Atlanta, of wondering what was going on at work, of needing to feel in control…at the helm. But something about cuddling a warm baby helped to freeze time. As though any considerations outside of this particular moment were less than urgent.

As he'd told Phoebe, he wasn't a complete novice when it came to being around kids. Luc and Hattie adopted Hattie's niece after they married last year. The little girl was almost two years old now. And last Valentine's Day, Hattie gave birth to the first "blood" Cavallo of the new generation, a dark-haired, dark-eyed little boy.

Leo appreciated children. They were the world's most concrete promise that the globe would keep on spinning. But in truth, he had no real desire to father any of his own. His lifestyle was complicated, regimented, full. Children deserved a healthy measure of their parents' love and attention. The Cavallo empire was Leo's baby. He knew on any given day what the financial bottom line was. During hard financial times, he wrestled the beast that was their investment and sales strategy and demanded returns instead of losses.

He was aware that some people called him hard…unfeeling. But he did what he did knowing how many employees around the world depended on the Cavallos for their livelihoods. It irked the hell out of him to think that another man was temporarily sitting in his metaphorical chair. The vice president Luc had chosen to keep tabs on the money in Leo's absence was solid and capable.

But that didn't make Leo feel any less sidelined.

He glanced at his watch. God in heaven. It was only ten-thirty in the morning. How was he going to survive being on the back burner for two months? Did he even want to try becoming the man his family thought he could be? A balanced, laid-back, easygoing guy?

He rested his free arm across the back of the sofa and closed his eyes, reaching for something Zen. Something peaceful.

Damn it, he didn't want to change. He wanted to go home. At least he had until he met Phoebe. Now he wasn't sure what he wanted.

Hoping that the boy wasn't picking up on his frustration and malcontent thoughts, Leo focused on the only thing capable of diverting him from his problems. Phoebe. Tall, long-legged Phoebe. A dark-haired, dark-eyed beauty with an attitude.

If Phoebe could be lured into an intimate relationship, then this whole recuperative escape from reality had definite possibilities. Leo sensed a spark between them. And he was seldom wrong about things like that. When a man had money, power and reasonably good looks, the female sex swarmed like mosquitoes. That wasn't ego speaking. Merely the truth.

As young men in Italy, he and Luc had racked up a number of conquests until they realized the emptiness of being wanted for superficial reasons. Luc had finally found his soul mate in college. But things hadn't worked out, and it had been ten years before he achieved happiness with the same woman.

Leo had never even made it that far. Not once in his life had he met a female who really cared about who he was as a person. Would-be "Mrs. Cavallos" saw the external trappings of wealth and authority and wanted wedding rings. And the real women, the uncomplicated, good-hearted ones, steered clear of men like Leo for fear of having their hearts broken.

He wasn't sure which category might include Phoebe Kemper. But he was willing to find out.

Four

Phoebe took her time showering, drying her hair and dressing. If Leo wasn't going to live up to his end of the bargain, she wanted to know it now. Leaving Teddy in his temporary care was no risk while she enjoyed a brief respite from the demands of surrogate parenthood. Despite Leo's protestations to the contrary, he was a man who could handle difficult situations.

It was hard to imagine that he had been ill. He seemed impervious to the things that lesser mortals faced. She envied him his confidence. Hers had taken a serious knock three years ago, and she wasn't sure if she had ever truly regained it. A younger Phoebe had taken the world by storm, never doubting her own ability to craft outcomes to her satisfaction.

But she had paid dearly for her hubris. Her entire world had crumbled. Afterward, she had chosen to hide from life, and only in the past few months had she finally begun to understand who she was and what she wanted. The lessons had been painful and slow in coming.

Unfortunately, her awakening had also made her face her own cowardice. Once upon a time she had taken great pleasure in blazing trails where no other women had gone.

Back then, she would have seen a man like Leo as a challenge, both in business and in her personal life.

Smart and confident, she had cruised through life, never realizing that on any given day, she—like any other human being—was subject to the whims of fate. Her perfect life had disintegrated in the way of a comet shattering into a million pieces.

Things would never be as they were. But could they be equally good in another very different way?

She took more care in dressing than she did normally. Instead of jeans, she pulled out a pair of cream corduroy pants and paired them with a cheery red scoop-necked sweater. Christmas was on the way, and the color always lifted her mood.

Wryly acknowledging her vanity, she left her hair loose on her shoulders. It was thick and straight as a plumb line. With the baby demanding much of her time, a braid was easier. Nevertheless, today she wanted to look nice for her guest.

When she finally returned to the living room, Teddy was asleep on Leo's chest, and Leo's eyes were closed, as well. She lingered for a moment in the doorway, enjoying the picture they made. The big, strong man and the tiny, defenseless baby.

Her chest hurt. She rubbed it absently, wondering if she would always grieve for what she had lost. Sequestering herself like a nun the past few years had given her a sort of numb peace. But that peace was an illusion, because it was the product of not living.

Living hurt. If Phoebe were ever going to rejoin the human race, she would have to accept being vulnerable. The thought was terrifying. The flip side of great love and joy was immense pain. She wasn't sure the first was worth risking the prospect of the last.

Quietly she approached the sofa and laid a hand on Leo's

arm. His eyes opened at once as if he had perhaps only been lost in thought rather than dozing. She held out her arms for the baby, but Leo shook his head.

"Show me where to take him," he whispered. "No point in waking him up."

She led the way through her bedroom and bathroom to a much smaller bedroom that adjoined on the opposite side. Before Teddy's arrival she had used this space as a junk room, filled with the things she was too dispirited to sort through when she'd moved in.

Now it had been tamed somewhat, so that half the room was full of neatly stacked plastic tubs, while the other half had been quickly transformed into a comfy space for Teddy. A baby bed, rocking chair and changing table, all with matching prints, made an appealing, albeit temporary, nursery.

Leo bent over the crib and laid Teddy gently on his back. The little boy immediately rolled to his side and stuck a thumb in his mouth. Both adults smiled. Phoebe clicked on the monitor and motioned for Leo to follow her as they tiptoed out.

In the living room, she waved an arm. "Relax. Do whatever you like. There's plenty of wood if you feel up to building us a fire."

"I told you. I'm not sick."

The terse words had a bite to them. Phoebe flinched inwardly, but kept her composure. Something had happened to Leo. Something serious. Cancer maybe. But she was not privy to that information. So conversation regarding the subject was akin to navigating a minefield.

Most men were terrible patients. Usually because their health and vigor were tied to their self-esteem. Clearly, Leo had been sent here or had agreed to come here because he needed rest and relaxation. He didn't want Phoebe hovering or commenting on his situation. Okay. Fine. But she was still going to keep an eye on him, because whatever had given him a wallop was serious enough to warrant a two-month hiatus from work.

That in itself was telling. In her past life, she had interacted with lots of men like Leo. They were alpha animals, content only with the number one spot in the pack. Their work was their life. And even if they married, familial relationships were kept in neatly separated boxes.

Unfortunately for Phoebe, she possessed some of those same killer instincts…or she had. The adrenaline rush of an impossible-to-pull-off business deal was addictive. The more you succeeded, the more you wanted to try again. Being around Leo was going to be difficult, because like a recovering alcoholic who avoided other drinkers, she was in danger of being sucked into his life, his work issues, whatever made him tick.

Under no circumstances could she let herself be dragged back into that frenzied schedule. The world was a big, beautiful place. She had enough money tucked away to live simply for a very long time. She had lost herself in the drive to achieve success. It was better now to accept her new lifestyle.

Leo moved to the fireplace and began stacking kindling and firewood with the precision of an Eagle Scout. Phoebe busied herself in the kitchen making a pot of chili to go with sandwiches for their lunch. Finally, she broke the awkward silence. "I have a young woman who babysits for me when I have to be gone for a short time. It occurred to me that I could see if she is free and if so, she could stay here in the house and watch Teddy while you and I do an initial damage assessment on the other cabin."

Leo paused to look over his shoulder, one foot propped on the raised hearth. "You sound very businesslike about this."

She shrugged. "I used to work for a big company. I'm accustomed to tackling difficult tasks."

He lit the kindling, stood back to see if it would catch, and then replaced the fire screen, brushing his hands together to remove the soot. "Where did you work?"

Biting her lip, she berated herself inwardly for bringing up a subject she would rather not pursue. "I was a stockbroker for a firm in Charlotte, North Carolina."

"Did they go under? Is that why you're here?"

His was a fair assumption. But wrong. "The business survived the economic collapse and is expanding by leaps and bounds."

"Which doesn't really answer my question."

She grimaced. "Maybe when we've known each other for more than a nanosecond I might share the gory details. But not today."

Leo understood her reluctance, or he thought he did. Not everyone wanted to talk about his or her failures. And rational or not, he regarded his heart attack as a failure. He wasn't overweight. He didn't smoke. Truth be told, his vices were few, perhaps only one. He was type A to the max. And type A personalities lived with stress so continuously that the condition became second nature. According to his doctor, no amount of exercise or healthy eating could compensate for an inability to unwind.

So maybe Leo was screwed.

He joined his hostess in the kitchen, looking for any excuse to get closer to her. "Something smells good." *Smooth, Leo. Real smooth.*

Last night he had dreamed about Phoebe's braid. But today...wow. Who knew within that old-fashioned hairstyle was a shiny waterfall the color of midnight?

Phoebe adjusted the heat on the stove top and turned to

face him. "I didn't ask. Do you have any dietary restrictions? Any allergies?"

Leo frowned. "I don't expect you to cook for me all the time I'm here. You claimed that civilization is close by. Why don't I take you out now and then?"

She shot him a pitying look that said he was clueless. "Clearly you've never tried eating at a restaurant with an infant. It's ridiculously loud, not to mention that the chaos means tipping the server at least thirty percent to compensate for the rice cereal all over the floor." She eyed his sweater. "I doubt you would enjoy it."

"I know kids are messy." He'd eaten out with Luc and Hattie and the babies a time or two. Hadn't he? Or come to think of it, maybe it was always at their home. "Well, not that then, but I could at least pick up a pizza once a week."

Phoebe smiled at him sweetly. "That would be lovely. Thank you, Leo."

Her genuine pleasure made him want to do all sorts of things for her…and *to* her. Something about that radiant smile twisted his insides in a knot. The unmistakable jolt of attraction was perhaps inevitable. They were two healthy adults who were going to be living in close proximity for eight or nine weeks. They were bound to notice each other sexually.

He cleared his throat as he shoved his hands into his pockets. "Is there a boyfriend who won't like me staying here?"

Again, that faint, fleeting shadow that dimmed her beauty for a moment. "No. You're safe." She shook her head, giving him a rueful smile. "I probably should say yes, though. Just so you don't get any ideas."

He tried to look innocent. "What ideas?" All joking aside, he was a little worried about having sex for the first time since… Oh, hell. He had a hard time even saying it in his head. Heart attack. There. He wasn't afraid of two stupid words.

The doctor had said *no restrictions,* but the doctor hadn't seen Phoebe Kemper in a snug crimson sweater. She reminded Leo of a cross between Wonder Woman and Pocahontas. Both of whom he'd fantasized about as a preteen boy. What did that say about his chances of staying away from her?

She shooed him with her hands. "Go unpack. Read one of those books. Lunch will be ready in an hour."

Leo enjoyed Phoebe's cooking almost as much as her soft, feminine beauty. If he could eat like this all the time, maybe he wouldn't skip meals and drive through fast-food places at nine o'clock at night. Little Teddy sat in his high chair playing with a set of plastic keys. It wasn't time for another bottle, so the poor kid had to watch the grown-ups eat.

They had barely finished the meal when Allison, the babysitter, showed up. According to Phoebe, she was a college student who lived at home and enjoyed picking up extra money. Plus, she adored Teddy, which was a bonus.

Since temperatures had warmed up enough to melt the ice, Leo went out to the car for his big suitcase, brought it in and rummaged until he found winter gear. Not much of it was necessary in Atlanta. It did snow occasionally, but rarely hung around. Natives, though, could tell hair-raising stories about ice storms and two-week stints without power.

When he made his way back to the living room, Allison was playing peekaboo with the baby, and Phoebe was slipping her arms into a fleece-lined sheepskin jacket. Even the bulky garment did nothing to diminish her appeal.

She tucked a notepad and pen into her pocket. "Don't be shy about telling me things you see. Construction is not my forte."

"Nor mine, but my brother and I did build a tree house once upon a time. Does that count?"

He followed her out the door, inhaling sharply as the icy wind filled his lungs with a jolt. The winter afternoon enwrapped them, blue-skied and damp. From every corner echoed the sounds of dripping water as ice gave way beneath pale sunlight.

Lingering on the porch to take it all in, he found himself strangely buoyed by the sights and sounds of the forest. The barest minimum of trees had been cleared for Phoebe's home and its mate close by. All around them, a sea of evergreen danced in the brisk wind. Though he could see a single contrail far above them, etched white against the blue, there was little other sign of the twenty-first century.

"Did you have these built when you moved here?" he asked as they walked side by side up the incline to the other cabin.

Phoebe tucked the ends of her fluttering scarf into her coat, lifting her face to the sun. "My grandmother left me this property when she died a dozen years ago. I had just started college. For years I held on to it because of sentimental reasons, and then much later…"

"Later, what?"

She looked at him, her eyes hidden behind dark sunglasses. Her shoulders lifted and fell. "I decided to mimic Thoreau and live in the woods."

Phoebe didn't expand on her explanation, so he didn't push. They had plenty of time for sharing confidences. And besides, he was none too eager to divulge all his secrets just yet.

Up close, and in the unforgiving light of day, the damage to the cabin was more extensive than he had realized. He put a hand on Phoebe's arm. "Let me go first. There's no telling what might still be in danger of crumbling."

They were able to open the front door, but just barely. The tree that had crushed the roof was a massive oak, large enough around that Leo would not have been able to encircle it with his arms. The house had caved in so dramatically that the floor was knee-deep in rubble—insulation, roofing shingles, branches of every size and, beneath it all, Phoebe's furnishings.

She removed her sunglasses and craned her neck to look up at the nonexistent ceiling as she followed Leo inside. "Not much left, is there?" Her voice wobbled a bit at the end. "I'm so grateful it wasn't *my* house."

"You and me, both," he muttered. Phoebe or Teddy or both could have been killed or badly injured…with no one nearby to check on them. The isolation was peaceful, but he wasn't sure he approved of a defenseless woman living here. Perhaps that was a prehistoric gut feeling. Given the state of the structure in which they were standing, however, he did have a case.

He just didn't have any right to argue it.

Taking Phoebe's hand to steady her, they stepped on top of and over all the debris and made their way to the back portion of the cabin. The far left corner bedroom had escaped unscathed…and some pieces of furniture in the outer rooms were okay for the moment. But if anything were to be salvaged, it would have to be done immediately. Dampness would lead to mildew, and with animals having free rein, further damage was a certainty.

Phoebe's face was hard to read. Finally she sighed. "I might do better to bulldoze it and start over," she said glumly. She bent down to pick up a glass wildflower that had tumbled from a small table, but had miraculously escaped demolition. "My friends cautioned me to furnish the rental cabin with inexpensive, institutional stuff that would not be a big deal to replace in case of theft or carelessness on the part of the tenants. I suppose I should have listened."

"Do you have decent insurance?" He was running the numbers in his head, and the outcome wasn't pretty.

She nodded. "I don't remember all the ins and outs of the policy, but my agent is a friend of my sister's, so I imagine he made sure I have what I need."

Phoebe's discouragement was almost palpable.

"Sometimes things work out for a reason," he said, wanting to reassure her, but well aware that she had no reason to lean on him. "I need something to do to keep me from going crazy. You have a baby to care for. Let me handle this mess, Phoebe. Let me juggle and schedule the various contractors. Please. You'd be doing me a favor."

Five

Phoebe was tempted. So tempted. Leo stood facing her, legs planted apart in a stance that said he was there to stay. Wearing an expensive quilted black parka and aviator sunglasses that hid his every emotion, he was an enigma. Why had a virile, handsome, vigorous male found his way to her hidden corner of the world?

What was he after? Healing? Peace? He had the physique of a bouncer and the look of a wealthy playboy. Had he really been sick? Would she be committing a terrible sin to lay this burden on him from the beginning?

"That's ridiculous," she said faintly. "I'd be taking advantage of you. But I have to confess that I find your offer incredibly appealing. I definitely underestimated how exhausting it would be to take care of a baby 24/7. I love Teddy, and he's not really a fussy child at all, but the thought of adding all this…" She flung out her arm. "Well, it's daunting."

"Then let me help you," he said quietly.

"I don't expect you to actually do the work yourself."

He pocketed his sunglasses and laughed, making his rugged features even more attractive. "No worries there. I'm aware that men are known for biting off more than they can chew, but your cabin, or what's left of it, falls into the category of catastrophe. That's best left to the experts."

She stepped past him and surveyed the large bed with the burgundy-and-navy duvet. "This was supposed to be your room. I know you would have been comfortable here." She turned to face him. "I'm sorry, Leo. I feel terrible about shortchanging you."

He touched her arm. Only for a second. The smile disappeared, but his eyes were warm and teasing. "I'm pretty happy where I ended up. A gorgeous woman. A cozy cabin. Sounds like I won the jackpot."

"You're flirting," she said, hearing the odd and embarrassingly breathless note in her voice.

His gaze was intent, sexy…leaving no question that he was interested. "I've been admonished to stop and smell the roses. And here you are."

Removing her coat that suddenly felt too hot, she leaned against the door frame. The odd sensation of being inside the house but having the sunlight spill down from above was disconcerting. "You may find me more of a thorn. My sister says that living alone up here has made me set in my ways." It was probably true. Some days she felt like a certified hermit.

Once a social animal comfortable at cocktail parties and business lunches, she now preferred the company of chipmunks and woodpeckers and the occasional fox. Dull, dull, dull…

Leo kicked aside a dangerously sharp portion of what had been the dresser mirror. "I'll take my chances. I've got nowhere to go and nobody to see, as my grandfather used to say. You and Teddy brighten the prospect of my long exile considerably."

"Are you ever going to tell me why you're here?" she asked without censoring her curiosity.

He shrugged. "It's not a very interesting story...but maybe...when it's time."

"How will you know?" This odd conversation seemed to have many layers. Her question erased Leo's charmingly flirtatious smile and replaced it with a scowl.

"You're a pain in the butt," he said, the words a low growl.

"I told you I'm no rose."

He took her arm and steered her toward the front door. "Then pretend," he muttered. "Can you do that?"

Their muted altercation was interrupted by the arrival of the insurance agent. The next hour was consumed with questions and photographs and introducing Leo to the agent. The two men soon had their heads together as they climbed piles of rubble and inspected every cranny of the doomed cabin.

Phoebe excused herself and walked down the path, knowing that Allison would be ready to go home. As she opened the door and entered the cabin, Teddy greeted her with a chortle and a grin. Envy pinched her heart, but stronger still was happiness that the baby recognized her and was happy to see her.

Given Phoebe's background, her sister had been torn about the arrangement. But Phoebe had reassured her, and eventually, her sister and brother-in-law gave in. Dragging a baby across the ocean was not an easy task in ideal circumstances, and facing the disposal of an entire estate, they knew Teddy would be miserable and they would be overwhelmed.

Still, Phoebe knew they missed their small son terribly. They used FaceTime to talk to him when Phoebe went into town and had a decent phone signal, and she sent them constant, newsy updates via email and texts. But they were so far away. She suspected they regretted their decision to leave him. Probably, they were working like fiends to take care of all the estate business so they could get back to the U.S. sooner.

When Allison left, Phoebe held Teddy and looked out the window toward the other cabin. Leo and the insurance agent were still measuring and assessing the damage. She rubbed the baby's back. "I think Santa has sent us our present early, my little man. Leo is proving to be a godsend. Now all I have to do is ignore the fact that he's the most attractive man I've seen in a long, long time, and that he makes it hard to breathe whenever I get too close to him, and I'll be fine."

Teddy continued sucking his thumb, his long-lashed eyelids growing heavy as he fought sleep.

"You're no help," she grumbled. His weight was comfortable in her arms. Inhaling his clean baby smell made her womb clench. What would it be like to share a child with Leo Cavallo? Would he be a good father, or an absent one?

The man in question burst through the front door suddenly, bringing with him the smell of the outdoors. "Honey, I'm home." His humor lightened his face and made him seem younger.

Phoebe grinned at him. "Take off your boots, *honey.*" She was going to have to practice keeping him at arm's length. Leo Cavallo had the dangerous ability to make himself seem harmless. Which was a lie. Even in a few short hours, Phoebe had recognized and assessed his sexual pull.

Some men simply oozed testosterone. Leo was one of them.

It wasn't just his size, though he was definitely a bear of a man. More than that, he emanated a gut-level masculinity that made her, in some odd way, far more aware of her own carnal needs. She would like to blame it on the fact that they were alone together in the woods, but in truth, she would have had the same reaction to him had they met at the opera or on the deck of a yacht.

Leo was a man's man. The kind of male animal who caught women in his net without even trying. Phoebe had thought herself immune to such silly, pheromone-driven impulses, but with Leo in her house, she recognized an appalling truth. She needed sex. She wanted sex. And she had found just the man to satisfy her every whim.

Her face heated as she pretended to be occupied with the baby. Leo shed his coat and pulled a folded piece of paper from his pocket. "Here," he said. "Take a look. I'll hold the kid."

Before Phoebe could protest, Leo scooped Teddy into his arms and lifted him toward the ceiling. Teddy, who had been sleepy only moments before, squealed with delight. Shaking her head at the antics of the two males who seemed in perfect accord, Phoebe sank into a kitchen chair and scanned the list Leo had handed her.

"Ouch," she said, taking a deep breath for courage. "According to this, I was probably right about the bulldozer."

Leo shook his head. "No. I realize the bottom line looks bad, but it would be even worse to build a new cabin from the ground up. Your agent thinks the settlement will be generous. All you have to provide is an overabundance of patience."

"We may have a problem," she joked. "That's not my strong suit."

Teddy's shirt had rucked up. Leo blew a raspberry against the baby's pudgy, soft-skinned stomach. "I'll do my best to keep you out of it. Unless you want to be consulted about every little detail."

Phoebe shuddered. "Heavens, no. If you're foolish enough to offer me the chance to get my property repaired without my lifting a finger, then far be it from me to nitpick."

Teddy wilted suddenly as Leo cuddled him. What was it about the sight of a big, strong man being gentle with a baby that made a woman's heart melt? Phoebe told herself she shouldn't be swayed by such an ordinary thing, but she couldn't help it. Seeing Leo hold little Teddy made her insides mushy with longing. She wanted it all. The man. The baby. Was that too much to ask?

Leo glanced over at her, hopefully not noticing the way her eyes misted over.

"You want me to put him in his bed?" he asked.

"Sure. He takes these little forty-five-minute catnaps on and off instead of one long one. But he seems happy, so I go with the flow."

Leo paused in the hallway. "How long have you had him?"

"Two weeks. We've settled into a routine of sorts."

"Until I came along to mess things up."

"If you're fishing for compliments, forget it. You've already earned your keep, and it hasn't even been twenty-four hours yet."

He flashed her a grin. "Just think how much you'll love me when you get to know me."

Her knees went weak, and she wasn't even standing. "Go put him down, Leo, and behave."

He kissed the baby's head, smiling down at him. "She's a hard case, kiddo. But I'll wear her down."

When Leo disappeared from sight, Phoebe exhaled loudly. She'd been holding her breath and hadn't even realized it. Rising to her feet unsteadily, she went from window to window closing the curtains. Darkness fell early in this mountain *holler,* as the old generation called it. Soon it would be the longest night of the year.

Phoebe had learned to dread the winter months. Not just the snow and ice and cold, gray days, but the intense loneliness. It had been the season of Christmas one year when she lost everything. Each anniversary brought it all back. But even before the advent of Leo, she had been determined to make this year better. She had a baby in the house. And now a guest. Surely that was enough to manufacture holiday cheer and thaw some of the ice that had kept her captive for so long.

Leo returned, carrying his laptop. He made himself at home on the sofa. “Do you mind giving me your internet password?” he asked, opening the computer and firing it up.

Uh-oh. “Um…” She leaned against the sink for support. “I don’t have internet,” she said, not sure there was any way to soften that blow.

Leo’s look, a cross between horror and bafflement, was priceless. “Why not?”

“I decided I could live my life without it.”

He ran his hands through his hair, agitation building. His neck turned red and a pulse beat in his temple. “This is the twenty-first century,” he said, clearly trying to speak calmly. “*Everybody* has internet.” He paused, his eyes narrowing. “This is either a joke, or you’re Amish. Which is it?”

She lifted her chin, refusing to be judged for a decision that had seemed entirely necessary at the time. “Neither. I made a choice. That’s all.”

“My sister-in-law would never have rented me a cabin that didn’t have the appropriate amenities,” he said stubbornly.

“Well,” she conceded. “You’re right about that. The cabin I rent out has satellite internet. But as you saw for yourself, everything was pretty much demolished, including the dish.”

She watched Leo’s good humor evaporate as he absorbed the full import of what she was saying. Suddenly he pulled his smartphone from his pocket. “At least I can check email with this,” he said, a note of panic in his voice.

“We’re pretty far back in this gorge,” she said. “Only one carrier gets a decent signal and it’s—”

"Not the one I have." He stared at the screen and sighed. "Unbelievable. Outposts in Africa have better connectivity than this. I don't think I can stay somewhere that I have to be out of touch from the world."

Phoebe's heart sank. She had hoped Leo would come to appreciate the simplicity of her life here in the mountains. "Is it really that important? I have a landline phone you're welcome to use. For that matter, you can use *my* cell phone. And I do have a television dish, so you're welcome to add the other service if it's that important to you." If he were unable to understand and accept the choices she had made, then it would be foolish to pursue the attraction between them. She would only end up getting hurt.

Leo closed his eyes for a moment. "I'm sorry," he said at last, shooting her a look that was half grimace, half apology. "It took me by surprise, that's all. I'm accustomed to having access to my business emails around the clock."

Was that why he was here? Because he was *too* plugged in? Had he suffered some kind of breakdown? It didn't seem likely, but she knew firsthand how tension and stress could affect a person.

She pulled her cell phone from her pocket and crossed the room to hand it to him. "Use mine for now. It's not a problem."

Their fingers brushed as she gave him the device. Leo hesitated for a moment, but finally took it. "Thank you," he said gruffly. "I appreciate it."

Turning her back to give him some privacy, she went to the kitchen to rummage in the fridge and find an appealing dinner choice. Now that Leo was here, she would have to change her grocery buying habits. Fortunately, she had chicken and vegetables that would make a nice stir-fry.

Perhaps twenty minutes passed before she heard a very ungentlemanly curse from her tenant. Turning sharply, she witnessed the fury and incredulity that turned his jaw to steel and his eyes to molten chocolate. "I can't believe they did this to me."

She wiped her hands on a dish towel. "What, Leo? What did they do? Who are you talking about?"

He stood up and rubbed his eyes with the heels of his hands. "My brother," he croaked. "My black-hearted, devious baby brother."

As she watched, he paced, his scowl growing darker by the minute. "I'll kill him," he said with far too much relish. "I'll poison his coffee. I'll beat him to a pulp. I'll grind his wretched bones into powder."

Phoebe felt obliged to step in at that moment. "Didn't you say he has a wife and two kids? I don't think you really want to murder your own flesh and blood…do you? What could he possibly have done that's so terrible?"

Leo sank into an armchair, his arms dangling over the sides. Everything about his posture suggested defeat. "He locked me out of my work email," Leo muttered with a note of confused disbelief. "Changed all the passwords. Because he didn't trust me to stay away."

"Well, it sounds like he knows you pretty well, then. 'Cause isn't that exactly what you were doing? Trying to look at work email?"

Leo glared at her, his brother momentarily out of the crosshairs. "Whose side are you on anyway? You don't even know my brother."

"When you spoke of him earlier…he and your sister-in-law and the kids…I heard love in your voice, Leo. So that tells me he must love you just as much. Following that line of reasoning, he surely had a good reason to do what he did."

A hush fell over the room. The clock on the mantel ticked loudly. Leo stared at her with an intensity that made the hair on the back of her neck stand up. He was pissed. Really angry. And since his brother wasn't around, Phoebe might very well be his default target.

She had the temerity to inch closer and perch on the chair opposite him. "Why would he keep you away from work, Leo? And why did he and your sister-in-law send you here? You're not a prisoner. If being with me in this house is so damned terrible, then do us both a favor and go home."

Six

Leo was ashamed of his behavior. He'd acted like a petulant child. But everything about this situation threw him off balance. He was accustomed to being completely in charge of his domain, whether that be the Cavallo empire or his personal life. It wasn't that he didn't trust Luc. He did. Completely. Unequivocally. And in his gut, he knew the business wouldn't suffer in his absence.

Perhaps that was what bothered him the most. If the company he had worked all of his adult life to build could roll along just fine during his two-month hiatus, then what use was Leo to anyone? His successes were what he thrived on. Every time he made an acquisition or increased the company's bottom line, he felt a rush of adrenaline that was addictive.

Moving slot by slot up the Fortune 500 was immensely gratifying. He had made more money, both for the company and for himself, by the time he was thirty than most people earned in a lifetime. He was damned good at finance. Even in uncertain times, Leo had never made a misstep. His grandfather even went so far as to praise him for his genius. Given that eliciting a compliment from the old dragon was as rare as finding unicorn teeth, Leo had been justifiably proud.

But without Cavallo…without the high-tech office… without the daily onslaught of problems and split-second decisions…who was he? Just a young man with nowhere to go and nothing to do. The aimlessness of it all hung around his neck like a millstone.

Painfully aware that Phoebe had observed his humiliating meltdown, he stood, grabbed his coat from the hook by the door, shoved his feet in his shoes and escaped.

Phoebe fixed dinner with one ear out for the baby and one eye out the window to see if Leo was coming back. His car still sat parked out front, so she knew he was on foot. The day was warm, at least by December standards. But it *was* possible to get lost in these mountains. People did it all the time.

The knot in her stomach eased when at long last, he reappeared. His expression was impossible to read, but his body language seemed relaxed. "I've worked up an appetite" he said, smiling as if nothing had happened.

"It's almost ready. If we're lucky we'll be able to eat our meal in peace before Teddy wakes up."

"He's still asleep?"

She nodded. "I can never predict his schedule. I guess because he's still so small. But since I'm flexible, I'm fine with that."

He held out a chair for her and then joined her at the table. Phoebe had taken pains with the presentation. Pale green woven place mats and matching napkins from a craft cooperative in Gatlinburg accentuated amber stoneware plates and chunky handblown glass goblets that mingled green and gold in interesting swirls.

She poured each of them a glass of pinot. "There's beer in the fridge if you'd prefer it."

He tasted the wine. "No. This is good. A local vintage?"

"Yes. We have several wineries in the area."

Their conversation was painfully polite. Almost as awkward as a blind date. Though in this case there was nothing of a romantic nature to worry about. No *will he* or *won't he* when it came time for a possible good-night kiss at the front door.

Even so, she was on edge. Leo Cavallo's sexuality gave a woman ideas, even if unintentionally. It had been a very long time since Phoebe had kissed a man, longer still since she had felt the weight of a lover's body moving against hers in urgent passion. She thought she had safely buried those urges in her subconscious, but with Leo in her house, big and alive and so damned sexy, she was in the midst of an erotic awakening.

Like a limb that has gone to sleep and then experienced the pain of renewed blood flow, Phoebe's body tingled with awareness. Watching the muscles in his throat as he swallowed. Inhaling the scent of him, warm male and crisp outdoors. Inadvertently brushing his shoulder as she served him second helpings of chicken and rice. Hearing the lazy tempo of his speech that made her think of hot August nights and damp bodies twined together beneath a summer moon.

All of her senses were engaged except for taste. And the yearning to do just that, to kiss him, swelled in her chest and made her hands shake. The need was as overwhelming as it was unexpected. She fixated on the curve of his lips as he spoke. They were good lips. Full, but masculine. What would they feel like pressed against hers?

Imagining the taste of his mouth tightened everything inside her until she felt faint with arousal. Standing abruptly, she put her back to him, busying herself at the sink as she rinsed plates and loaded the dishwasher. Suddenly, she felt him behind her, almost pressing against her.

"Let me handle cleanup," he said, the words a warm breath of air at her neck. She froze. Did he sense her jittery nerves, her longing?

She swallowed, clenching her fingers on the edge of the counter. "No. Thank you. But a fire would be nice." She was already on fire. But what the heck…in for a penny, in for a pound.

After long seconds when it seemed as if every molecule of oxygen in the room vaporized, he moved away. "Whatever you want," he said. "Just ask."

Leo was neither naive nor oblivious. Phoebe was attracted to him. He knew, because he felt the same inexorable pull. But he had known her for barely a day. Perhaps long enough for an easy pickup at a bar or a one-night stand, but not for a relationship that was going to have to survive for a couple of months.

With a different woman at another time, he would have taken advantage of the situation. But he was at Phoebe's mercy for now. One wrong move, and she could boot him out. There were other cabins…other peaceful getaways. None of them, however, had Phoebe. And he was beginning to think that she was his talisman, his lucky charm, the only hope he had of making it through the next weeks without going stark raving mad.

The fire caught immediately, the dry tinder flaming as it coaxed the heavier logs into the blaze. When he turned around, Phoebe was watching him, her eyes huge.

He smiled at her. "Come join me on the sofa. We're going to be spending a lot of time together. We might as well get to know each other."

At that very moment, Teddy announced his displeasure with a noisy cry. The relief on Phoebe's face was almost comical. "Sorry. I'll be back in a minute."

While she was gone, he sat on the hearth, feeling the heat

from the fire sink into his back. Beneath his feet a bearskin pelt covered the floor. He was fairly certain it was fake, but the thick, soft fur made him imagine a scenario that was all too real. Phoebe…nude…her skin gilded with firelight.

The vivid picture in his mind hardened his sex and dried his mouth. Jumping to his feet, he went to the kitchen and poured himself another glass of wine. Sipping it slowly, he tried to rein in his hunger. Something might develop during this time with Phoebe. They could become friends. Or even more than that. But rushing his fences was not the way to go. He had to resist the temptation to bring sex into the picture before she had a chance to trust him.

Regardless of Phoebe's desires, or even his own, this was a situation that called for caution. Not his first impulse, or even his last. But if he had any hope of making her his, he'd bide his time.

His mental gyrations were interrupted by Phoebe's return. "There you are," he said. "I wondered if Teddy had kidnapped you."

"Poopy diaper," she said with a grimace. She held the baby on her hip as she prepared a bottle. "He's starving, poor thing. Slept right through dinner."

Leo moved to the sofa and was gratified when Phoebe followed suit. She now held the baby as a barricade between them, but he could wait. The child wasn't big enough to be much of a problem.

"So tell me," he said. "What did you do with yourself before Teddy arrived?"

Phoebe settled the baby on her lap and held the bottle so he could reach it easily. "I moved in three years ago. At first I was plenty busy with decorating and outfitting both cabins. I took my time and looked for exactly what I wanted. In the meantime, I made a few friends, mostly women I met at the gym. A few who worked in stores where I shopped."

"And when the cabins were ready?"

She stared down at the baby, rubbing his head with a wistful smile on her face. He wondered if she had any clue how revealing her expression was. She adored the little boy. That much was certain.

"I found someone to help me start a garden," she said. "Buford is the old man who lives back near the main road where you turned off. He's a sweetheart. His wife taught me how to bake bread and how to can fruits and vegetables. I know how to make preserves. And I can even churn my own butter in a pinch, though that seems a bit of a stretch in this day and age."

He studied her, trying to get to the bottom of what she wasn't saying. "I understand all that," he said. "And if I didn't know better, I'd guess you were a free spirit, hippie-commune, granola-loving Earth Mother. But something doesn't add up. How did you get from stockbroker to this?"

Phoebe understood his confusion. None of it made sense on paper. But was she willing to expose all of her painful secrets to a man she barely knew? No…not just yet.

Picking her words carefully, she gave him an answer. Not a lie, but not the whole truth. "I had some disappointments both personally and professionally. They hit me hard…enough to make me reconsider whether the career path I had chosen was the right one. At the time, I didn't honestly know. So I took a time-out. A step backward. I came here and decided to see if I could make my life simpler. More meaningful."

"And now? Any revelations to report?"

She raised an eyebrow. "Are you mocking me?"

He held up his hands. "No. I swear I'm not. If anything, I have to admire you for being proactive. Most people simply slog away at a job because they don't have the courage to try something new."

"I wish I could say it was like that. But to be honest,

it was more a case of crawling in a hole to hide out from the world."

"You don't cut yourself much slack, do you?"

"I was a mess when I came here."

"And now?"

She thought about it for a moment. No one had ever asked her straight-out if her self-imposed exile had borne fruit. "I think I have a better handle on what I want out of life. And I've forgiven myself for mistakes I made. But do I want to go back to that cutthroat lifestyle? No. I don't."

"I know this is a rude question, but I'm going to ask it anyway. What have you done for money since you've been out of work?"

"I'm sure a lot of people wonder that." She put the baby on her shoulder and burped him. "The truth is, Leo. I'm darned good at making money. I have a lot stashed away. And since I've been here, my weekly expenses are fairly modest. So though I can't stay here forever, I certainly haven't bankrupted myself."

"Would you say your experience has been worth it?"

She nodded. "Definitely."

"Then maybe there's hope for me after all."

Phoebe was glad to have Teddy as a buffer. Sitting with Leo in a firelit room on a cold December night was far too cozy. But when Teddy finished his bottle and was ready to play, she had no choice but to get down on the floor with him and let him roll around on the faux bearskin rug. He had mastered flipping from his back to his tummy. Now he enjoyed the increased mobility.

She was truly shocked when Leo joined them, stretching out on his right side and propping his head on his hand. "How long 'til he crawls?"

"Anytime now. He's already learned to get his knees up under him, so I don't think it will be too many more weeks." Leo seemed entirely relaxed, while Phoebe was in danger of hyperventilating. Anyone watching them might assume they were a family…mom, dad and baby. But the truth was, they were three separate people who happened to be occupying the same space for the moment.

Teddy was her nephew, true. But he was on loan, so to speak. She could feed him and play with him and love him, but at the end of the day, he wasn't hers. Still, what could it hurt to pretend for a while?

She pulled her knees to her chest and wrapped her arms around her legs. Ordinarily, she would have lain down on her stomach and played with Teddy at his level. But getting horizontal with Leo Cavallo was not smart, especially since he was in touching distance. She'd give herself away, no doubt. Even with a baby between them, she couldn't help thinking how nice it would be to spend an unencumbered hour with her new houseguest.

Some soft music on the radio, another bottle of wine, more logs on the fire. And after that…

Her heartbeat stuttered and stumbled. Dampness gathered at the back of her neck and in another, less accessible spot. Her breathing grew shallow. She stared at Teddy blindly, anything to avoid looking at Leo. Not for the world would she want him to think she was so desperate for male company that she would fall at his feet.

Even as she imagined such a scenario, he rolled to his back and slung an arm across his face. Moments later, she saw the steady rise and fall of his chest as he gave in to sleep.

Teddy was headed in the same direction. His acrobatics had worn him out. He slumped onto his face, butt in the air, and slept.

Phoebe watched the two males with a tightness in her chest that was a combination of so many things. Yearning for what might have been. Fear of what was yet to come.

Hope that somewhere along the way she could have a family of her own.

Her sleepless night caught up with her, making her eyelids droop. With one wary look at Leo to make sure he was asleep, she eased down beside her two companions and curled on her side with Teddy in the curve of her body. Now she could smell warm baby and wood smoke, and perhaps the faint scent of Leo's aftershave.

Closing her eyes, she sighed deeply. She would rest for a moment....

Seven

Leo awoke disoriented. His bed felt rock-hard, and his pillow had fallen on the floor. Gradually, he remembered where he was. Turning his head, he took in the sight of Phoebe and Teddy sleeping peacefully beside him.

The baby was the picture of innocence, but Phoebe… He sucked in a breath. Her position, curled on her side, made the neckline of her sweater gape, treating him to an intimate view of rounded breasts and creamy skin. Her hair tumbled around her face as if she had just awakened from a night of energetic sex. All he had to do was extend his arm and he could stroke her belly beneath the edge of her top.

His sex hardened to the point of discomfort. He didn't know whether to thank God for the presence of the kid or to curse the bad timing. The strength of his desire was both surprising and worrisome. Was he reacting so strongly to Phoebe because he was in exile and she was the only woman around, or had his long bout of celibacy predisposed him to want her?

Either way, his hunger for her was suspect. It would be the height of selfishness to seduce her because of boredom or propinquity. Already, he had taken her measure. She was loving, generous and kind, though by no means a pushover.

Even with training in what some would call a nonfeminine field, she nevertheless seemed completely comfortable with the more traditional roles of childcare and homemaking.

Phoebe was complicated. That, more than anything else, attracted him. At the moment a tiny frown line marked the space between her brows. He wanted to erase it with a kiss. The faint shadowy smudges beneath her eyes spoke of her exhaustion. He had been around his brother and sister-in-law enough to know that dealing with infants was harrowing and draining on the best of days.

He also knew that they glowed with pride when it came to their children, and he could see in Phoebe the same self-sacrificial love. Even now, in sleep, her arms surrounded little Teddy, keeping him close though he was unaware.

Moving carefully so as not to wake them, he rolled to his feet and quietly removed the screen so he could add wood to the smoldering fire. For insurance, he tossed another handful of kindling into the mix and blew on it gently. Small flames danced and writhed as he took a medium-size log and positioned it across the coals.

The simple task rocked him in an indefinable way. How often did he pause in his daily schedule to enjoy something as elemental and magical as an honest-to-God wood fire? The elegant gas logs in his condo were nothing in comparison.

As he stared into the hearth, the temperature built. His skin burned, and yet he couldn't move away. Phoebe seemed to him more like this real fire than any woman he had been with in recent memory. Energetic…messy… mesmerizing. Producing a heat that warmed him down to his bones.

Most of his liaisons in Atlanta were brief. He spent an enormous amount of time, perhaps more than was warranted, growing and protecting the Cavallo bottom line. Sex was good and a necessary part of his life. But he had never been tempted to do what it took to keep a woman in his bed night after night.

Kneeling, he turned and looked at Phoebe. Should he wake her up? Did the baby need to be put to bed?

Uncharacteristically uncertain, he deferred a decision. Snagging a pillow from the sofa, he leaned back against the stone hearth, stretched out his legs and watched them sleep.

Phoebe awoke slowly, but in no way befuddled. Her situation was crystal clear. Like a coward, she kept her eyes closed, even though she knew Leo was watching her. Apparently, her possum act didn't fool him. He touched her foot with his. "Open your eyes, Phoebe."

She felt at a distinct disadvantage. There was no graceful way to get up with him so close. Sighing, she obeyed his command and stared at him with as much chutzpah as she could muster. Rolling onto her back, she tucked her hands behind her head. "Have I brought a voyeur into my home?" she asked with a tart bite in her voice. It would do no good to let him see how much he affected her.

Leo yawned and stretched, his eyes heavy-lidded. "It's not my fault you had too much wine at dinner."

"I did not," she said indignantly. "I'm just tired, because the baby—"

"Gotcha," he said smugly, his eyes gleaming with mischief.

She sat up and ran her hands through her hair, crossing her legs but being careful not to bump Teddy. "Very funny. How long was I out?"

He shrugged. "Not long." His hot stare told her more clearly than words what he was thinking. They had rocketed from acquaintances to sleeping partners at warp speed. It was going to be difficult to pretend otherwise.

Her breasts ached and her mouth was dry. Sexual tension

shimmered between them like unseen vines drawing them ever closer. The only thing keeping them apart was a baby.

A baby who was her responsibility. That reality drew her back from the edge, though the decision to be clear-headed was a painful one. "I think we'll say good-night," she muttered. "Feel free to stay up as long as you like. But please bank the fire before you go to bed."

His gaze never faltered as she scooped up Teddy and gathered his things. "We have to talk about this," he said, the blunt words a challenge.

It took a lot, but she managed to look him straight in the eyes with a calm smile. "I don't know what you mean. Good night, Leo."

At two o'clock, he gave up the fight to sleep. He was wired, and his body pulsed with arousal, his sex full and hard. Neither of which condition was conducive to slumber. The *New York Times* bestseller he had opened failed to hold his attention past the first chapter. Cursing as he climbed out of his warm bed to pace the floor, he stopped suddenly and listened.

Faintly, but distinctly, he heard a baby cry.

It was all the excuse he needed. Throwing a thin, gray wool robe over his navy silk sleep pants, he padded into the hall, glad of the thick socks that Hattie had packed for him. Undoubtedly she had imagined him needing them if it snowed and he wore his boots. But they happened to be perfect for a man who wanted to move stealthily about the house.

In the hallway, he paused, trying to locate his landlady. There was a faint light under her door, but not Teddy's. The kid cried again, a fretful, middle-of-the-night whimper. Without weighing the consequences, Leo knocked.

Seconds later, the door opened a crack. Phoebe peered

out at him, her expression indiscernible in the gloom. "What's wrong? What do you want?"

Her stage whisper was comical given the fact that Teddy was clearly awake.

"You need some backup?"

"I'm fine." She started to close the door, but he stuck his foot in the gap, remembering at the last instant that he wasn't wearing shoes.

She pushed harder than he anticipated, and his socks were less protection than he expected. Pain shot up his leg. He groaned, jerking backward and nearly falling on his ass. Hopping on one foot, he pounded his fist against the wall to keep from letting loose with a string of words definitely not rated for kid ears.

Now Phoebe flung the door open wide, her face etched in dismay. "Are you hurt? Oh, heavens, of course you are. Here," she said. "Hold him while I get ice."

Without warning, his arms were full of a squirmy little body that smelled of spit-up and Phoebe's light floral scent. "But I..." He followed her down the hall, wincing at every step, even as Teddy's grumbles grew louder.

By the time he made it to the living room, Phoebe had turned on a couple of lamps and filled a dish towel with ice cubes. Her fingers curled around his biceps. "Give me the baby and sit down," she said, sounding frazzled and irritated, and anything but amorous. She pushed him toward the sofa. "Put your leg on the couch and let me see if you broke anything."

Teddy objected to the jostling and cried in earnest. Leo lost his balance and flopped down onto the sofa so hard that the baby's head and Leo's chin made contact with jarring force.

"Damn it to hell." He lay back, half-dazed, as Phoebe plucked Teddy from his arms and sat at the opposite end of the sofa. Before he could object, she had his leg in her lap and was peeling off his sock.

When slim, cool fingers closed around the bare arch of his foot, Leo groaned again. This time for a far different reason. Having Phoebe stroke his skin was damned arousing, even if he was in pain. Her thumb pressed gently, moving from side to side to assess the damage.

Leo hissed, a sharp involuntary inhalation. Phoebe winced. "Sorry. Am I hurting you too badly?"

She glanced sideways and her eyes grew big. His robe had opened when he lost his balance. Most of his chest was bare, and it was impossible to miss the erection that tented his sleep pants. He actually saw the muscles in her throat ripple as she swallowed.

"It feels good," he muttered. "Don't stop."

But Teddy shrieked in earnest now, almost inconsolable.

Phoebe dropped Leo's foot like it was a live grenade, scooting out from under his leg and standing. "Put the ice on it," she said, sounding breathless and embarrassed. "I'll be back."

Phoebe sank into the rocker in Teddy's room, her whole body trembling with awareness. The baby curled into her shoulder as she rubbed his back and sang to him quietly. He wasn't hungry. She had given him a bottle barely an hour ago. His only problem now was that his mouth hurt. She'd felt the tiny sharp edge of a tooth on his bottom gum and knew it was giving him fits. "Poor darling," she murmured. Reaching for the numbing drops, she rubbed a small amount on his sore mouth.

Teddy sucked her fingertip, snuffled and squirmed, then gradually subsided into sleep. She rocked him an extra five minutes just to make sure. When he was finally out, she laid him in his crib and tiptoed out of the room.

Her bed called out to her. She was weaving on her feet,

wrapped in a thick blanket of exhaustion. But she had told Leo she would come back. And in truth, nothing but cowardice could keep her from fulfilling that promise.

When she returned to the living room, it was filled with shadows, only a single lamp burning, though Leo had started another fire in the grate that gave off some illumination. He was watching television, but he switched it off as soon as she appeared. She hovered in the doorway, abashed by the sexual currents drawing her to this enigma of a man. "How's the foot?"

"See for yourself."

It was a dare, and she recognized it as such. Her legs carried her forward, even as her brain shouted, *Stop. Stop.* She wasn't so foolish this time as to sit down on the sofa. Instead, she knelt and removed the makeshift ice pack, setting it aside on a glass dish. Leo's foot was bruising already. A thin red line marked where the sharp corner of the door had scraped him.

"How does it feel?" she asked quietly.

Leo sat up, wincing, as he pulled his thick wool sock into place over his foot and ankle. "I'll live."

When he leaned forward with his forearms resting on his knees, he was face-to-face with her. "Unless you have an objection," he said, "I'm going to kiss you now." A lock of hair fell over his forehead. His voice was husky and low, sending shivers down her spine. The hour was late, that crazy time when dawn was far away and the night spun on, seemingly forever.

She licked her lips, feeling her nipples furl tightly, even as everything else in her body loosened with the warm flow of honey. "No objections," she whispered, wondering if he had woven some kind of spell over her while she was sleeping.

Slowly, gently, perhaps giving her time to resist, he cupped her cheeks with his hands, sliding his fingers into her hair and massaging her scalp. His thumbs ran along her jawline, pausing when he reached the little indentation beneath her ear.

"God, you're beautiful," he groaned, resting his forehead against hers. She could feel the heat radiating from his bare chest. All on their own, her hands came up to touch him, to flatten over his rib cage, to explore miles of warm, smooth skin. Well-defined pectoral muscles gave way to a thin line of hair that led to a flat belly corded with more muscles.

She felt drunk with pleasure. So long…it had been so long. And though she had encountered opportunities to be intimate with men during the past three years, none of them had been as tempting as Leo Cavallo. "What are we doing?" she asked raggedly, almost beyond the point of reason.

He gathered handfuls of her hair and played with it, pulling her closer. "Getting to know each other," he whispered. His mouth settled over hers, lips firm and confident. She opened to him, greedy for more of the hot pleasure that built at the base of her abdomen and made her shift restlessly.

When his tongue moved lazily between her lips, she met it with hers, learning the taste of him as she had wanted to so badly, experimenting with the little motions that made him shudder and groan. He held her head tightly now, dragging her to him, forcing her neck to arch so he could deepen the kiss. He tasted of toothpaste and determination.

Her hands clung to his wrists. "You're good at this," she panted. "A little too good."

"It's you," he whispered. "It's you." He moved down beside her so that they were chest to chest. "Tell me to stop, Phoebe." Wildly he kissed her, his hands roving over her back and hips. They were so close, his erection pressed into her belly.

She was wearing her usual knit pajamas, nothing sexy about them. But when his big hands trespassed beneath the elastic waistband and cupped her butt, she felt like a desirable woman. It had been so long since a man had touched her. And this wasn't just any man.

It was Leo. Big, brawny Leo, who looked as if he could move mountains for a woman, and yet paradoxically touched her so gently she wanted to melt into him and never leave his embrace. "Make love to me, Leo. Please. I need you so much…."

He dragged her to her feet and drew her closer to the fireplace. Standing on the bearskin rug, he pulled her top over her head. As he stared at her breasts, he cradled one in each hand, squeezing them carefully, plumping them with an expression that made her feel wanton and hungry.

At last looking at her face, he rubbed her nipples lightly as he kissed her nose, her cheeks, her eyes. His expression was warmly sensual, wickedly hot. "You make a man weak," he said. "I want to do all sorts of things to you, but I don't know where to start."

She should have felt awkward or embarrassed. But instead, exhilaration fizzed in her veins, making her breathing choppy. His light touch was not enough. She twined her arms around his neck, rubbing her lower body against his. "Does this give you any ideas?"

Eight

Leo was torn on a rack of indecision. Phoebe was here… in his arms…willing. But some tiny shred of decency in his soul insisted on being heard. The timing wasn't right. *This* wasn't right.

Cursing himself inwardly with a groan of anguish for the effort it took to stop the train on the tracks, he removed her arms from around his neck and stepped back. "We can't," he said. "I won't take advantage of you."

Barely able to look at what he was saying no to, he grabbed her pajama top and thrust it toward her. "Put this on."

Phoebe obeyed instantly as mortification and anger colored her face. "I'm not a child, Leo. I make my own decisions."

He wanted to comfort her, but touching her again was out of the question. An explanation would have to suffice. He hoped she understood him. "A tree demolished one of your cabins. You're caring for a teething baby, who has kept you up big chunks of the past two nights. Stress and exhaustion are no basis for making decisions." He of all people should know. "I don't want to be that man you regret when the sun comes up."

She wrapped her arms around her waist, glaring at him with thinly veiled hurt. "I should toss you out on your ass," she said, the words holding a faint but audible tremor.

His heart contracted. "I hope you won't." There were things he needed to tell her before they became intimate, and if he wasn't ready to come clean, then he wasn't ready to have sex with Phoebe. He hurt just looking at her. With her hair mussed and her protective posture, she seemed far younger than he knew her to be. Achingly vulnerable.

She lifted her chin. "We won't do this again. You keep to yourself, and I'll keep my end of the bargain. Good night, Leo." Turning on her heel, she left him.

The room seemed cold and lonely in her absence. Had he made the most colossal mistake of his life? The fire between the two of them burned hot and bright. She was perfection in his arms, sensual, giving, as intuitive a lover as he had ever envisaged.

Despite his unfilled passion, he knew he had done the right thing. Phoebe wasn't the kind of woman who had sex without thinking it through. Despite her apparent willingness tonight to do just that, he knew she would have blamed both herself and him when it was all over.

What he wanted from her, if indeed he had a chance of ever getting close to her again, was trust. He had secrets to share. And he suspected she did, as well. So he could wait for the other, the carnal satisfaction. Maybe....

Phoebe climbed into her cold bed with tears of humiliation wetting her cheeks. No matter what Leo said, tonight had been a rejection. What kind of man could call a halt when he was completely aroused and almost at the point of penetration? Only one who wasn't fully involved or committed to the act of lovemaking.

Perhaps she had inadvertently stimulated him with her foot massage. And maybe the intimacy of their nap in front of the fire had given him a buzz. But in the end, Phoebe simply wasn't who or what he wanted.

The fact that she could be badly hurt by a man she had met only recently gave her pause. Was she so desperate? So lonely? Tonight's debacle had given her some painful truths to examine.

But self-reflection would have to wait, because despite her distress, she could barely keep her eyes open....

Leo slept late the next morning. Not intentionally, but because he had been up much of the night pacing the floor. Sometime before dawn he had taken a shower and pleasured himself, but it had been a hollow exercise whose only purpose was to allow him to find oblivion in much-needed sleep.

The clock read almost ten when he made his way to the front of the house. He liked the open floor plan of the living room and kitchen, because it gave fewer places for Phoebe to hide.

Today, however, he was dumbstruck to find that she was nowhere in the house. And Teddy's crib was empty.

A twinge of panic gripped him until he found both of them out on the front porch chatting with the man who had come to remove the enormous fallen oak tree. When he stepped outside, Phoebe's quick disapproving glance reminded him that he had neither shaved nor combed his hair.

The grizzled workman who could have been anywhere from fifty to seventy saluted them with tobacco-stained fingers and headed down the lane to where he had parked his truck.

"I'm sorry," Leo said stiffly. "I was supposed to be handling this."

Phoebe's lips smiled, but her gaze was wintry. "No problem. Teddy and I dealt with it. If you'll excuse me, I have to get him down for his morning nap."

"But I—"

She shut the door in his face, leaving him out in the cold…literally.

He paused on the porch to count to ten, or maybe a hundred. Then, when he thought he had a hold on his temper, he went back inside and scavenged the kitchen for a snack to hold him until lunch. A couple of pieces of cold toast he found on a plate by the stove would have to do. He slathered them with some of Phoebe's homemade strawberry jam and sat down at the table. When Phoebe returned, he had finished eating and had also realized that he needed a favor. Not a great time to ask, but what the heck.

She ignored him pointedly, but he wasn't going to let a little cold shoulder put him off. "May I use your phone?" he asked politely.

"Why?"

"I'm going to order a new phone from your carrier since mine is virtually useless, and I also want to get internet service going. I'll pay the contract fees for a year, but when I leave you can drop it if you want to."

"That's pretty expensive for a short-term solution. It must be nice to be loaded."

He ground his teeth together, reminding himself that she was still upset about last night. "I won't apologize for having money," he said quietly. "I work very hard."

"Is it really that important to stay plugged in? Can't you go cold turkey for two months?" Phoebe was pale. She looked at him as if she would put him on the first plane out if she could.

How had they become combatants? He stared at her until her cheeks flushed and she looked away. "Technology and business are not demons," he said. "We live in the information age."

"And what about your recovery?"

"What about it?"

"I got the impression that you were supposed to stay away from business in order to rest and recuperate."

"I can do that and still have access to the world."

She took a step in his direction. "Can you? Can you really? Because from where I'm standing, you look like a guy who is determined to get what he wants when he wants it. Your doctor may have given you orders. Your brother may have, as well. But I doubt you respect them enough to really do what they've asked."

Her harsh assessment hit a little too close to home. "I'm following doctor's orders, I swear. Though it's really none of your business." The defensive note in his voice made him cringe inwardly. Was he honestly the ass she described?

"Do what you have to do," she said, pulling her phone from her pocket and handing it to him. Her expression was a mix of disappointment and resignation. "But I would caution you to think long and hard about the people who love you. And why it is that you're here."

At that moment, Leo saw a large delivery truck pull up in front of the cabin. Good, his surprise had arrived. Maybe it would win him some brownie points with Phoebe. And deflect her from the uncomfortable subject of his recuperation.

She went to the door as the bell rang. "But I didn't order anything," she protested when the man in brown set a large box just inside the door.

"Please sign here, ma'am," he said patiently.

The door slammed and Phoebe stared down at the box as if it possibly contained dynamite.

"Open it," Leo said.

Phoebe couldn't help being a little anxious when she tore into the package. It didn't have foreign postage, so it was not from her sister. She pulled back the cardboard flaps and stared in amazement. The box was full of food—an expensive ham, casseroles preserved in freezer packs, desserts, fresh fruit, the list was endless.

She turned to look at Leo, who now lay sprawled on the sofa. "Did you do this?"

He shrugged, his arms outstretched along the back of the couch. "Before I lost my temper yesterday about my work email, I scrolled through my personal messages and decided to contact a good buddy of mine, a cordon bleu chef in Atlanta who owes me a favor. I felt bad about you agreeing to cook for me all the time, so I asked him to hook us up with some meals. He's going to send a box once a week."

Her mind reeled. Not only was this a beautifully thoughtful gesture, it was also incredibly expensive. She stared at the contents, feeling her dismal mood slip away. A man like Leo would be a lovely companion for the following two months, even if all he wanted from her was friendship.

Before she could lose her nerve, she crossed the room, leaned down and kissed him on the cheek. His look of shock made her face heat. "Don't worry," she said wryly. "That was completely platonic. I merely wanted to say thank-you for a lovely gift."

He grasped her wrist, his warm touch sending ripples of heat all the way up her arm. "You're welcome, Phoebe. But of course, it's partially a selfish thing. I get to enjoy the bounty, as well." His smile could charm the birds off the trees. In repose, Leo's rugged features seemed austere, even intimidating. But when he smiled, the force of his charisma increased exponentially.

Feeling something inside her soul ease at the cessation of hostilities, she returned the smile, though she pulled away and put a safe distance between them. It was no use being embarrassed or awkward around Leo. She wasn't so heartless as to throw him out, and truthfully, she didn't want to. Teddy was a sweetheart, but having another adult in the house was a different kind of stimulation.

Suddenly, she remembered what she had wanted to ask Leo before last night when everything ended so poorly. "Tell me," she said. "Would you object to having Christmas decorations in the house?"

"That's a strange segue, but why would I object?" he asked. "I'm not a Scrooge."

"I never thought you were, but you might have ethnic or religious reasons to abstain."

"No problems on either score," he chuckled. "Does this involve a shopping trip?"

"No. Actually, I have boxes and boxes of stuff in the attic. When I moved here, I wasn't in the mood to celebrate. Now, with Teddy in the house, it doesn't seem right to ignore the holiday. I wasn't able to take it all down on my own. Do you mind helping? I warn you…it's a lot of stuff."

"Including a tree?"

She smiled beseechingly. "My old one is artificial, and not all that pretty. I thought it might be fun to find one in the woods."

"Seriously?"

"Well, of course. I own thirty acres. Surely we can discover something appropriate."

He lifted a skeptical eyebrow. *"We?"*

"Yes, we. Don't be so suspicious. I'm not sending you out in the cold all on your own. I have one of those baby carrier things. Teddy and I will go with you. Besides, I don't think men are the best judge when it comes to locating the perfect tree."

"You wound me," he said, standing and clutching his chest. "I have excellent taste."

"This cabin has space limitations to consider. And admit it. Men always think bigger is better."

"So do women as a rule."

His naughty double entendre was delivered with a straight face, but his eyes danced with mischief. Phoebe knew her cheeks had turned bright red. She felt the heat. "Are we still talking about Christmas trees?" she asked, her throat dry as the Sahara.

"You tell me."

"I think you made yourself pretty clear last night," she snapped.

He looked abashed. "I never should have let things go that far. We need to take baby steps, Phoebe. Forced proximity makes for a certain intimacy, but I respect you too much to take advantage of that."

"And if *I* take advantage of you?"

She was appalled to hear the words leave her mouth. Apparently her libido trumped both her pride and her common sense.

Leo's brows drew together in a scowl. He folded his arms across his broad chest. With his legs braced in a fighting stance, he suddenly seemed far more dangerous. Today he had on old jeans and a cream wool fisherman's sweater.

Everything about him from his head to his toes screamed wealth and privilege. So why hadn't he chosen some exclusive resort for his sabbatical? A place with tennis courts and spas and golf courses?

He still hadn't answered her question. The arousal swirling in her belly congealed into a small knot of embarrassment. Did he get some kind of sadistic kick out of flirting with women and then shutting them down?

"Never mind," she said, the words tight. "I understand."

He strode toward her, his face a thundercloud. "You don't understand a single damn thing," he said roughly. Before she could protest or back up or initiate any other of a dozen protective moves, he dragged her to his chest, wrapped one arm around her back and used his free hand to anchor her chin and tip her face up to his.

His thick-lashed brown eyes, afire with emotion and seemingly able to peer into her soul, locked on hers and dared her to look away. "Make no mistake, Phoebe," he said. "I want you. And Lord willing, I'm going to have you. When we finally make it to a bed—or frankly any flat surface, 'cause I'm not picky—I'm going to make love to you until we're both too weak to stand. But in the meantime, *you're* going to behave. *I'm* going to behave. Got it?"

Time stood still. Just like in the movies. Every one of her senses went on high alert. He was breathing hard, his chest rising and falling rapidly. When he grabbed her, she had braced one hand reflexively on his shoulder, though the idea of holding him at bay was ludicrous. She couldn't manage that even if she wanted to. His strength and power were evident despite whatever illness had plagued him.

Dark stubble covered his chin. He could have been a pirate or a highwayman or any of the renegade heroes in the historical novels her sister read. Phoebe was so close she could inhale the warm scent of him. A great bear of a man not long from his bed.

She licked her lips, trembling enough that she was glad of his support. "Define *behave*." She kissed his chin, his wrist, the fingers caressing her skin.

Leo fought her. Not outwardly. But from within. His struggle was written on his face. But he didn't release her. Not this time.

The curse he uttered as he gave in to her provocation was heartfelt and earthy as he encircled her with both arms and half lifted her off her feet. His mouth crushed hers, taking…giving no quarter. His masculine force was exhilarating. She was glad she was tall and strong, because it gave her the ability to match him kiss for kiss.

Baby steps be damned. She and Leo had jumped over miles of social convention and landed in a time of desperation, of elemental reality. Like the prehistoric people who had lived in these hills and valleys centuries before, the base human instinct to mate clawed its way to the forefront, making a mockery of soft words and tender sentiments.

This was passion in its most raw form. She rubbed against him, desperate to get closer. “Leo,” she groaned, unable to articulate what she wanted, what she needed. “Leo…”

Nine

He was lost. Months of celibacy combined with the uncertainty of whether his body would be the same after his attack walloped him like a sucker punch. In his brain he repeated a frenzied litany. *Just a kiss. Just a kiss, just a kiss...*

His erection was swollen painfully, the taut skin near bursting. His lungs had contracted to half capacity, and black dots danced in front of his eyes. Phoebe felt like heaven in his arms. She was feminine and sinfully curved in all the right places, but she wasn't fragile. He liked that. No. Correction. He loved that. She kissed him without apology, no half measures.

Her skin smelled like scented shower gel and baby powder. This morning her hair was again tamed in a fat braid. He wrapped it around his fist and tugged, drawing back her head so he could nip at her throat with sharp love bites.

The noise she made, part cry, part moan, hit him in the gut. He lifted her, grunting when her legs wrapped around his waist. They were fully clothed, but he thrust against her, tormenting them both with pressure that promised no relief.

Without warning, Phoebe struggled to get away from him. He held her more tightly, half crazed with the urge to take her hard and fast.

She pushed at his chest. “Leo. I hear the baby. He’s awake.”

Finally, her breathless words penetrated the fog of lust that chained him. He dropped her to her feet and staggered backward, his heart threatening to pound through the wall of his chest.

Afraid of his own emotions, he strode to the door where his boots sat, shoved his feet into them, flung open the door and left the cabin, never looking back.

Phoebe had never once seen Teddy’s advent into her life as anything but a blessing. Until today. Collecting herself as best she could, she walked down the hall and scooped him out of his crib. “Well, that was a short nap,” she said with a laugh that bordered on hysteria. Teddy, happy now that she had rescued him, chortled as he clutched her braid. His not-so-nice baby smell warned her that he had a messy diaper, probably the reason he had awakened so soon.

She changed him and then put him on a blanket on the floor while she tidied his room. Even as she automatically carried out the oft-repeated chores, her mind was attuned to Leo’s absence. He had left without a coat. Fortunately, he was wearing a thick sweater, and thankfully, the temperature had moderated today, climbing already into the low fifties.

She was appalled and remorseful about what had happened, all of it her fault. Leo, ever the gentleman, had done his best to be levelheaded about confronting their attraction amidst the present situation. But Phoebe, like a lonely, deprived spinster, had practically attacked him. It was no wonder things had escalated.

Men, unless they were spoken for—and sometimes not even then—were not physically wired to refuse women who threw out such blatant invitations. And that’s what

Phoebe had done. She had made it abysmally clear that she was his for the taking.

Leo had reacted. Of course. What red-blooded, straight, unattached male wouldn't? *Oh, God.* How was she going to face him? And how did they deal with this intense but ill-timed attraction?

A half hour later she held Teddy on her hip as she put away the abundance of food Leo's chef friend had sent. She decided to have the chimichangas for lunch. They were already prepared. All she had to do was thaw them according to the directions and then whip up some rice and salad to go alongside.

An hour passed, then two. She only looked out the window a hundred times or so. What if he was lost? Or hurt? Or sick? Her stomach cramped, thinking of the possibilities.

Leo strode through the forest until his legs ached and his lungs gasped for air. It felt good to stretch his physical limits, to push himself and know that he was okay. Nothing he did, however, erased his hunger for Phoebe. At first he had been suspicious of his immediate fascination. His life had recently weathered a rough patch, and feminine companionship hadn't even been on his radar. That was how he rationalized his response to Phoebe, even on the day they'd met.

But he knew it was more than that. She was a virus in his blood, an immediate, powerful affliction that was in its own way as dangerous as his heart attack. Phoebe had the power to make his stay here either heaven or hell. And if it were the latter, he might as well cut and run right now.

But even as he thought it, his ego *and* his libido shouted a vehement *hell, no.* Phoebe might be calling the shots as his landlady, but when it came to sex, the decision was already made. He and Phoebe were going to be lovers. The only question was when and where.

His head cleared as he walked, and the physical exertion gradually drained him to the point that he felt able to go back. He had followed the creek upstream for the most part, not wanting to get lost. In some places the rhododendron thickets were so dense he was forced to climb up and around. When he finally halted, he was partway up the mountainside. To his surprise, he could see a tiny section of Phoebe's chimney sticking up out of the woods.

Perhaps Luc had been right. Here, in an environment so antithetical to Leo's own, he saw himself in a new light. His world was neither bad nor good in comparison to Phoebe's. But it was different.

Was that why Phoebe had come here? To get perspective? And if so, had she succeeded? Would she ever go back to her earlier life?

He sat for a moment on a large granite boulder, feeling the steady pumping of his heart. Its quiet, regular beats filled him with gratitude for everything he had almost lost. Perhaps it was the nature of humans to take life for granted. But now, like the sole survivor of a plane crash, he felt obliged to take stock, to search for meaning, to tear apart the status quo and see if it was really worthy of his devotion.

Amidst those noble aspirations, he shamefully acknowledged if only to himself that he yearned to be back at his desk. He ran a billion-dollar company, and ran it well. He was Leo Cavallo, CFO of a textile conglomerate that spanned the globe. Like a recovering addict, his hands itched for a fix…for the pulse-pumping, mentally stimulating, nonstop schedule that he understood so intimately.

He knew people used *workaholic* as a pejorative term, often with a side order of pitying glances and shakes of the head. But, honest to God, he didn't see anything wrong with having passion for a job and doing it well. It irritated the hell out of him to imagine all the balls that were being dropped in his absence. Not that Luc and the rest of the team weren't as smart as he was…it wasn't that.

Leo, however, gave Cavallo his everything.

In December, the prep work began for year-end reports. Who was paying attention to those sorts of things while Leo was AWOL? It often became necessary to buy or sell some smaller arms of the business for the appropriate tax benefit. The longer he thought about it, the more agitated he became. He could feel his blood pressure escalating.

As every muscle in his body tensed, he had to force himself to take deep breaths, to back away from an invisible cliff. In the midst of his agitation, an inquisitive squirrel paused not six inches from Leo's boot to scrabble in the dirt for an acorn. Chattering his displeasure with the human who had invaded his territory, the small animal worked furiously, found the nut and scampered away.

Leo smiled. And in doing so, felt the burden he carried shift and ease. He inhaled sharply, filling his lungs with clean air. As a rule, he thrived on the sounds of traffic and the ceaseless hum of life in a big city. Yet even so, he found himself noticing the stillness of the woods. The almost imperceptible presence of creatures who went about their business doing whatever they were created to do.

They were lucky, Leo mused wryly. No great soul-searching for them. Merely point A to point B. And again. And again.

He envied them their singularity of purpose, though he had no desire to be a hamster on a wheel. As a boy, his teachers had identified him as gifted. His parents had enrolled him in special programs and sent him to summer camps in astrophysics and geology and other erudite endeavors.

All of it interested and engaged him, but he never quite fit in anywhere. His size and athletic prowess made him a target of suspicion in the realm of the nerds, and his academic successes and love for school excluded him from the jock circle.

His brother became, and still was, his best friend. They squabbled and competed as siblings did, but their bond ran deep. Which was why Leo was stuck here, like a storybook character, lost in the woods. Because Luc had insisted it was important. And Leo owed his brother. If Luc believed Leo needed this time to recover, then it was probably so.

Rising to his feet and stretching, he shivered hard. After his strenuous exercise, he had sat too long, and now he was chilled and stiff. Suddenly, he wanted nothing more than to see Phoebe. He couldn't share his soul-searching and his minor epiphanies with her, because he hadn't yet come clean about his health. But he wanted to be with her. In any way and for any amount of time fate granted him.

Though it was not his way, he made an inward vow to avoid the calendar and to concentrate on the moment. Perhaps there was more to Leo Cavallo than met the eye. If so, he had two months to figure it out.

Phoebe couldn't decide whether to cry or curse when Leo finally came through the door, his tall, broad silhouette filling the doorway. Her giddy relief that he was okay warred with irritation because he had disappeared for so long without an explanation. Of course, if he had been living in his own cabin, she would not have been privy to his comings and goings.

But this was different. He and Phoebe were cohabiting. Which surely gave her some minimal rights when it came to social conventions. Since she didn't have the guts to chastise him, her only choice was to swallow her pique and move forward.

As he entered and kicked off his muddy boots, he smiled sheepishly. "Have you already eaten?"

"Yours is warming in the oven." She returned the smile,

but stayed seated. It wasn't necessary to hover over him like a doting housewife. Leo was a big boy.

Teddy played with a plastic straw while Phoebe enjoyed a second cup of coffee. As Leo joined her at the table, she nodded at his plate. "Your friend is a genius. Please thank him for me. Though I'm sure I'll be ruing the additional calories."

Leo dug into his food with a gusto that suggested he had walked long and hard. "You're right. I've even had him cater dinner parties at my home. Makes me very popular, I can tell you."

As he finished his meal, Phoebe excused herself to put a drooping Teddy down for his nap. "I have a white noise machine I use sometimes in his room, so I think we'll be able to get the boxes down without disturbing him," she said. "And if he takes a long afternoon nap like he sometimes does, we can get a lot of the decorating done if you're still up for it."

Leo cocked his head, leaning his chair back on two legs. "I'm definitely *up* for it," he said, his lips twitching.

She couldn't believe he would tease about their recent insanity. "That's not funny."

"You don't have to tell me." He grinned wryly. "I realize in theory that couples with young children have sex. I just don't understand how they do it."

His hangdog expression made Phoebe burst into laughter, startling Teddy, who had almost fallen asleep on her shoulder. "Well, you don't have to worry about it," she said sharply, giving him a look designed to put him in his place. "All I have on the agenda this afternoon is decking the halls."

Leo had seldom spent as much time alone with a woman as he had with Phoebe. He was beginning to learn her expressions and to read them with a fair amount of accuracy.

When she reappeared after settling the baby, her excitement was palpable.

"The pull-down steps to the attic are in that far corner over there." She dragged a chair in that direction. "I'll draw the cord and you get ready to steady the steps as they come down."

He did as she asked, realizing ruefully that this position put him on eye level with her breasts. Stoically, he looked in the opposite direction. Phoebe dragged on the rope. The small framed-off section of the ceiling opened up to reveal a very sturdy set of telescoping stairs.

Leo grabbed the bottom section and pulled, easing it to the floor. He set his foot on the first rung. "What do you want me to get first?"

"The order doesn't really matter. I want it all. Except for the tree. That can stay. Here," she said, handing him a flashlight from her pocket. "I almost forgot."

Leo climbed, using the heavy flashlight to illuminate cobwebs so he could swat them away. Perhaps because the cabin was fairly new, or maybe because Phoebe was an organized sort, her attic was not a hodgepodge of unidentified mess. Neatly labeled cardboard cartons and large plastic tubs had been stacked in a tight perimeter around the top of the stairs within easy reach.

Some of the containers were fairly heavy. He wondered how she had managed to get them up here. He heard a screech and bent to stick his head out the hole. "What's wrong?"

Phoebe shuddered. "A spider. I didn't think all this stuff would have gotten so icky in just three years."

"Shall I stop?"

She grimaced. "No. We might as well finish. I'll just take two or three showers when we're done."

He tossed her a small box that was light as a feather. In neat black marker, Phoebe had labeled *Treetop Angel*.

When she caught it, he grinned at her. "I'd be glad to help with that body check. I'll search the back of your hair for creepy-crawlies."

"I can't decide if that's revolting or exciting. Seems like you made a similar offer when you were convincing me to let you stay. Only then, you promised to kill *hypothetical* bugs."

"Turns out I was right, doesn't it?" He returned to his task, his body humming with arousal. He'd never paid much attention to the holidays. But with Phoebe, suddenly all the chores surrounding Christmas took on a whole new dimension.

By the time he had brought down the last box and stored away the stairs, Phoebe was elbows-deep into a carton of ornaments.

She held up a tiny glass snowman. "My grandmother gave me this when I was eight."

He crouched beside her. "Is she still alive?"

"No. Sadly."

"And your parents?" He was close enough to brush his lips across the nape of her neck, but he refrained.

Phoebe sank back on her bottom and crossed her legs, working to separate a tangle of glittery silver beads. "My parents were hit by a drunk driver when my sister and I were in high school. A very kind foster family took us in and looked after us until we were able to graduate and get established in college."

"And since then?"

"Dana and I are very close."

"No significant others in your past?"

She frowned at the knot that wouldn't give way. "What about your family, Leo?"

He heard the unspoken request for privacy, so he backed off. "Oddly enough, you and I have that in common. Luc and I were seventeen and eighteen when we lost our parents. Only it was a boating accident. My father loved his nautical toys, and he was addicted to the adrenaline rush of speed. We were in Italy visiting my grandfather one spring break. Dad took a friend's boat out, just he and my mom. On the way back, he hit a concrete piling at high speed as they were approaching the dock."

"Oh, my God." Her hands stilled. "How dreadful."

He nodded, the memory bleak even after all this time. "Grandfather insisted on having autopsies done. My mother wasn't wearing a life jacket. She drowned when she was flung into the water. I took comfort in the fact that she was probably unconscious when she died, because she had a severe head wound."

"And your father?"

Leo swallowed. "He had a heart attack. That's what caused him to lose control of the boat." Repeating the words stirred something dark and ugly in his gut. To know that he was his father's son had never pained him more than in the past few months.

Phoebe put a hand on his arm. "But wasn't he awfully young?"

"Forty-one."

"Oh, Leo. I'm so very sorry."

He shrugged. "It was a long time ago. After the funerals, Grandfather took Luc and I back to Italy to live with him. He insisted we attend college in Rome. Some would say we were lucky to have had such an education, but we were miserable for a long time. Our grief was twofold, of course. On top of that, Grandfather is not an easy man to love." He hesitated for a moment. "I don't tell many people that story, but you understand what it feels like to have the rug ripped out from under your feet."

"I do indeed. My parents were wonderful people. They always encouraged Dana and me to go for any goal we wanted. Never any question of it being *too hard* or *not a girl thing.* Losing them changed our lives."

Silence fell like a pall. Leo tugged at her braid. "Sorry. I didn't mean to take us down such a dismal path."

She rested her head against his hand. "It's hard not to think of family at this time of year, especially the ones we've lost. I'm glad you're here, Leo."

Ten

She wasn't sure who initiated the intimate contact. Their lips met briefly, sweetly. The taste of him was as warm and comfortable as a summer rain. She felt the erotic river of molten lava hidden just beneath the surface, but as if by unspoken consent, the kiss remained soft and easy.

Leaning into him, she let herself be bolstered by his strength. One big arm supported her back. He was virile and sexy. She couldn't be blamed for wanting more. "Leo," she muttered.

All she said was his name, but she felt the shudder that ran through him. "What?" he asked hoarsely. "What, Phoebe?"

A million different answers hovered at the tip of her tongue. *Undress me. Touch my bare skin. Make love to me.* Instead, she managed to be sensible. "Let me put some music on to get us in the mood for decorating."

"I *am* in the mood," he grumbled. But he smiled when he said it and kissed the tip of her nose. Then he sobered. "To be absolutely clear, I want you in my bed, tonight, Phoebe. When the little man is sound asleep and not likely to interrupt us."

His eyes were dark chocolate, sinful and rich and designed to make a woman melt into their depths. She stared at him, weighing the risks. As a financial speculator, she played hunches and often came out on top. But taking Leo as a lover was infinitely more dangerous.

He was here only for a short while. And though Phoebe had made peace with her demons and embraced her new lifestyle, she was under no illusions that Leo had done the same. He was anxious to return home. Coming to the mountains had been some sort of penance for him, a healing ritual that he accepted under protest.

Leo would never be content to stagnate. He had too much energy, too much life.

She touched his cheek, knowing that her acquiescence was a forgone conclusion. "Yes. I'd like that, too. And I'm sorry that we can't be more spontaneous. A new relationship should be hot and crazy and passionate." *Like this morning when you nearly took me standing up.* Her pulse tripped and stumbled as her thighs tightened in remembrance.

Leo cupped her hand to his face with one big palm. "It will be, Phoebe, darlin'. Don't you worry about that."

To Phoebe's surprise and delight, the afternoon became one long, drawn-out session of foreplay. Leo built a fire so high and hot they both had to change into T-shirts to keep cool. Phoebe found a radio station that played classic Christmas songs. She teased Leo unmercifully when she realized he never remembered any of the second verses, and instead made up his own words.

Together, they dug out a collection of balsam-scented candles, lit them and set them on the coffee table. During the summer, the trapped heat in the attic had melted the wax a bit, so the ones that were supposed to be Christmas trees looked more like drunken bushes.

Phoebe laughed. "Perhaps I should just throw them away."

Leo shook his head. "Don't do that. They have *character.*"

"If you say so." She leaned down and squinted at them. "They look damaged to me. Beyond repair."

"Looks can be deceiving."

Something in his voice—an odd note—caught her attention. He was staring at the poor trees as if all the answers to life's great questions lay trapped in green wax.

What did Leo Cavallo know about being damaged? As far as Phoebe could see, he was at the peak of his physical strength and mental acuity. Sleek muscles whispered of his ability to hold a woman…to protect her. And in a contest of wits, she would need to stay on her toes to best him. Intelligence crackled in his eyes and in his repartee.

Leo was the whole package, and Phoebe wanted it all.

Gradually, the room was transformed. With Leo's assistance, Phoebe hung garland from the mantel and around the doorways, intertwining it with tiny white lights that sparkled and danced even in the daytime. She would have preferred fresh greenery. But with a baby to care for and a cabin to repair, she had to accept her limits.

Leo spent over an hour tacking silver, green and gold snowflakes to the ceiling. Far more meticulous than she would have been, he measured and arranged them until every glittering scrap of foil was perfectly placed. The masculine satisfaction on his face as he stood, neck craned, and surveyed his handiwork amused her, but she was quick to offer the appropriate accolades.

In addition to the misshapen candles, the coffee table now sported a red wool runner appliquéd in reindeer. The *Merry Christmas* rug she remembered from her home in Charlotte now lay in front of a new door. The kitchen table boasted dark green place mats and settings of Christmas china.

At long last, Leo flopped down on the sofa with a groan. "You *really* like Christmas, don't you?"

She joined him, curling into his embrace as naturally as if they were old friends. "I lost the spirit for a few years, but with Teddy here, this time I think it will be pretty magical." Weighing her words, she finally asked the question she had been dying to have him answer. "What about you, Leo? Your sister-in-law made your reservation for two months. But you'll go home for the holidays, won't you?"

Playing lazily with the ends of her braid, he sighed. "I hadn't really thought about it. Many times in the past six or eight years, Luc and I flew to Italy to be with Grandfather for Christmas. But when Luc and Hattie married the year before last, Grandfather actually came over here, though he swore it wouldn't be an annual thing, because the trip wore him out. Now, with two little ones, I think Luc and Hattie deserve their own family Christmas."

"And what about you?"

Leo shrugged. "I'll have an invitation or two, I'm sure."

"You could stay here with Teddy and me." Only when she said the words aloud did she realize how desperately she wanted him to say yes.

He half turned to face her. "Are you sure? I wouldn't want to intrude."

Was he serious? She was a single woman caring for a baby that wasn't hers in a lonely cabin in the woods. "I think we can make room," she said drily. Without pausing to think of the ramifications, she ran a hand through his thick hair. The color, rich chestnut shot through with dark gold, was far too gorgeous for a man, not really fair at all.

Leo closed his eyes and leaned back, a smile on his face, but fine tension in his body. "That would be nice…" he said, trailing off as though her gentle scalp massage was making it hard to speak.

She put her head on his chest. With only a thin navy

T-shirt covering his impressive upper physique, she could hear the steady *ka-thud, ka-thud, ka-thud* of his heart. "Perhaps we should wait and see how tonight goes," she muttered. "I'm out of practice, to be honest." Better he know now than later.

Moving so quickly that she never saw it coming, he took hold of her and placed her beneath him on the sofa, his long, solid frame covering hers as he kissed his way down her throat. One of his legs lodged between her thighs, opening her to the possibility of something reckless. She lifted her hips instinctively. "Don't stop," she pleaded.

He found her breasts and took one nipple between his teeth, wetting the fabric of her shirt and bra as he tormented her with a bite that was just short of pain. Fire shot from the place where his mouth touched her all the way to her core. Shivers of pleasure racked her.

Suddenly, Leo reared back, laughing and cursing.

Blankly, she stared up at him, her body at a fever pitch of longing. "What? Tell me, Leo."

"Listen. The baby's awake."

When a knock sounded at the door minutes later, Leo knew he and Phoebe had narrowly escaped embarrassment on top of sexual frustration. She was out of sight tending to Teddy, so Leo greeted the man at the door with a smile. "Can I help you?"

The old codger in overalls looked him up and down. "Name's Buford. These sugared pecans is from my wife. She knowed they were Miss Phoebe's favorite, so she made up an extra batch after she finished the ones for the church bazaar. Will you give 'em to her?"

Leo took the paper sack. "I'd be happy to. She's feeding the baby a bottle, I think, but she should be finished in a moment. Would you like to come in?"

"Naw. Thanks. Are you the fella that was going to rent the other cabin?"

"Yes, sir, I am."

"Don't be gettin' any ideas. Miss Phoebe's pretty popular with the neighbors. We look out fer her."

"I understand."

"You best get some extra firewood inside. Gonna snow tonight."

"Really?" The afternoon sunshine felt more like spring than Christmas.

"Weather changes quicklike around here."

"Thanks for the warning, Buford."

With a tip of his cap, the guy ambled away, slid into a rust-covered pickup truck and backed up to turn and return the way he had come.

Leo closed the door. Despite feeling like a sneaky child, he unfolded the top of the sack and stole three sugary pecans.

Phoebe caught him with his hand in the bag…literally. "What's that?" she asked, patting Teddy on the back to burp him.

Leo chewed and swallowed, barely resisting the urge to grab another handful of nuts. "Your farmer friend, Buford, came by. How old is he anyway?"

"Buford is ninety-eight and his wife is ninety-seven. They were both born in the Great Smoky Mountains before the land became a national park. The house Buford and Octavia now live in is the one he built for her when they married in the early 1930s, just as the Depression was gearing up."

"A log cabin?"

"Yes. With a couple of rambling additions. They still used an actual outhouse up until the mid-eighties when their kids and grandkids insisted that Buford and Octavia were getting too old to go outside in the dead of winter to do their business."

"What happened then?"

"The relatives chipped in and installed indoor plumbing."

"Good Lord." Leo did some rapid math. "If they married in the early thirties, then—"

"They'll be celebrating their eightieth anniversary in March."

"That seems impossible."

"She was seventeen. Buford one year older. It happened all the time."

"Not their ages. I mean the part about eighty years together. How can anything last that long?"

"I've wondered that myself. After all, even a thirty-five-year marriage is becoming harder to find among my peers' parents."

Leo studied Phoebe, trying to imagine her shoulders stooped with age and her beautiful skin lined with wrinkles. She would be lovely still at sixty, and even seventy. But closing in on a hundredth birthday? Could any couple plan on spending 85 percent of an entire life looking at the same face across the breakfast table every morning? It boggled the mind.

Somehow, though, when he really thought about it, he *was* able see Phoebe in that scenario. She was strong and adaptable and willing to step outside her comfort zone. He couldn't imagine ever being bored by her. She had a sharp mind and an entertaining sense of humor. Not to mention a body that wouldn't quit.

Leo, himself, had never fallen in love even once. Relationships, good ones, took time and effort. Until now, he'd never met a woman capable of making him think long term.

Phoebe was another story altogether. He still didn't fully understand the decision that had brought her to the mountains, but he planned on sticking around at least long enough to find out. She intrigued him, entertained him and aroused him. Perhaps it was their isolation, but he felt a connection that transcended common sense and entered the realm of the heart. He was hazy about what he wanted from her in the long run. But tonight's agenda was crystal clear.

He desired Phoebe. Deeply. As much and as painfully as a man could hunger for a woman. Barring any unforeseen circumstances, she was going to be his.

To Phoebe's eyes, Leo seemed to zone out for a moment. She didn't feel comfortable demanding an explanation, not even a joking "Penny for your thoughts." Instead, she tried a distraction. "Teddy is fed and dry and rested at the moment. If we're going to get a tree, the time is right."

Leo snapped out of his fog and nodded, staring at the baby. "You don't think it will be too cold?"

"I have a snowsuit to put on him. That should be plenty of insulation for today. I'll get the two of us ready. If you don't mind going out to the shed, you can get the ax. It's just inside the door."

"You have an ax?" He was clearly taken aback.

"Well, yes. How else would we cut down a tree?"

"But you told me you haven't had a Christmas tree since you've been here. Why do you need an ax?"

She shrugged. "I split my own wood. Or at least I did in the pre-Teddy days. Now I can't take the chance that something might happen to me and he'd be in the house helpless. So I pay a high school boy to do it."

"I'm not sure how wise it is for you to be so isolated and alone. What if you needed help in an emergency?"

"We have 911 access. And I have the landline phone in addition to my cell. Besides, the neighbors aren't all that far away."

"But a woman on her own is vulnerable in ways a man isn't."

She understood what he wasn't saying. And she'd had those same conversations with herself in the beginning. Sleeping had been difficult for a few months. Her imagination had run wild, conjuring up rapists and murderers and deviants like the Unabomber looking for places to hide out in her neck of the woods.

Eventually, she had begun to accept that living in the city carried the same risks. The only difference being that they were packaged differently.

"I understand what you're saying," Phoebe said. "And yes, there have been nights, like the recent storm for instance, when I've questioned my decision to live here. But I decided over time that the benefits outweigh the negatives, so I've stayed."

Leo looked as if he wanted to argue the point, but in the end, he shook his head, donned his gear and left.

It took longer than she expected to get the baby and herself ready to brave the outdoors. That had been the biggest surprise about keeping Teddy. Everything about caring for him was twice as complicated and time-consuming as she had imagined. Finally, though, she was getting the hang of things, and already, she could barely remember her life without the little boy.

Eleven

It was the perfect day for an excursion. Since men were still working at the cabin removing the last of the tree debris and getting ready to cover the whole structure with a heavy tarp, Phoebe turned in the opposite direction, walking side by side with Leo back down the road to a small lane which turned off to the left and meandered into the forest.

She had fastened Teddy into a sturdy canvas carrier with straps that crisscrossed at her back. Walking was her favorite form of exercise, but it took a quarter mile to get used to the extra weight on her chest. She kept her hand under Teddy's bottom. His body was comfortable and warm nestled against her.

Leo carried the large ax like it weighed nothing at all, when Phoebe knew for a fact that the wooden-handled implement was plenty heavy. He seemed pleased to be out of the house, whistling an off-key tune as they strode in amicable silence.

The spot where she hoped to find the perfect Christmas tree was actually an old home site, though only remnants of the foundation and the chimney remained. Small weather-roughened headstones nearby marked a modest family cemetery. Some of the writing on the stones was still legible, including several that read simply, Beloved Baby. It pained her to think of the tragic deaths from disease in those days.

But she had suffered more than her share of hurt. She liked to think she understood a bit of what those families had faced.

Leo frowned, seeing the poignant evidence of human lives loved and lost. "Does this belong to you?" The wind soughed in the trees, seeming to echo chattering voices and happy laughter of an earlier day.

"As much as you can own a graveyard, I guess. It's on my property. But if anyone ever showed up to claim this place, I would give them access, of course. If descendants exist, they probably don't even know this is here."

One of the infant markers caught his attention. "I can't imagine losing a child," he said, his expression grim. "I see how much Luc and Hattie love their two, and even though I'm not a parent, sometimes it terrifies me to think of all the things that happen in the world today."

"Will you ever want children of your own?" Her breath caught in her throat as she realized that his answer was very important to her.

He squatted and brushed leaves away from the base of the small lichen-covered stone. "I doubt it. I don't have the time, and frankly, it scares the hell out of me." Looking up at her, his smile was wry. But despite the humor, she realized he was telling the absolute truth.

Her stomach tightened in disappointment. "You're still young."

"The business is my baby. I'm content to let Luc carry on the family lineage."

Since she had no answer to that, the subject lapsed, but she knew she had been given fair warning. Not from any intentional ultimatum on Leo's part. The problem was, Phoebe had allowed her imagination to begin weaving fantasies. Along the way, her heart, once broken but well on the way to recovery, had decided to participate.

The result was an intense and sadly dead-end infatuation with Leo Cavallo.

She stroked Teddy's hair, smiling to see the interest he demonstrated in his surroundings. He was a happy, inquisitive baby. Since the day he was born, she had loved him terribly. But this time alone, just the two of them, and now with Leo, had cemented his place in her heart. Having to return him to his parents was going to be a dreadful wrench. The prospect was so dismal, she forced the thought away. Much more of this, and she was going to start quoting an infamous Southern belle. *I'll think about that tomorrow.*

Leo stood and stretched, rolling his shoulders, the ax on the ground propped against his hip. "I'm ready. Show me which one."

"Don't be silly. We have to make a careful decision."

"This is the world's biggest Christmas tree farm. I'd say you won't have too much trouble. How about that one right there?" He pointed at a fluffy cedar about five feet tall.

"Too small and the wrong variety. I'll know when I see it."

Leo took her arm and steered her toward a grouping of evergreens. "Anything here grab your fancy?"

She and Leo were both encased in layers of winter clothes. But she fancied she could feel the warmth of his fingers on her skin. A hundred years ago, Leo would have worked from dawn to dusk, providing for his family. At night, when the children were asleep in the loft, she could see him making love to his wife on a feather tick mattress in front of the fire. Entering *her,* Phoebe, with a fire, a passion he had kept banked during the daylight hours. Saving those special moments of intimacy for the dark of night.

Wishing she could peel out of her coat, she stripped off her gloves and removed her scarf. The image of a more primitive Leo was so real, her breasts ached for his touch. She realized she had worn too many clothes. The day was warm for a winter afternoon. And thoughts of Leo's expertise in bed made her feel as if she had a fever.

She cleared her throat, hoping he wouldn't notice the hot color that heated her neck and cheeks. "Give me a second." Pretending an intense interest in the grouping of trees, she breathed deeply, inhaling the scent of the fresh foliage. "This one," she said hoarsely, grabbing blindly at the branches of a large Fraser fir.

At her back, Leo stood warm and tall. "I want you to have your perfect Christmas, Phoebe. But as the voice of reason I have to point out that your choice is a little on the big side." He put his hands on her shoulders, kissing her just below the ear. "If it's what you want, though, I'll trim it or something."

She nodded, her legs shaky. "Thank you."

He set her aside gently, and picked up the ax. "Move farther back. I don't know how far the wood chips will fly."

Teddy had dozed off, his chubby cheeks a healthy pink. She kept her arms around him as Leo notched the bottom of the tree trunk and took a few practice chops. At the last minute, he shed his heavy parka, now clad above the waist in only a thermal weave shirt, green to match his surroundings.

It was ridiculous to get so turned on by a Neanderthal exhibition of strength. But when Leo took his first powerful swing and the ax cut deeply into the tree, Phoebe felt a little faint.

Leo was determined to make Phoebe happy. The trunk of this particular fir was never going to fit into a normal-size tree stand. He'd have to cobble something together with a large bucket and some gravel. Who knew? At the moment, his first task was to fell the sucker and drag it home.

At his fifth swing, he felt a twinge in his chest. The feeling was so unexpected and so sharp, he hesitated half a second, long enough for the ax to lose its trajectory and land out of target range. Now, one of the lower branches was about two feet shorter than it had been.

Phoebe, standing a good ten feet away, called out to him. "What's wrong?"

"Nothing," he said, wiping his brow with the back of his hand. Tree chopping was damned hard work. Knowing that her eyes were on him, he found his stride again, landing four perfect strikes at exactly the same spot. The pain in his chest had already disappeared. Probably just a muscle. His doctor had reassured him more than once that Leo's health was perfect. Trouble was, when a man had been felled by something he couldn't see, it made him jumpy.

Before severing the trunk completely, he paused before the last swing and tugged the tree to one side. The fragrance of the branches was alluring. Crisp. Piquant. Containing memories of childhood days long forgotten. Something about scent leaped barriers of time and place.

Standing here in the forest with sap on his hands and his muscles straining from exertion, he felt a wave of nostalgia. He turned to Phoebe. "I'm glad you wanted to do this. I remember Christmases when I begged for a real tree. But my dad was allergic. Our artificial trees were always beautiful—Mom had a knack for that—but just now, a whiff of the air brought it all back. It's the smell of the holidays."

"I'm glad you approve," she said with a charming grin. Standing as she was in a splash of sunlight, her hair glistened with the sheen of a raven's wing. The baby slept against her breast. Leo wondered what it said about his own life that he envied a little kid. Phoebe's hand cradled Teddy's head almost unconsciously. Every move she made to care for her sister's child spoke eloquently of the love she had for her nephew.

Phoebe should have kids of her own. And a husband. The thought hit him like a revelation, and he didn't know why it was startling. Most women Phoebe's age were looking to settle down and start families. But maybe she wasn't. Because, clearly, she had hidden herself away like the unfortunate heroine in Rapunzel's castle. Only in Phoebe's case, the incarceration was voluntary.

Why would a smart, attractive woman isolate herself in an out-of-the-way cabin where her nearest neighbors were knocking on heaven's door? When was the last time she'd had a date? Nothing about Phoebe's life made sense, especially since she had admitted to working once upon a time in a highly competitive career.

A few thin clouds had begun to roll in, dropping the temperature, so he chopped one last time and had the satisfaction of hearing the snap that freed their prize. Phoebe clapped softly. "Bravo, Paul Bunyan."

He donned his coat and lifted an eyebrow. "Are you making fun of me?"

She joined him beside the tree and reached up awkwardly to kiss his cheek, the baby tucked between them. "Not even a little. You're my hero. I couldn't have done this on my own."

"Happy to oblige." Her gratitude warmed him. But her next words gave him pause.

"If we eat dinner early, we can probably get the whole thing decorated before bedtime."

"Whoa. Back up the truck. I thought we had *plans* for bedtime." He curled a hand behind her neck and stopped her in her tracks by the simple expedient of kissing her long and slow. Working around the kid was a challenge, but he was motivated.

Phoebe's lashes fluttered downward as she leaned into him. "We do," she whispered. The fact that she returned his kiss was noteworthy, but even more gratifying was her enthusiasm. She went up on tiptoes, aligned their lips perfectly and kissed him until he shuddered and groaned. "Good Lord, Phoebe."

She smoothed a strand of hair behind his ear, her fingers warm against his chilled skin. "Are you complaining, Mr. Cavallo?"

"No," he croaked.

"Then let's get crackin'."

Even though Phoebe carried a baby, and had been for some time, Leo was equally challenged by the difficulty of dragging the enormous tree, trunk first, back to the house. He walked at the edge of the road in the tall, dead grass, not wanting to shred the branches on gravel. By the time they reached their destination, he was breathing hard. "I think this thing weighs a hundred pounds."

Phoebe looked over her shoulder, her smile wickedly teasing. "I've seen your biceps, Leo. I'm sure you can bench-press a single measly tree." She unlocked the front door and propped it open. "I've already cleared a spot by the fireplace. Let me know if you need a hand."

Phoebe couldn't remember the last time she'd had so much fun. Leo was a good sport. Chopping down the large tree she had selected was not an easy task, but he hadn't complained. If anything, he seemed to get a measure of satisfaction from conquering *O Tannenbaum.*

Phoebe unashamedly used Teddy as a shield for the rest of the day. It wasn't that she didn't want to be alone with Leo. But there was something jarring about feeling such wanton, breathless excitement for a man when she was, at the same time, cuddling a little baby.

It would probably be different if the child were one they shared. Then, over Teddy's small, adorable head, she and Leo could exchanges smiles and loving glances as they remembered the night they created this precious bundle of joy. With no such scenario in existence, Phoebe decided her feelings were fractured…much like the time she'd had a high school babysitting job interrupted by the arrival of her boyfriend. That long-ago night as a sixteen-year-old, it had been all she could do to concentrate on her charges.

Almost a decade and a half later, with Leo prowling the interior of the cabin, all grumpy and masculine and gorgeous, she felt much the same way. Nevertheless, she focused on entertaining her nephew.

Fortunately, the baby was in an extremely good mood. He played in his high chair while Phoebe threw dinner together. Thanks to the largesse of Leo's buddy—which Leo no doubt cofunded—it was no trouble to pick and choose. Chicken Alfredo. Spinach salad. Fruit crepes for dessert. It would be easy to get spoiled by having haute cuisine at her fingertips with minimal effort. She would have to resist, though. Because, like Leo's presence in her life, the four-star meals were temporary.

Leo, after much cursing and struggling, and with a dollop of luck, finally pronounced himself satisfied with the security of their Christmas pièce de résistance. After changing the baby's diaper, Phoebe served up two plates and set them on the table. "Hurry, then. Before it gets cold."

Leo sat down with a groan. "Wouldn't matter to me. I'm starving."

She ended up sitting Teddy in his high chair and feeding him his bottle with one hand while she ate with the other. At the end of the meal, she scooped Teddy up and held him out to Leo. "If you wouldn't mind playing with him on the sofa for a little while, I'll clean up the kitchen, and we can start on the tree."

A look of discomfort crossed Leo's face. "I'm more of an observer when it comes to babies. I don't think they like me."

"Don't be silly, Leo. And besides, you did offer to help with Teddy when I let you stay. Remember?"

He picked up his coat. "Buford says it's going to snow tonight. I need to move half of that pile of wood you have out by the shed and stack it on the front porch. If it's a heavy snow, we might lose power." Before Phoebe could protest, he bundled up in his winter gear and was gone.

Phoebe felt the joy leach out of the room. She wanted Leo to love Teddy like she did, but that was silly. Leo had his own family, a brother, a sister-in-law, a niece, a nephew and a grandfather. Besides, he'd been pretty clear about not wanting kids. Some people didn't get all warm and fuzzy when it came to infants.

Still, she felt a leaden sense of disappointment. Leo was a wonderful man. Being squeamish about babies was hardly a character flaw.

She put Teddy back in the high chair. "Sorry, kiddo. Looks like it's you and me on KP duty tonight. I'll be as quick as I can, and then I'll read you a book. How about that?"

Teddy found the loose end of the safety strap and chewed it. His little chortling sounds and syllables were cute, but hardly helpful when it came to the question of Leo.

Tonight was a big bridge for Phoebe to cross. She was ready. She wanted Leo, no question. But she couldn't help feeling anxiety about the future. In coming to the mountains, she had learned to be alone. Would agreeing to be Leo's lover negate all the progress she had made? And would ultimately losing him—as she surely would—put her back in that dark place again?

Even with all her questions, tonight's outcome was a foregone conclusion. Leo was her Christmas present to herself.

Twelve

Leo pushed himself hard, carrying five or six heavy logs at a time. He took Buford's warning seriously, but the real reason he was out here was because staying in the cabin with Phoebe was torture. It was one thing to casually say, "We'll wait until bedtime." It was another entirely to keep himself reined in.

Every time she bent over to do something with the baby or to put something in the oven, her jeans cupped a butt that was the perfect size for a man's hands to grab hold of. The memory of her naked breasts lodged in his brain like a continuous, R-rated movie reel.

Earlier, he had called Luc, explaining the isolation of Phoebe's cabin and promising to stay in touch. His new phone should arrive in the morning, and the satellite internet would be set up, as well. By bedtime *tomorrow* night, Leo would be plugged in, all of his electronic devices at his fingertips. A very short time ago, that notion would have filled him with satisfaction and a sense of being on track. Not today. Now he could think of nothing but taking Phoebe to bed.

When he had a healthy stack of logs tucked just outside the front door in easy reach, he knew it was time to go in and face the music. His throat was dry. His heart pounded far harder than warranted by his current task. But the worst part was his semipermanent erection. He literally ached all over…wanting Phoebe. *Needing* her with a ferocious appetite that made him grateful to be a man with a beating heart.

He told himself he was close to having everything he craved. All he had to do was make it through the evening. But he was jittery with arousal. Testosterone charged through his bloodstream like a devil on his shoulder. Urging him on to stake a claim. Dismissing the need for gentleness.

Phoebe was his for the taking. She'd told him as much. A few more hours, and everything he wanted would be his.

Phoebe moved the portable crib into the living room near the fireplace, on the opposite side from the tree. Her hope was that Teddy would amuse himself for a while. He'd been fed, changed, and was now playing happily with several of his favorite teething toys.

When Leo came through the door on a blast of cold air, her stomach flipped. She'd given herself multiple lectures on remaining calm and cool. No need for him to know how agitated she was about the evening to come. Her giddiness was an odd mixture of anticipation and reservation.

Never in her life had she been intimate with a man of whom she knew so little. And likewise, never had she contemplated sex with someone for recreational purposes. She and Leo were taking advantage of a serendipitous place and time. Neither of them made any pretense that this was more. No passionate declarations of love. No tentative plans for the future.

Just sex.

Did that cheapen what she felt for him?

As he removed his coat and boots, she stared. The look in his eyes was hot and predatory. A shiver snaked down her spine. Leo was a big man, both in body and in personality. His charisma seduced her equally as much as his honed, masculine body.

She licked her lips, biting the lower one. "Um…there's hot chocolate on the stove. I made the real stuff. Seemed appropriate."

He rubbed his hands together, his cheeks ruddy from the cold. "Thanks."

The single syllable was gruff. Phoebe knew then, beyond the shadow of a doubt, that Leo was as enmeshed in whatever was happening between them as she was. The knowledge settled her nerves. She had been afraid of seeming gauche or awkward. Leo's intensity indicated that he was perhaps as off balance as she felt.

As he poured his drink, she expected him to come sit on the sofa. Instead, he lingered in the kitchen. She dragged a large red plastic tub nearer the tree. "If you'll do the lights, I'll sort through the ornaments and put hangers on them so that part will go quickly."

He set his mug in the sink. "Lights?"

She shot him an innocent look. "It's the man's job. Always."

"And if there were no man around?"

"I'd have to handle it. But I'm sure the tree would not look nearly as pretty."

Finally, he joined her, his body language somewhat more relaxed. "You are so full of it," he said with a fake glower as he bent and picked up the first strand. "You realize, don't you, that many people buy pre-lit trees these days."

"True." She plugged in the extension cord and handed him the end. "But not live ones. Think how proud you're going to be when we're finished, how satisfied with a job well done."

Tugging her braid, he deliberately brushed the backs of his fingers down her neck. "I'm a long way from satisfied."

His chocolate-scented breath was warm on her cheek. If she turned her head an inch or two, their lips would meet.

She closed her eyes involuntarily, her body weak with longing. Leo had to know what he was doing to her. And judging by the smirk on his face when she finally managed to look at him, he was enjoying her discomfiture.

Turnabout was fair play. “Good things come to those who wait,” she whispered. She stroked a hand down the middle of his rib cage, stopping just above his belt buckle.

Leo sucked in a sharp breath as his hands clenched on her shoulders. “Phoebe…”

“Phoebe, what?” Toying with the hem of his shirt, she lifted it and touched his bare skin with two fingertips. Teasing him like this was more fun than she could have imagined. Her long-buried sensual side came out to play. Taking one step closer so that their bodies touched chest to knee, she laid her cheek against him, hearing the steady, though rapid, beat of his heart.

Between them, she felt the press of his erection, full and hard, at her stomach. For so long she had hidden from the richness of life, afraid of making another tragic misstep. But one lesson she had learned well. No matter how terrible the mistake and how long the resultant fall, the world kept on turning.

Leo might well be her next blunder. But at least she was living. Feeling. Wanting. Her emotions had begun to thaw with the advent of Teddy. Leo’s arrival in the midst of her reawakening had been fortuitous. Six months ago, she would not have had the courage to act on her attraction.

Now, feeling the vestiges of her grief slide into the realm of the past, her heart swelled with joy in the realization that the Phoebe Kemper she had once known was still alive. It had been a long road. And she didn’t think she would ever want to go back and reclaim certain remnants of that woman’s life.

But she was ready to move forward. With Leo.

He set her away from him, his expression strained. "Give me the damn lights."

Leo was at sixes and sevens, his head muddled with a million thoughts, his body near crippled with desire. Fortunately for him, Phoebe was the meticulous sort. There were no knots of wire to untangle. Every strand of lights had been neatly wrapped around pieces of plywood before being stored away. He sensed that this Christmas decorating ritual was far more important to Phoebe than perhaps he realized. So despite his mental and physical discomfort, he set his mind to weaving lights in amongst the branches.

Phoebe worked nearby, unwrapping tissue-wrapped ornaments, discarding broken ones, tending to Teddy now and again. Music played softly in the background. One tune in particular he recognized. He had always enjoyed the verve and tempo of the popular modern classic by Mariah Carey. But not until this exact minute had he understood the songwriter's simple message.

Some things were visceral. It was true. He needed no other gift but Phoebe. When a man was rich enough to buy anything he wanted, the act of exchanging presents took on new meaning. He had always given generously to his employees. And he and Luc knew each other well enough to come up with the occasional surprise gift that demonstrated thought and care.

But he couldn't remember a Christmas when he'd been willing to strip the holiday down to its basic component. Love.

His mind shied away from that thought. Surely a man of his age and experience and sophistication didn't believe in love at first sight. The heart attack had left him floundering, grasping at things to stay afloat in a suddenly changing world. Phoebe was here. And it was almost Christmas.

He wanted her badly. No need to tear the situation apart with questions.

He finished the last of the lights and dragged one final tub over to the edge of the coffee table so he could sit and sift through the contents. Though the tree was large, he wasn't sure they were going to be able to fit everything on the limbs.

Spying a small, unopened green box, he picked it up and turned it over. Visible through the clear plastic covering was a sterling sliver rocking horse with the words *Baby's First Christmas* engraved on the base. And a date. An old date. His stomach clenched.

When he looked up, Phoebe was staring at the item in his hands, her face ashen. Cursing himself for not moving more quickly to tuck it out of sight, he stood, not knowing what to say. A dozen theories rushed through his mind. But only one made sense.

Tears rolled from Phoebe's huge pain-darkened eyes, though he was fairly certain she didn't know she was crying. It was as if she had frozen, sensing danger, not sure where to run.

He approached her slowly, his hands outstretched. "Phoebe, sweetheart. Talk to me."

Her eyes were uncomprehending...even when she wiped one wet cheek with the back of her hand.

"Let me see it," she whispered, walking toward the tub of ornaments.

He put his body in front of hers, cupping her face in his hands. "No. It doesn't matter. You're shaking." Wrapping his arms around her and holding her as tightly as he could, he tried to still the tremors that tore through her body cruelly.

Phoebe never weakened. She stood erect, not leaning into him, not accepting his comfort. He might as well have been holding a statue. At last, he stepped back, staring into her eyes. "Let me get you a drink."

"No." She wiped her nose.

Leo reached into his pocket for a handkerchief and handed it to her. He was torn, unsure if talking about it would make things better or worse. As he stood there, trying to decide how to navigate the chasm that had opened at his feet, the fraught moment was broken by a baby's cry.

Phoebe whirled around. "Oh, Teddy. We were ignoring you." She rushed to pick him up, holding him close as new tears wet her lashes. "It's your bedtime, isn't it, my sweet? Don't worry. Aunt Phoebe is here."

Leo tried to take the boy. "You need to sit down, Phoebe." He was fairly certain she was in shock. Her hands were icy cold and her lips had a blue tinge.

Phoebe fought him. "No. You don't like babies. I can do it."

The belligerence in her wild gaze shocked him, coming as it did out of nowhere. "I never said that." He spoke softly, as though gentling a spooked animal. "Let me help you."

Ignoring his plea, she exited the room, Teddy clutched to her chest. He followed the pair of them down the hall and into the baby's nursery cum storage room. He had never seen this door open. Phoebe always used her own bedroom to access Teddy's.

She put the child on the changing table and stood there. Leo realized she didn't know what to do next.

Quietly, not making a fuss, he reached for the little pair of pajamas hanging from a hook on the wall nearby. The diapers were tucked into a cheerful yellow plastic basket at the boy's feet. Easing Phoebe aside with nothing more than a nudge of his hip, he unfastened what seemed like a hundred snaps, top and bottom, and drew the cloth up over Teddy's head. Teddy cooed, smiling trustingly as Leo stripped him naked. The baby's skin was soft, his flailing arms and legs pudgy and strong.

The diaper posed a momentary problem, but only until Leo's brain clicked into gear and he saw how the assembly worked. Cleaning the little bottom with a baby wipe, he gave thanks that he was only dealing with a wet diaper, not a messy one.

Phoebe hadn't moved. Her hands were clenched on the decorative edge of the wooden table so hard that her knuckles were white.

Leo closed up the diaper, checked it for structural integrity, and then held up the pajamas. He couldn't really see much difference between these pj's and the daytime outfits the kid wore, but apparently there was one. This piece of clothing was even more of a challenge, because the snaps ran from the throat all the way down one leg. It took him three tries to get it right.

Through it all, Phoebe stood unaware. Or at least it seemed that way.

Cradling the child in one arm, Leo used his free hand to steer Phoebe out of the room. "You'll have to help me with the bottle," he said softly, hoping she was hearing him.

Her brief nod was a relief.

Leo installed Phoebe in a kitchen chair. Squatting in front of her, he waited until her eyes met his. "Can you hold him?"

She took the small, squirmy bundle and bowed her head, teardrops wetting the front of the sleeper. "I have a bottle ready," she said, the words almost inaudible. "Put it in a bowl of hot water two or three times until the formula feels warm when you sprinkle it on your wrist."

He had seen her perform that task several times, so it was easy to follow the instructions. When the bottle was ready, he turned back to Phoebe. Her grip on Teddy was firm. The child was in no danger of being dropped. But Phoebe had ceased interacting with her nephew.

Leo put a hand on her shoulder. "Would you like to feed him, or do you want me to do it? I'm happy to."

Long seconds ticked by. Phoebe stood abruptly, handing him the baby. "You can. I'm going to my room."

He grabbed her wrist. "No. You're not. Come sit with us on the sofa."

Thirteen

Phoebe didn't have the emotional energy to fight him. Leo's gaze was kind but firm. She followed him to the living room and sat down with her legs curled beneath her. Leo sat beside her with Teddy in his arms. Fortunately, Teddy didn't protest the change in leadership. He took his bottle from Leo as if it were an everyday occurrence.

Despite the roaring fire that Leo had built, which still leaped and danced vigorously, she felt cold all over. Clenching her jaw to keep her teeth from chattering, she wished she had thought to pick up an afghan. But the pile neatly folded on the hearth was too far away. She couldn't seem to make her legs move.

Trying to distract her thoughts, she studied Leo out of the corner of her eye. The powerful picture of the big man and the small baby affected her at a gut-deep level. Despite Leo's professed lack of experience, he was doing well. His large hands were careful as he adjusted Teddy's position now and again or moved the bottle to a better angle.

Beyond Leo's knee she could see the abandoned ornaments. But not the little green box. He must have shoved it out of sight beneath the table. She remembered vividly the day she'd purchased it. After leaving her doctor's office, she was on her way back to work. On a whim, she stopped by the mall to grab a bite of lunch and to walk off some of her giddy euphoria.

It was September, but a Christmas shop had already opened its doors in preparation for the holidays. On a table near the front, a display of ornaments caught her eyes. Feeling crazily joyful and foolishly furtive, she picked one out and paid for it.

Until this evening she had suppressed that memory. In fact, she didn't even realize she had kept the ornament and moved it three years ago.

Leo wrapped an arm around her shoulders, pulling her closer to his side. "Lean on me," he said.

She obeyed gladly, inhaling the scent of his aftershave and the warm "man" smell of him. Gradually, lulled by the fire and the utter security of Leo's embrace, she closed her eyes. Pain hovered just offstage, but she chose not to confront it at the moment. She had believed herself to be virtually healed. As though all the dark edges of her life had been sanded away by her sojourn in the woods.

How terribly unfair to find out it wasn't true. How devastating to know that something so simple could trip her up.

Perhaps because the afternoon and evening had been so enjoyable, so delightfully *homey,* the harshness of being thrust into a past she didn't want to remember was all the more devastating.

Teddy drained the last of the bottle, his little eyelashes drooping. Leo coaxed a muffled burp from him and then put a hand on Phoebe's knee. "Is it okay for me to lay him down? Anything I need to know?"

"I'll take him," she said halfheartedly, not sure if she could make the effort to stand up.

He squeezed her hand. "Don't move. I'll be right back."

She stared into space, barely even noticing when he returned and began moving about the kitchen with muffled sounds. A few minutes later he handed her a mug of cocoa. She wrapped her fingers around the warm stoneware, welcoming the heat against her frozen skin.

Leo had topped her serving with whipped cream. She sipped delicately, wary of burning her tongue.

He sat down beside her and smiled. "You have a mustache," he teased. Using his thumb, he rubbed her upper lip. Somewhere deep inside her, regret surfaced. She had ruined their sexy, fun-filled evening.

Leo appeared unperturbed. He leaned back, his legs outstretched, and propped his feet on the coffee table. With his mug resting against his chest, he shot her a sideways glance. "When you're ready, Phoebe, I want you to tell me the story."

She nodded, her eyes downcast as she studied the pale swirls of melted topping in the hot brown liquid. It was time. It was beyond time. Even her sister didn't know all the details. When the unthinkable had happened, the pain was too fresh. Phoebe had floundered in a sea of confused grief, not knowing how to claw her way out.

In the end, her only choice had been to wait until the waves abated and finally receded. Peace had eventually replaced the hurt. But her hard-won composure had been fragile at best. Judging by today, she had a long way to go.

Leo got up to stoke the fire and to add more music to the stereo. She was struck by how comfortable it felt to have him in her cabin, in her life. He was an easy man to be with. Quiet when the occasion demanded it, and drolly amusing when he wanted to be.

He settled back onto the couch and covered both of them with a wool throw. Fingering the cloth, he wrinkled his nose. "We should burn this," he said with a grin. "Imported fabric, cheap construction. I could hook you up with something far nicer."

"I'll put it on my Christmas list." She managed a smile,

not wanting him to think she was a total mental case. "I'm sorry I checked out on you," she muttered.

"We're all entitled now and then."

The quiet response took some of the sting out of her embarrassment. He was being remarkably patient. "I owe you an explanation."

"You don't *owe* me anything, sweet Phoebe. But it helps to talk about it. I know that from experience. When our parents were killed, Grandfather was wise enough to get us counseling almost immediately. We would never have shown weakness to him. He was and still is a sharp-browed, blustering tyrant, though we love him, of course. But he knew we would need an outlet for what we were feeling."

"Did it work?"

"In time. We were at a vulnerable age. Not quite men, but more than boys. It was hard to admit that our world had come crashing down around us." He took her hand. She had twisted one piece of blanket fringe so tightly it was almost severed. Linking their fingers, he raised her hand to his lips and kissed it. "Is that what happened to you?"

Despite her emotional state, she was not above being moved by the feel of his lips against her skin. Hot tears stung her eyes, not because she was so sad, but in simple recognition of his genuine empathy. "You could say that."

"Tell me about your baby."

There was nothing to be gained from denial. But he would understand more if she began elsewhere. "I'll go back to the beginning if you don't mind."

"A good place to start." He kissed her fingers again before tucking her hand against his chest. The warmth of him, even through his clothing, calmed and comforted her.

"I told you that I was a stockbroker in Charlotte."

"Yes."

"Well, I was good, really good at my job. There were a half dozen of us, and competition was fierce. Gracious for the most part, but inescapable. I had a knack for putting together portfolios, and people liked working with me, because I didn't make them feel stupid or uninformed about their money. We had a number of very wealthy clients with neither the time nor the inclination to grow their fortunes, so we did it for them."

"I'm having a hard time reconciling *killer* Phoebe with the woman who bakes her own bread."

His wry observation actually made her laugh. "I can understand your confusion. Back then I focused on getting ahead in my profession. I was determined to be successful and financially comfortable."

"Perhaps because losing your parents left you feeling insecure in so many other ways."

His intuitive comment was impressive. "You should hang out a shingle," she said. "I'm sure people would pay for such on-the-mark analysis."

"Is that sarcasm I hear?"

"Not at all."

"I can't take too much credit. You and I have more in common than I realized. Getting the foundations knocked out from under you at a time when most young people are getting ready to step out into the big wide world breeds a certain distrust in the system. Parents are supposed to help their children with the shift into adulthood."

"And without them, everything seems like a scary gamble at best."

"Exactly. But there's more, isn't there?"

She nodded, fighting the lump in her throat. "I was engaged," she croaked. "To another broker. We had an ongoing battle to see who could bring in the most business. I thought we were a team, both professionally *and* personally, but it turns out I was naive."

"What happened?"

Taking a deep breath, she ripped off the Band-Aid of her

old wound and brought it all back to life…to ugly life. "We had plans to get married the following year, but no specific date. Then—in the early fall—I found out I was pregnant."

"Not planned, I assume?"

"Oh, gosh, no. I assumed that motherhood, if it ever rolled around, was sometime *way* in the future. But Rick and I—that was his name—well…once we got over the shock, we started to be happy about it. Freaked-out, for sure. But happy nevertheless."

"Did you set a date then for a wedding?"

"Not at first. We decided to wait a bit, maybe until we knew the sex of the baby, to tell our coworkers. I thought everything was rocking along just fine, and then Rick began dropping subtle and not-so-subtle hints that I should think about taking a leave for a while."

"Why? It wasn't a physically demanding job, was it?"

"No. But he kept bringing up the stress factor. How my intensity and my long hours could be harmful to the baby. At first, I was confused. I honestly didn't see any problem."

"And was there?"

"Not the one he was trying to sell to me. But the truth was, Rick knew he could be top dog at the company if I were gone. And even when I came back after maternity leave, he would have made so much progress that I would never catch up."

"Ouch."

She grimaced. "It was a nasty smack in the face. We had a huge fight, and he accused me of being too ambitious for my own good. I called him a sexist pig. Things degenerated from there."

"Did you give the ring back?"

"How could I? Even if I now knew that my fiancé was a jerk, he was the father of my baby. I decided I had no choice but to make it work. But no matter how hard I tried, things only got worse."

"Did you have an abortion?"

Leo's quiet query held no hint of judgment, only a deep compassion. From where he was standing, that assumption made perfect sense.

She swallowed. The trembling she had managed to squelch started up again. "No. I wanted the baby by then. Against all odds. I was three and a half months along, and then..." Her throat tightened. Leo rubbed her shoulder, the caress comforting rather than sexual.

"What happened, Phoebe?"

Closing her eyes, she saw the moment as if it had been yesterday. "I started bleeding at work one day. Terribly. They rushed me to the hospital, but I lost the baby. All I could think about when I was lying in that bed, touching my empty belly, was that Rick had been right."

"You were young and healthy. I can't imagine there was a reason you shouldn't have been working."

"That's what my doctor said. She tried to reassure me, but I wasn't hysterical. Just cold. So cold. They told me the baby had developed with an abnormality. I would never have carried it to term. One of those random, awful things."

She didn't cry again. The emptiness was too dry and deep for that...a dull, vague feeling of loss.

Leo lifted her onto his lap, turning her sideways so her cheek rested on his chest. His arms held her tightly, communicating without words his sympathy and his desire to comfort her. He brushed a stray hair from her forehead. "I'm so sorry, Phoebe."

She shrugged. "Lots of people lose babies."

"But usually not a fiancé at the same time. You lost everything. And that's why you came here."

"Yes. I was a coward. I couldn't bear people staring at me with pity. And with Rick still working at the company, I knew I was done. My boss wasn't happy about it. I think he would have liked to fire Rick and keep me, but you can't terminate a guy for being a selfish, self-absorbed bastard."

"I would have." The three words encompassed an icy intensity that communicated his anger toward a man he had never met. "Your boss shouldn't have been so spineless. You were good at your job, Phoebe. If you had stayed, you might have recovered from your loss much sooner. The work would have been a healthy distraction. Perhaps even fulfilling in a new way."

Here was the crux of the matter. "The thing is," she said slowly. "I have my doubts. Looking back, I can see that I had all the makings of a workaholic. It's bad enough when a man falls into that trap. But women are traditionally the caregivers, the support system for a spouse or a family. So even though the doctor told me I had done nothing wrong, I felt as if I had betrayed my child by working nonstop."

Leo's arms tightened around her, his chest heaving in a startled inhalation. "Good Lord, Phoebe. That's totally irrational. You were an unencumbered woman on the upswing of your career. Female pioneers have fought for decades so you could be exactly where you were."

"And yet we still have battles within the sisterhood between stay-at-home moms and those who work outside the home. I've seen both groups sneer at each other as though one choice is more admirable than the other."

"I'll give you that one. In reality, though, I assume women work for many reasons. Fulfillment. Excitement. Or in some cases, simply to put food on the table."

"But it's about balance, Leo. And I had none. It's not true that women can have it all. Life is about choices. We only have twenty-four hours in a day. That never changes. So if I don't learn how to fit *work* into a box of the appropriate size, I don't know that I'll ever be able to go back."

"That's it, then? You're never going to be employed

again? Despite the fact that you've been gifted with financial talents and people skills?"

"I'd like to have a family someday. And even more importantly, find peace and contentment in the way I live my life. Is that so wrong?"

"How are you supposed to accomplish that by hiding out? Phoebe, you're not doing what you're good at…and borrowing a baby from your sister isn't exactly going after what you want."

"I don't know if I'm ready yet. It sounds like a cliché, but I've been trying to find myself. And hopefully in the process learning something about balance."

"We all have to live in the real world. Most of the life lessons I've learned have come via failure."

"Well, that's depressing."

"Not at all. You have to trust yourself again."

"And if I crash and burn?"

"Then you'll pick yourself up and start over one more time. You're more resilient than you think."

Fourteen

Leo was more bothered by Phoebe's soul-searching than he should have been. Her self-evaluation proved her to be far more courageous than he was in facing up to painful truths. But in his gut, he believed she was missing the bigger picture. Phoebe had clearly excelled in her previous career. And had loved the work, even with overt competition…perhaps *because* of it.

She was lucky to have had the financial resources to fund her long sabbatical. In the end, though, how would she ever know if it was time to leave the mountains? And what if she decided to stay? She had proved her independence. And in her eyes and in her home he saw peace. Did that mean she couldn't see herself finding happiness—and perhaps a family—anywhere but here?

He played with her hair, removing the elastic band that secured her braid. Gently, he loosened the thick ropes, fanning out the dark, shiny tresses until they hung down her back, covering his hand in black silk. Holding her in his arms as a friend and not a lover was difficult, but he couldn't push her away.

Phoebe saw herself as a coward, but that was far from the truth. Though she had been at the top of her game, she had wanted the baby that threatened to disrupt her life. Even in the face of disappointment, knowing that her fiancé was not the man she thought he was, she had been prepared to work at the relationship so they could be a family.

Leo admired her deeply.

Her eyes were closed, her breathing steady. It had been a long, busy day, and an emotional one for her. Leo knew their timing was off. Again. Even with Teddy sleeping soundly, Phoebe was in no shape to initiate a sexual relationship with a new partner. Perhaps if they had been a couple for a long time, Leo could have used the intimacy of sex to comfort and reassure her. As it was, his role would have to be that of protector.

A man could do worse when it came to Phoebe Kemper.

He stood, prepared to carry her to her room. Phoebe stirred, her long lashes lifting to reveal eyes that were still beautiful, though rimmed in red. "What are you doing?"

"You need to be in bed. Alone," he clarified, in case there was any doubt about his intentions.

She shook her head, a stubborn expression he had come to know all too well painting her face with insistence. "I want to sleep in here so I can see the tree. I'll keep the monitor with me. You go on to bed. I'm fine."

He nuzzled her nose with his, resisting the urge to kiss her. Her aching vulnerability held him back. "No," he said huskily. "I'll stay with you." He set her on her feet and went to his room to get extra blankets and a pillow. The bearskin rug in front of the fire would be a decent enough bed, and from there, he'd be able to keep the fire going. He brushed his teeth and changed into his pajama pants and robe.

By the time he returned, Phoebe had made the same preparations. It was colder tonight. Instead of her knit pj's, she had donned a high-necked flannel nightgown that made her look as if she had stepped right out of the pages of *Little*

House on the Prairie. The fabric was pale ivory with little red reindeer cavorting from neck to hemline.

The old-fashioned design should have made her look as asexual as a nun. But with her hair spilling around her shoulders and her dark eyes heavy-lidded, all Leo could think about was whether or not she had on panties beneath that fortress of a garment.

If the utilitarian cloth and enveloping design was meant to discourage him, Phoebe didn't know much about men. When the castle was barricaded, the knights had to fight all the harder to claim their prize.

She clutched a pillow to her chest, her cheeks turning pink. "You don't have to stay with me. I'm okay…really."

"What if I want to?" The words came out gruffer than he intended.

Her eyes widened. He could swear he saw the faint outline of pert nipples beneath the bodice of her nightwear. She licked her lips. "You've been very sweet to me, Leo. I'm sorry the night didn't go the way we planned. But maybe it's for the best. Perhaps we were rushing into this."

"You don't want me?" He hadn't meant to ask it. Hated the way the question revealed his need.

Phoebe's chin wobbled. "I don't know. I mean, yes. Of course I want you. I think that's painfully obvious. But we're not…"

"Not what?" He took the pillow from her and tossed it on the couch. Gathering her into his arms, he fought a battle of painful scale. It seemed as if he had wanted her for a lifetime. "Only a fool would press you now…when you've dealt with so much tonight. But make no mistake, Phoebe. I'm going to have you. No matter how long the wait." He stroked his hands down her back, pulling her hips to his, establishing once and for all that she was *not* wearing underwear.

Had he detected any resistance at all on her part, he

would have been forced to release her. But she melted into him, her body warm and soft and unmistakably feminine through the negligible barrier of her gown. He had belted his robe tightly before leaving his bedroom, not wanting to give any appearance of carnal intent.

To his intense shock and surprise, a small hand made its way between the thin layers of cashmere and found his bare chest. Within seconds his erection lifted and thickened. His voice locked in his throat. He was positive that if he spoke, the words would come out wrong.

Phoebe's hand landed over his heart and lingered as if counting the beats. Could she hear the acceleration? Did she feel the rigidity of his posture? He gulped, his breathing shallow and ragged. There was no way she could miss his thrusting sex, even through her pseudo armor.

The woman in his arms sighed deeply. "You should go to your room," she whispered. "The floor will be too hard."

"I'll manage." He thrust her away, hoping the maneuver wasn't as awkward as it felt. Turning his back, he added logs to the fire and then prepared his makeshift bed.

In his peripheral vision he saw Phoebe ready the sofa with a pile of blankets and her own pillow. When she sat down, removed her slippers and swung her legs up onto the couch, he caught one quick glimpse of bare, slender thighs. *Holy hell.*

A shot of whiskey wouldn't come amiss, but Phoebe's fridge held nothing stronger than beer. Quietly, keeping a wide perimeter between himself and temptation, he went about the cabin turning off lights. Soon, only the glow of the fire and the muted rainbow colors of the tree illuminated the room.

He checked the lock on the front door and closed a gap in the drapes. When he could think of nothing else as a distraction, he turned reluctantly and surveyed the evocative scene Phoebe's love of Christmas had created. Even the most hardened of "Scrooge-ish" hearts surely couldn't resist the inherent emotion.

Peace. Comfort. Home. All of it was there for anyone with eyes to see. Had his luxurious condo in Atlanta ever been as appealing?

Phoebe's eyes were closed, a half smile on her lips. She lay like a child with one hand tucked beneath her cheek. He didn't know if she was already asleep or simply enjoying the smell of the outdoors they had managed to capture in a tree. Perhaps it was the sound of the fire she savored, the same life-affirming heat that popped and hissed as it had for generations before.

Exhaustion finally overrode his lust-addled brain and coaxed him toward sleep. He fashioned his bed in front of the hearth and climbed in. It wasn't the Ritz-Carlton, but for tonight, there was nowhere he would rather be. After no more than five minutes, he realized that his robe was going to be far too warm so close to the fire.

Shrugging out of it, he tossed it aside and lay back in the covers with a yawn. A month ago if anyone had told him he'd be camping out on a hard floor in dangerous proximity to a fascinating woman he wanted desperately, he'd have laughed. Of course, he would have had a similar reaction if that same someone had told him he'd have a heart attack at thirty-six.

He had to tell Phoebe the truth about why he had come to the Smoky Mountains…to her cabin in the woods. She had bared her soul to him. Perhaps tomorrow he would find the opportunity and the words to reveal the truth. The prospect made him uneasy. He hated admitting weakness. Always had. But his pride should not stand in the way of his relationship to a woman he had come to respect as much or more than he desired her.

He shifted on the furry pallet, searching for a position that was comfortable. With Phoebe in the same room, he didn't even have the option of taking his sex in hand and finding relief. Hours passed, or so it seemed, before he slept....

Phoebe jerked awake, her heart pounding in response to some unremembered dream. It took her several seconds to recognize her surroundings. In the next instant, she glanced at the baby monitor. Reassurance came in the form of a grainy picture. Teddy slept in his usual position.

Sighing shakily as adrenaline winnowed away, she glanced at the clock on the far wall. Two in the morning. The fire burned brightly, so Leo must have been up tending to it recently. The room was warm and cozy. Despite her unaccustomed bed and the late hour, she felt momentarily rested and not at all sleepy.

Warily, she lifted her head a couple of inches, only enough to get a clear view of Leo over the top of the coffee table. Her breath caught at the picture he made. Sprawled on his back on the bearskin rug, he lay with one arm flung outward, the other bent and covering his eyes.

He was bare-chested. Firelight warmed skin that was deep gold dusted with a hint of dark hair that ran down the midline of his rib cage. Smooth muscles gave definition to a torso that was a sculptor's dream.

Arousal swam in her veins, sluggish and sweet, washing away any vestige of sadness from earlier in the evening. A wave of yearning tightened her thighs. Moisture gathered in her sex, readying her for his possession. Leo would never have made a move on her this evening in light of what she had shared with him.

Which meant that Phoebe had to take the initiative.

Telling herself and her houseguest that intimacy between them wasn't a good idea was as realistic as commanding the moon not to rise over the mountain. She *wanted* Leo. She trembled with the force of that wanting. It had been aeons since she had felt even the slightest interest in a man, longer still since she had paid any attention to the sexual needs of her body.

It was foolish to miss this chance that might never come her way again. Leo was not only physically appealing, he was also a fascinating and complex man. She was drawn to him with a force that was as strong as it was unexpected. Some things in life couldn't be explained. Often in her old life, she had picked stocks based on hunches. Nine times out of ten she was right.

With Leo, the odds might not be as good. Heartbreak and loss were potential outcomes. But at this barren time in her life, she was willing to take that chance.

Before she could change her mind, she drew her gown up and over her head. Being naked felt wanton and wicked, particularly in the midst of winter. Too long now she had bundled herself up in every way…mentally…emotionally. It was time to face life and be brave again.

She knelt beside him and sat back on her haunches, marveling at the beauty of his big, elegant body. His navy sleep pants hung low on his hips, exposing his navel. The tangle of bedding, blankets and all, reached just high enough to conceal his sex. Though she was pushing her limits, she didn't quite have the courage to take a corner of the sheet and pull.

Would he reject her, citing her emotional distress and bad timing? Or was Leo's need as great as hers? Did he want her enough to ignore all the warning signs and go for it regardless of possible catastrophe?

There was only one way to find out. Slipping her hand beneath the blanket, she encountered silk warmed by his skin. Carefully, she stroked over the interesting mound that was his sex. She had no more than touched him when he began to swell and harden.

Fifteen

Leo was having the most amazing dream. One of Phoebe's hands touched him intimately, while the other moved lightly over his chest, toying with his navel, teasing his nipples with her thumb. He groaned in his sleep, trying not to move so the illusion wouldn't shatter.

He sensed her leaning over him, her hair brushing his chest, his shoulders, his face, as she found his mouth. The kiss tasted sweet and hot. Small, sharp teeth nipped his bottom lip. He shuddered, bound in thrall to a surge of arousal that left him weak and gasping for breath. His chest heaved as he tried to pull air into his lungs.

His heart pounded like the hooves of a racehorse in the last turn. For a split second, a dash of cold fear dampened his enthusiasm. He hadn't had sex since his heart attack. All medical reassurances to the contrary, he wasn't sure what would happen when he was intimate with a woman. His hand—and the process of self-gratification—he trusted. Would the real deal finish him off?

But this was a dream. No need for heartburn. He laughed inwardly at his own pun. Nothing mattered but hanging onto the erotic fantasy and enjoying it until the end.

He felt Phoebe slide his loose pants down his legs and

over his feet. In the next second she was up on her knees straddling him. Grabbing one smooth, firm thigh, he tugged, angling her leg over his shoulder so he could pleasure her with his mouth. When he put his tongue at her center and probed, he shot from the realm of slumber to delicious reality in a nanosecond. The taste of Phoebe's sweet, hot sex was all too authentic.

His hands cupped her ass to hold her steady, even as his brain struggled to catch up. "Phoebe?" The hoarse word was all he could manage. Blinking to clear his sleep-fogged eyes, he looked up and found himself treated to the vision of soft, full breasts half hidden in a fall of silky black hair. Curvy hips nipped into a narrow waist.

Phoebe's wary-eyed gaze met his. She licked her lips, uncertainty in every angle of her body. "I didn't ask," she said, looking delightfully guilty.

"Trust me, honey. There's not a man living who would object. But you should have woken me up sooner. I don't want to miss anything." He loved the fact that she had taken the initiative in their coming together, because it told him she was as invested in this madness as he was. He scooted his thumb along the damp crevice where her body was pink and perfect. When he concentrated on a certain spot, Phoebe moaned.

Inserting two fingers, he found her swollen and wet. *Sweet Lord.* The driving urge he had to take her wildly and immediately had to be subdued in favor of pleasuring such an exquisite creature slowly. Making her yearn and burn and ultimately reach the same razor-sharp edge of arousal on which he balanced so precariously.

"Put your hair behind your shoulders," he commanded.

Phoebe lifted her arms and obeyed.

"Link your hands behind your back."

A split second of hesitation and then compliance. The

docile acquiescence gave him a politically incorrect rush of elation. She was his. She was his.

Watching her face for every nuance of reaction, he played with her sex…light, teasing strokes interspersed with firmer pressure. Her body bloomed for him, the spicy sent of her making him drunk with hunger. Keeping his thumb on the little bud that encompassed her pleasure center, he entered her with three fingers this time, stretching her sheath.

Phoebe came instantly, with a keening cry. He actually felt the little flutters inside her as she squeezed. Imagining what that would feel like on his shaft made him dizzy.

When the last ripple of orgasm released her, he sat up, settling Phoebe in his lap and holding her tightly. His eager erection bumped up against her bottom. Her thighs were draped over his, her ankles linked at his back.

Emotions hit him hard and fast. The one he hadn't anticipated was regret. Not for touching her, never that. But sorrow that they hadn't met sooner. And fear that she would be dismissive of their intimacy because their time together had been so brief.

He waited as long as he could. At least until her breathing returned to normal. Then he pulled back and searched her face. "Don't think for a minute that we're almost done. That was only a tiny prelude. I'm going to devote myself to making you delirious with pleasure."

Her smile was smug. "Been there, done that, bought the T-shirt."

Leo knew that if things were to progress he had to get up. But knowing and doing were two different matters. "Can I ask you a very important question, my Phoebe?"

She rested her forehead on his shoulder. "Ask away."

"If I go fetch a bushel of condoms, will you change your mind about this while I'm gone?"

He felt her go still. “No.” The voice was small, but the sentiment seemed genuine.

“And if Teddy wakes at an inopportune moment, will that be an excuse? Or even a sign from the universe that we should stop?”

She lifted her head, her eyes searching his. For what? Encouragement? Sincerity? “If that happens,” she said slowly, “we’ll settle him back to sleep and pick up where we left off.”

“Good.” He told himself to release her. Until he rustled up some protection, he couldn’t take her the way he wanted to. But holding her like this was unutterably sweet. A real conundrum, because he couldn’t ever remember feeling such a thing with another lover. This mix of shivering need and overwhelming tenderness.

Phoebe smiled. “Shall I go get them?”

He shook his head. “No. Just give me a minute.” The actual fire had died down, and he needed to take care of that, as well.

While he sat there, desperately trying to find the will to stand up, Phoebe reached behind her bottom and found his shaft, giving it a little tug. The teasing touch was almost more than he could stand. The skin at the head was tight and wet with fluid that had leaked in his excitement.

Her fingers found the less rigid part of his sex and massaged him gently. “Don’t. Ah, God, don’t,” he cried. But it was too late. He came in a violent climax that racked him with painful, fiery release. Gripping Phoebe hard enough to endanger her ribs, he groaned and shuddered, feeling the press of her breasts against his chest.

In the pregnant silence that followed, the witch had the temerity to laugh. “Perhaps we should quit while we’re ahead. I don’t think you’re going to make it down the hall anytime soon.”

He pinched her ass, gasping for breath. "Impertinent hussy."

"Well, it's true. I suppose I should have thought through all the ramifications before I jumped your bones."

"You *were* a tad eager," he pointed out, squeezing her perfectly plump butt cheeks.

Phoebe wriggled free and wrapped a blanket around her shoulders. "Go, Leo. Hurry. I'm getting cold."

Dragging himself to his feet, he yawned and stretched. Just looking at her had his erection bobbing hopefully again. *Down, boy.* He removed the fire screen, threw on a couple of good-size logs and poked the embers until they blazed up again. "Don't go anywhere," he ordered. "I'll be right back."

Phoebe watched him walk away with stars in her eyes. This was bad. This was very bad. Leo in the buff was one spectacular sight. Aside from his considerable *assets,* the view from the rear was impressive, as well. Broad shoulders, trim waist, taut buttocks, nicely muscled thighs. Even his big feet were sexy.

Despite everything they had done in the last forty-five minutes, her body continued to hum with arousal. She still couldn't believe she had stripped naked and attacked him in his sleep. That was something the old Phoebe might have done. But only if the man in question were Leo. He had the ability to make a woman throw caution to the wind.

She tidied the pile of bedding and smoothed out the wrinkles. Just like a cavewoman preparing for the return of her marauding spouse. It struck her as funny that Leo really had provided food for her. Not by clubbing anything over the head, but still…

Now that he was gone, she felt a bit bashful. She had seen the size of his sex. Wondering how things would fit together made her nipples furl in anticipation.

His return was rapid and startling. From his hand dangled a long strip of connected condom packages. She licked her lips. "I don't think the night is that long."

Dropping down beside her, he bit her shoulder. "Trust me, sweetheart."

He took her chin in his hand, the lock of hair falling across his forehead making him look younger and more carefree. "I'm thinking we'll go hard and fast the first time and then branch out into variations."

As he cupped her breast, her eyelids fluttered shut all of their own accord. Despite the fact that he had paraded nude through the house, his skin was as warm as ever. She burrowed closer. "Merry Christmas to me," she muttered.

"Look at me, Phoebe."

When she obeyed, she saw that every trace of his good humor had fled. His face was no more than planes and angles, painted by firelight to resemble an ancient king. Eyes so dark they appeared black. Still he held her chin. "I'm looking," she quipped with deliberate sass. "What am I supposed to see?" His intensity aroused and agitated her, but she wouldn't let him know how his caveman antics affected her. Not yet.

He flipped her onto her back without warning, her brief fall cushioned by the many-layered pallet. Instead of answering her provocative question, he *showed* her. Kneeling between her thighs, he yanked a single packet free, ripped it open with his teeth and extracted the contents. Making sure she watched him—by the simple expedient of locking her gaze to his—he rolled the condom over his straining erection.

She doubted he meant for her to see him wince. But the evidence of his arousal lit a fire low in her belly. Leo was in pain. Because of her. He wanted her so badly his hands were shaking. That meant he was more vulnerable than she had imagined. And knowing she was not the only one falling apart calmed her nerves.

Clearly, Leo did not see her as one in a line of faceless women. Whatever their differences in lifestyle, or world view, or even sexual experience, tonight was special.

She grabbed his wrist. "Tell me what you're going to do to me." She breathed the words on a moan as his legs tangled with hers and he positioned the head of his sex at her opening.

Still he didn't smile. His expression was a mask of frayed control…jaw clenched, teeth ground together. "I'm going to take you, my sweet. To heaven and back."

At the first push of his rigid length, she lost her breath. Everything in the room stood still. Her body strained to accommodate him. Though she was more than ready, she had been celibate a long time, and Leo was a big man.

He paused, though the effort brought beads of perspiration to his forehead. "Too much?" he asked, his voice raw.

"No." She concentrated on relaxing, though everything inside her seemed wound tight. "I want all of you."

Her declaration made him shudder as though the mental picture was more stimulating than the actual joining of their flesh. Steadily, he forced his way in. Phoebe felt his penetration in every inch of her soul. She knew in that instant that she had been deceiving herself. Leo was more than a mere fling. He was the man who could make her live again.

When he was fully seated, he withdrew with a hoarse shout and slammed into her, making her grab the leg of the coffee table as a brace. "I don't want to hurt you," he rasped.

"Then don't stop, Leo. I can handle whatever you have to give."

Sixteen

Leo was out of control. In some sane corner of his mind, he knew it. But Phoebe…God, Phoebe…she milked the length of him every time he withdrew, and on the down-stroke arched her back, taking him a centimeter deeper with each successive thrust.

Her legs had his waist in a vise. Her cloud of night-dark hair fanned out around them. He buried his face in it at one point, stilling his frantic motions, desperately trying to stave off his release. She smelled amazing. Though he couldn't pinpoint the fragrance, he would have recognized her scent in a pitch-black room.

Her fingernails dug into his back. He relished the sting-ing discomfort…found his arousal ratcheting up by a de-gree each time she cried out his name and marked his flesh.

But nothing prepared him for the feel of her climax as she tightened on his shaft and came apart in release. He held her close, feeling the aftershocks that quivered in her sex like endless ripples of sensation.

When he knew she was at peace, he lost it. Slamming into her without finesse or reason, he exploded in a white-hot flash of lust. He lost a few seconds in the aftermath, his mouth dry and his head pounding.

Barely conscious, he tried to spare her most of his weight. He had come twice in quick succession, and his brain was muddled, incredulous that he wanted her still.

Phoebe stirred restlessly. "We should get some sleep." Her words were barely audible, but he caught the inference.

No way. She wasn't leaving him. No way in hell. Rolling onto his side, he scooped her close, spooning her with a murmur of satisfaction. Though her soft bottom pressed into the cradle of his thighs, his arousal was a faint whisper after two incredible climaxes. The need he felt was more than physical.

Her head pillowed on his arm, he slept.

He couldn't mark the moment consciousness returned, but he knew at once that he was alone. Sunlight peeked in around the edges of the drapes, the reflection strangely bright. He could hear the furnace running, and although the fire had long since burned out, he was plenty warm.

Sitting up with a groan, he felt muscle twinges that came from a night of carnal excess. Thinking about it made him hard. He cursed, well aware that any repeat of last night's sexual calisthenics was hours in the future.

Phoebe had put away all the bedding she had used on the sofa. But on the kitchen counter he saw a pot of coffee steaming. He stood up, feeling as if he'd been on a weekend bender. Grabbing his robe that had gotten wedged beneath the edge of the sofa, he slid his arms into the sleeves and zeroed in on the life-saving caffeine.

After two cups he was ready to go in search of his landlady. He found her and Teddy curled up on Phoebe's bed reading books. She sat up when she saw him, her smile warm but perhaps tinged with reserve. "I hope we didn't wake you."

He put his hands on top of the door frame and stretched

hard, feeling the muscles loosen bit by bit. "I didn't hear a thing. Has he been up long?"

"An hour maybe. I gave him his bottle in here."

They were conversing like strangers. Or perhaps a married couple with nothing much to say.

He sat down on the edge of the bed and took her hand. "Good morning, Phoebe."

Hot color flushed her cheeks and reddened her throat. "Good morning."

He dragged her closer for a scorching kiss. "It sure as hell is."

That surprised a laugh from her, and immediately he felt her relax. "Have you looked outside?" she asked.

He shook his head. "No. Why? Did it snow?"

She nodded. "We got three or four inches. Buford's grandson will plow the driveway by midmorning. I know you were expecting some deliveries."

Shock immobilized him. It had been hours since he had checked his email on Phoebe's phone or even sent his brother a text. Never in his adult life could he remember going so long without his electronic lifelines. Yet with Phoebe, tucked away from the world, he had gradually begun to accept the absence of technology as commonplace.

Not that she was really rustic in her situation. She had phones and television. But beyond that, life was tech-free. He frowned, not sure he was comfortable with the knowledge that she had converted him in a matter of days. It was the sex. That's all. He'd been pleasantly diverted. Didn't mean he wanted to give up his usual M.O. on a permanent basis.

Smiling to cover his unease, he released her. "I'm going to take a shower. I can play with the kid after that if you want to clean up."

* * *

Phoebe watched him go, her heart troubled. Something was off, but she couldn't pinpoint it. Maybe nothing more than a bad case of *morning after.*

By the time both adults were clean and dressed, the sound of a tractor echoed in the distance. Soon the driveway was passable, and in no time at all, vehicles began arriving. A truck dealing with Leo's satellite internet. The express delivery service with his new phone. A large moving van that somehow managed to turn and back up to the damaged cabin.

With the felled tree completely gone now, a small army of men began carrying out everything salvageable to place into storage until the repairs were complete. Leo didn't even linger for breakfast. He was out the door in minutes, wading into the midst of chaos…coordinating, instructing, and generally making himself indispensable. Phoebe wasn't sure what she would have done without his help. If she had not been laden with the responsibility of Teddy, she would have managed just fine. But caring for a baby and trying to deal with the storm damage at the same time would have made things extremely difficult.

She was amazed that she could see a difference in the baby in two weeks. He was growing so quickly and his personality seemed more evident every day. This morning he was delighting himself by blowing bubbles and babbling nonsense sounds.

After tidying the kitchen, Phoebe picked him up out of his high chair and carried him over to the tree. "See what Leo and I did, Teddy? Isn't it pretty?" The baby reached for an ornament, and she tucked his hand to her cheek. "I know. It isn't fair to have so many pretty baubles and none of them for you to play with."

Teddy grabbed a strand of her hair that had escaped her braid and yanked. She'd been in a hurry that morning after her shower and had woven her hair in its usual style with less than her usual precision. It was beginning to be clear to her why so many young mothers had simple hairstyles. Caring for an infant didn't leave much time for primping.

In another half hour Teddy would be ready for a nap. Already his eyes were drooping. After last night's excess, Phoebe might try to sneak in a few minutes of shut-eye herself. Thinking about Leo made her feel all bubbly inside. Like a sixteen-year-old about to go to prom with her latest crush.

Even in the good days with her fiancé, sex had never been like that. Leo had devoted himself to her pleasure, proving to her again and again that she had more to give and receive. Her body felt sensitized…energized…eager to try it all over again.

She walked the baby around the living room, humming Christmas carols, feeling happier than she had felt in a long time.

When the knock sounded at the front door, she looked up in puzzlement. Surely Leo hadn't locked himself out. She had made sure to leave the catch undone when he left. Before she could react, the door opened and a familiar head appeared.

"Dana!" Phoebe eyed her sister with shock and dismay. "What's wrong? Why are you here?"

Leo jogged back to the cabin. He was starving, but more than that, he wanted to see Phoebe. He didn't want to give her time to think of a million reasons why they shouldn't be together. When he burst through the front door, he ground to a halt, immediately aware that he had walked into a tense situation. He'd seen an unfamiliar car outside, but hadn't paid much attention, assuming it belonged to one of the workmen.

Phoebe's eyes met his across the room. For a split second, he saw into her very soul. Her anguish seared him, but the moment passed, and now her expression seemed normal. She smiled at him. "You're just in time. My sister, Dana, arrived unexpectedly. Dana, this is Leo."

He shook hands with the other woman and tried to analyze the dynamic that sizzled in the room. Dana was a shorter, rounder version of her sister. At the moment, she seemed exhausted and at the point of tears.

Phoebe held Teddy on her hip. "What are you doing here, Dana? Why didn't you let me know you were coming? I would have picked you up at the airport. You look like you haven't slept in hours."

Dana plopped onto the sofa and burst into tears, her hands over her face. "I knew you would try to talk me out of it," she sobbed. "I know it's stupid. I've been on a plane for hours, and I have to be back on a flight at two. But I couldn't spend Christmas without my baby. I thought I could, but I can't."

Leo froze, realizing at once what was happening. Phoebe…dear, beautiful, strong Phoebe put whatever feelings she had aside and went to sit beside her sister. "Of course you can't. I understand. Dry your eyes and take your son." She handed Teddy over to his mother as though it were the most natural thing in the world.

Leo knew it was breaking her heart.

Dana's face when she hugged her baby to her chest would have touched even the most hardened cynic. She kissed the top of his head, nuzzling the soft, fuzzy hair. "We found a lady in the village who speaks a little English. She's agreed to look after him while we work."

Phoebe clasped her hands in her lap as if she didn't know what to do with them. "How are things going with your father-in-law's estate?"

Dana made a face. "It's a mess. Worse than we thought. So stressful. The house is chock-full of junk. We have to go through it all so we don't miss anything valuable. I know it doesn't make sense to take Teddy over there, but if I can just have him in the evenings and be able to see him during the day when we take breaks, I know I'll feel so much better."

Phoebe nodded. "Of course you will."

Dana grabbed her sister's wrist. "You don't know how much we love you and appreciate all you've done for Teddy. I have an extra ticket on standby if you want to come back with me...or even in a day or two. I don't want you to be alone at Christmas, especially because it was that time of year when you lost—" She clapped her hand over her mouth, her expression horrified. "Oh, God, honey. I'm sorry. I'm exhausted and I don't know what I'm saying. I didn't mean to mention it."

Phoebe put an arm around the frazzled woman and kissed her cheek. "Take a deep breath, Dana. Everything's fine. I'm fine. If you're really on such a time crunch, let's start packing up Teddy's things. He'll nap in the car while you drive."

Phoebe paused in the back hallway, leaning against the wall and closing her eyes. Her smile felt frozen in place. Leo wasn't fooled. She could see his concern. But the important thing was for Dana not to realize what her unexpected arrival had done to Phoebe's plans for a cozy Christmas.

In less than an hour from start to finish, Dana came and went, taking Teddy with her. The resultant silence was painful. The only baby items left behind were the high chair in the kitchen and the large pieces of furniture in Teddy's room. Without asking, Leo took the high chair, put it in with the other stuff and shut the door. Phoebe watched him, her heart in pieces at her feet.

When he returned, she wrapped her arms around her

waist, her mood as flat as a three-day-old helium balloon. "I knew he wasn't my baby."

"Of course you did."

Leo's unspoken compassion took her close to an edge she didn't want to face. "Don't be nice to me or I may fall apart."

He grinned, taking her in his arms and resting his cheek on her head. "I'm very proud of you, Phoebe."

"For what?"

"For being such a good sister and aunt. For not making Dana feel guilty. For doing what had to be done."

"I was looking forward to Christmas morning," she whispered, her throat tight with unshed tears. "His presents are all wrapped." She clung to Leo, feeling his warm presence like a balm to her hurting spirit.

He squeezed her shoulders. "I have an idea to cheer you up."

She pulled back to look at him, only slightly embarrassed that her eyes were wet. "Having recently participated in some of your ideas, I'm listening," she said.

He wiped the edge of her eye with his thumb. "Get your mind out of the gutter, Ms. Kemper. I wanted to propose a trip."

"But you just arrived."

Putting a finger over her lips, he drew her to the sofa and sat down with her, tucking her close to his side. "Let me get it all out before you interrupt."

Phoebe nodded. "Okay."

"You asked me earlier about my plans for Christmas, and I had pretty much decided to stay here with you and Teddy. But I did feel a twinge of sadness and guilt to be missing some things back home. This weekend is the big Cavallo Christmas party for all our employees and their families. We have it at Luc's house. I'd like you to go with me."

She opened her mouth to speak, but he shushed her.

"Hear me out," he said. "I have an older friend who retired from Cavallo ten years ago, but he likes to keep busy. So now and again when the need arises, he does jobs for me. I know he would jump at the chance to come up here and oversee your cabin renovation. I trust him implicitly. He could stay in my room if it's okay with you. What do you think?"

"So I'm allowed to speak now?" She punched his ribs.

He inclined his head. "You have my permission."

"Where would *I* stay?"

"You mean in Atlanta?"

She nodded. "Yes."

"I was hoping you'd be at my place. But I can put you up at a nice hotel if you'd rather do that."

She scooted onto his lap, facing him, her hands on his shoulders. "But what about all my decorations and the tree?"

He pursed his lips. "Well, we could replicate the ambience at my place. You *do* like decorating. But I was also thinking that maybe you and I could come back here in time for Christmas Eve. Just the two of us. I know it won't be the same without Teddy, so if that's a bad idea, you can say so."

Seventeen

Leo held his breath, awaiting her answer. The fact that she felt comfortable enough with him to be sitting as she was reassured him. Last night a noticeable dynamic between them had shifted. She felt a part of him now. In ways he couldn't quite explain.

It had killed him to know she was so hurt this morning. Yet in the midst of her pain, she had handled herself beautifully, never once letting her sister realize how much Phoebe had been counting on Christmas with her nephew. By Phoebe's own admission, this was the first time in three years she had felt like celebrating. Yet when everything seemed to be going her way, she was blindsided by disappointment and loss.

Not a tragedy or a permanent loss, but deeply hurtful nevertheless.

Phoebe ran her fingers across his scalp, both hands… messing up his hair deliberately. "Do I have to decide now?"

"You mean about Christmas Eve?"

"Yes."

"I think that can wait. But does that mean you'll go with me?"

"I suppose I'll need a fancy dress." She traced the outer edges of his ears, making him squirm restlessly.

"Definitely. Is that a problem?" Holding her like this was a torment he could do without at the moment. He heard too much activity going on outside to be confident of no interruptions. When she slid a hand inside his shirt collar, he shivered. His erection was trapped uncomfortably beneath her denim-clad butt.

"No problem at all," she said breezily, unfastening the top two buttons of his shirt. "I have a whole closet full of nice things from my gainfully employed days."

"Define nice...."

She kissed him softly, sliding her tongue into his mouth and making him crazy. "Backless," she whispered. "Not much of a front. Slit up the leg. How does that sound?"

He groaned. "Lord, have mercy." He wasn't sure if he was talking about the dress or about the way her nimble fingers were moving down his chest. "Phoebe," he said, trying to sound more reasonable and less desperate. "Was that a *yes?*"

She cupped his face in her hands, her expression suddenly sweet and intense. "Thank you, Leo. You've saved Christmas for me. As hard as it was to say goodbye to little Teddy, you're the only other male of my acquaintance who could make me want to enjoy the season. So yes. I'd love to go with you to Atlanta."

He had to talk fast, but he managed to convince her they should leave that afternoon. Already he was fantasizing about making love to her in his comfy king-size bed. Last night's spontaneous lunacy had been mind-blowing, but there was something to be said for soft sheets and a firm mattress. Not to mention the fact that he wanted to wine and dine her and show her that the big city had its own appeal.

When she finally emerged from her bedroom, he stared.

Phoebe had one large suitcase, two smaller ones and a garment bag.

He put his hands on his hips, cocking his head. "You did understand that this was a *brief* visit…right?"

She was hot and flushed and wisps of hair stood out from her head like tiny signals saying, *Don't mess with me!* Dumping the bags at his feet, she wiped her forehead with the back of her hand. "I want to be prepared for any eventuality."

He nudged the enormous bag with his toe. "The NASA astronauts weren't *this* prepared," he joked. But inside he was pleased that the sparkle was back in her eyes. "Anything else I should know about? You do know I drive a Jag."

Phoebe smiled sweetly. "We could take my van."

He shuddered theatrically. "Leo Cavallo has a reputation to uphold. No, thank you."

While Phoebe went through the cabin turning off lights and putting out fresh sheets and towels, Leo studied the phone he had ordered. No point in taking it with him. He would only need it if he came back. If. Where had that thought come from? His reservation was fixed until the middle of January with a possible two-week extension.

Simply because he and Phoebe were going to make an appearance at the Christmas party didn't mean that his doctor and Luc were going to let him off the hook. He was painfully aware that he still hadn't told Phoebe the truth. And the reasons were murky.

But one thing stood out. Vanity. He didn't want her to see him as weak or broken. It was a hell of a thing to admit. But would she think of him differently once she knew?

By the time the car was loaded and they had dropped off the keys at Buford's house, Leo was starving. In blissful disregard of the calendar date, Phoebe had packed a picnic. To eat in the car, she insisted.

Instead of the way he had come in before, Phoebe suggested another route. "If you want to, we can take the scenic route, up over the mountains to Cherokee, North Carolina, and then we'll drop south to Atlanta from there. The road was closed by a landslide for a long time, but they've reopened it."

"I'm game," he said. "At least this time it will be daylight."

Phoebe giggled, tucking her legs into the car and waiting for him to shut the door. "You were so grumpy that night."

"I thought I was never going to get here. The rain and the fog and the dark. I was lucky I didn't end up nose deep in the creek."

"It wasn't that bad."

He shook his head, refusing to argue the point. Today's drive, though, was the complete opposite of his introduction to Phoebe's home turf. Sun shone down on them, warming the temperatures nicely. The winding two-lane highway cut through the quaint town of Gatlinburg and then climbed the mountain at a gentle grade. The vistas were incredible. He'd visited here once as a child, but it had been so long ago he had forgotten how peaceful the Smokies were… and how beautiful.

The trip flew by. Part of the time they talked. At other moments, they listened to music, comparing favorite artists and arguing over the merits of country versus pop. If driving to Tennessee had initially seemed like a punishment, today was entirely the opposite. He felt unreasonably lucky and blessed to be alive.

As they neared the city, he felt his pulse pick up. This was where he belonged. He and Luc had built something here, something good. But what if the life he knew and loved wasn't right for Phoebe?

Was it too soon to wonder such a thing?

All day he had been hyperaware of her…the quick flash of her smile, her light flowery scent, the way she moved her hands when she wanted to make a point. He remained in a state of constant semi-arousal. Now that they were almost at their destination, he found himself subject to a surprising agitation.

What if Phoebe didn't like his home?

She was silent as they pulled into the parking garage beneath his downtown high-rise building and slowed to a halt beside the kiosk. "Hey, Jerome," he said, greeting the stoop-shouldered, balding man inside the booth with a smile. "This is where we get out, Phoebe." He turned back to Jerome. "Do you mind asking one of the boys to unload the car and bring up our bags?"

"Not at all, Mr. Cavallo. We'll get them right up."

Leo took Phoebe's elbow and steered her toward the elevator, where he used his special key to access and press the penthouse button. "Jerome's a retired army sergeant. He runs this place with an iron fist."

Phoebe clutched her purse, her expression inscrutable. Because the video camera in this tiny space was recording everything they said, Leo refrained from personal chitchat. He preferred to keep his private life private.

Upstairs, they stepped out into his private hallway. He generally took the recessed lighting and sophisticated decor for granted, but Phoebe looked around with interest. Once inside, he tossed his keys on a console table and held out a hand. "Would you like the tour?"

Phoebe felt like Alice in Wonderland. To go from her comfortable though modest cabin to this level of luxury was the equivalent of situational whiplash. She had realized on an intellectual level that Leo must be wealthy. Though she hadn't known him personally before he arrived on her doorstep, she was well aware of the Cavallo empire and the pricey goods it offered to high-end consumers. But somehow, she hadn't fully understood *how* rich Leo really was.

The floors of his penthouse condo, acres of them it seemed, were laid in cream-colored marble veined with gold. Expensive Oriental rugs in hues of cinnamon and deep azure bought warmth and color to what might otherwise have been too sterile a decorating scheme.

Incredible artwork graced the walls. Some of the paintings, to Phoebe's inexperience gaze, appeared to be priceless originals. Two walls of the main living area were made entirely of glass, affording an unparalleled view of Atlanta as far as the eye could see. Everything from the gold leaf–covered dome of the Capitol building to the unmistakable outline of Stone Mountain in the far distance.

A variety of formal armchairs and sofas were upholstered in either pale gold velvet or ecru leather. Crimson and navy pillows beckoned visitors to sit and relax. Overhead, a massive modern chandelier splayed light to all corners of the room.

Undoubtedly, all of the fabrics were of Italian Cavallo design. Phoebe, who had always adored vivid color and strong statements in decor, fell in love with Leo's home immediately. She turned in a circle. "I'm speechless. Should I take off my shoes?"

He stepped behind her, his hands on her shoulders. Pushing aside her hair, left loose for a change, he kissed her neck just below her ear. "It's meant to be lived in. May I say how glad I am that you're here?"

She turned to face him, wondering if she really knew him at all. At her old job, she had earned a comfortable living. But in comparison to all this, she was a pauper. How did Leo know she was not interested in him for his money? Unwilling to disclose her unsettling thoughts, she linked her arms around his neck. "Thank you for inviting me."

She tugged at his bottom lip with the pad of her thumb. "Surely there are bedrooms I should see."

His eyes darkened. "I didn't want to rush you."

Her hand brushed the front of his trousers. "I've noticed this fellow hanging around all day."

The feel of her slim fingers, even through the fabric of his pants, affected him like an electric shock. "Seems to be a permanent condition around you."

"Then I suppose it's only fair if I offer some…um…"

His grin was a wicked flash of white teeth. "While you're thinking of the appropriate word, my sweet," Leo said, scooping her into his arms, "I could show you my etchings."

She tweaked his chin. "Not in here, I presume?"

"Down the hall." He held her close to his chest, his muscular arms bearing her weight as if she were no more than a child.

Being treated like Scarlett O'Hara seemed entirely appropriate here in the Peach State. Leo's power and strength seduced her almost as much as the memory of last night's erotic play. "The sofa is closer," she whispered, noting the shadow of his stubble and the way his golden-skinned throat moved when he spoke huskily.

He nodded his head, hunger darkening his eyes. "I like the way you think." He kissed her cheek as he strode across the room.

"No one knows you're home, right?"

"Correct."

"And there's no one else on this floor?"

He shook his head, lowering her onto the soft cushions. "No."

"So I can be as loud as I like?"

He stared at her in shock as her outrageous taunt sank in. "Good God Almighty." Color crept from his throat to his hairline. "I thought you were a sweet young thing when I first met you. But apparently I was wrong."

"Never judge a book by its cover, Mr. Cavallo." She ripped her sweater off over her head. "Please tell me you have some more of those packets."

Leo seemed fixated on the sight of her lace-covered breasts, but he recovered. "Damn it." His expression leaned toward desperation.

"What's wrong?"

"All of our luggage is downstairs."

"Your bathroom. Here?"

"Well, yes, but somebody will be coming up that elevator any moment now."

"Leo…" she wailed, not willing to wait another second. "Call them back. Tell them we're in the shower."

"Both of us?" He glanced at the door and back at her, frustration a living, breathing presence between them. An impressive erection tented his slacks. "It won't be long. Fifteen minutes tops."

The way she felt at the moment, five minutes was too long. She wanted Leo. Now.

Fortunately for both of them, a quiet chime sounded, presumably a doorbell, though it sounded more like a heavenly harp. Leo headed for the entrance and stared back at her. "You planning on staying like that?"

Her jaw dropped. She was half naked and the doorknob was turning in Leo's hand. With a squeak, she clutched her sweater to her breasts and ran around the nearest wall, which happened to conceal the kitchen. Not even bothering to envy the fabulous marble countertops and fancy appliances, she listened with bated breath as Leo conversed with the bellman. At long last, she heard the door close, and the sound of footsteps.

As she hovered amidst gourmet cookware and the scent of unseen spices, Leo appeared. "He's gone." In his hand he held a stack of condoms. "Is this what you wanted?"

Eighteen

Leo had never particularly considered his kitchen to be a sexy place. In truth, he spent little time here. But with Phoebe loitering half naked, like a nymph who had lost her way, he suddenly began to see about a zillion possibilities.

He leaned a hip against the counter. "Take off the rest of your clothes." Would she follow his lead, or had he come on too strong?

When perfect white teeth mutilated her bottom lip, he couldn't decide if she was intending to drive him crazy by delaying or if she was perhaps now a bit shy. Without responding verbally, she tugged off her knee-length boots and removed her trim black slacks. The only article of clothing that remained, her tiny panties, was a perfect match to her blush-pink bra.

"The floor is cold," she complained as she kicked aside the better part of her wardrobe.

His hands clenched the edge of the counter behind him. Lord, she was a handful. And gorgeous to boot. "You're not done," he said with far more dispassion than he felt.

Phoebe thrust out her bottom lip and straightened her shoulders. "I don't know why you have to be so bossy."

"Because you like it." He could see the excitement building in her wide-eyed stare as she reached behind her back and unfastened her bra. It fell to the floor like a wispy pink cloud. Though she hesitated for a brief moment, she continued disrobing, stepping out of her small undies with all the grace of a seasoned stripper.

She twirled the panties on the end of her finger. "Come and get me."

He literally saw red. His vision hazed and he felt every molecule of moisture leach from his mouth. Quickly, with razor-sharp concentration that belied the painful ache in his groin, he assessed the possibilities. Beside the refrigerator, some genius architect had thought to install a desk that matched the rest of the kitchen. The marble top was the perfect height for what Leo had in mind.

Forget the sofa or the bedroom or any other damned part of his house. He was going to take her here.

He could barely look at Phoebe without coming apart at the seams. Young and strong and healthy, she was the epitome of womanhood. Her dark hair fell over one shoulder, partially veiling one raspberry nipple. "You're beautiful, Phoebe."

The raw sincerity in his strained voice must have told her that the time for games was over. Surprised pleasure warmed her eyes. "I'm glad you think so." She licked her lips. "Do you plan on staying over there forever?"

"I don't know," he said in all seriousness. "The way I feel at the moment, I'm afraid I'll take you like a madman."

Her lips curved. "Is that a bad thing?"

"You tell me." Galvanized at last into action by a yearning that could no longer be denied, he picked her up by the waist and sat her on the desk. Phoebe yelped when the cold surface made contact with her bottom, but she exhaled on a long, deep sigh as the sensation subsided.

He ripped at his zipper and freed his sex. He was as hard as the marble that surrounded them, but far hotter. Sheathing himself with fumbling hands, he stepped between her legs. "Prop your feet on the desk, honey."

Phoebe's cooperation was instant, though her eyes rounded when she realized what he was about to do.

He positioned himself at the opening of her moist pink sex and shoved, one strong thrust that took him all the way. He held her bottom for leverage and moved slowly in and out. Phoebe's arms linked around his neck in a strangle-hold. Her feet lost their purchase and instead, she linked her ankles behind his waist.

It would be embarrassing if she realized that his legs were trembling and his heart was doing weird flips and flops that had nothing to do with his recent health event. Phoebe made him forget everything he thought was important and forced him to concentrate on the two of them. Not from any devious machinations on her part, but because she was so damned cute and fun.

Even as he moved inside her, he was already wondering where they could make love next. Heat built in his groin, a monstrous, unstoppable force. "I'm gonna come," he groaned.

She had barely made a sound. In sudden dismay, he leaned back so he could see her face. "Talk to me, Phoebe." Reaching down, he rubbed gently at the swollen nub he'd been grazing again and again with the base of his sex. When his fingers made one last pass, Phoebe arched her back and cried out as she climaxed. Inside, her body squeezed him with flutters that threatened to take off the top of his head because the feeling was so intense.

With his muscles clenched from head to toe, he held back his own release so he could relish every moment of her shuddering finale. As she slumped limp in his embrace, he cursed and thrust wildly, emptying himself until he was wrung dry. With one last forceful thrust, he finished, but as he did, his forehead met the edge of the cabinet over Phoebe's head with enough force to make him stagger backward.

"Hell..." His reverse momentum was halted by the large island in the center of the kitchen. He leaned there, dazed.

Phoebe slid to her feet. "Oh, Leo. You're bleeding." Her face turned red, and she burst out laughing. Mortification and remorse filled her eyes in addition to concern, but she apparently couldn't control her mirth, despite the fact that he had been injured in battle.

Okay. So it *was* a little funny. His lips quirking, he put a hand to his forehead and winced when it came away streaked in red. "Would you please put some clothes on?" he said, trying not to notice the way her breasts bounced nicely when she laughed.

Phoebe rolled her eyes. "Take them off. Put them on. You're never satisfied."

He looked down at his erection that was already preparing for duty. "Apparently not." When she bent over to step into her underwear and pants, it was all he could do not to take her again.

Only the throbbing in his head held him back. When she was decent, he grimaced. "We're going to a party tomorrow night. How am I going to explain this?"

Phoebe took his hand and led him toward the bedrooms. "Which one is yours?" she asked. When he pointed, she kept walking, all the way to his hedonistic bathroom. "We'll put some antibiotic ointment on it between now and then. Plus, there's always makeup."

"Great. Just great."

She opened the drawer he indicated and gathered the needed supplies. "Sit on the stool."

He zipped himself back into his trousers, more to avoid temptation than from any real desire to be dressed. "Is this going to hurt?"

"Probably."

The truth was the truth. When she moistened a cotton ball with antiseptic and dabbed at the cut, it stung like fire. He glanced in the mirror. The gash, more of a deep scrape really, was about two inches long. And dead in the center of his forehead. Now, every time he saw his reflection for the next week or so, all he would remember was debauching Phoebe in his kitchen.

She smeared a line of medicated cream along the wound and tried covering it with two vertical Band-Aids. Now he looked like Frankenstein.

Their eyes met in the large mahogany-framed mirror. Phoebe put a hand over her mouth. "Sorry," she mumbled. But she was shaking all over, and he wasn't fooled. Her mirth spilled out in wet eyes and muffled giggles.

"Thank God you didn't go into nursing," he groused. He stood up and reached for a glass of water to down some ibuprofen. "Are you hungry, by any chance?" The kitchen episode had left him famished. Maybe it was the subliminal message in his surroundings.

Phoebe wiped her eyes and nodded. "That picnic food was a long time ago."

"In that case, let me show you to your room and you can do whatever you need to do to get ready. The place I want to take you is intimate, but fairly casual. You don't really have to change if you don't want to. But I'll drag your three dozen suitcases in there to be on the safe side."

Phoebe wasn't sure what to think about the opulent suite that was apparently hers for the duration of her visit. It was amazing, of course. Yards of white carpet. French country furniture in distressed white wood. A heavy cotton bedspread that had been hand embroidered with every wildflower in the world. And a bathroom that rivaled Leo's. But in truth, she had thought she would be sleeping with him.

Nevertheless, when Leo disappeared, she wasted no time

in getting ready. She took a quick shower, though she made sure to keep her hair dry. It had grown dramatically in three years, far longer than she had ever worn it. Once wet, it was a pain to dry. She brushed it quickly and bound it loosely at the back of her neck with a silver clasp.

Given Leo's description of their destination, she chose black tights and black flats topped with a flirty black skirt trimmed at the hem in three narrow layers of multicolored chiffon. With a hot-pink silk chemise and a waist-length black sweater, she looked nice, but not too over-the-top.

She had forgotten how much fun it was to dress up for a date. Fastening a silver chain around her neck, she fingered the charm that dangled from it. The letter *P* was engraved on the silver disc in fancy cursive script. Her mother's name had started with the same letter as Phoebe's. And Phoebe had decided that if her baby was a girl, she wanted to name her Polly. An old-fashioned name maybe, but one she loved.

It was hard to imagine ever being pregnant again. Would she be terrified the entire nine months? The doctor had insisted there was no reason her next pregnancy shouldn't be perfectly normal. But it would be hard, so hard, not to worry.

Pregnancy was a moot point now. There was no man in her life other than Leo. And the two of them had known each other for no time at all. Even if the relationship were serious—which it definitely was not—Leo wasn't interested in having kids. It hadn't been difficult to pick up on that.

He clearly loved his niece and nephew, and he had been great with Teddy. But he was not the kind of guy to settle for home and hearth. Running the Cavallo conglomerate required most of his devotion. He loved it. Was proud of it. And at the level of responsibility he carried, having any substantive personal life would be tricky.

His brother, Luc, seemed to have mastered the art of balance, from what Leo had said. But maybe Luc wasn't quite as single-mindedly driven as his intense brother.

When she was content with her appearance, she returned to the living room. Leo was standing in front of the expanse of glass, his hands clasped behind his back. He turned when he heard her footsteps. "That was quick."

He looked her over from head to toe. "I'll be the envy of every guy in the restaurant."

She smiled, crossing the room to him and lightly touching his forehead. "You okay?"

"A little headache, but I'll live. Are you ready?"

She nodded. "Perhaps we should stop by a pharmacy and grab some tiny Band-Aids so you don't scare children."

"Smart-ass." He put an arm around her waist and steered her toward the door.

"I'm serious."

"So am I…."

Nineteen

After a quick stop for medical supplies, they arrived at a small bistro tucked away in the heart of downtown Atlanta. The maître d' recognized Leo and escorted them to a quiet table in the corner. "Mr. Cavallo," he said. "So glad to see you are well."

An odd look flashed across Leo's face. "Thank you. Please keep our visit quiet. I hope to surprise my brother tomorrow."

"At the Christmas party, yes?" The dumpy man with the Italian accent nodded with a smile. "My nephew works in your mail room. He is looking forward to it."

"Tell him to introduce himself if he gets a chance."

Leo held Phoebe's chair as she was seated and then joined her on the opposite side of the table. He handed her a menu. "I have my favorites, but you should take a look. They make everything from scratch, and it's all pretty amazing."

After they ordered, Phoebe cocked her head and stared at him with a smile. "Does everyone in Atlanta know who you are?"

"Hardly. I'm just the guy who writes the checks."

"Modest, but suspect."

"It's true," he insisted. "I'm not a player, if that's what you're thinking."

"You don't have the traditional little black book full of names?"

"My phone is black. And a few of the contacts are women."

"That's not an answer."

"I'll plead the Fifth Amendment."

Phoebe enjoyed the dinner immensely. Leo was wearing a beautiful navy-and-gray tweed blazer with dark slacks. Even battle-scarred, he was the most impressive man in the room. Despite his size, he handled his fragile wineglass delicately, his fingers curled around the stem with care.

Thinking about Leo's light touch made Phoebe almost choke on a bite of veal. When she had drained her water glass and regained her composure, Leo grinned. "I don't know what you were thinking about, but your face is bright red."

"You're the one with the sex injury," she pointed out.

"Fair enough." His lips twitched, and his gaze promised retribution later for her refusal to explain.

On the way home, it started to rain. Phoebe loved the quiet swish of the wipers and the fuzzy glow of Christmas decorations in every window. Leo turned down a side street and parked at the curb. He stared through the windshield, his expression oddly intent, his hands clenched on the steering wheel.

"What is it?" she asked. "What's wrong?"

He glanced at her, eyes hooded. "Nothing's *wrong.* Would you mind if we go up to my office?"

She craned her neck, for the first time seeing the Cavallo name on the building directory. "Of course not." He was acting very strangely.

Leo exited the car, opened an umbrella and came around the car to help her out. Fortunately her shoes were not expensive, because her feet tripped through the edge of a puddle as they accessed the sidewalk.

She shivered while he took a set of keys from his pocket and opened the main door. The plate glass clunked shut behind them. "Over there," Leo said. Again, using his private keys, they entered a glossy-walled elevator.

Phoebe had seen dozens of movies where lovers used a quick ride to sneak a passionate kiss. Leo clearly didn't know the plot, because he leaned against the wall and studied the illuminated numbers as they went higher and higher. Cavallo occupied the top twelve floors.

When they arrived at their destination, Phoebe was not surprised to see all the trappings of an elite twenty-first-century business. A sleek reception area decorated for the season, secretarial cubicles, multiple managerial offices and, at the far end of the floor on which they entered, an imposing door with Leo's name inscribed on a brass panel.

Another key, another entry. They skirted what was obviously the domain of an executive assistant and walked through one last door.

Leo stopped so suddenly, she almost ran into his back. She had a feeling he had forgotten her presence. He moved forward slowly, stopping to run a hand along the edge of what was clearly *his* desk. The top was completely bare, the surface polished to a high sheen.

Leo turned to her suddenly, consternation on his face. "Make yourself comfortable," he said, pointing to a leather chair and ottoman near the window. "That's where I like to sit when I have paperwork to read through. I won't be long."

She did as he suggested, noting that much like his sophisticated home, his place of business, arguably the epicenter of his life, had two transparent walls. The dark, rainy night beyond the thick glass was broken up by a million pinpoints of light, markers of a city that scurried to and fro.

As she sat down and propped her feet on the ottoman,

she relaxed into the soft, expensive seat that smelled of leather and Leo's distinctive aftershave. The faint aroma made her nostalgic suddenly for the memory of curling up with him on her sofa, enjoying the Christmas tree and watching the fire.

Leo prowled, tension in the set of his shoulders. He opened drawers, shuffled papers, flicked the leaves of plants on the credenza. He seemed lost. Or at the very least confused.

Hoping to give him the semblance of privacy, she picked up a book from the small table at her elbow. It was a technical and mostly inaccessible tome about third-world economies. She read the first two paragraphs and turned up her nose. Not exactly escape reading.

Next down the pile was a news magazine. But the date was last month's, and she was familiar with most of the stories. Finally, at the bottom, was a collection of Sunday newspapers. Someone had taken great care to stack them in reverse order. Again, they were out of date, but that same someone had extracted the "Around Town" section of the most recent one and folded it to a story whose accompanying photograph she recognized instantly. It was Leo.

Reading automatically, her stomach clenched and her breathing grew choppy. No. This had to be a mistake.

She stood up, paper in her hand, and stared at him. Disbelief, distress and anger coursed through her veins in a nauseating cocktail. "You had a heart attack?"

Leo froze but turned around to face her, his shoulders stiff and his whole body tensed as if facing an enemy. "Who told you that?"

She threw the paper at him, watching it separate and rain down on the thick pile carpet with barely a sound. "It's right there," she cried, clutching her arms around her waist. Prominent Atlanta Businessman Leo Cavallo, Age 36, Suffers Heart Attack. "My God, Leo. Why didn't you tell me?"

He opened his mouth to speak, but she interrupted him with an appalled groan. “You carried wood for me. And chopped down a tree. I made you drag heavy boxes from the attic. Damn it, Leo, how could you not tell me?”

“It wasn’t that big a deal.” His expression was blank, but his eyes burned with an emotion she couldn’t fathom.

She shivered, her mind a whirl of painful thoughts. He could have died. He could have died. He could have died. And she would never have known him. His humor. His kindness. His incredibly sexy and appealing personality. His big, perfect body.

“Trust me,” she said slowly. “When a man in his thirties has a heart attack, it’s a big freaking deal.”

He shoved his hands into his pockets, the line of his mouth grim. “I had a very mild heart attack. A minor blockage. It’s a hereditary thing. I’m extraordinarily healthy. All I have to do now is keep an eye on certain markers.”

As she examined the days in the past week, things kept popping up, memories that made her feel even worse. “Your father,” she whispered. “You said he had a heart attack. And that’s why the boat crashed.”

“Yes.”

“That’s it. Just *yes?* Did it ever occur to you when you were screwing me that your medical history was information I might have wanted to know? Hell, Leo, I gave you every intimate detail of my past and you couldn’t be bothered to mention something as major as a heart attack?” She knew she was shouting and couldn’t seem to stop. Her heart slammed in her chest.

“I’ve never heard you curse. I don’t like it.”

“Well, that’s just too damn bad.” She stopped short, appalled that she was yelling like a shrew. Hyperventilation threatened. “That’s why you came to my cabin, isn’t it? I thought maybe you’d had a bad case of the flu. Or complications from pneumonia. Or even, God forbid, a mental breakdown of some sort. But a heart attack…" Her legs gave out, and she sank back into the chair, feeling disappointed and angry and, beneath it all, so scared for him. "Why didn't you tell me, Leo? Why couldn't you trust me with the truth? Surely I deserved that much consideration."

But then it struck her. He hadn't shared the intimate details of his illness with her because she didn't matter. The bitter realization sat like a stone in her stomach. Leo had kept his secrets, because when all was said and done, Phoebe was nothing more than a vacation romance of sorts. Leo wasn't serious about any kind of a future with her. He fully planned to return to his old life and take up where he left off. As soon as his doctor gave permission.

He came to her then, sat on the ottoman and put a hand on her leg. "It wasn't something I could easily talk about, Phoebe. Try to understand that. I was a young man. One minute I was standing in a room, doing my job, and the next I couldn't breathe. Strangers were rushing me out to an ambulance. It was a hellish experience. All I wanted to do was forget."

"But you didn't want to come to the mountains."

"No. I didn't. My doctor, who happens to be a good friend, and my brother, who I consider my *best* friend, gave me no choice. I was supposed to learn how to control my stress levels."

She swallowed, wishing he wasn't touching her. The warmth of his hand threatened to dissolve the fragile hold she had on her emotions. "We had *sex,* Leo. To me, that's pretty intimate. But I can see in retrospect that I was just a piece of your convalescent plan, not dictated by your doctor friend, I'm sure. Did it even cross your mind to worry about *that?*"

He hesitated, and she knew she had hit a nerve.

She saw him swallow. He ran a hand through his hair, unintentionally betraying his agitation. "The first time I was with you…in that way, I hadn't had sex since my heart attack. And to be honest, not for several months before that. Do you want me to tell you I was scared shitless? Is that going to make you feel better?"

She knew it was the nature of men to fear weakness. And far worse was having someone witness that vulnerability. So she even understood his angry retort to some extent. But that didn't make her any less despairing. "You haven't taken any of this seriously, have you, Leo? You think you're invincible and that your exile to Tennessee was just a momentary inconvenience. Do you even want to change your ways?" Coming to the office tonight said louder than words what he was thinking.

"It's not that easy."

"Nothing important ever is," she whispered, her throat almost too tight for speech. She stood up and went to the window, blinking back tears. If he couldn't admit that he needed a life outside of work, and if he couldn't be honest with himself *or* with her, then he wasn't ready for the kind of relationship she wanted.

In that moment, she knew that any feeble hope she had nurtured for intimacy with Leo, even in the short term, was futile. "May we leave now?" she asked, her emotions at the breaking point. "I'm tired. It's been a long day."

Twenty

Leo knew he had hurt Phoebe. Badly. But for the life of him, he couldn't see a way to fix things. She disappeared into her room as soon as they got home from his office. The next day, they barely spoke. He fooled around on the internet and watched MSNBC and CNN, particularly the financial pundits.

Being in his office last night had unsettled him. The room had been cold and clinically clean, as if the last occupant had died and the desk was awaiting a new owner.

Somehow he'd thought he might get some kind of revelation about his life if he could stand where he'd once stood. As though in the very air itself he would be able to make sense of it all.

If he had gone straight home from the restaurant, he and Phoebe would no doubt have spent the night in bed dreaming up one way after another to lose themselves in pleasure.

Instead, his impulsive action had ruined everything.

He didn't blame her for being upset. But if he had it to do over again, he still wouldn't have told her about his heart attack. It wasn't the kind of news a man shared with the woman he wanted to impress.

And there it was. He wanted to impress Phoebe. With

his intellect, his entrepreneurial success, his life in general. As if by comparison she could and would see that her hermitlike retreat was not valid. That she was the one with lessons to learn.

As he remembered his brief time in Phoebe's magical mountain home, suddenly, everything clicked into focus. The reason his office had seemed sterile and empty last night was not because Leo had been gone for several weeks. The odd feelings he had experienced were a reluctant recognition of the difference between his work domain and the warm, cheerful home Phoebe had created.

In the midst of her pain and heartbreak, she hadn't become a bitter, angry woman. Instead, she had stretched her wings. She'd had the courage to step out in faith, trusting that she would find the answers she needed. Her solitude and new way of life had taught her valuable lessons about what was important. And she'd been willing to share her wisdom with Leo. But he had been too arrogant to accept that her experience could in any way shed light on his own life.

What a jackass he had been. He had lied to her by omission and all along had been patronizing about her simple existence. Instead of protecting his macho pride, he should have been begging her to help him make a new start.

He *needed* to find balance in his life. His brother, Luc, had managed that feat. Surely Leo could follow his example. And even beyond that, Leo needed Phoebe. More than he could ever have thought possible. But by his selfish actions, he had lost her. Perhaps forever. It would take every ounce of genius he possessed to win back her trust.

The magnitude of his failure was humbling. But as long as there was life, there was hope.

At his request, she consented to stay for the party. He knew she had booked a flight home for the following morning, because he had eavesdropped unashamedly at her door while she made the reservation.

When she appeared in the foyer at a quarter 'til seven that evening, his heart stopped. But this time he recognized the interruption. A lightning bolt of passion or lust or maybe nothing more complicated than need shattered his composure.

She wore a dress that many women would avoid for fear they couldn't carry it off. The fabric was red. An intense crimson that spoke for itself. And Phoebe hadn't been teasing when she described it. Cut low in the back and the front and high on the leg, it fit her as if it had been created with exactly her body in mind.

Stiletto heels in matte black leather put her almost on eye level with him. As equals.

Her hair was stunning. She had braided two tiny sections from the front and wound them at her crown. The rest cascaded in a sleek fall halfway down her back. On her right upper arm she wore a three-inch wide hammered silver band. Matching earrings dangled and caught the light.

He cleared his throat. "You look sensational."

"Thank you." Her expression was as remote as the Egyptian queen she resembled.

He had hoped tonight to strengthen the connection between them by showing her a slice of his life. His family. His employees. The way the company was built on trust and integrity. But now there was this chasm between Phoebe and him.

He hated the emotional distance, but he would use their physical attraction to fight back, to get through to her, if he had to. She had accused him of not taking his recovery seriously, but by God, he was serious now. His future hung in the balance. Everything he had worked for up until this point was rendered valueless. Without Phoebe's love and trust, he had nothing.

* * *

Fortunately his brother's home was close…on West Paces Ferry Road, an old and elegant established neighborhood for Atlanta's wealthy and powerful. But Luc and Hattie had made their home warm and welcoming amidst its elegant personality, a place where children could run and play, though little Luc Jr. was still too small for that.

Leo handed the keys of his Jag to the attendant and helped Phoebe out of the car. The college kid's eyes glazed over as he caught a glimpse of Phoebe's long, toned legs. Glaring at the boy, Leo wrapped her faux fur stole around her shoulders and ushered her toward the house.

Every tree and bush on the property had been trimmed in tiny white lights. Fragrant greenery festooned with gold bows wrapped lampposts and wrought-iron porch rails.

Phoebe paused on the steps, taking it all in. "I love this place," she said simply. "It feels like a classy Southern lady."

"Luc and Hattie will probably be at the door greeting their guests, but perhaps we can sit down with them later and catch up." The timing was off. Phoebe was leaving in the morning, and their relationship was dead in the water, but he still wanted her to meet his brother.

As it turned out, Leo was correct. His dashing brother took one look at Leo and wrestled him into a long bear hug that brought tears to Phoebe's eyes. Leo's sister-in-law wore the very same expression as she watched the two men embrace. Both brothers wore classic formal attire, and in their tuxes, they were incredibly dashing, almost like old film stars with their chiseled features.

Luc shook Phoebe's hand as they were introduced. "I wasn't sure Leo was going to come back for the holidays, or even if he should. I'm happy to see he has such a lovely woman looking after him."

Leo's jaw tightened, though his smile remained. "Phoebe's my date, not my nurse."

Phoebe saw from Luc's abashed expression that he knew he had stepped in it. Hattie whispered something in his ear, and he nodded.

Other people crowded in behind them, but Leo lingered for a moment longer. "Can we see the kids?"

Hattie touched his cheek, her smile warm and affectionate. "We have them asleep upstairs with a sitter, but you're welcome to take a peek." She smiled at Phoebe. "Leo dotes on our babies. Lord help us when he has some of his own. I've never known a man with a softer heart."

"Hey," Luc said, looking indignant. "I'm standing right here."

Hattie kissed his cheek. "Don't worry, sweetheart. I'll always love you best."

On the cloud of laughter that followed, Leo and Phoebe moved into the thick of the party. It was soon clear to her that Leo Cavallo was popular and beloved. Despite his reputation as a hard-hitting negotiator in the boardroom, everyone under Luc's roof treated Leo not only with respect, but with genuine caring and concern.

After an hour, though, she sensed that his patience was wearing thin. Perhaps he hadn't anticipated the many questions about his recovery. At any rate, she recognized his growing tension. She hated the unmistakable awkwardness between them as the evening progressed, but despite her hurt, she couldn't stop wanting to help him. Even if he couldn't be hers, she wanted him to be happy.

In a lull between conversations, she touched his arm. "Do you want to go upstairs and see your niece and nephew?"

He nodded, relief in his harried gaze.

Luc and Hattie's home was far different than Leo's, but spectacular in its own right. Phoebe experienced a frisson of envy for the couple who had created such a warm and nurturing family environment. The little girl's room was done in peach and cream with Disney fairies. The baby boy's nursery sported a delightful zoo animal theme.

Leo stroked his nephew's back and spoke to him softly, but he stayed the longest in Deedee's room. His eyes were somber as he watched the toddler sleep. "She's not their biological child, you know. When Hattie's sister died, Hattie took her baby to raise, and then after the wedding, Luc and Hattie adopted her."

"Has your brother been married long?"

"Less than two years. He and Hattie were pretty serious back in college. The relationship didn't work out, but they were lucky enough to find their way back to each other."

Phoebe stared at Leo's bent head as he sat carefully on the corner of the bed and touched his niece's hand. He took her tiny fingers in his and brought them to his lips. It would have been clear to a blind man that Leo was capable of great love and caring. He felt about these two little ones the way Phoebe did about Teddy.

He turned his head suddenly and caught her watching him, probably with her heart in her eyes. "Will you take a walk with me?" he asked gravely.

"Of course."

Tiny flurries of snow danced around them when they exited the back of the house. Leo had retrieved her wrap, but even so, the night was brisk. In the center of the upper terrace a large, tiled fire pit blazed with vigor, casting a small circle of warmth. Other than the old man adding logs now and again, Leo and Phoebe were alone. Apparently no one else was eager to brave the cold.

A wave of sadness, deep and poignant, washed over Phoebe. If only she and Leo had met under other circumstances. No pain and heartache in her past. No devastating illness in his. Just two people sharing a riveting attraction.

They could have enjoyed a sexual relationship that might have grown into something more.

Now, they stood apart, when only twenty-four hours ago, give or take, Leo had been turning her world upside down with his lovemaking. Their recent fight echoed in her mind. She had accused Leo of not wanting to change, but wasn't she just as cowardly? She had gone from one extreme to the other. Workaholic to hermit. Such a radical swing couldn't be considered balance at all.

In the faces of the crowd tonight, she saw more than the bonhomie of the season. She saw a kinship, a trust that came from working side by side. That was what she had given up, and she realized that she missed it. She missed all of it. The hard challenges, the silly celebrations, the satisfaction of a job well done.

So lost in her thoughts was she, that she jumped when Leo took her by the shoulders and turned her to face him. Again, as at her cabin, firelight painted his features. His eyes were dark, unfathomable. "I have a proposition for you, Phoebe, so hear me out before you say anything."

Her hands tightened on her wrap. "Very well." A tiny piece of gravel had found its way into her shoe. And she couldn't feel her toes. But not even a blizzard could have made her walk away.

He released her as though he couldn't speak freely when they were touching. She thought she understood. Passion had flared so hot and so quickly between them when they first met, its veracity was suspect given the length of their acquaintance.

"First of all," he said quietly, "I'm sorry I didn't tell you about the heart attack. It was an ego thing. I didn't want you to think less of me."

"But I…" She bit her lip and stopped, determined to listen as he had requested.

He ran a hand across the back of his neck. "I was angry

and bitter and confused when I met you. I'd spent a week at the hospital, a week here at Luc's, and then to top it all, they exiled me to Tennessee."

"Tennessee is a very nice state," she felt bound to point out.

A tiny smile flickered across his lips. "It's a lovely state, but that's not the point. I looked at you and saw a desirable woman. You had your hang-ups. We all do. But I didn't want you to look too closely at mine. I wanted you to see me as a strong, capable man."

"And I did."

"But you have to admit the truth, Phoebe. Last night in my office. You stared at me and saw something else." The defeat in his voice made her ill with regret.

"You don't understand," she said, willing him to hear her with an open mind. "I was upset, yes. It terrified me that you had been in such a dangerous situation. And I was angry that you didn't trust me enough to share that with me. But it never changed the way I saw you. If you felt that, then you were wrong."

He paced in silence for several long minutes. She wondered if he believed her. Finally, he stopped and lifted a hand to bat away the snowflakes that were increasing in size and frequency. "We jumped too far ahead," he said. "I want to say things to you that are too soon, too serious."

Her heart sank, because she knew he was right. "So that's it?" she asked bleakly. "We just chalk this up to bad timing and walk away?"

"Is that what you want?" He stood there…proud, tall and so alone her heart broke for him.

"No. That's not what I want at all," she said, daring to be honest with so much at stake. "So if you have a plan, I'm listening."

He exhaled noisily as if he'd been holding his breath. "Well, okay, then. Here it is. I propose that we go back to your place and spend Christmas Eve together when it rolls around. I'll stay with you for the remainder of the time I have reserved and work on learning how not to obsess about business."

"Is that even possible?" She said it with a grin so he would know she was teasing. Mostly.

"God, I hope so. Because I want you in my life, Phoebe. And you deserve a man who will not only make a place for you, but will put you front and center."

One hot tear rolled down her cheek. "Is there more?"

"Yes. And this is the scary part. At the end of January, assuming we haven't killed each other or bored each other to death, I want you to come back to Atlanta and move in with me…as my fiancée. Not now," he said quickly. "As of this moment, we are simply a man and a woman who are attracted to each other."

"Very attracted," Phoebe agreed, her heart lifting to float with the snowflakes.

She took a step in his direction, but he held up a hand. "Not yet. Let me finish."

His utter seriousness and heartfelt sincerity gave her hope that what had begun as a serendipitous fling might actually have substance and a solid foundation. Cautious elation fluttered inside her chest. But she kept her cool… barely. "Go on."

"I'm not criticizing you, Phoebe, but you have to admit—you have issues with balance, too. Work is valid and important. But when you left Charlotte, you cut off that part of yourself."

She grimaced, feeling shame for the holier-than-thou way she had judged his life. "You're right. I did. But I'm not sure how to step back in the opposite direction."

A tiny smile lifted the corners of his mouth. "When we get back to Atlanta, I want you to work for Cavallo. I could use someone with your experience and financial instincts.

Not only that, but it would make me very happy for us to share that aspect of who we are. I understand why you ran away to the mountains. I do. And I strongly suspect that knowing each of us, we'll need your cabin as an escape when work threatens to become all-encompassing."

Anxiety dampened her burgeoning joy. "I'm afraid, Leo. I messed things up so badly before."

He shook his head. "You had a man who didn't deserve you and you lost your baby, a miscarriage that was one of those inexplicable tragedies of life. But it's time to live again, Phoebe. I want that for both of us. It's not wrong to have a passion for work. But we can keep each other grounded. And I think together we can find that balance and peace that are so important." He paused. "There's one more thing."

She was shaking more on the inside than she was on the outside. Leo was so confident, so sure. Could she take another chance at happiness? "What is it?" she asked.

At last, he took her in his arms, warming her with his big, solid frame. He cupped her cheeks in his hands, his gaze hot and sweet. "I want to make babies with you, Phoebe. I thought my life was great the way it was. But then I had the heart attack, and I met you, and suddenly I was questioning everything I had ever known about myself. Watching you with Teddy did something to me. And now tonight, with Luc and Hattie's babies upstairs asleep, I see it all clearly. You and I, Phoebe, against all odds…we have a shot at the brass ring. Having the whole enchilada. I think you were wrong about that, my love. I think with the right person, life can be just about perfect."

He bent his head and took her mouth in a soft, firm kiss that was equal parts romance and knee-weakening passion. "Will you be my almost-fiancée?" he whispered, his voice hoarse and ragged. His hands slid down the silky fabric of her dress all the way to her hips. Dragging her closer still, he buried his face in her neck. She could feel him trembling.

Emotions tumbled in her heart with all the random patterns of the snowflakes. She had grieved for so long, too long in fact. Cowardice and the fear of being hurt again had constrained her equally as much as Leo's workaholic ways had hemmed him in.

The old man tending the fire had gone inside, probably to get warm. Phoebe gasped when Leo used the slit in her skirt to his advantage, placing a warm palm on her upper thigh. His fingers skated perilously close to the place where her body ached for him.

Teasing her with outrageous caresses, he nibbled her ear, her neck, the partially exposed line of her collarbone. "I need an answer, my love. Please."

Heat flooded her veins, negating the winter chill. Her body felt alive, spectacularly alive. Leo held her tightly, as if he were afraid she might run. But that was ludicrous, because there was no place she would rather be.

She gave herself a moment to say goodbye to the little child she would never know. So many hopes and dreams she had cherished had been ripped away. But the mountains had taught her much about peace, and in surviving, she had been given another chance. A wonderful, exciting, heart-pounding second chance.

Laying her cheek against Leo's crisp white shirt, feeling the steady beat of his wonderfully big heart, she nodded. "Yes, Leo Cavallo. I believe I will."

Epilogue

Leo paced the marble floor, his palms damp. "Hurry, Phoebe. They'll be here in a minute." He was nervous about his surprise, and if Phoebe lollygagged too much longer, it would be ruined. He gazed around his familiar home, noting the addition this year of a gigantic Christmas tree, its branches heavy with ornaments. In the chandelier overhead, tiny clumps of mistletoe dangled, tied with narrow red velvet ribbons.

His body tightened and his breath quickened as he recalled the manner in which he and Phoebe had christened that mistletoe, making love on the rug beneath. In truth, they had christened most of his condo in such a way. Including a repeat of what he liked to call "the kitchen episode."

He tugged at his bow tie, feeling much too hot all of a sudden.

At long last, his beloved wife appeared, her usual feminine stride hampered by a certain waddling movement. She grimaced. "This red dress makes me look like a giant tomato."

He pulled her in close for a kiss, running his hand over the fascinating swell of her large abdomen. "Red is my new favorite color. And besides, it's Christmas." Feeling the life growing inside his precious Phoebe tightened his throat and wet his eyes. So many miracles in his life. So much love.

She returned the kiss with passion. The force that drew them together in the beginning had never faded. In fact, it grew deeper and more fiery with each passing month.

This evening, though, they were headed for a night out on the town with Luc and Hattie. Dinner, followed by a performance of *The Nutcracker*.

Phoebe rubbed her back. "I hope I'm going to fit into a seat at the theater."

He grinned broadly. "Quit fishing for compliments. You know you're the sexiest pregnant woman in the entire state. But sit down, my love. I have something I want to give you before they get here."

Phoebe eased into a comfy armchair with a grimace. "It's five days 'til Christmas."

"This is an *early* present."

From his jacket pocket he extracted a ruby velvet rectangle. Flipping it open, he handed it to her. "I had it made especially for you."

Phoebe took the box from him and stared. Inside, nestled on a bed of black satin, was an exquisite necklace. Two dozen or more tiny diamond snowflakes glittered with fire on a delicate platinum chain. She couldn't speak for the emotion that threatened to swamp her with hormonal tears.

Leo went down on one knee beside her, removed the jewelry from the box and gently fastened it around her neck.

She put a hand to her throat, staring at his masculine beauty, feeling the tangible evidence of his boundless, generous love. "Thank you, Leo. It's perfect."

He wrapped a hand in her hair and fingered it. "I could have waited until our anniversary. But tonight is special to me. It was exactly a year ago that you stood in the snow and gave me a new life. A wonderful life."

Running one hand through his hair, she cupped his neck with the other and pulled him back for another kiss. “Are you channeling Jimmy Stewart now?” she teased, her heart full to bursting.

He laid a hand on her round belly, laughing softly when their son made an all too visible kick. “Not at all, my dear Phoebe. I’m merely counting my blessings. And I always count you twice.”

* * * * *

CHRISTMAS BABY FOR THE GREEK

JENNIE LUCAS

CHAPTER ONE

WAS THERE ANYTHING worse than a wedding on Christmas Eve, with glittering lights sparkling against the snow, holly and ivy decking the halls and the scent of winter roses in the air?

If there was, Holly Marlowe couldn't think of it.

"You may now kiss the bride," the minister said, beaming between the newly married couple.

Heartbroken, Holly watched as Oliver—the boss she'd loved in devoted silence for three years—beamed back and lowered his head to kiss the bride.

Her younger sister, Nicole.

The guests in the pews looked enchanted at the couple's passionate embrace, but Holly felt sick. Fidgeting in her tight red maid-of-honor dress, she looked up at the grand stained-glass windows, then back at the nave of the old New York City church, lavishly decorated with flickering white candles and red roses.

Finally, the newly married couple pulled apart from the kiss. Snatching her bouquet back from Holly's numb fingers, the bride lifted her new husband's hand triumphantly in the air.

"Best Christmas ever!" Nicole cried.

There was a wave of adoring laughter and applause. And though Holly had always loved Christmas, striving to make it magical and full of treats each year for her little sister since their parents had died, she thought she'd hate it for the rest of her life.

No. A lump rose in Holly's throat. She couldn't think that way. She couldn't be selfish. Nicole and Oliver were in love. She should be happy for them. She forced herself to smile as the "Hallelujah" Chorus pounded from the organ in the alcove above.

Smiling, the bride and groom started back down the aisle. And Holly suddenly faced the best man. Oliver's cousin, and his boss. Which made him her boss's boss.

Stavros Minos.

Dark, tall and broad-shouldered, the powerful Greek billionaire seemed out of place in the old stone church. The very air seemed to vibrate back from him, moving to give him space. *He* hadn't been forced to wear some ridiculous outfit that made him look like a deranged Christmas lounge singer. Of course not. She looked over his sleek suit enviously. She couldn't imagine anyone forcing Stavros Minos to do anything.

Then Holly looked up, and the Greek's black eyes cut through her soul.

He glanced with sardonic amusement between her and the happy couple, as they continued to walk down the aisle to the cheers of their guests. And his cruel, sensual lips curved up at the edges, as if he knew exactly how her heart had been broken.

Holly's mouth went dry. No. No, he couldn't. No one must ever know that she'd loved Oliver. Because he wasn't just her boss now. He was her sister's husband. She had to pretend it never happened.

The truth was nothing *had* happened. She'd never said a word about her feelings to anyone, especially Oliver. The man had no idea that while working as his secretary, Holly had been secretly consumed by pathetic, unrequited love.

No one had any idea. No one, it seemed, except Stavros Minos.

But it shouldn't surprise her the billionaire Greek playboy might see things no other person could. Nearly twenty years ago, as a teenager, he'd single-handedly started a tech company that now owned half the world. He was often in the news, both for his high-powered business dealings and conquests of the world's most beautiful women. Now, as organ music thundered relentlessly around them, Stavros looked at Holly with a strange knowing in his eyes.

Wordlessly, he held out his arm.

Reluctantly, Holly took it, and tried not to notice how muscled his arm was beneath his sleek black jacket. His biceps had to be bigger than her thigh! It seemed ridiculously unfair that a man so rich and powerful could also be so good-looking. It was why she'd carefully avoided looking at him whenever she'd liaised with his executive assistants—he had three of them—at work.

Shivering, she avoided looking at him again now as they followed Oliver and Nicole. The faces of the guests slid by as Holly smiled blindly at everyone in the packed wooden pews until she thought her face might crack.

Outside the old stone church, on a charming, historical lane in the Financial District, more guests waited to cheer for the couple, tossing red and white rose petals that fell against the thin blanket of snow on the ground.

The afternoon sunlight was weak and gray against the lowering clouds when Holly reached the safety of the waiting limo. Dropping Stavros's arm, she scrambled inside and turned to stare fiercely out the window, blinking fast so no one would see her tears.

She couldn't be sad. Not today. Not ever. She was happy for her sister and Oliver, happy they'd be leaving her today to start new adventures together around the world. *Happy.*

"Whew." Nicole flopped into the seat across from her

in a wave of white tulle that took most of the space in the back of the limo. She grinned at her new husband beside her. "We did it! We're married!"

"Finally," Oliver drawled, all lazy charm as he looked down at his bride. "That was a lot of work. But then, I never thought I'd let anyone put the marriage noose round my neck."

"'Til you met me," Nicole murmured, turning her face up to be kissed.

Smiling, he lowered his head. "Exactly."

Holly felt her own seat move as Stavros Minos sat beside her. As the door closed behind him, and the limo pulled away from the curb, she unwillingly breathed in his intoxicating scent of musk and power.

Oliver turned smugly to his cousin. "How about it, Stavros? Did the ceremony give you any ideas?"

The Greek tycoon's handsome face was colder than the icy winter air outside. "Such as you can't imagine."

How dare he be so rude? Holly thought incredulously. But then, the commitment-phobic playboy famously despised weddings. He obviously was unhappy to be forced to attend his cousin's wedding. And unlike Holly, he didn't feel any compunction to hide his feelings. Luckily, the happy couple didn't seem to notice.

Oliver snorted. "I was going to invite Uncle Aristides today, him being family and all that, but I knew you wouldn't like it."

"Generous of you." His voice was flat.

Holly envied Stavros Minos's coldness right now, when she herself felt heartbroken and raw. Her sister's pressure for Holly to move with them to Hong Kong after they returned from their honeymoon in Aruba had been ratcheted up to an explosive level. Oliver had already quit at Minos International. If Holly stayed, she'd soon be working for the notoriously unpleasant VP of Operations. Or else she had a standing offer from a previous employer who'd moved back to Europe.

But if she was going to leave New York, shouldn't she move to Hong Kong, and work for Oliver in his new job? Shouldn't she devote herself to her baby sister's happiness, forever and ever?

"You really hate weddings, don't you, Stavros?" Oliver grinned at his cousin. "At least I won't have to see your grouchy face at the office anymore, old man. Your loss is Sinistech's gain."

"Right." Stavros shrugged. "Let another company deal with your three-hour martini lunches."

"Quite." Oliver's grin widened, then he licked his lips. "I can hardly wait to explore Hong Kong's delights."

"Me, too," Nicole said.

Oliver nearly jumped, as if he'd forgotten his bride beside him. "Naturally." He suddenly looked at Holly. "Did Nicole convince you yet? Will you come and work as my secretary there?"

Feeling everyone's eyes on her, her cheeks went red-hot. She stammered, "D-don't be silly."

"You mustn't be selfish," Oliver insisted. "I can't cope without you. Who else can keep me organized in my new job?"

"And I might get pregnant soon," Nicole said anxiously. "Who will take care of the baby if you're not around?"

The ache in Holly's throat sharpened to a razor blade. Watching her sister marry the man she loved and then leave for the other side of the world was hard enough. But the suggestion that Holly should live with them and raise their children was pure cruelty.

As of her birthday yesterday, she was a twenty-seven-year-old virgin. She was a secretary, a sister, and perhaps soon, an aunt. But would she ever be more? A wife? A mother?

Would she ever meet a man she could love, who would love her in return? Would she ever be the most important person in the world to anyone?

At twenty-seven, it was starting to seem unlikely. She'd spent nearly a decade raising her sister since their parents died. She'd spent the last three years taking care of Oliver at work. Maybe that was all she was meant to do. Take care of Nicole and Oliver, watch them love each other and raise their children. Maybe Holly was meant only to be support staff in life. Never the star. The thought caused a stab of pain through her heart.

She choked out, "You'll be fine without me."

"Fine!" Indignantly, Nicole shook her head. "It would be a disaster! You have to come with us to Hong Kong, Holly. *Please!*"

Her sister spoke with the same wheedling tone she'd used since she was a child to get her own way. The same one she'd used four weeks ago to convince Holly to arrange her sudden wedding—using the same Christmas details that Holly had once dreamed of for her own wedding someday.

Until she'd realized there was no point in saving all her own Christmas wedding dreams for a marriage that would never happen. If any man was ever going to be interested in her, it would have happened by now. And it hadn't. Her sister was the one with the talent in that arena. Blonde, tiny and beautiful, Nicole had always had a strange power over men, and at twenty-two, she'd learned how to use it well.

But even Holly had never imagined, when she'd introduced her to Oliver last summer at a company picnic, that it would end like this.

Looking at her sister, Holly suddenly noticed Nicole's bare neck. "Where's Mom's gold-star necklace, Nicole?"

Touching her bare collarbone above her neckline, her sister ducked her head. "It's somewhere in all the boxes. I'm sure I'll find it when I unpack in Hong Kong."

"You lost Mom's necklace?" Holly felt stricken. It was bad enough their parents hadn't lived to see their youngest daughter get married, but if Nicole had lost the precious gold-star necklace their mother had always worn…

"I didn't lose it," Nicole said irritably. She shrugged. "It's somewhere."

"And don't try to change the subject, Holly," Oliver said sharply. "You're being stubborn and selfish to stay in New York, when I need you so badly."

Selfish. The accusation hit Holly like a blow. Was she being selfish to stay, when they needed her? Selfish to still hope she could find her own happiness, instead of putting their needs first forever?

"I… I'm not trying to be," she whispered. As the limo drove north toward Midtown, Holly looked out the window, toward the bright Christmas lights and colorful window displays as the limo passed the department stores on Sixth Avenue. The sidewalks were filled with shoppers carrying festive bags and wrapped packages, rushing to buy gifts to put under the Christmas tree and fill stockings tomorrow morning. She saw happy children wearing Santa hats and beaming smiles.

A memory went through her of Nicole at that age, her smiling, happy face missing two front teeth as she'd hugged Holly tight and cried, "I wuv you, Howwy!"

A lump rose in Holly's throat. Nicole was her only family. If her baby sister truly needed her, maybe she *was* being selfish, thinking of her own happiness. Maybe she should just—

"Let me get this straight." Stavros Minos's voice was acidic as he suddenly leaned forward. "You want Miss Marlowe to quit her job at Minos International and move to Hong Kong? To do your office work for you, Oliver, all day, then take care of your children all night?"

Oliver scowled. "It's none of your business, Stavros."

"Your concern does you credit, Mr. Minos," Nicole interceded, giving him a charming smile, "but taking care of people is what Holly does best. She's taken care of me since I was twelve. I can't imagine her ever wanting to stop taking care of me."

"Of us," Oliver said.

Stavros lifted his sensual lips into a smile that showed the white glint of his teeth as he turned to Holly. "Is that true?"

He was looking at her so strangely. She stammered, "A-anyone would feel the same."

"I wouldn't."

"Of course you wouldn't," Oliver said with a snort, leaning back in the seat. "Minos men are selfish to the bone. We do what we like, and everyone else be damned."

"What is that supposed to mean?" his wife said.

He winked. "It's part of our charm, darling."

But Nicole didn't seem terribly charmed. With a flare of her nostrils, she turned to Holly. "I can't just leave you in New York. You wouldn't know what to do with yourself. You'd be so alone."

She stiffened. "I have friends..."

"But not family," she said impatiently. "And it's not very likely you ever will, is it?"

"Will what?"

"Have a husband or children of your own. I mean, come on." She gave a good-natured snort. "You've never even had a serious boyfriend. Do you really want to die alone?"

Holly stared at her sister in the back of the limo.

Nicole was right. And tomorrow, for the first time in her life, Holly would spend Christmas Day alone.

Christmas, and the rest of her life.

Her eyes met Stavros's in the back of the limo. His handsome features looked as hard and cold as a marble statue, his black eyes icy as a midwinter's night. Then his expression suddenly changed.

"I'm afraid Miss Marlowe can't possibly go to Hong Kong," he said. "Because I need another executive assistant. So I'm giving her a promotion."

"What?" gasped Oliver.

"What?" gasped Nicole.

Holly looked at him sharply, blinking back tears. "What?"

His expression gentled. "Will you come work directly for me, Miss Marlowe? It will mean long hours, but a sizable raise. I'll double your salary."

"But—" Swallowing, Holly whispered, "Why me?"

"Because you're the best." His jaw, dark with five-o'clock shadow, tightened. "And because I can."

Stavros hadn't meant to get involved. Oliver was right. This was none of his business.

He didn't care about his cousin. Cousin or not, the man was a useless bastard. Stavros regretted the day he'd hired him. Oliver had done a poor job as VP of Marketing. He'd been within a day of being fired when he'd taken the "surprise offer" from Hong Kong. Stavros was glad to see him go. He suspected Oliver might be surprised when his new employers actually expected him to work for his salary.

Stavros didn't much care for his cousin's new bride, either. In spite of his own turmoil last night, he'd actually tried to warn Nicole about Oliver's cheating ways at the rehearsal dinner. But the blonde had just cut him off. So she knew what she was getting into; she just didn't care.

He didn't give a damn about either of them.

But Holly Marlowe—she was different.

Stavros suspected it was only through the hardworking secretary's efforts that Oliver had managed to stay afloat these last three years. Holly worked long hours at the office then probably nights and weekends at home, doing Oliver's job for him. Everyone at the New York office loved kind, dependable Miss Marlowe, from the janitors to the COO. Tender-hearted, noble, self-sacrificing… Holly Marlowe was the most respected person in the New York office, Stavros included.

But she was totally oppressed by these two selfish people, who, instead of thanking her for all she'd done, seemed intent on taking her indentured servitude with them to Hong Kong.

Two days ago, Stavros might have shrugged it off. People had the right to make their own choices, even stupid ones.

But not after the news he'd received yesterday. Now, for the first time he was thinking about what his own legacy would be after he was gone. And it wasn't a pretty picture.

"You can't have Holly! I need her!" Oliver exploded. At Stavros's fierce glare, his cousin glanced uneasily at his wife. "*We* need her."

"You don't want some stupid promotion, do you, Holly?" Nicole wailed.

But Holly's face was shining as she looked at Stavros. "Do—do you mean it?"

"I never say anything I don't mean." As they drove north, past bundled-up tourists and sparkling lights and brightly decorated department-store windows, his gaze unwillingly traced over her pretty face and incredible figure. Until he'd stood across from her in the old stone church by candlelight, he'd never realized how truly beautiful Holly Marlowe was.

The truth was, he hadn't *wanted* to notice. Beautiful women were a dime a dozen in his world, while truly competent, highly driven secretaries were few. And Holly had hidden her beauty, making herself nearly invisible at the office, yanking her fiery red hair in a matronly bun, never wearing makeup, working quietly behind the scenes in loose-cut beige skirt suits and sensible shoes.

Was this what she'd looked like all the time? Right under his nose?

Her bright, wide-set green eyes looked up at him, luminous beneath dramatic black lashes. Her skin was pale except for a smattering of freckles over her nose. Her lips were red and delectable as she nibbled them with white, even teeth. Her thick, curly red-gold hair spilled over her shoulders. And that tight red dress—

That dress—

Stavros obviously wasn't dead yet, because it set his pulse racing.

The bodice was low-cut, clinging to full, delicious breasts he'd never imagined existed beneath those baggy beige suits. As she moved, the knit fabric clung to her curves. He'd gotten a look at her deliciously full backside as they'd left the church, too.

All things he would have to ignore once she worked for him. Deliberately, he looked away. He didn't seduce women who worked for him. Why would he, when beautiful women were so plentiful in his world, and truly spectacular employees more precious than diamonds?

Sex was an amusement, nothing more. But for years, his company had been his life.

And the reason Holly chose to dress so plainly in the office was obviously that she wanted to be valued for her accomplishments and hard work, not her appearance. In that, they were the same. From the time he was a child, Stavros had wanted to do important things. He'd wanted to change the world.

But that wasn't all they had in common. He'd seen her tortured expression as she'd looked at Oliver. So Stavros and Holly each had secrets they didn't want to talk about.

To anyone.

Ever.

But her inexplicable infatuation for Oliver couldn't possibly last. When she recovered from it, like someone healing from a bad cold, she'd realize she'd dodged a bullet.

As for Stavros's secret, people would figure it out for themselves when he dropped dead. Which, according to his doctor's prognosis, would happen in about six to nine months. He blinked.

All the life he'd left unlived...

Just a few days ago, Stavros had vaguely assumed he'd have another fifty years. Instead, he'd be unlikely to see his thirty-seventh birthday next September.

He would die alone, with no one but his lawyers and stockholders to mourn him. His company would be his only legacy. Estranged from his father, and feeling as he did about Oliver, Stavros would likely leave his shares to charity.

Poor Stavros, his ex-mistresses would say. Then they'd roll over and enjoy their hot new lovers in bed.

Poor Minos, his business associates would say. Then they'd focus on exciting new technology to buy and sell.

And he'd be dirt in the ground. Never once knowing what it felt like to commit to anything but work. Not even leaving a son or daughter to carry on his name.

Looking back, Stavros saw it all with painful clarity, now that his life was coming to an end. And he had only himself to blame. Nicole's thoughtlessly cruel words floated back to him. *Do you really want to die alone?*

Christmas lights sparkled on Sixth Avenue, as yellow taxis filled with people on the way to family dinners rushed past in the rapidly falling twilight. The limo turned east, finally pulling into the entrance of the grand hotel overlooking Central Park.

"This isn't over, Holly," Oliver said firmly. "I'm going to persuade you."

"You'll come with us," Nicole said, smiling as she smoothed back her veil.

The uniformed driver opened the back door of the limousine. Oliver got out first, then gallantly reached back to assist his glamorous bride. Nicole's white tulle skirts swirled in a train with her fluttery white veil, her diamond tiara sparkling. Tourists gaped at them on the sidewalk. A few lifted their phones for pictures, clearly believing they were seeing royalty. The new Mr. and Mrs. Oliver Minos waved at them regally as they swept into the grand hotel to take photos before the guests arrived for a ballroom reception.

Silence fell in the back of the limo. For a moment, Holly didn't move. Stavros looked at her.

"Don't give in to them, Holly," he urged in a low voice. It was the first time he'd used her first name. "Stick up for yourself. You're worth so much more than they are."

Her green eyes widened, then suddenly glistened with tears. She whispered, "How can you say that?"

"Because it's true," he said harshly. He got out of the limo and held out his hand for her.

Blinking fast, she slowly placed her hand in his.

And it happened.

Stavros had slept with many women, beautiful and famous and powerful, models and starlets and even a Nobel laureate.

But when he touched Holly's hand to help her from the limo, he felt something he'd never experienced before. An electric shock sizzled him to his core.

He looked down at her as he pulled her to the sidewalk, his heart pounding strangely as he helped her to her feet. Snowflakes suddenly began falling as she looked up, lingering in his arms.

Then Holly's gaze fell on the lacy white snowflakes. With a joyous laugh, she dropped his hand, looking up with wonder at the gray lowering sky.

Without her warmth, Stavros again felt the winter chill beneath his tuxedo jacket. The world became a darker place, freezing him, reminding him he'd soon feel nothing at all. He stood very still, watching her. Then he lifted his face to the sky, wondering if this would be the last time he'd feel snowflakes on his skin.

If only he could have at least left a child behind. He suddenly wanted that so badly it hurt. If only he could have left some memory of his existence on earth.

But the women he knew were as ambitious and heartless as he was. He couldn't leave an innocent child in their care. Children needed someone willing to put their needs above her own. He knew no woman like that. None at all.

Then he heard a laugh of pure delight, and Stavros looked down at Holly Marlowe's beautiful, shining, tenderhearted eyes.

"Can you believe it?" Stretching her arms wide, laughing like a child, she whirled in a circle, holding out her tongue to taste the snowflakes. She looked like an angel. Her eyes danced as she cried, "It's snowing at my sister's wedding! On Christmas Eve!"

And all of the busy avenue, the tourists, the horse-drawn carriages, the taxis blaring Christmas music, faded into the background. Stavros saw only her.

CHAPTER TWO

THE GRAND TWO-STORY hotel ballroom was a winter wonderland, filled with white-and-silver Christmas trees twinkling like stars. Each of the twenty big round tables had centerpieces of red roses, deep scarlet against the white. It was even more beautiful than Holly had dreamed. A lump rose in her throat as she slowly looked around her.

She'd imagined a wedding reception like this long ago, as a lonely nineteen-year-old, cutting out photographs from magazines and putting them in an idea book each night while her little sister slept in the dark apartment. Holly had been alone, her friends all in college or partying in clubs.

Holly didn't regret her choice to give up her college scholarship and come home. After their parents had died in the car accident on their anniversary, she'd known she couldn't leave Nicole to foster care. But sometimes, she'd felt so trapped, chained by the responsibilities of love. She'd felt so lonely, without a partner, and with a teenaged sister who'd often shouted at Holly in her own grief and frustrated rage.

So to comfort herself, Holly had created the dream book. It had kept her company, until Nicole had left for college three years ago, and Holly had started working for Oliver.

In her romantic fantasy of long ago, she'd always imagined she'd be the bride in the white princess dress, dancing with an adoring groom. Now, as she watched Nicole and Oliver dance their first dance as husband and wife, surrounded by all their adoring friends, she told herself she'd never been so happy.

"They really do make a perfect couple." Stavros's low, husky voice spoke beside her. Somehow, his tone made the words less than complimentary.

"Yes," Holly said, moving slightly to make sure they didn't accidentally touch. When he'd helped her from the limo earlier, her whole body had trembled. It was totally ridiculous. She was sure Stavros Minos hadn't felt anything. Why would he? While Holly, hours later, still felt burning hot, lit up from within, whenever the Greek billionaire drew close. Whenever he even looked at her. She had to get ahold of herself, if she was going to be his assistant!

What was wrong with her? Holly didn't understand. How could she feel so—so aware of Stavros, when she was in love with Oliver?

She was, wasn't she?

But she didn't want to love Oliver anymore. It had done nothing but hurt her. And now he was her brother-in-law, it felt slimy and wrong. She wanted to reach inside her soul and turn off her feelings like a light—

"You arranged the reception, too, didn't you?" Stavros said, looking at the Christmas fantasy around them.

She forced herself to smile. "I wanted my sister to have a dream wedding. I did my best."

Stavros abruptly turned to look at the happy couple, dancing now in front of the largest white-flocked tree, decorated with white lights and silver stars. He took a long drink of the amber-colored liquid he'd gotten from the open bar. "You are a good person."

Again, the words should have been a compliment, but they weren't. Not the way he said them. She tried to read his expression, but his darkly handsome face was inscrutable. She shook her head. "You must hate all this."

"This?"

"Being best man at a wedding." Holly shrugged. "You're the most famously commitment-phobic bachelor in the city."

He took another deliberate drink. "Let's just say love is something I've never had the good fortune to experience."

More irony, she thought. Then his black eyes burned through her, reminding her he knew about her secret love for Oliver. Her cheeks burned.

Looking toward the beautiful bride and handsome groom slow-dancing in the center of the ballroom, the very picture of fairy-tale love, she mumbled, "You're right. They do make a perfect couple."

"Stop it," he said sharply, as if he was personally annoyed.

"Stop what?"

"Take off the rose-colored glasses."

Her mouth dropped. "What?"

"You'd have to be stupid to love Oliver. And whatever you are, Miss Marlowe, you're not stupid."

The conversation had taken a strangely personal turn. Her heart pounded. But there seemed no point in trying to lie. She'd never dared to give voice to her feelings before. She whispered, "How did you guess?"

He rolled his eyes. "You wear your heart on your face." He paused. "I'm sure Oliver knows exactly how you feel."

Horror went through her. "Oh, no—he couldn't possibly—"

"Of course he knows," Stavros said brutally. "How else could he have taken advantage of you all these years?"

"Advantage?" Astonished, she looked up at him. "Of me?"

He looked down at her seriously. "I have ten thousand employees around the world. And from what everyone tells me, you're the hardest working one."

"Mr. Minos—"

"Call me Stavros," he ordered.

"Stavros." She blushed. "I'm sure that's not true. I go home at six every night—"

"Yes, home to do Oliver's paperwork. Never asking for a raise, even though you were paying for your sister to go to college. Which, by the way, she could have gotten a job and paid for herself."

Her blush deepened in confusion. "I take care of my sister because—because she's my responsibility. I take care of Oliver because, because," she continued, faltering, "I'm his employee. At least I was…"

"And because you're in love with him."

"Yes," she whispered, her heart in her throat.

"And now he's impulsively married your sister, and instead of being angry—" he motioned at the winter wonderland around them "—you arranged all this."

"Except for this dress." She looked down ruefully at the tight red dress, wishing she was dressed in that modest burgundy gown she'd selected. "Nicole picked it out. She said my dress was the frumpiest thing she'd ever seen and she wasn't going to let it ruin her wedding photographs."

"They really do deserve each other, don't they?" he murmured. Then he glanced down at her and growled, "You look beautiful in that dress."

Another compliment that didn't sound like a compliment. If anything, he sounded angry about it. His jaw was tight as he looked away.

Was he mocking her? She didn't understand why he would tell her she was beautiful but sound almost furious about it. Her cheeks burned as she muttered, "Thanks."

For a moment, the two of them stood apart from the crowd, watching as the bridal couple finished their dance with a long, flashy kiss. The guests applauded then went out to join them on the dance floor. Feeling awkward, Holly started to turn away.

Stavros stopped her, his dark eyes glittering as he said huskily, "Dance with me."

"What? No."

Broad-shouldered and powerful in his tuxedo, he towered over her like a dark shadow. Lifting a sardonic eyebrow, he just held out his hand, waiting.

What was he playing at? Stavros took starlets and models to his bed. Why would he be interested in dancing with a plain, ordinary girl like her? She looked up at him. His handsome face was arrogant, as untouchable and distant as a star.

"You don't have to feel sorry for me," she said stiffly.

"I don't."

"Or if you think it's a requirement, because you're best man and I'm maid of honor—"

"Do I strike you as a man who gives a damn about other people's rules?" he asked, cutting her off. "I just want you to see the truth."

"What's that?" Half-mesmerized, she let him pull her into his powerful arms. Electricity crackled up her arm as she felt the heat of his palm against hers. She looked up at his face. His jawline was dark with five-o'clock shadow below razor-sharp cheekbones. There was a strange darkness in his black eyes, a vibrating tension from his muscular body beneath the well-cut tuxedo.

"You don't love my cousin. You never did."

She tried to pull away. "You have some nerve to—"

Holding her hand implacably in his own, he led her out onto the dance floor, where guests swayed to the slow romantic Christmas music of the orchestra.

She felt everyone looking at her. The women, with a mix of envy and bewilderment, the men, with interest, their eyes lingering on her uncomfortably low neckline.

Even Nicole and Oliver paused to gape at the sight of Stavros leading her out on the dance floor. Holly felt equally bewildered. Stavros could dance with anyone. Why would he choose her? Had he lost some kind of bet?

Surely this couldn't just be to convince Holly she had no real feelings for Oliver.

But if he could, how wonderful would that be?

Suddenly, Holly wanted it more than anything in the world.

Stavros led her confidently to the center of the dance floor, forcing others to move aside to make way for them. Pulling her against his chest, he looked down at her. She felt his dark gaze burn through her body, all the way to her toes. He looked at her almost as if he—

Desired her?

No. Holly's cheeks went hot. That was a step too far. No man had ever desired her. Not Oliver. Not even Albert from Accounting, who'd asked her on a date a few months ago, then stood her up for some playoff game.

But there was heat in Stavros's gaze as he moved her in his arms.

"You don't love my cousin," he whispered, tightening his hold on her. "Admit it. He was just a dream you had to keep you warm at night."

Could it be true? How she wanted to be convinced! "How can you say that?"

His sensual lips curved. "Because as little as I know about love, it seems to involve really knowing someone, flaws and all. And you don't even know him."

She rolled her eyes. "I've worked for him for three years. Of course I know Oliver. I know everything about him."

"Are you sure?" Stavros said, glancing at the dancing couple.

Following his gaze, Holly saw Oliver give a flirtatious smile to a pretty girl over his wife's shoulder. She saw Nicole notice, scowl, then deliberately step on her new husband's foot with her wicked stiletto heel.

"So he's a little flirty," she said. "It doesn't mean anything."

Now Stavros was the one to roll his eyes. "He sleeps with every woman he possibly can."

"He never tried to sleep with me," she protested.

"Because you're special."

Holly sucked in her breath. "I am?"

"Get that dying-cow look off your face," he said irritably. "Yes, special. His secretary before you filed a sexual harassment suit against him. I told Oliver if that ever happened again, I'd fire him, cousin or not. And he's a Minos man to the core. Like he said, selfish to the bone. Why would he want to risk losing an amazing secretary slaving away for him night and day, just for some cheap sex he can—and does—get everywhere else?"

"Cheap!" Holly had never even been naked with a man before. How dare Stavros imply she offered cheap sex to all comers? She glared at him. "What right do you have to criticize him? You're just as bad. You sleep with a new actress or model every week!"

Stavros's jaw tightened. "That's not true..." Then something made the anger drain out of his handsome face, replaced by stark, raw emotion. "But you're right. I have no right to criticize him. And I wouldn't, except he's trying to take your life. Don't let him do it," he said fiercely. He pulled her closer, looking down at her as they swayed to the slow music. "Oliver is using you. Look past your dream. See him for the man he really is."

Looking back at Oliver, now arguing with his new bride as they left the dance floor, Holly suddenly thought of all the times that he'd stopped her as she left the office on Friday nights, putting stacks of files into her arms. "You don't mind taking care of this over the weekend, do you, Holly?" he'd say, flashing her his most charming, boyish, slightly sheepish grin. "Thanks, you're the best!"

She thought of all the times he'd mysteriously disappear when an unpleasant conversation was required, leaving Holly to do his dirty work for him. And not just work like firing someone. Frequently she'd be left alone to sort out weeping, heartbroken women who appeared at the office, begging to see him, railing about broken promises.

At the time, Holly had convinced herself it was proof of his faith in her that he'd relied on her to handle such important matters.

But now…

She looked at Oliver and Nicole, who'd gone back to sit at the head table. There was still a smudge of white frosting on her sister's cheek. Earlier, when they'd cut the wedding cake, Nicole had delicately fed her new husband his slice, holding the pose beautifully for pictures. Immediately afterward, Oliver had smashed the piece into his bride's face to make the crowd laugh.

Now, sitting on the dais, they were arguing fiercely over champagne. She was trying to pull the bottle away from him. Yanking it back, Oliver tilted back his head and vengefully drank it straight from the bottle.

And this was supposed to be the happiest day of their lives.

Holly's body flashed hot, then cold, from her scalp to her toes. With an intake of breath, she looked up at Stavros as they danced. "My sister—"

"She's made her bed. Now she'll have to lie in it." His hands tightened as he said, "But you don't have to."

Holly desperately tried to remember the feelings she'd once had for Oliver, all the lonely nights she'd spent in her tiny apartment, with only her romantic fantasies about her boss to keep her warm. But those memories had disappeared like mist against the cold reality of this wedding, and the hot feel of Stavros's hand over hers. The dream was gone.

"Why are you forcing me to see the truth?" she said helplessly. "Why do you care?"

Stavros abruptly stopped dancing. He looked down at her, his black eyes searing through her soul.

"Because I want you, Holly," he said huskily. "On my arm. In my bed." His hand trailed through her hair and down her back as he whispered, "I want you for my own."

He was going to hell for this.

Or at the very least, his conscience warned, he shouldn't hire her as his secretary. Because as hard as he'd tried to ignore her beauty—he *couldn't.*

Stavros looked down at her. Her emerald eyes widened. Her curly red hair looked like fire tumbling over her shoulders. Her petite body felt so soft and sensual in his arms.

But he wanted to keep her as his secretary. He wanted to keep her for everything. He wanted Holly more than he'd ever wanted anyone.

Why her? He didn't know. It couldn't just be her luscious beauty. He'd bedded beautiful women before.

Holly Marlowe was different. The supermodels and actresses seemed as glittery as tinsel, cold as snowflakes. Holly was real. She was warm and alive. Her heart shone from her beautiful green eyes. She didn't even try to guard her heart. He could read her feelings on her face.

And her body…

As they'd danced, he'd watched the tight red fabric slide against her ripe, curvaceous body, and his mouth had gone dry as he'd imagined feeling her naked skin against his own. With his hand against her lower back, he'd felt her hips move, felt the sway of her tiny waist. He'd watched her blush and shiver at his touch, and wondered how innocent she might be. Could she even be a virgin?

No. In this day and age? Surely not.

And yet he'd known then he had to make Holly his, if it was the last thing he did. Which it well could be.

His gaze fell to her pink lips, tracing down to her low-cut neckline, where with each sharp rise and fall of her breath he half expected the red fabric to tear, setting her deliciously full breasts free. He repeated huskily, "I want you."

Holly gave a sudden jagged intake of breath. "How can you be so cruel?"

Frowning, Stavros pulled back. "Cruel?"

"All right, so I'm just a secretary. I'm plain and boring and nothing special. That gives you no right to—no right to—"

"To what?" he said, mystified.

"Make fun of me!" Her voice ended with a sob, and she turned and fled, leaving him standing alone on the dance floor.

A low curse twisted his lips. Make fun of her? He'd never been more serious about anything in his life. Make fun of her? Was she insane?

Grimly, he turned through the crowd, trying to pursue her. But other people suddenly blocked his path on the dance floor, business acquaintances desperate to ingratiate themselves, women hoping for a shot at dancing in his arms.

He barely knew what he said to them as his eyes searched the crowds for Holly. His heart was racing and his body was in a cold sweat. Symptoms of his condition? His body shutting down?

All the things he'd never get the chance to do…

All the things he'd never thought of…

His eyes fell on Oliver, chatting with a trashy-looking girl by the open bar. As much as he despised his cousin's boorish behavior, Stavros realized in some ways he'd been just like him.

He'd never cheated or lied to a girlfriend, it was true. But that was hardly an amazing virtue when Stavros's relationships rarely lasted longer than a month. Whenever the pull of work became greater than the pull of lust, or if a mistress demanded any emotional involvement from him, Stavros would simply end the affair.

For nearly two decades, he'd worked eighteen hours a day, building his tech company. Unlike Oliver, he wasn't afraid of hard work. At first, he'd only wanted to succeed as a big middle finger to his estranged father, who'd cut off his mother without a penny and excluded Stavros from the Minos fortune. But by the time he was twenty, he'd learned the pleasures of work: the intensity, the focus, the thrill of victory. He'd become addicted to it.

But the truth was, he still wasn't so different from Oliver. Like his cousin, Stavros had spent all his adult life focusing on money and power and sleeping with beautiful women, while avoiding emotional entanglement. Stavros had just been better at it.

It was a blow for him to realize that Oliver, as weak and shallow as he was, had managed to do something he hadn't: he'd taken a wife.

Two years younger, and Oliver was already ahead. While Stavros had so little time left…

His eyes narrowed when he finally focused on Holly, speaking urgently with the bride on the other side of the ballroom. "Excuse me," he said shortly, and began pushing through the crowds, ignoring anyone who tried to talk to him.

He came up behind Holly just in time to hear the bride tell her angrily, "How dare you say such a thing!"

Holly flinched, but her voice was low as she pleaded, "I'm sorry, Nicole, I'm just scared for you…"

"I don't care what you imagine, or what Stavros Minos says. Oliver would never cheat. Not on me!" Nicole lifted her chin, her long white veil fluttering as her eyes flashed. "You don't deserve to be my maid of honor. I should have asked Yuna, not you! Better an old college roommate than a jealous old maid of a sister!"

"Nicole!"

"Forget it." Her sister's eyes sparkled as coldly as her tiara. "I want you out of here."

Holly took a deep breath. "Please. I wasn't trying to—"

"Get out!" Nicole shouted, loud enough to be heard over the orchestra, causing everyone nearby to turn and look.

Holly's shoulders flinched. She took a deep breath, then slowly turned away. Stavros had a brief glimpse of her stricken face before she walked through the silent, staring crowds.

He turned to Nicole.

"Your sister loves you," he said in a low voice. "She was trying to warn you."

"Warn me?" Nicole's perfect pink lip curled as she lifted her chin derisively. "Excuse me. I've never been so happy."

Stavros stared at her in disbelief.

"Good luck with that," he said, and went after Holly.

He found her shivering in front of the hotel, hopelessly trying to wave down a yellow taxi in the cold, snowy evening. As Christmas Eve deepened, the traffic on Central Park South had dissipated, leaving the city strangely quiet, tucked in to sleep beneath a blanket of snow, as the stars twinkled in the black sky.

When Holly saw him coming out of the hotel, her expression blanched. Turning, she stumbled away, across the empty street toward wintry, quiet Central Park. When he followed her, she shouted back desperately, "Leave me alone!"

"Holly, wait."

"No!"

Stavros caught up with her on the sidewalk near an empty horse carriage, festooned with holly and red bows, waiting patiently for customers. He grabbed her shoulder.

"Damn you..."

Then he saw her miserable face. Choking back his angry words, he pulled her into his arms. She cried against his chest, and he felt her shivering from grief and cold.

"I told her too late. I should have seen... I should have warned her long ago!"

"It's not your fault." Inwardly cursing both his cousin and her sister, Stavros gently stroked her long red hair until the crying stopped.

She looked up at him, her lovely face desolate, tearstained with streaks of mascara as she wiped her eyes. "I'm not going back."

"Good."

She took a deep breath. "Nicole didn't send you after me?"

Stavros shook his head.

Her shoulders sagged for a moment, then she lifted her chin. "So what do you want?"

He came closer, looking down at her as scattered snowflakes whirled around them on the sidewalk in front of the dark, snowy park. "I told you."

Her eyes widened, and her lips parted. Then she turned her head sharply away. "Don't."

"Don't what?"

"Just don't." She swallowed hard, her green eyes glistening with tears as she looked at him beneath the moonlight. "All right, I was a fool over Oliver. I see now it was just a dream to stave off loneliness." Her voice broke. "But you don't have to be cruel to prove your point. I know I'm not your type, but I do still have feelings!"

"You think I'm toying with you?" Searching her gaze, he said quietly, "I want you, Holly. As I've never wanted anyone."

Looking away, she mulishly shook her head.

As she shivered, he took off his sleek black tuxedo jacket

and draped it gently over her shoulders. Reaching out, he cupped her cheek, running the tip of his thumb over her tender, trembling lower lip. "Holly, look at me."

Her eyes were huge in the moonlight as she flashed him a troubled glance. Behind her he could see the snowy park stretching out forever beneath the wintry, starlit night. She said haltingly, "You can't expect me to believe—"

"Believe this," he whispered. And, grabbing the lapels of the oversize tuxedo jacket around her, he pulled her hard against him, and swiftly lowered his mouth to hers.

CHAPTER THREE

EVEN IN HER wildest dreams, Holly had never imagined a kiss like this.

The few anemic kisses she'd had in her life, the forgettable ends of unsatisfying dates in high school and her one semester of college, had been nothing like this.

But then, she'd never been kissed by a man like Stavros.

His lips moved expertly as his tongue swept hers, taking command, taking possession. Held fast against his powerful, muscular body, she felt herself respond, felt her body rise.

Beneath his passionate, ruthless embrace, a spark of desire built inside her to a sudden white-hot flame.

She'd never felt like this before. The memory of her childish infatuation with Oliver melted away in a second beneath the intensity of this fire. A moment before, she'd been heartsick and despondent over her sister's harsh words. But now, she was lost in a sensual dream, her whole body tight with a sweet, savage yearning she never wanted to end.

When he finally pulled away, Holly looked up at him in shock. Behind him, the bright lights of Midtown skyscrapers illuminated his dark hair like a halo.

"Agape mou," he said hoarsely, stroking the edge of her cheekbone gently with his thumb. "You are everything I want in life. Everything."

Her throat went dry. Trying to smile, she said unevenly, "I bet you say that to all the girls."

"I've never said it to anyone." He looked toward the park's black lace of bare trees against the sweep of moonlit snow. "But life doesn't last forever. I can't waste a moment." He looked at her. "Will you?"

She bit her lip, feeling as if she was in a dream. "But you could have anyone you want. I'm so different..."

"Yes, different. I've watched you. You're warm and loving and kind. And so damned beautiful," he whispered, running a hand through her long red hair. His gaze dropped to her low-cut red dress. "And so sexy you'd make any man lose his mind."

Sexy? *Her?*

He cupped her cheek, kissing her forehead, her cheek, her lips, with butterfly kisses. Drawing back, he looked at her. "You're the only one I want."

Lowering his lips to hers, he kissed her again until she forgot all her insecurity and doubts, until she forgot her own name.

When he released her, she was still lost in the heat of his embrace. Lifting his phone to his ear, he said unsteadily, "Pick me up on Central Park South."

"You're leaving?" she whispered, oddly crestfallen.

"I'm taking you home."

"You don't need to take me home. I have my MetroCard. I can—"

"Not your home." His eyes burned through her. "To mine."

The thought of going home with him, of what that could mean, caused her to shiver as images of unimaginable delights filled her mind. Her breathing quickened. "Why?"

His sensual lips quirked at the edges. *"Why?"*

"I mean...do you need something typed, or...?"

"Is that all you think you are?"

She blushed beneath his gaze. She bit her lip, then forced herself to respond. "You want to seduce me...?"

"How clearly must I say it?" he said huskily. He cupped her cheek, searching her gaze. "I want you, Holly. In my bed." He ran his hand through her hair as he whispered, "In my life."

And those three last words were the most shocking of all.

She stared at him. Once, she'd thought that working all hours and having a secret crush on her boss was the most she could expect out of life. Even earlier today, as she'd watched Oliver marry her little sister, Holly had been sure her future would be one of self-sacrifice, self-abnegation, caring for others, trying to ignore her own loneliness and misery.

Now, in Stavros's arms, wrapped in his tuxedo jacket, looking up at the handsome Greek billionaire's hungry black eyes, she felt like she'd suddenly traded a small black-and-white dream for a big Technicolor one.

His hand tightened on her shoulder. "Unless you still think you're in love with Oliver."

Holly took a deep breath, then slowly shook her head. In all her years working for Oliver, she'd seen only what she wanted to see: his boyish good looks, his cheerful, sly charm. She'd deliberately chosen to be blind to the rest: the laziness, the constant womanizing. "You were right," she said quietly. "It was just a ridiculous dream."

Stavros exhaled. "Then come home with me tonight."

"I can't..." Her heart was pounding. "I've never done anything like that."

"You've played by the rules for your whole life. So have I." His jaw tensed with an anger she didn't understand as he looked up toward the moon, icy and crystalline in the frozen black sky. "The tycoon's playbook. Dating models whose names I can barely remember now. Working twenty hours a day to build a fortune, and for what? To buy another Ferrari?" His lips twisted bitterly. "What has my life even been for?"

Holly stared at him, shocked that Stavros would allow himself to appear so vulnerable in front of anyone. It threw her into confusion. She'd thought of him as her all-knowing and powerful boss. But now, she realized, he was also just a man. With a beating heart, like hers.

"You're not giving yourself enough credit." Gently, she put her hand over his. "You've created jobs all over the world. You've built amazing tech that—"

"It doesn't matter. Not anymore."

"It matters a lot…"

"Not to me."

She took a deep breath. "Then what does?"

"This," he said simply, and lowered his lips to hers.

This time, his kiss was gentle and deep, wistful as a whisper. Could this really be happening? Was she dreaming? Or could she be totally drunk on half a glass of champagne?

Her heart filled with longing as his powerful body enveloped hers.

"Come home with me," he murmured against her lips.

She sucked in her breath, looking up at his handsome, shadowed face. "It's Christmas Eve…"

His dark gaze burned through her. "There's no one else I'd rather have in my arms when I wake on Christmas morning." His hand slowly traced down her cheek to the edge of her throat to her shoulder shivering beneath the oversize tuxedo jacket. "Unless you don't want me…"

Her—not want *him*? Just the ridiculousness of that suggestion made her gasp. "You can't think that…"

His shoulders relaxed, and his dark eyes met hers. "Then live like we're alive."

Live like we're alive. What a strange thing to say.

He was right, she'd followed the good-girl playbook her whole life, Holly thought suddenly. What had being sensible and safe and good ever done for her, except to leave her working overtime for free for a manipulative boss and sacrificing all her dreams to spoil her little sister—only to feel used and taken for granted by both?

"Say yes," Stavros urged huskily, stroking his hands slowly through her hair. "Come away with me. Be free."

A Rolls-Royce pulled up to the curb. She looked at him, her heart pounding.

"Yes," she breathed.

A trace of silvery moonlight caressed the edge of his sculpted, sensual lips as he drew back to make sure she meant it. "Yes?"

"Let's live like we're alive," she whispered.

Glancing back at the waiting car, he held out his hand. "Are you ready?"

Holly nodded, her heart pounding. But as she took his hand, she didn't feel ready. At all.

As she sat next to him in the back of the limo, she barely noticed the driver in front. She didn't notice anything but Stavros beside her. The journey seemed like mere seconds before they pulled in front of a famous luxury hotel in Midtown.

"This is where you live?" Holly said, looking up at the skyscraper.

He smiled wryly. "You don't like it?"

"Of course I do, but…you live in a hotel?"

"It's convenient."

"Oh." Convenient? She supposed her shabby one-bedroom walk-up in Queens was convenient, too. She only had to change trains once to get to work. "But where is your home?"

He shrugged. "Everywhere. I travel a lot. I prefer not to keep permanent live-in staff."

"Right." She nodded sagely. "I prefer that, too."

His lips quirked, then he turned back toward the glamorous hotel, all decorated and sparkling with Christmas lights.

"Mr. Minos!" a uniformed doorman called desperately, rushing to hold open the door. "Thank you again. My wife hasn't stopped crying since she opened your Christmas card."

"It was nothing."

"Nothing!" The burly man swore under his breath. "Because of your Christmas gift, we can finally buy a house. Which means we can finally start trying to have a baby..." His voice choked off.

Stavros briefly put his hand on the burly man's shoulder. "Merry Christmas, Rob."

"Merry Christmas, Mr. Minos," he replied, unchecked tears streaming down his face.

Holding Holly's hand tightly, Stavros led her through the gilded door into the luxurious lobby, which had at its center an enormous gold Christmas tree decorated with red stars stretching two stories high. All around them, glamorous guests walked, some briskly and others strolling, many trailing assistants and bodyguards and holding little pampered dogs. But Holly only looked at the dark, powerful man beside her.

"That must have been some Christmas gift."

"It was just money," he said shortly, leading her through the lobby.

"The doorman—did he do a big favor for you or something?"

As he led her to the elevator, he gave an awkward shrug that made him look almost embarrassed. "Rob holds the door for me. Always smiles and says hello. Sometimes arranges for a car."

"And for that, you bought him and his wife a house?"

Pushing the elevator button, Stavros said again, "It was nothing. Really."

"Nothing to you," she said softly as the door slid open with a ding. "But everything to them."

Wordlessly, he walked into the elevator. She followed him.

"Why did you do it?"

"Because I could."

The same reason he offered me a job as his secretary, she thought. "Stavros," she said, "is it possible that, deep down, you're actually a good guy?"

She saw a flash of something bleak in his dark eyes, quickly veiled. He turned his face toward the sensor then pressed the button for the penthouse. "I'm a selfish bastard. Everyone knows that."

But there was something vulnerable in the tone of his voice. "I'm finding it hard to believe that. Unless there's something else," she said slowly. "Something you're not telling me. Is there—"

Her voice cut off as Stavros pressed her against the elevator wall, and hungrily lowered his mouth to hers.

He kissed her with such hot demand that the questions starting to form in her mind disappeared as if they had never been. All that was left was heat. She felt molten with desire.

With a ding, the elevator door slid open.

Gripping her hand, he pulled her forward. Knees still weak, she followed, looking around her.

The enormous, starkly decorated penthouse was dark except for the white lights glittering from a ten-foot fresh-cut Christmas tree, which stood in front of the floor-to-ceiling windows overlooking the sparkling lights of the city below.

Still shivering from the intensity of his kiss, she looked at him. "Nice tree."

Stavros glanced at it as if he hadn't noticed it 'til now. "The hotel staff arranged that."

She looked around the apartment. There were no photographs on the walls. Nothing personal at all. The white-and-black decor looked like something out of a magazine, curated by a museum. "Did you just move in?"

"I bought this place five years ago."

She looked at him, startled. "Five *years*?"

"So?"

Holly thought of her own shabby walk-up apartment, filled with photos of family and friends, her comfortable, beat-up old furniture, her grandma's old quilt, the tangled-up yarn from her hopeless efforts to learn how to knit. "It seems unlived in."

"I hired the top designer in the city." He sounded a little disgruntled. "It's a look."

"Um." She bit her lip, then turned with a bright smile. "It's nice."

He pulled her into his arms. "You don't really think that."

"No." Butterflies flew through her belly as she stared at his beautiful mouth. Her gaze fell to his thick neck above his black tuxedo tie, to his broad shoulders in the white bespoke shirt, down all the way to the taut waistline of his black trousers to his powerful thighs. Butterflies? The crackle in her core felt more like the sizzle of lightning, burning through every nerve.

"Tell me the truth."

Biting her lip, she said, "I think your apartment is horrible."

"Better," he breathed, and he lowered his mouth to hers.

She tasted the sweetness of his mouth, and surrendered to the strength and power of his larger body wrapped around hers. Surrendered? She hungered for more.

Stavros kissed her for hours, or maybe just minutes, holding her body tightly against his as they stood in his shadowy, stark penthouse, beside the lights of the Christmas tree.

Heart pounding, dizzy from his passionate embrace, she pulled away with a shuddering breath. "This doesn't seem real."

"Lots of things don't feel real to me right now." Brushing tendrils of red hair away from her face, he said softly, "Except you."

As he pulled her tight against his body, his tuxedo jacket fell off her shoulders, dropping silently to the floor. His hands ran slowly through her hair and down her back, over her red dress.

Pulling away, her eyes fell to the floor as she warned him, "I don't have much experience."

"You're a virgin."

Her cheeks flamed. "How did you know?" she whispered. "Is it the way I kissed you?"

"Yes. And the way you shiver when I pull you into my arms. The first time I kissed you, I felt how new it was to you." He gently stroked her cheek, down the edge of her throat, to her breast. Her hard nipple ached even at that slight brush of contact. "That made it new to me, too."

Thinking of the gossip about his previous mistresses, all gorgeous sophisticated women no doubt with amazing, gymnastlike sexual skills, she suddenly couldn't meet his eyes. She bit her swollen lip. "What if I don't please you?"

With a low laugh, he gently lifted her chin as he countered, "What if I don't please you?"

"Are you crazy?" Her eyes went wide. "That's impossible!"

His lips twisted with an emotion she couldn't quite identify.

"That's how I feel about you, Holly," he said in a low voice. "You deserve better."

Stavros felt like *she* deserved better—better than the most famous Greek billionaire playboy in the world? But as she looked into his dark eyes, she saw he believed every word.

With a deep breath, she said quietly, "I can't work for you, Stavros. Not after this."

His expression fell. "You can't?"

Shaking her head, she gave him a crooked smile. "It's all right. Working for the VP of Operations won't be so bad."

His jaw tightened. "As you wish. You will, of course, still get your raise."

"I wouldn't feel comfortable—"

"Nonnegotiable." He cut her off. "You've more than earned it by being the company's hardest-working employee for years. In fact, you should be *demanding* a raise, not just accepting it. Damn it, Holly, you need to realize your value..."

Impulsively, she lifted up on her toes and kissed him. It was the briefest of kisses, feather-light, but it felt daring and terrifying to make the first move. As she started to draw back, he caught her, pulling her against him urgently. He kissed her hungry and hard, as if she was a life raft, and he was a drowning man.

Her body felt tight with need. Her breasts felt heavy, her nipples aching, sending electric sparks rushing through her every time they brushed against his hard chest. Tension coiled low and deep inside her, and she wanted him even closer. Reaching up, she pulled his head down harder to deepen the kiss.

With a growl, he lifted her up into his arms, and carried her down the hallway to an enormous bedroom.

The room was huge, but as sparsely decorated as the great room. Shadows filled the room, with a white gas fire shimmering like candlelight in the stark modern fireplace. Next to the windows, an artificial white tree gleamed with white lights.

Setting her down beside the bed, Stavros stroked her cheek. "You're so beautiful, Holly," he whispered. "I never imagined anyone could be so beautiful. Like an angel."

"I'm no angel."

He paused, looking at her in the winter moonlight flooding in through the window. "No." Reaching around her, he slowly unzipped her red maid-of-honor dress. "You're all woman."

Noiselessly, the dress dropped to the floor. Leaving her standing before him in only a bra, panties and high-heeled shoes.

She should have felt cold, standing nearly naked in front of him in the large bedroom. But beneath the heat of his gaze, she felt lit with an intoxicating fire as he slowly looked her over, from her full breasts plumped up by the white silk demi bra, past the softly curved plane of her belly, to her white silk panties, edged with lace. Taking her courage in her hands, she lifted her gaze.

Cupping her face in both hands, he lowered his head to hers and kissed her until the whole world swirled around her as she was lost in the sweet maelstrom of his embrace. His hands roamed feather-light over her body, stroking her breasts, her tiny waist, her big hips, the full curve of her backside. When his hands stroked over the silk bra, she held her breath until he reached around her to unhook the clasp, springing her free. With an intake of breath, he cupped her breasts, tweaking her taut nipples. She shuddered, vibrating with need.

Reaching down, he pulled off her high-heeled shoes, one by one, sending each skittering across the black floor. Pushing her back against the white comforter of the king-size bed, he undid the cuff links of his shirt.

Never taking his eyes off her, he loosened the buttons, and she had her first flash of his hard chest. He dropped the shirt to the floor, and she got her full view of it, in all its tanned, muscular glory. A trail of dark hair led to his flat, taut belly.

He unzipped his dark trousers, and slowly pulled them down his thighs, along with his underwear, revealing his muscular, powerful legs laced with more dark hair. She sucked in her breath as he straightened, and she saw how big he was, and how hard for her.

She wasn't a total innocent. She'd seen pictures of the male form. There had been that sex education course in high school, gag gifts in shops, and working in an office, she'd once stumbled over a coworker watching porn on his computer. She wasn't totally naive.

But in this moment, seeing him naked in all his physical power and brute force, she felt nervous. Swallowing, she pulled the white comforter up to her chin, squeezing her eyes shut, suddenly shaking.

She felt the mattress move beneath her.

"Holly." His voice was low. His hand, warm and gentle, was on her shoulder. "Look at me."

Biting her lip, she looked up at him, wondering what she should do, what she should say. Stavros's darkly handsome face was intense, lost in desire.

"Are you afraid?" he asked in a low voice.

Biting her lip, she looked away. "I don't want to displease you. I—I don't know what to do."

"Holly," he repeated huskily. Slowly, he ran a fingertip down her bare shoulder above the comforter. Just that simple touch caused a sizzle of electricity to go through her. "Look at me. All of me. And see if you please me."

She looked down as he'd commanded, and saw how large he was, how hard and thick and smooth. He wanted her. There could be no doubt of that.

Trembling, she lifted her mouth toward his. Holding her tenderly, he kissed her.

With his lips on hers, all rational thought disappeared again in molten heat, in the rising need that made her forget everything else. She was dimly aware of the comforter disappearing. As his naked body covered hers, as she felt his weight and strength on her, she sighed with pleasure and a sense of rightness—of being part of something, half of a whole. Entwining her tongue with his own, he teased her, toyed with her, made her gasp. The kiss was so perfect, so deep, when he pulled away she was left with a sense of loss and longing.

He nibbled her chin, then slowly worked his way down her naked body with hot kisses, as his hands caressed her bare skin. He licked her neck, her collarbone. He cupped her full, bare breasts and lowered his mouth slowly to the valley between them, making her grip the white cotton sheet beneath her as she felt his hot breath against her skin.

He wrapped his lips around her taut, aching nipple. His mouth was wet and hot as he suckled her, pulling her deep into his mouth, swirling her with his tongue. She gasped with pleasure, closing her eyes.

He moved to the other breast, suckling that nipple in turn, as his hands stroked slowly down her body, caressing her belly, her hips, her thighs. He lowered his head, kissing where his hands had just caressed her, seducing her with feather-light touches that made her skin burn. She felt his fingertips lift the edge of her panties from her hips.

"Do you want me?" he whispered, his voice so low it made her tremble.

"Yes," she breathed.

"Louder."

"Yes!" she cried, her cheeks burning.

Then Stavros suddenly pulled away, looking down at her. And he spoke words she'd never expected. Words that nearly made her heart stop.

"Marry me, Holly." Stavros cupped her cheek, his dark eyes burning in the Christmas-Eve night. "Have a child with me."

Her eyes widened with shock. "Are you serious?"

"I've never been more serious."

Holly couldn't believe it. Even a one-night stand with a

man like Stavros seemed like a dream. But he wanted to marry her? Have a baby with her?

Tears came to her eyes.

"I've shocked you," he said grimly.

"No…yes." Lifting her chin, she whispered, "It's like all my most impossible dreams are suddenly coming true."

Exhaling, he ran his thumb lightly along her cheekbone, brushing a tear away. "Is that a yes?"

"Yes," she breathed.

He smiled, and it was brighter than the sun, even as she saw a suspicious sheen in his black eyes. "You'll never regret it. I swear it on my life."

"I'll do my best to make you happy…"

"You already have." Lowering his head, he kissed her. "I want you, *agape mou*," he groaned against her lips. "I'll want you until the day I die."

She held her breath as he kissed down her throat, to her breasts, then her belly. She shivered, lost in a sensual dream. He wanted to marry her. He wanted to fill her with his child…

He slowly pulled her white silk panties down her legs, and tossed them away. Kneeling between her legs on the bed, he pushed her thighs apart. She felt the warmth of his breath against the most sensitive part of her body, a place no man had ever touched.

Lowering his head, he spread her wide with his hands. For a moment, she couldn't breathe, as he teased her with the warmth of his breath.

Then he tasted her, delicately with the tip of his tongue, swirling against the core of her pleasure. Even as she gasped in shock at the intensity of the sensation, he moved, deepening his possession, reaching around her to hold her tight, as he lapped her with the full width of his tongue.

She cried out, grasping the bed beneath her as electricity whipped through her, causing her back to arch, lifting off the mattress.

He moaned, his hands tightening on her thighs, holding her down as her whole body strained to fly. Her breasts felt tight, her whole body aching with need. Then he pushed a single thick fingertip inside her, stretching her.

Pleasure built inside her, whirling her in every direction, pleasure she'd never imagined. She held her breath, closing her eyes as her head tilted back. Her body arched off the bed as he worked her with his tongue—then, just as she tightened with pleasure almost too great to bear, he pushed a second fingertip inside her. And she exploded into a thousand chiming diamonds, in a million colors, soaring through the sky.

She was only dimly aware as he reached for a condom from a nearby nightstand. But as he started to tear it open, she covered it with her hand.

"No," she panted, still dizzy beneath waves of pleasure.

"No?" He looked stunned.

"You don't need that." She smiled. "Live like you're alive."

Savage joy lit up his dark eyes as he threw the condom to the floor. "This is my first time without one," he whispered, lowering his head to kiss her. "My first time ever."

"For both of us," she breathed, closing her eyes with a delicious shiver as he gently bit the corner of her neck. Prickles of desire raced through her body.

"I'll end the pain as quickly as I can," he said huskily.

Pain? What pain? All she felt was bliss—

Gripping her hips, he positioned himself between her legs. In a swift, deliberate movement, he sheathed himself deeply inside her.

She gasped as he broke the barrier inside her. But he held himself utterly still, holding her as the sudden pang of pain lessened, then disappeared. His weight was heavy on hers, his hard-muscled chest sliding sensually over her breasts as he lowered his head to kiss her, gently at first, then with rising passion as she started to return his embrace.

Only then did he slowly begin to move inside her, thrusting deeper, inch by inch. And to her shock, a delicious new tension began to coil, low and deep inside her belly.

Reaching up to his shoulders, Holly pulled him down tighter against her, wanting him deeper, wanting more. Wanting everything.

CHAPTER FOUR

HE WAS ALREADY deep inside her, so deliciously deep. Stavros fought to keep control as she gripped his shoulders, pulling his naked body down against her. He felt her move beneath him, tightening with new desire.

"Yes," she'd whispered. He shuddered at the memory.

When Holly had told him she'd marry him and have his child, that single word had nearly unmanned him. And now it was almost impossible to hold himself back, when just the feel of her and the sight of her were enough to make him explode. Especially when he was bare inside her, a pleasure he'd never experienced before. He was a breath from losing control.

But he couldn't. Not yet. He set his jaw, desperately trying to keep hold of the reins in a ruthless grip.

Stavros felt like a virgin himself.

He'd spoken the forbidden words that seared his heart, words he'd never said to any woman. Outlandish words, asking her to marry him and have his baby. It was his one last chance to leave something of himself behind. An adoring wife, and a son or daughter to carry on his name.

She should have refused him, laughed in his face. After all, they were barely more than strangers to each other.

Instead, she'd accepted him, as if she'd dreamed her whole life of marrying Stavros and having his child.

All he'd wanted to do was possess her, to thrust inside her, hard and fast. But he'd known the first time would be painful for her. So he'd forced himself to go slow, to take his time, to seduce her. To make it good for her.

When he'd first pushed himself inside her, he'd hated to see sudden pain wipe out the joy in her beautiful face. So he'd held her, until her pain passed, though it was total agony to hold himself still, so hard with need, so deep inside her. But he managed it—for her. He'd kissed her sweaty forehead, her soft cheek, and held her close until he felt her shoulders relax, and a sigh came from her lips.

Now, the raw intensity of his desire for her was almost too much to bear. As he felt her move beneath him, her every gasp of pleasure was pure torture.

She was soft, so soft. And so sensual. He was on a razor's edge of control.

Holly Marlowe was a sensual goddess. He wondered how he hadn't recognized her beauty and sensuality from the moment he'd first seen her, three years before. He should have seen past the mousy bun and baggy, unflattering clothes. He should have known what they really were—a disguise.

She was his now, and she would be his for as long as he lived. She would be his wife. He would fill her with his child—

With a shudder of need, he kissed her lips, tenderly at first, then with building passion. As her hands gripped his shoulders, pushing him tighter against her, he panted with need, beads of sweat rising on his forehead as he continued to thrust slowly, gently, letting her feel every inch of him moving inside her.

The pleasure was incredible. Some of his control began to slip. But he wasn't ready for it to end, not yet. He wanted to make it amazing for her.

He looked down. Holly's face was sweetly lifted, her eyes closed with ecstasy. He almost exploded right then. With a shudder, he gripped her hips and slowly began to increase his pace. Her lips parted as she sucked in her breath, her fingernails raking slowly down his naked back.

When he finally felt her tighten around him as her gasp of pleasure turned into a scream, he could hold himself back no longer. He plunged deep into her, and his own hoarse shout melded with hers, echoing against the windows overlooking the sparkling lights of the city. The white tree twinkled amid the dark shadows of the bedroom, as the clock struck midnight on Christmas Eve.

When Stavros woke, the soft light of dawn was coming through his bedroom's floor-to-ceiling windows. Outside, the wintry city looked gray on Christmas morning.

He'd been lost in the best dream he'd ever had. Holly had been kissing him, and she'd been heavily pregnant. Emotion shone from her vulnerable eyes as she'd told him she loved him—

Now, he looked at the soft, warm woman in his arms. Both of them were still naked beneath the white comforter. He realized he'd slept all night, holding her in his arms. They were still facing each other, their foreheads almost touching on the pillow, her curly red hair stretched out behind her. Even in sleep, his arms had been wrapped protectively around her.

I love you, Stavros, she'd whispered in the dream, her heart and soul in her eyes.

It was just a dream, he reminded himself harshly. Totally meaningless. But in the cold light of reality, he felt her imagined words like an ice pick through his soul. *I love you.*

When he'd imagined leaving her behind after his death, he'd pictured a pregnant wife dressed in black, standing stoically beside his grave.

He hadn't thought of how it might feel to be the widow left behind. How Holly's warm, generous, loving heart might react to all that grief. It could destroy her.

Could? It *would.*

His conscience, buried and repressed for so long, suddenly came out in full force. Could he really be so selfish? Was he a Minos man through and through after all?

I'll leave her all my fortune, he argued with himself.

But Holly wouldn't care about that, not really. After all, she'd spent three years working for Oliver without asking for the raise and promotion she deserved. When she'd walked into his twenty-million-dollar penthouse, with its elegant decor created at great expense by Manhattan's foremost interior designer, she'd been left utterly unmoved.

Holly, alone of all women on earth, didn't seem to give a damn about money.

So his billions would bring her little pleasure. Far from it. With her kind, sympathetic heart, his widow's fortune would make her an easy target for unscrupulous fortune hunters. First and foremost: his greedy cousin and her spoiled sister.

Stavros looked back at Holly, sleeping so sweetly and trustingly in his arms.

I'll leave her with a child, he tried to tell himself. That, at least, was something he knew she wanted.

But a child she would raise alone?

He felt sick. He'd seduced Holly under false pretenses. His dream had only shown the stark truth: he'd soon make her love him. He'd already started to make her care. Her heart was innocent; she had no defense against love, not like Stavros. Only he knew what love really meant: surrender or possession. Being the helpless conquered or tyrannical conqueror. No one came out of it unscathed.

Just the fact that she'd convinced herself, even for a moment, that she could love a man as unworthy of it as Oliver only proved how open her heart was. She was not guarded. She had no walls.

So when Stavros died, which he would before next

Christmas, he would not leave behind him a dignified wife in a black veil and chic black mourning suit standing stoically beside his grave, as he'd imagined.

Instead, he'd leave a broken woman, bewildered and lost, perhaps with a child to raise on her own. For all he knew, she might already be pregnant. Stavros would soon be dead and buried, forgotten. But Holly would remain, a widow with a broken heart, bitterly cursing him as the liar who'd seduced her with false promises of forever and changed her life in ways she'd never imagined.

A razor blade lifted to his throat as he looked at her, still sleeping trustingly in his arms. He had no choice. He had to tell her the truth. Explain about his fatal brain tumor before it was too late for her to change her mind about marrying him.

If it wasn't already too late.

"You're awake." Holly's voice was soft and warm as she drowsily opened her eyes, smiling up at him with love shining from her face. "Merry Christmas."

Stavros looked down at her. His lips parted to choke out the truth. Then he stopped.

He suddenly realized with horrifying clarity that even if he told her about his illness *she would marry him, anyway.*

As that sister of hers had said, taking care of other people was what Holly did best. She gave and gave and gave, leaving nothing for herself. From the time her parents had died, she'd put her little sister first. From the moment she'd started working at Minos International, she'd put Oliver first. She sacrificed herself for others, even if they didn't deserve it.

And if Stavros told her he was dying she would do the same for him. She'd take care of him. She'd hold his hand through chemotherapy appointments. She'd love him. She'd never leave him.

Even if it destroyed her.

"Holly," he said hoarsely, struggling to know what to do, "there's something you need to…"

He felt a sharp pain behind his right eye, so sudden and savage he jerked back from her. The bed seemed like it was swaying beneath him.

Holding the comforter over her chest, Holly sat up with a frown. "Stavros?"

The pain was nearly blinding, spreading through his head, causing a rough throbbing in his skull. He put a trembling hand against his forehead. How long did he have? Even his doctor had hedged his bets when he'd given him the news two days before.

"No one can say for sure how long you'll live, Mr. Minos," Dr. Ramirez had said gravely. But when Stavros had pressed him, he'd admitted six to nine months might be typical for a patient at his advanced stage.

But Stavros wasn't a typical man. He'd always prided himself on it. He'd always beaten others, proving himself stronger and smarter and faster. His tumor was part of him. All his worst sins bottled up into one fleshy mass rapidly spreading through his brain.

"What is it?" Holly cried. "What's wrong?"

Slowly getting out of bed, he stood still, blinking until the blurriness passed and he could see again in the dim early light of his penthouse's master bedroom. Wearily, he stumbled across the room, opened a drawer and pulled on some loosely slung knit pants. He felt as if he was a million years old.

Going to the wall of windows, he stared out at the cold gray city beneath him. So very cold. So very gray.

All these years he'd hated his father as heartless and cruel. All these years he'd despised his cousin as a selfish bastard.

What Stavros had just done proved him to be the worst of them all.

He was dying, so in a pathetic attempt to make his life matter, to be important to someone other than his shareholders, he'd proposed marriage to this trusting girl. He'd taken her virginity. That was bad enough.

But he'd wanted to do so much more.

He'd wanted to crush her heart and spirit and make her suffer with him as he declined, and failed, and died. Clinging to her like a drowning man, like a filthy coward, he'd wanted to drag her down with him.

Most women he knew might have been happy to exchange six months of holding his hand and watching him die for a vast pot of gold at the end. Those women guarded their souls—if they even *had* souls.

But not Holly. He'd seen it in her warm, trusting face. From the first moment he'd taken her arm at her sister's wedding, when they'd danced at the reception, when he'd first kissed her in the snowy darkness of Central Park, he'd seen how quickly her opinion of him had changed, from resentment, to curiosity, to bewildered desire. And finally, when she'd opened her eyes just now in the gray light of Christmas morning in his bed, he'd seen the way her soft emerald eyes glowed. And he'd known.

He could break her.

"Stavros, you're scaring me." From behind him on the bed, the tone of her voice suddenly changed, becoming artificially bright. "You've changed your mind about marrying me, haven't you? You're scared to tell me. But don't be. I wouldn't blame you if—"

"Yes." His voice was harsh as he turned to face her. "I've changed my mind."

"You have?"

Her lovely face went pale, but she spoke the words as if this was exactly what she'd expected all along. As if she'd known her joy and ecstasy could only be a brief fantasy.

Setting his shoulders, forcing himself not to feel, he said shortly, "Last night was a mistake."

Holly's shoulders sagged, and she looked away, toward the twinkling white tree. Holding the comforter over her naked breasts, she whispered, "Was it something I did, or…?"

"I was drunk last night," he lied harshly, knowing the fastest way through this was to hit her at her most vulnerable point, so she wouldn't fight it. One hard painful wrench, and it would all be over. "I mean—" he shrugged, the stereotype of a casually cruel playboy "—let's face it. Like you said, you aren't my usual type."

The blow hit her squarely. The last color drained from her cheeks, leaving her pale as a ghost beneath her fiery hair. She swallowed, tried to speak, failed. She was lost in pain and insecurity and couldn't see past it. Wordlessly, she looked down at her hands, clasped together tightly over the comforter. "I…"

"You should go," he said coldly.

Not meeting his eyes, Holly slowly got out of bed. Picking up her bra and panties, and her crumpled red gown from the floor, she covered her amazing body. Her face held the pure, unmitigated heartbreak of youth, and he hated himself at that moment more than he'd ever hated anyone. Which was saying something.

"My driver will take you home. He could stop at the drugstore, if you like."

"What for?"

"Emergency contraception," he said coldly.

"That's not necessary."

"It's not?"

Stepping into her high-heeled shoes, she lifted her chin. With a deep breath, she looked back at him. "I told you. I can take the subway."

His stomach churned at the bleakness in her eyes. “Holly—”

She cut him off with a harsh gesture. Then she gave a forced smile. “It’s my fault. I knew all along you couldn’t possibly— I never should have come here.”

Holly was apologizing…to him. It took all of Stavros’s willpower not to reach for her, pull her into his arms, tell her how he was to blame for everything. But the habits of a lifetime held him in good stead. His hands tightened into fists at his sides. “I’ll make sure you still get the promotion and raise you deserve,” was all he said. “But it’s better we don’t work together in the future.”

“Yes.” Looking back at him, her eyes suddenly glittered with a strange ferocity he’d never seen before. “You’re right. Goodbye.” She turned away.

But he couldn’t let her go, not like this. Not when he suddenly wondered if he’d ever see her again.

Stavros grabbed her arm. “Wait.”

“What else is there to say?” she asked, her voice catching.

His fingers tightened over her wrist. Last night had been the most incredible sexual experience of his life—and more than sexual. Their eyes locked, and all Stavros wanted to do was pull her back into his arms. Into his bed. Into his life.

But not at the cost of hers.

He dropped her wrist.

“It’s unlikely you’re pregnant after just one night. But if anything happens,” he drawled, “you’ll let my lawyers know, won’t you?”

Her lips parted in confusion. “Your lawyers?”

“Yes. If you’re pregnant, they’ll take care of it.”

Her face went white, then red. Then her green eyes narrowed with cold fury. “You’re too kind.”

Stavros had played the part of a coldhearted, womanizing louse to perfection, insinuating that he would have his lawyers pay her off if there was a child. Insinuating he was too busy and important to even be bothered with such a minor detail.

No wonder she was now looking at him as if he was the most despicable human being on earth.

"That's all." He tilted his head, making his eyes as frozen and gray as the world outside. "Now get out."

With an intake of breath, Holly said in a trembling voice, "I wish I'd never met you."

And turning on her heel, she left his penthouse, taking all the warmth and light with her, leaving Stavros alone in the coldest Christmas he'd ever known.

CHAPTER FIVE

Eleven months later

HOLLY PAUSED IN shoveling snow, taking a deep breath that turned to smoke in the chill air. All around her, sunshine illuminated the snow, making the white blanket sparkle like diamonds.

It was the day after Thanksgiving, and for the first time in her life, she was spending it alone—and in Switzerland, of all places. Farther from home than she could ever have imagined last Christmas, when her heart had been so savagely broken.

She leaned against the shovel. A soft smile lifted to her face as she looked toward the porch. But she wasn't alone, not truly. She'd never be alone again.

Late November snow was nearly four feet deep around the winding path that led from her tiny chalet, just a rustic cabin really, to the sliver of main road. The nearest village was a mile away, tucked in a remote valley of the Swiss Alps, and even that was nearly deserted in winter. The nearest real market town was Zedermatt, where the festive outdoor Christmas market would open today. A friend had begged her to accompany him there this afternoon. Somewhat hesitantly, she'd agreed. Why not enjoy the season?

Holly's days of working long hours in an office, always filled with stress and urgency, now seemed like a strange dream from long ago. Here, there was only tranquility and peace, and of course, snow, but she'd gotten used to that, shoveling the path to her door every day, and listening to the quiet sound of snowflakes each night against the slanted roof.

In the last year, everything had changed. Her old life in New York, the person she'd once been, were all gone. So much lost. But even more gained.

A baby's gurgle came from the small porch of her chalet, and Holly looked up tenderly, with a familiar joy in her heart.

"Are you hungry, sweet boy?" Shoveling the last few scoops of wet snow from the path to the road, she carried the shovel back toward the chalet. She tromped her winter boots heavily to knock off the snow, then climbed the steps to the porch and smiled down at her sweet two-month-old baby, Freddie, named after her own beloved father.

The baby gurgled and waved his arms happily, at least as much as he could do, bundled up as he was in a one-piece winter fleece that covered him from mittens to hood, tucked snugly into the baby seat with a blanket over the top.

"We'll get you fed," Holly promised, smiling. Setting down the shovel nearby, she lifted the baby seat's handle and carried him inside.

Inside the rustic cabin, a fire blazed in the old stone fireplace. This chalet was two hundred years old, with low ceilings braced with hand-hewn wooden beams. The furniture wasn't quite as old, but close. And the place was tiny: there was only one bedroom. But every day since she'd arrived here, pregnant and heartbroken, last February, she'd blessed her former employer, who'd offered her free lodging in exchange for keeping an eye on the place.

Coming inside, Holly set down the baby carrier then pushed the door closed behind her to keep out the frozen air. She yanked off her heavy winter coat and colorful hand-knitted hat, hanging them on the coat rack while she shook errant snowflakes out of her long red braid. Pulling off her boots, she left them on towels placed just inside the door and stepped nimbly into the room, wearing a loose green sweater and snug black leggings ending in thick warm socks.

Unbuckling Freddie out of the carrier, she changed his diaper then wrapped him snugly in a soft baby blanket. Cradling him in her arms, she carried him to the worn sofa near the fire. As she fed the baby, he looked up at her with big wondering eyes, nestling his tiny hand between her breasts.

Holly had arrived here in a panic in February, wondering how she'd ever cope with raising a child on her own. Then she'd remembered: she already had. She'd raised her baby sister when Holly was barely more than a child herself.

After Stavros had coldly thrown her out of his bed last Christmas morning, she'd never gone back to her job at Minos International. She hadn't even gone back to collect her carefully tended plant or framed photos of her sister. A friend had collected them for her, along with her last check.

Holly had had money in her savings account. She'd learned to be careful with money the hard way, at eighteen, when she'd found herself with a little sister to raise and very little money from her parents' life insurance to support them. Ever since, she'd always been careful.

That saved her when, in mid-January as she'd started her job search, she'd discovered the real source of the stomach flu she hadn't been able to shake: she was pregnant.

And the memory of Stavros's words in bed on Christmas morning chilled her. *If you're pregnant, let my lawyers know...they'll take care of it.*

That, more than anything, had destroyed any lingering illusions she'd had about Stavros Minos being a decent human being.

She'd, of course, heard stories about men lying to get a woman into bed. But she'd never imagined it would happen to her. When he'd desired her, Stavros had been romantic beyond belief, seducing her with sweet words, passionate kisses and, most astonishing of all, proposing marriage and having a child together.

But from the moment he'd gotten what he wanted, he'd expected her to disappear.

Holly had known she wouldn't let him make the baby disappear, too. She couldn't take the risk of seeing Stavros Minos again, even accidentally, or letting him know she was pregnant.

So she'd left New York.

She'd been happy in Switzerland. She was lucky. All right, so Thanksgiving, the traditional American kickoff to the Christmas season, had felt a little quiet yesterday, since the holiday wasn't celebrated in Switzerland. Growing up, Holly's mother had always spent the whole day cooking turkey and baking pies that smelled heavenly, while the two girls stretched out in the morning on the carpet of the family room, watching the Thanksgiving Day parade on TV. In the afternoon, during commercials of his football game, their father inevitably wandered into the kitchen, hoping to sneak a taste of mashed potatoes and cranberry sauce, before their mother shooed him away with a playful smack of a Santa-decorated towel.

Christmas had always been Holly's favorite time of year. At least until last year. Now, with her heartbreaking memories of Stavros last Christmas Day, she was almost afraid to face the holidays this year.

Holly steadied herself. She had so much to be thankful for now. This warm, cozy chalet, her baby, her health. And after nearly a year of estrangement, when she'd phoned her sister to wish her happy Thanksgiving yesterday, for the first time her sister had actually answered the phone.

All right, so Nicole had mostly just yelled at her during the ten-minute call. Apparently Oliver had been fired from three different jobs over the past year, causing the newlyweds to move from Hong Kong to Los Angeles, then back to New York, where he was now unemployed. Her sister blamed Holly.

"It's your fault," Nicole had shouted. "His bosses expect too much. You should be here taking care of things for him. And for me!"

Feeling guilty, Holly tried to change the subject. "I've been busy this year, too..." And she'd finally told her sister the happy news about the baby.

But if she'd hoped it would make Nicole forgive her, or have any joy at the news of a baby nephew, Holly was soon disappointed.

Her sister had been shocked, then furious, then demanded to know the identity of the father. Swearing her to secrecy, Holly had shivered as she'd whispered Stavros's name into the phone. It had been the first time she'd spoken his name aloud in almost a year.

But knowing that secret only seemed to enrage Nicole more.

"So now you're a baby mama for a billionaire?" she'd cried. "You selfish cow—you never have to worry about anything, do you?"

And her sister had slammed down the phone.

At least they were talking again, Holly told herself now, trying to remain cheerful. It was a start. And who knew what the future could hold? After all, they were coming into the season of miracles.

Her baby was the biggest miracle of all. She could never be sad about anything for long, not when she had him. She smiled down at Freddie, who was all bright eyes and plump cheeks. And if, with his dark eyes and black hair, her baby strongly resembled a man she didn't want to remember, she blocked it from her mind with harsh determination.

Freddie was hers. He had no father. Holly would be the only parent he'd ever need.

The baby, born a week late in a Zurich hospital, had been over four kilos—nine pounds, two ounces—and continued to gain weight at a healthy clip. As Holly looked down at her precious child, her heart twisted with love such as she'd never known.

And Stavros would never even know he existed.

Holly looked into the fire. She'd had no choice, she reminded herself fiercely, as she'd done many times over the past year. Stavros had made his feelings clear. The morning after he'd seduced her with promises and lies, she'd woken up on the happiest Christmas morning she'd ever known, only to be tossed out with the trash.

After she'd found out she was pregnant, she'd fled New York in fear that his lawyers might try to force her to end the pregnancy. She'd gone to London, where her former employer had made it clear she had a standing job offer. He'd been bewildered when, instead of accepting a high-paying office job, she'd asked about being a caretaker to his family's old chalet in Switzerland.

"It's not St. Moritz, you know," he'd replied doubtfully, stroking his white beard. "The village is deserted in winter. It was my great-grandfather's cabin. It's a bit of a wreck. Are you sure?"

Holly had been sure. And she'd never regretted her choice. She'd made friends with her elderly neighbors down the road, kind people who'd delighted in showering lonely, pregnant Holly with advice and *Älplermagronen*, and since her baby's birth, with babysitting offers and cake. Holly's high-school German was rapidly improving. As far as she was concerned, she'd be happy to live here forever. Happy enough.

How could she ever admit she felt lonely sometimes, or that she didn't think her heart would ever completely heal from her brief affair with Stavros? It would be the height of ingratitude to ever feel sad, when she had so much: home, friends and Freddie.

It was enough. It had to be enough.

She looked down at the sleeping baby in her arms. Stroking his rosy cheek, her heart full of love, she whispered, "I'm going to make your first Christmas perfect, Freddie. See if I don't."

The baby yawned in reply, drowsy and sleepy with a full belly and a warm fire. Carefully, Holly rose to her feet and settled the baby into a small bassinet in the cabin's bedroom. Leaving him in the darkened room to nap, she softly closed the door behind her.

Back in the main room, the fire crackled. Untying her braid to shake her hair free, she went to the closet and dug to the back, where she found a large box.

It was time to reclaim Christmas.

Reaching into her family's old box of treasures, Holly pulled out her grandmother's old quilt, the chipped ceramic Santa cookie jar, a garland of colorful felt stars and the Christmas recipe book with her mother's faded handwriting. Vintage ornaments from her childhood. She touched the hand-knitted stockings, and her heart lifted to her throat.

She decorated the small main room, putting the ornaments on the wooden mantel above the fire, and then stepped back to look. That would have to do, at least until she got a tree at the Christmas market. A lump rose in her throat. She'd make sure Freddie had a wonderful Christmas—

There was a hard knock at the door, making her jump. Then she shook her head, smiling. Who was it? Elke with freshly baked gingerbread? Horst, offering to shovel snow? Brushing off some errant Christmas glitter from her black leggings, Holly opened the door.

And her smile dropped.

"Holly." Stavros's coldly handsome face glowered down at her. His voice was low, barely more than a growl.

Her lips parted in a silent gasp.

"Is it true?" he demanded. Moving closer, he narrowed his eyes, black as night. His jawline was dark with five-o'clock shadow, and his powerful form filled the door, all broad shoulders and muscle. Behind him, parked on the edge of the snowy road, she saw his driver waiting inside a black luxury SUV that looked totally out of place in this rural Swiss valley.

Terror went through her. Her baby. He'd come for her baby! Instinctively she started to close the door in his face. "I don't want to see you—"

"Too bad." Reaching out a powerful arm, he blocked the door, and pushed his way inside.

Shivering with sickening fear, she stepped back as he closed the door behind him. He calmly shook the snowflakes from his Italian cashmere coat.

He was even more handsome than she remembered. Even more dangerous.

"I heard a rumor." Stavros looked slowly around the cabin, with its roaring fireplace and homemade Christmas decorations. Pulling off his black leather gloves, he tucked them into his pockets and turned to her with narrowed eyes. His voice was colder than the frigid winter air outside. "Is it true?"

"Is what true?" she whispered, with a sinking heart.

Stavros's jaw was tight as he looked right through her. "Did you have my baby, Holly?"

Her blood went cold. Teeth chattering, she stared at him. The man who'd once seduced her, who'd wooed her with words and languorous kisses, was now looking at her with hatred in his eyes.

She tried to laugh. "Where did you hear that?"

"You're a terrible liar," he said softly. "Is it possible you've lied to me for nearly a year?"

Her heart lifted to her throat. It was all she could do not to turn and rush into the bedroom, to grab their sleeping baby and try to run before it was too late.

But it was already too late. She'd never outrun Stavros. Especially with his driver outside. There was no escape.

Her mouth went dry as she tried to think of a lie he might believe. Something, anything. She could say Freddie was another man's son. Stavros knew she'd been a virgin in his bed, but maybe she'd slept with someone else right afterward. A hookup after Christmas! A drunken one-night stand on New Year's Eve! Anything!

But as her eyes met Stavros's, she couldn't force any lie from her trembling lips.

"Who told you?" she whispered, her voice barely audible.

Stavros staggered back, his dark eyes wide. For a split second, he did not move.

Then he took a deep breath. Reaching out, he cupped her cheek. She felt the rough warmth of his palm against her skin. His touch was tender, but his expression was cruel.

"Who told me? Oliver. Who heard it from your sister." He said softly, "He enjoyed telling me. He's never been able to make me feel like a fool before." Blinding sunlight from the window, amplified by the snow, suddenly bathed the hard edges of his cheekbones and jawline in golden light. "But he's not to blame. You are."

Shivering, she licked her lips. "I..."

"You promised to tell me if there was a pregnancy." His dark eyes were aflame with cold fury. "You're a liar, Holly. A filthy, despicable liar."

But at that, sudden rage filled her, chasing away the shadows of fear.

"*I'm* a liar?" she said incredulously.

His lip curled scornfully. "You hid your pregnancy and ran away like a thief—"

Holly was past listening as nearly a year of grief and rage exploded from her heart.

"*You're* the liar, Stavros. When you wanted me in your bed, you promised the sun and the moon! You asked me to marry you!" Her body shook with pain and anger. "But as soon as you were done, you couldn't throw me away fast enough on Christmas morning!"

He started to speak, then abruptly cut himself off. He looked away, his jaw clenching. He said in a low voice, "I had a good reason."

"Yeah, right!" Holly, who'd never lost her temper in her life, truly lost it now. "You'd had your fun and you were done. You didn't care what it did to me. You're selfish to the bone. Why would I ever let a man like you near my son?"

"Son?" He slowly turned to her. Then his eyes narrowed. "I want to meet him."

"No."

"I'm his father."

"Father?" She lifted her chin incredulously. "You're a sperm donor, nothing more. I don't want anything to do with you. We're better off without you." She jabbed her finger toward the door. "Now get out!"

Stavros clawed his hands through his dark, tousled hair. His black eyes looked weary, almost bleak. "You don't understand. I wasn't myself last year—"

"You were exactly yourself," she interrupted coldly. "The lying, coldhearted bastard everyone else claimed you were." Holly was surprised he'd even bother trying to make excuses. It didn't seem like his style. But it didn't matter. She wouldn't let herself get suckered into caring about him ever again. She shook her head. "You're selfish and cruel. Just like Oliver said—Minos men only care about themselves!"

Abruptly, Stavros turned to face her.

"I was dying, Holly," he said flatly. "That's why I sent you away on Christmas morning. I thought I was dying." He narrowed his eyes. "And now I want to see my son."

Stavros wasn't prepared for the shock he'd felt, seeing her in the doorway of the Alpine chalet.

He was even less prepared for the shock of learning that the rumor was true, and he was a father.

A father. And the baby had to be around two months old. All those months of the pregnancy, and he hadn't known. He felt dizzy with the revelation.

Dizzy, and angry. But not just at Holly.

So much had happened over the last year. He'd been unusually emotional last Christmas, convinced he'd been about to die. That must have been why he'd acted so foolishly, seducing her with such wild longing, proposing marriage, even begging her to have his child.

It embarrassed him now to remember it. All that rank sentimentality, the desperation he'd felt for love and family and home.

Thank God, he'd recovered from that, along with the cancer. Holly Marlowe was nothing to him now.

Or so he'd thought. But now they had a child together. That meant they'd be linked forever, even after death.

And looking at Holly now, Stavros felt the same punch in the gut that he remembered from last Christmas. If anything, she looked more beautiful, more impossibly desirable.

Her curly red hair tumbled over her shoulders of her soft green tunic, and the angry pant of her breath showed off breasts grown fuller and even more womanly than he remembered. Tight leggings revealed the delicious shape of her hips and backside. Her emerald eyes sparkled with fury as they narrowed in disbelief.

"Dying?" she said incredulously.

"It's true. Last Christmas I thought I only had months to live."

He waited for her to react, but her face was stony.

"Didn't you hear me?" he demanded. She shrugged.

"I'm waiting for the punch line," she said coldly.

"Damn you. I'm trying to tell you something I haven't shared with anyone."

"Lucky me."

Turning away, Stavros paced, staring briefly at the crackling fire in the fireplace, then out of the frosted window toward the sun sparkling on the snow. He took a deep breath. "I had a brain tumor. I was told I was dying."

"And that inspired you to seduce me and lie to me?"

"Dying inspired me to want more," he said softly. "To make one last attempt to leave something behind. A wife. A child." He turned back to her. "That's why I slept with you, Holly. That's why I said I wanted to marry you and have a child with you. I wasn't lying. I did want it."

She clenched her hands, glaring at him. "So what happened?"

"I couldn't go through with it. I couldn't be that selfish. I knew you would fall in love with me. You were so…innocent. So trusting. I didn't want to break your heart and make you collapse with grief after I died."

She pulled back, looking strangely outraged. He'd forgotten that about her, how she wore her emotions so visibly on her face. Most people he knew hid their emotions behind iron walls. Including and especially himself, notwithstanding Christmas Eve last year, which he still tried not to think about.

"So you said those horrible things," Holly said, "and sent me away for my sake. You're such a good guy."

Her tone was acid. Staring at her in shock, Stavros realized he'd taken her innocence in more ways than one.

He'd kept the secret of his illness entirely to himself for a year. Even when his hair had fallen out, he'd shaved his head and pretended it was a fashion choice. When his skin had turned ashy and he lost weight, he'd blamed it on the stress of mergers and acquisitions.

Until this moment, only his doctors had known the truth. Literally no one else. Stavros had thought, if he ever opened up to Holly about that night, he would be instantly forgiven. Because, damn it, he'd been *dying.*

He'd obviously thought wrong.

"Why didn't you die, then?" Holly said scornfully. She tilted her head in mild curiosity, as if asking why he'd missed breakfast. "Why didn't your tumor kill you?"

Stavros thought of the months of painful treatment, getting radiation and chemotherapy. After he'd abandoned his dream of leaving behind a wife and child, he'd decided to give up his dying body to an experimental new therapy. He'd thought he might at least benefit science by his death.

Instead, in August, he'd been informed by shocked doctors that the inoperable tumor had started to shrink.

Now, Stavros shrugged, as if it didn't matter. "It was a miracle."

Holly snorted. "Of course it was." She rolled her eyes. "Men like you always have miracles, don't they?"

"Men like me?"

"Selfish and richer than the earth."

The scorn in her voice set his teeth on edge. "Look, I'm getting a little tired of you calling me selfish—"

"The truth hurts, does it?"

"Stop trying to put all the blame on me," he growled. "You're the one who has kept my son from me. I told you to contact my lawyers if you were pregnant!"

"I wasn't going to let you force me into having an abortion!"

Shocked, Stavros stared at her, his forehead furrowed. "What?"

"Christmas morning, you told me you'd changed your mind. You didn't want a child. You said if I was pregnant, I should contact your lawyers and they'd *take care of it*!" An angry sob choked her voice. "Did you think I didn't know what you meant?"

Furious, he grabbed her shoulders. "I *meant* I'd provide for my child with a great deal of *money*," he growled. "Damn you!"

As Holly stared at him, Stavros abruptly dropped his hands, exhaling.

Finally, he understood. Since Oliver had phoned him yesterday, he'd wondered how it could be true. Why would Holly not tell him about a pregnancy? Was it some kind of nefarious attempt at revenge for his seduction and subsequent rejection? Holly had apparently kept the news from her sister as well. She'd only told her yesterday, obviously knowing Nicole would tell Oliver and he'd tell Stavros. But why?

Now it was clear. Holly had been afraid. He gritted his teeth at that insult. But now, with her baby safely born, she was ready to claim the fortune that was due her.

Stavros looked around the ramshackle old cabin, saw the cracks between the logs where the cold wind blew. Holly was no gold digger, but any mother would want the best for her child. She was ready for them to live in greater comfort, and who could blame her?

Now that he understood her motivation, Stavros relaxed. "You have nothing to worry about," he proclaimed. "I will provide for the baby, if he's mine."

"If?" she repeated in fury.

"I want to meet him."

Holly glared at him. "No."

Stavros blinked. "What?"

"You came here to find out if I'd had your baby. Fine. Now you know. Your lawyers probably gave you papers for me to sign. Some kind of settlement to make sure neither I nor my baby would ever make a claim on your full fortune."

"How did you know—" He cut himself off too late. She gave him a cold smile.

"I was a secretary for many years to powerful men. I know how you all think. You're no different from the rest." She came closer, her eyes glowing intently. "I don't want your money. I'll take nothing from you. And nothing is what you'll get in return. Freddie is mine. You will relinquish all parental rights."

"Relinquish?" he breathed in shock. All his earlier smug confidence had disappeared. Surely Holly couldn't hate him so much, when all he'd been trying to do last Christmas was protect her from her own weakness? There was no reason for her to toss him out like this, without even letting him see the baby. Unless—

A thought hit him like hard kick in the gut from a steel-toed boot.

"Is there another man?" he said slowly.

An odd smile lifted the corner of her lovely lips. "What difference would it make to you?"

"None," he lied coldly.

But against his will, he was enraged at the thought.

He'd spent the year as celibate as monk, exhausted after too many hours at the hospital alone, getting medical treatment that sucked away his life and energy. Why had he imagined, just because he'd taken her virginity, that a beautiful young woman like Holly would have spent the last year celibate as well?

For the last year, he'd tried not to think about her, or how out of control she'd made him feel last year. He'd told himself that he'd done the noble thing, the hard thing, setting her free. Since he'd gone into complete remission last month, he'd tried to forget that their night together had been the single greatest sensual experience of his life.

Because Holly made him lose control. She made him weak. He'd couldn't risk seeing her again.

Until he'd gotten the call from Oliver yesterday. Then he'd had no choice.

Because whatever Holly might think of him, Stavros would never abandon his child. Even if he wasn't sure he was ready to be a father, he would provide for him.

His lawyers had warned him if the baby rumor was true, he should immediately ask for a paternity test, and insist that Holly sign papers to recuse herself and her child from any other claim on his billions before he paid her a dime.

His lawyers had never told Stavros what to do if Holly scorned him, his money, and the horse he rode in on.

"You…don't even want my son to know me?" he asked.

She gave a single short shake of her head.

"So why tell me about the baby at all?" he said harshly. "Just to punish me?"

"I never intended for you to know. I swore my sister to secrecy."

Holly hadn't intended for him to know about his son? Ever? Shock left him scrambling. "But my son needs a father!"

She lifted her chin. "Better no father at all than someone who will let him down, and teach him all the wrong lessons about how to be a man. How to lie. How to make meaningless promises. How to be ruthless and selfish and care only about himself!"

Stavros hadn't thought he had much of a heart left, but her words stabbed him deep. He thought of his own childhood, growing up without a father. Having to figure out for himself how to be a man.

Hardly aware of what he was saying, he insisted, "But

what if I want to be in his life? What if I want to help raise him?"

Holly's eyes widened.

Then her lips twisted scornfully. "I've heard that lie before."

"This is different…"

"You might have lured me once into some romantic fantasy. Never again." Crossing the cabin, she wrenched open the door. A blast of cold air flew inside, whipping the fire with its icy fingers. "Please go. Don't come back. Have your lawyers send me the papers." She looked at him coldly. "There's no reason for us to ever meet again."

"Holly, you're not being fair—"

It was the wrong word to use.

"Fair?" Turning, she called out to the driver parked in front of the cabin. "Your boss is ready to leave."

Stavros's head was spinning. He needed time. He hadn't even seen his baby, or held him in his arms. He wasn't sure what he wanted anymore. But Holly was already making the decision for both of them.

She didn't want any part of him. Not as a husband. Not as a father. Even his money wasn't good enough.

Fine, he told himself coldly. He'd keep his money. He didn't need her. Or their baby.

"Fine. You'll have the papers by the end of the day," he told her grimly.

"Good," she said in the same tone.

Stavros set his jaw, glaring at her. Then he stalked out of the cabin without a word, his long dark coat flying behind him as he breathed a Greek curse that left a whisper of white smoke in the icy air. The frozen snow crackled beneath his Italian leather shoes as he passed his waiting driver and got into the back seat of the Rolls-Royce Cullinan.

"Let's go," he growled to his driver.

"Where to, Mr. Minos?"

"Back to the airport," Stavros barked. He'd tried to take responsibility, but she didn't want him in their baby's life. Fine. He'd give her exactly what she wanted. He'd call his lawyers and have them draw up the new papers, severing his parental rights, and giving Holly absolutely nothing.

All my most impossible dreams are suddenly coming true.

The memory of her trembling voice came back to him, whispered into the silent, sweet night last Christmas Eve. Leaning his head back against the leather seat, Stavros closed his eyes, pushing away the memory. Along with how it had felt to have her body against his that sacred, holy night.

But as the Rolls-Royce wound its way back through the Swiss valley, his shoulders only grew more tense. He stared out at the picturesque valley, blanketed by white snow sparkling beneath the sun.

For the past year, he'd hidden his illness from everyone, driving himself harder at work, so no one would know his secret. When he'd gotten the shocking news that he was going to live, he'd been alone in the medical clinic, with no one to share the miracle except for doctors eagerly planning to document the case to medical journals and astonish their colleagues.

Was this how he would spend that miracle? Abandoning the woman he'd seduced last Christmas…and the child they'd conceived together? Leaving a son to grow up without a father, and would despise Stavros as a heartless stranger?

If he did, he truly was a Minos to the core.

His eyes flew open.

"Stop," he said hoarsely.

CHAPTER SIX

HOLLY PUSHED HER stroller through the festive Christmas market in Zedermatt's tiny town square.

Sparkling lights were festooned over outdoor walkways filled with locals and tourists bundled up against the cold, browsing dozens of decorated outdoor stalls, filled with charming homemade items, centered around an enormous Christmas tree in the square. Sausages of every kind, *bockwurst* and *knockwurst* and every other kind of *wurst*, sizzled on outdoor grills, adding the delicious salty smell to scents of pine, fresh mountain air and hot spiced wine called *glühwein*. Smiles were everywhere on rosy cheeks.

Past the eighteenth-century buildings around the square, including a town hall with an elaborate cuckoo clock that rang the time, craggy, snow-covered Alps rose above the tiny valley.

As she pushed her baby's stroller through the crowds, everyone was welcoming. Gertrud and Karin, elderly sisters who ran a bakery in town, made a point of cooing over the baby. Gunther and Elfriede, selling scented homemade candles from their pine-decorated stall, generously praised Holly's improving language skills.

Holly was surrounded by friends. She'd made a home.

So why did she feel so miserable?

Stavros, she thought. Just his name caused her heart to twist. Seeing him had been more painful than she'd ever imagined. And more terrifying. Asking him to give up his parental rights to Freddie, she'd been shaking inside.

Why had she been so afraid? Even if he'd never actually meant to threaten her into terminating her pregnancy as she'd once feared, he'd still made his total lack of interest in fatherhood clear.

So if he'd seemed hurt by her words, it must have only been his pride, injured at being told he wasn't wanted. Obviously. What else could it be?

Dying inspired me to want more. To make one last attempt to leave something behind. A wife. A child. That's why I slept with you, Holly. That's why I said I wanted to marry you and have a child. I wasn't lying. I did want it.

Was it true? Had he really been dying?

She hadn't believed him at first. But a proud man like Stavros Minos wouldn't lie. Not about something like that, something that exposed weakness.

Holly's hands tightened on the stroller handle. It didn't matter. She wasn't going to let herself feel anything for him, ever again. Even if he'd thought he was dying, it was no excuse for how he'd treated her—seducing her, abandoning her!

But if he'd really thought he had only months to live…

Her heart twisted. What must that have been like for an arrogant tycoon to be helpless, facing death? What was it like for a powerful man to feel so powerless?

He'd kept his illness secret. She was the first person he'd told. He'd obviously thought it would make her forgive him.

But even if her traitorous heart might be tempted to feel some sympathy, how could she?

Because in spite of Stavros acting all shocked and upset that she'd never told him she was pregnant, he obviously didn't want to be a father. If he'd really wanted to be part of their son's life, he never would have let himself be scared off so easily today. He would have insisted on sticking around, whatever she said. But he hadn't. As soon as she'd given him an escape route, and told him they wouldn't try to claim any part of his fortune, he'd been off like a shot.

She and Freddie were better off without him. They *were*. Stavros was selfish and coldhearted. She'd never give him the chance to hurt their son like he'd hurt her. She'd done the right thing, sending Stavros away. She should be relieved, knowing he'd never bother her or the baby again.

So why, when Freddie suddenly whimpered in his stroller, did Holly feel like doing the same?

"Here's your hot chocolate." Coming toward her with an eager smile, Hans Müller handed her a steaming paper cup. The young Swiss man was sandy-haired and solidly built, with pale blue eyes.

"Thank you," she said, turning to him with a smile. "You're too kind."

"I would do anything for you, Holly." He looked at her. "You know that."

Sipping her cocoa, she shifted uneasily. She'd met Hans six months before, in a local café. He'd wanted to improve his English skills, and she her German. Back then, she'd been heavily pregnant, and their friendship had been easy. But something had changed lately. She feared he wanted more from her than she could give. It made her feel guilty. It wasn't Hans's fault Stavros had crushed all her romantic illusions forever.

"Hans," she said awkwardly, lifting the pacifier from Freddie's blanket to put it back in the fussing baby's mouth. "You know you're very dear to me..."

"And you're dear to me. So is Freddie." He looked at the baby, now sucking contentedly in the stroller. He paused. "He needs a father." He looked at her. "You need a husband."

"I—I..." She took a deep breath. The last thing she

wanted to do was hurt Hans, who'd been nothing but kind to her. *I don't think of you that way*, she prepared to say.

Then she stopped.

The only men she'd ever imagined as romantic partners had both been disasters—the three-year time-waster of imagining herself in love with Oliver, followed by the massive, life-changing fiasco last Christmas Eve with Stavros.

Maybe she should give Hans a chance. Maybe the fact that she was totally unattracted to him was actually a sign in his favor.

Because the only man who'd ever truly made her experience desire, who'd awakened her body and made her soul sing, had been a handsome, black-hearted liar who'd betrayed her before the sun rose on Christmas morning.

But as she looked at Hans's shining face, she knew she couldn't be that cruel. She couldn't destroy his illusions and ruin his life by letting him love her. Not when she knew she'd never love him—or any man—ever again.

Holly took a deep breath. It was hard, because she feared she'd lose his friendship. "I'm sorry, but you have to know—"

"Holly." The voice behind her was low and sensual. "Won't you introduce me to your friend?"

She turned with an intake of breath.

Stavros stood in the middle of the Christmas market, taller than anyone in the crowd, darkly handsome and powerful in his well-cut suit and cashmere coat. Her mouth went dry.

"What are you doing here?" she choked out. "I thought you were on your way back to New York—"

"Why would I leave?" Stavros's gaze fell longingly to the baby in the stroller. "When my son is here?"

"Freddie is your son?" Hans stammered.

He turned with a sharp-toothed smile. "Freddie?" He

lifted a sardonic eyebrow. "Yes. I'm his father." He extended his black-gloved hand. "You are?"

"Hans… Hans Müller." Shaking Stavros's hand, he nervously glanced at Holly. "I didn't know Freddie had a father. No, of course, I know everyone has a father. That is to say…"

He looked around helplessly.

"Indeed," Stavros said, his expression amused. Then he looked at Holly. "We need to talk."

"I have nothing else to say to you," she said stonily. "I'm here with Hans. I'm not going to be rude and—"

But the young man was already backing away from the powerful, broad-shouldered tycoon. "It's all right—you both have things to talk about. He's your baby's father." He looked at Holly reproachfully beneath his warm hat. "You should have told me."

"I'm sorry…" Her mouth went dry. "I never meant to…"

Hans lightly touched the top of the baby's dark head, then said softly, *"Auf wiedersehen."*

And sadly, Hans disappeared into the crowd.

Stavros said behind her, "That's the man you replaced me with?"

Holly whirled on him. "He's a friend! Nothing more!"

"He wanted more." Stavros looked down at the baby bundled up in a blanket, sucking drowsily on his pacifier. Kneeling beside the stroller, he tenderly stroked the baby's plump cheek. "My son," he whispered. "I am here. I'm your father, Freddie."

Against her will, she felt a violent twist in her heart. She took a deep breath. "Why did you come back? I told you! We don't want you here!"

Rising to his feet, Stavros glanced to the right and left. From the sweet-smelling bakery stall next door, Holly saw Gertrud watching them with a frown.

Taking her arm with one hand and the stroller handle

with the other, Stavros escorted her to a quiet spot on the other side of the massive, brightly decorated Christmas tree. His black eyes were cold. "Fine. You hate me. You don't care that I was dying. You don't want my money or anything to do with me."

"Exactly," she replied, pushing aside her feelings at the thought of him dying.

"Hating me doesn't give you the right to keep my son from me." Stavros looked down at the bundled-up baby, drowsing in the stroller as he sucked on his pacifier. "And whatever you say, I won't abandon him."

A chill went through her. "It's not your choice."

He smiled. "Ah, but it is," he said softly. "I'm his father. That means I have the right to be in his life. And I'm going to be. From now on."

She had no idea why he was pretending to care about Freddie. Out of a misguided sense of pride? Or just to hurt her?

But either way, he was correct. He did have rights, if he chose to fight for them. Fear gripped her heart as she faced him. "What do you intend to do?"

Stavros's expression was like ice. "I'm going to marry you, Holly."

Stavros hadn't intended to propose marriage like this. But it was logical. It was the best way to secure his son, and give the baby the future he deserved—with two parents in the same home.

When he'd returned to Holly's cabin an hour before, he'd intended to calmly insist on his parental rights, or perhaps threaten to sue for partial custody.

He'd arrived just in time to see Holly and the baby—dark-haired, tiny—climb into another man's car. And all his calm plans had gone up in smoke. He'd grimly had his driver follow them at a distance.

Meeting Hans in person at the Christmas market, Stavros was reassured that the man was no threat. Holly herself made that clear. There was no way the two of them had even kissed, for all the man's obvious interest in her.

But Holly was too bright, too beautiful, to be alone for long. As Stavros had watched her push the stroller through the Christmas market, her fiery red hair flying behind her, she'd looked effortlessly pretty in her black leggings and black puffy jacket. She smiled at everyone. And everyone smiled at her. She shone brighter than the star at the top of the Christmas tree.

He'd been mesmerized.

But he couldn't let her know that. He couldn't reveal his weakness. The one time he'd been weak enough to give in to foolish longings last Christmas, it had changed not just his life, but hers—permanent changes from a momentary whim.

He had a son. From the moment he'd seen his tiny, innocent baby, he'd known he would die to protect him. Just touching his cheek had made Stavros's heart expand in a way it never had before. He looked again at the sweetly drowsy baby in the stroller. He ached to take his son in his arms, but he'd never even held a baby before. He didn't know how. But there was one thing he could do: give Freddie the home he deserved, by marrying his mother.

Stavros tightened his hands at his sides.

"Well?" he said to Holly coldly. "What is your answer?"

He waited, wondering what her reply would be. Any other woman would have immediately said yes, but then, Holly wasn't like any other woman. She clearly despised him and didn't want him in her life. On the other hand, she'd agreed to marry him last Christmas. There was an even better reason for her to agree to it now. They had a child.

She stared at him, her emerald eyes wide. Then she did the one thing he'd never expected.

She burst into laughter.

"What's so funny?" he said grumpily.

"You." She wiped a tear from the corner of her eye. "Thank you for that."

"It's not a joke."

"You're wrong." She shook her head. "Do you really think I'd agree to marry a man I don't trust?"

Stavros ground his teeth. He'd been reasonable. He'd explained about his illness. He'd told her he wanted to take responsibility. He'd even asked her to marry him. What more could he do to convince her? He said shortly, "I have never lied to you."

"You lied about your illness last year."

"Damn it, Holly, what should I have done? Let you wreck your life holding my hand, watching me die?"

Her jaw tightened. "You should have given me the choice."

"Like you're giving me now, trying to cut me out of Freddie's life? I'm his father!" He narrowed his eyes. "I want to give him a name."

"He has one. Frederick Marlowe."

"No."

"It's a good name. My father's name!"

"His last name will be Minos."

"Why are you pretending to care?"

"I'm not pretending." Coming closer, he tried not to notice how her eyes sparkled beneath the Christmas lights in the festive outdoor market in the town square, with the snowy Alps soaring above. "I'm going to give my son the life he deserves. Marry me, or face the consequences."

"Is that a threat?"

"I will be part of my son's life, one way or another."

Glaring at him, she lifted her chin. "I won't be bullied into marriage. I don't care how rich or powerful you are. Family is what matters. Not money."

And as Stavros looked down at her in the cold mountain air, everything became crystal clear.

He had little experience managing tricky relationships. In the past, if a mistress ever got too demanding, he'd simply ended the relationship.

So think of it as a business deal. He coolly reassessed the situation. *A hostile takeover.* He looked down at the tiny dark-haired baby. He wanted to be a steady, permanent part of his child's life. Clearly, the best way to do that was to marry Holly. But she didn't want to marry him. She didn't want his money. She didn't want his name.

So how best to negotiate? How to win?

He could brutally fight her for custody. With his deep pockets, his lawyers would crush her. But inexperienced as Stavros was with long-term relationships, he didn't think this would ultimately lead to a happy home for their child.

How else could he get leverage?

Then he realized. She'd just revealed her weakness. *Family is what matters*, she'd said. And she'd shown that belief in every aspect of her life. She'd given up college and her own dreams, given up years of her life for that worthless sister of hers. She'd quit her job and fled to Europe when she'd thought she needed to protect her baby.

How could he use her own heart against her?

A sudden idea occurred to him. It made him feel sick inside. He tried to think of something else.

But Holly already looked as if she were ready to turn on her heel and stalk away, taking their child with her. He needed some way to spend time with her. To make her calm down and see reason. And he could think of only one way.

Since she was none too pleased with her sister at that moment, dragging her to New York wasn't an option.

But Freddie had a grandfather.

If Stavros tried to convince Holly that Aristides Minos deserved to meet the baby, he doubted her tender heart would resist. At least until she met the loathsome man. There was a reason Stavros despised his father to the core.

But a trip to Greece would give Stavros the time he needed to convince Holly to marry him. With any luck, he argued with himself, the old man wouldn't even be home.

Deliberately relaxing his shoulders, Stavros gave Holly his most charming smile. "I don't want to fight with you."

"Fine." Suspicion creased her forehead. "But I still won't marry you."

"Of course you won't," he said easily, still smiling. "You don't trust me. Because I treated you so badly."

Her lips parted. Then she narrowed her eyes. "Whatever you're doing, it's not going to work. My answer's still no."

She was too intuitive by half. "All right. So let's talk about Freddie. And what's best for him."

Holly snorted. "A father, you're going to say. But he doesn't need a father like you, who's selfish and—"

"My own father is honest to a fault," he interrupted. "Doesn't he have the right to meet his grandson?"

That stopped her angry words. She closed her mouth, then said uncertainly, "You have a father?"

Stavros gave her a crooked smile. "As your friend Hans said, everyone has a father."

"But you've never mentioned him. I assumed he was dead."

"You assumed wrong." Stavros had just *wished* his father was dead. Many, many times, after he'd divorced his mother and cut them off without a penny. After he'd ignored all of Stavros's frantic pleas for help when he was seventeen, and she'd gotten that fatal diagnosis. Pushing the awful memories away, Stavros said blandly, "I'm his only son." It was a guess. For all he knew, the man had ten other children he was ignoring or neglecting around the world. "Would you keep him from his only grandchild?"

Emotions crossed Holly's face. It was almost too easy to

read her. First, she wanted to angrily refuse. Then he saw sympathy, and regret.

"Is he like you?" she said finally. "Your father?"

"He's nothing like me."

"No?"

"Like I said. He's honest to a fault." Aristides definitely was authentic, that was true. He never tried to be anything but who he was. Social niceties like courtesy and kindness were utterly unknown to him.

"Really?" Holly said doubtfully, looking at him.

Stavros gave a humorless smile. "Really."

He tilted his head, waiting for her answer. On the other side of the towering Christmas tree, he could hear jaunty, festive music played by a brass band. How strange it would feel to see his father after all these years.

If he did, he would feel nothing. It had all happened so long ago. Stavros was no longer the boy who'd desperately craved a father's love, and been ruthlessly rejected. He was strong now, untouchable, with a heart of stone.

Taking a deep breath, he exhaled a cloud of smoke in the cold air. The tension eased in his shoulders. Feeling nothing was what Stavros did best.

Holly glared at him, gritting her teeth. "Fine," she sighed. "He can meet the baby." She paused. "Where? When?"

"He lives in Greece, I'm afraid."

"Greece!"

He gave her a smile he didn't feel. "The Minos villa on Minos Island."

"You grew up on your own island?"

"Until I was eight." Pulling his phone from his pocket, he dialed his pilot's number before she could change her mind. "We'll leave at once. My jet is waiting."

"I can't just leave," she protested weakly. "I'm the caretaker of my old boss's chalet."

Covering the phone's mouthpiece as the pilot answered the other end of the line, Stavros told her, "I'll handle it."

And he did. When she said their baby couldn't travel in the Rolls-Royce SUV without a baby seat, one miraculously materialized five minutes later. Before they'd returned to the chalet, where she packed an overnight bag for herself and the baby, Stavros had personally contacted the chalet's owner in London. The man sounded frankly astonished to get a direct call from the famous tech billionaire. "No one needs to stay there, really," he told Stavros. "It was empty for a year." And just like that, it was done.

"Does *everyone* do what you say?" Holly said resentfully as the SUV drove back over the winding road toward the private airport in St. Moritz. He lifted an eyebrow.

"Everyone but you."

"Everyone including me," she said softly, staring out her window at the snowy Alpine valley, with its picturesque, colorful chalets beneath sharp, brooding mountains. He watched her silently, hoping it was true.

She believed that they were heading to Greece for one night, which they were. What she didn't know was that, after their brief visit to his father's villa, Stavros intended to take both her and the baby back to live in New York.

He'd make her his wife. By any means necessary.

When they arrived at the tiny airport, his driver opened the SUV's door, then took their bags and folding stroller from the trunk. Holly carried the baby across the tarmac and up the air stairs to his new Gulfstream G650ER. As Stavros followed her, his gaze fell on the sweet curve of her backside in the snug black leggings, and he felt a flash of heat.

Eleven months. That was how long he'd been without a woman.

His night with Holly had been the most incredible sexual experience of his life.

She'd ruined him for all other women.

It was strange. He'd never thought of it in those terms. He'd assumed his lack of desire had been caused by radiation and chemotherapy treatments, while keeping up his workaholic schedule so no one would guess at his illness. Sex had been the last thing on his agenda.

But from the moment Holly had answered the door of that snowy chalet, her cheeks rosy and her sweater and leggings showing off her perfect hourglass shape, the whole past year of pent-up desire had exploded inside him with a vengeance.

Great, he thought resentfully. *Now* his libido chose to come alive? With the one woman on earth who seemed immune to him?

Or was she?

He looked at Holly, now sitting in an opposite chair inside the jet, as far away from him as possible, holding their baby in her lap.

The flight attendant appeared. "Would you like a drink, Mr. Minos? Your usual Scotch?"

Stavros's gaze remained on Holly, tracing the curve of her neck, her red hair curling down her shoulders, the fullness of her breasts beneath her loose sweater. Was she nursing, or had her breasts always been that big?

Holly looked up. "I'd like some sparkling water, please."

"Of course, madam. Sir?"

As Stavros looked at Holly, their eyes locked. The air between them sizzled. Images went through him of last Christmas, when she'd been naked in his bed. The heat of her body sliding against his own, her soft cry joining his hoarse shout as their mutual desire exploded. He was hard as a rock.

"Champagne," he said. "It's a celebration. A new start for us both."

Holly's eyes widened, her cheeks turning pink. Quickly, she turned her head away.

But it was too late. Because now he knew. In spite of her anger, in spite of her hatred, she was as sexually aware of him as he was of her.

And he suddenly realized there were additional benefits to taking her as his wife. Reasons that had nothing to do with taking care of their child.

He'd seduced her before. He would seduce her again. And this time, it would be forever.

CHAPTER SEVEN

SITTING IN A red convertible, as Stavros drove it down the coastal road clinging to the edge of the Aegean Sea, Holly looked out at the bright turquoise water. She felt the warm wind on her face. Felt Stavros's every move beside her. It was like torture. Holly's heart lifted to her throat.

Why had she ever agreed to this?

Guilt, she thought. Back in Switzerland, she'd convinced herself that however Stavros had betrayed her with his playboy ways and lying lips, her baby's grandfather was blameless. Now, she cursed the good intentions that had led her to come to this small Greek island.

Yes, she wanted Freddie to have a grandfather. Of course she did. She felt bad for the elderly man, who sounded like an honest, decent sort of person, to be stuck with such an obviously neglectful son as Stavros. He deserved to know he had a grandson.

Her motives hadn't been purely noble, it was true. Some part of her had hoped desperately, after Stavros spent a little time with their baby, he'd grow bored with the care of parenting a child, and decide to give up custody, and leave them alone.

But being this close to Stavros was difficult. Holly threw him a troubled glance. Every time he'd tried to speak with her on the trip from Switzerland, she'd coldly cut him off. But her own feelings frightened her. The truth was, part of her still desired him. Part of her, a very foolish part, still held on to the dream of being a family.

She'd never be that stupid again, she told herself fiercely. And they'd only be on this Greek island a single night before she returned to Switzerland. What damage could a single night do?

Hearing her baby chortling happily in the convertible's back seat, she looked back and shivered. One night could change everything.

"Almost there," Stavros murmured beside her, glancing at her sideways. She felt a flash of heat.

"Is Greece always this warm in November?" she said in a strangled voice.

"It is warmer than usual." His sensual lips curved up on the edges, as if he knew exactly how his nearness was affecting her. He lazily turned the wheel with one hand, driving the luxury convertible down the twisting road with no effort at all. Her gaze lingered on his powerful forearms, laced with dark hair below his rolled-up sleeves.

It was just the sun making her hot, she told herself. As it lowered toward the western horizon, she felt too warm in the sweater and leggings she'd worn from Switzerland. Her feet were roasting in their leather boots. "I didn't pack any summer clothes."

"Don't worry." Stavros glanced at her, his eyes traveling over her. "It's been arranged."

"You always arrange everything," she sighed.

"My assistant contacted my father's housekeeper and let her know we were on the way. She will provide anything you or Freddie might need."

Her cheeks flamed. "Uh… Thanks. I guess." She tried to smile. "What did your father say when he heard about the baby?"

He shrugged. "I didn't tell him."

"What?"

"I haven't spoken to my father for twenty years."

"Twenty—" Her jaw dropped. "Did you even tell him we were coming to visit?"

Stavros's hand tightened on the steering wheel as he drove the convertible swiftly around the thread of road clinging to the edge of the island's cliffs. He said evenly, "My assistant told the housekeeper. I presume she let him know."

Holly was scandalized. "But it's rude!"

"Rude," he growled. "What about—"

Stavros cut himself off, staring stonily ahead at the sea.

"What about what?"

"Nothing."

"It's not like you to censor yourself."

"Forget it," he said abruptly. "Ancient history."

But he stomped on the gas, driving the red convertible faster along the cliff road of this small island in the Aegean.

Holly looked at him, from his tight shoulders to the grim set of his jaw. She said slowly, "Why haven't you spoken to your—"

Her voice cut off as they went past a grove of olive trees to a guarded gate. A white-haired guard approached the convertible, scowling. Then his eyes went wide. "Stavi?"

"Vassilis," he replied, smiling up at him. They spoke in Greek. Stavros indicated Holly and Freddie, mentioning their names. The guard replied, nearly jumping in his excitement, before he waved them through.

"You know him?" Holly said as Stavros drove the car past the gate.

"He was kind to me when I was young." His voice seemed strained. He roared the convertible up the hill, finally parking in front of a grand villa, whitewashed and sprawling across the cliff, on the edge of the sea. With a deep breath, Stavros abruptly turned off the engine. He stared up at the villa.

"Are you all right?" Holly asked.

He seemed almost as if he dreaded what was ahead. Which Holly didn't understand. What could there be to dread about a lavish villa on a Greek island paradise?

Unless it was the same thing that had made Stavros not speak to his father in twenty years. Holly suddenly wondered what they were getting into.

"Stavros," she said slowly, "I feel like there's something you're not telling me."

Without looking at her, he got out of the car. Unlatching the baby seat in the back seat of the convertible, Holly followed with Freddie.

They hadn't even reached the imposing front door of the villa before it flew open, revealing a plump, white-haired woman. She cried out, clasping her hands over her heart. "Stavi!"

Looking at her, his eyes went wide.

"Eleni?" he whispered.

Rushing forward, the petite, round woman threw her arms around him with a sob. She was much shorter than Stavros. Awkwardly, he patted her on the back. His expression was stricken. Holly couldn't look away from the raw emotion on his usually stoic face.

The white-haired woman spoke in rapid Greek, tears filling her eyes. He answered her slowly in the same language. She turned to the baby in Holly's arms.

Stavros said in English, "Holly, this is my father's housekeeper, Eleni. She's worked here since I was a child." Reaching out, he stroked his baby's soft dark head. "Eleni, this is my son, Freddie."

"Your son!" the housekeeper cried in accented English. She patted the baby's plump cheek with tears in her eyes. Eleni turned to Holly. "You are Stavros's wife?"

"Uh, no," Holly said awkwardly, shifting her baby's

weight on her hip. "I'm Holly, his…" His what? Baby mama? Cast-off lover? "His, um, friend."

"Friend?" the housekeeper repeated with a frown.

Turning to Stavros, she said something sharply in Greek. Lips quirking, he answered her in the same language.

The old woman looked mollified. As servants collected their luggage and moved the convertible into the nearby garage, the housekeeper turned to Holly with an innocent smile. "You must be tired from your journey, Miss Holly, you and the baby. Everything is ready. Won't you come in, please?"

"Yes, thank you," Holly replied, throwing Stavros a confused glance as she followed them into the villa, cradling her baby in her arms.

Stavros's head tilted back as they walked through the foyer. "This place is smaller than I remember."

The housekeeper's wrinkled face smiled. "It is not smaller. You are bigger."

Small? Holly's eyes nearly popped out of her head as she looked around her. It was like a palace! The foyer opened directly into a huge room with a breathtaking view of the sun lowering into the sea with streaks of orange and red. An elegant chandelier hung high above the priceless antique furniture and marble floor.

Freddie gave a hungry whimper, and Eleni crooned, "Poor baby, you are tired. I will show you to your room."

Their room? As in, Holly and Stavros would be sharing one?

No. Surely not. Holly had made it very clear to Stavros that she had no interest in spending time with him. Especially not time of an intimate nature!

"Thank you, Eleni," Stavros said. He lifted a dark eyebrow. "When can I convince you to move to New York?"

"What would I do there? You live in a hotel!"

"Anything. Or nothing." He looked at her seriously. "You

deserve to rest, after taking care of us when I was young. You were my mother's only friend when she was here. At least accept a pension?"

"Oh, no." Blushing, the older woman ducked her head. "I won't take charity."

"It's not charity. It's gratitude."

"No. I couldn't. But thank you, Stavi. If you ever need a housekeeper, let me know. You're a good boy." She smiled at him, then turned as servants passed with their luggage. "Your room is this way, if you please."

As they followed the housekeeper down a long hallway, Holly whispered to Stavros, "What did you say to her earlier?"

He frowned. "When?"

Her cheeks went warm. "At the door when we arrived. When I said I was just your friend, she looked so upset. Until you said something to her in Greek."

"Oh." His black eyes gleamed with amusement. "I told Eleni not to worry. I will marry you soon."

His words caused a jolt that nearly made her trip. Then she rolled her eyes. "Funny."

Stavros raised an eyebrow. "You think I'm joking?"

He hadn't lost his arrogance, that was for sure. "I'll never marry you, Stavros. No way, no how."

He tilted his head with a crooked grin. "We'll see."

Holly's worst fears were confirmed when the housekeeper led them to a magnificent bedroom, with a balcony overlooking the sea. In the center of the room was a single enormous four-poster bed, and in the corner, a crib. Nearby, a changing table had been set up, with everything a baby could need. A rocking chair was placed by the windows.

"Perfect, yes?" Eleni said, smiling.

"It's beautiful, but..." Holly bit her lip as she looked around. "Where will I sleep?"

The housekeeper laughed, her eyes dancing. "I am not

so old-fashioned as to believe you sleep in separate rooms." Going to the enormous walk-in closet, she said to Stavros, "For your wife and baby."

Just hearing herself described as Stavros's wife caused a frisson of emotion to dart through Holly. She stuck out her chin. "I'm not—"

"Thank you, Eleni," Stavros interrupted as he looked into the closet. Reaching into his pocket, he pulled out a stack of bills from his wallet. "Will this cover the cost of the clothes?"

Eleni shifted uncomfortably. "It's not necessary. Your father still owes you and your mother for what he never—"

"No," he said grimly. He gently placed the money in her hands. "You know I'd never take money from him."

"I know," the woman agreed. She looked at the bills. "But this is too much."

"Keep it." With a smile that didn't meet his eyes, he said, "You made my life here endurable. For Mom, too."

Hearing the strained edge to his voice, Holly stared at him. His face looked almost…vulnerable.

What had happened in his childhood? Why hadn't he spoken to his father in twenty years?

Not even the most gossipy secretaries in the New York office, the ones who kept track of Stavros's every lavish date with starlets and models, had spoken about his childhood. Stavros's American mother had died when he was a teenager. That was all they knew.

Now Holly felt like there was some big secret. Some tragedy. She watched as the petite, elderly woman hugged him fiercely, tears in her eyes, saying something in Greek.

Stavros stiffened, then shrugged, and said in English, "It's fine. I'm fine."

"It is good of you to bring the baby here to meet him," the housekeeper responded.

"Is he here?"

Eleni looked embarrassed. "Not yet. I did tell him about the baby. He knew you were coming." Her cheeks went red. "He said he might be back for dinner, but he might not, depending…"

"I remember how he was. With Mom."

The housekeeper looked sad, then squeezed his arm as she said softly, "Your mother was a good lady, Stavi. I was so sorry when I heard she died. I wish she could have lived to see all your success."

"Thank you." His handsome face held no expression. He pulled his arm away. "There is no point in waiting for him. Perhaps we could have dinner on the terrace?"

"Of course." Eleni brightened. "Whenever you like."

Stavros looked at Holly. "Are you hungry?"

As if on cue, her stomach growled noisily. She blushed as the others laughed. But dinner wasn't what she was worried about. She bit her lip. "Er, about this bedroom—"

"We'll have dinner in an hour," Stavros told the housekeeper, who nodded and left, still smiling.

Holly turned on him. "Stavros, you can't imagine we can share a bedroom!"

Stavros tilted his head, a half smile on his lips. "Can't I?" He glanced toward the baby, who'd started to fuss. "Freddie, what's wrong?" He reached out for the baby. "Let me—"

Instinctively, Holly moved the baby out of Stavros's reach. "He's tired."

He asked quietly, "I know I don't have experience. But won't you let me try to hold my son?"

It was the first time he'd asked.

"I'm sorry, it's not a good time." Holly's cheeks went hot. She, who always prided herself on being kind, knew she was being a jerk. She was just protecting Freddie, she told herself. It was only a matter of time before Stavros realized he didn't want to be a father. He would let them down. Why pretend otherwise? Why even let herself hope?

"He's hungry. I need to give him a bath, then feed him and get him ready for bed."

"Of course," he said stiffly. Lowering his head, he tenderly kissed the baby's head. "Good night, my son."

Guilt built inside her, all the way to her throat.

He straightened, and said quietly to Holly, "Can you make your way to the terrace in an hour?"

"It's right outside that big room? By the foyer?"

He gave a short nod.

"I'll find it."

"Until then." With a small bow, he left. Holly looked after him, until the baby whimpered plaintively in her arms.

Was she being unkind, insisting on believing the worst of Stavros? Was it possible he actually wished to be a loving father to Freddie?

If he did, and Holly pushed him away from their son, then she would be the selfish one. Was she really protecting their baby? Or just wanting to punish Stavros, to make him suffer for the way he'd hurt her, by seducing and then abandoning her?

Lost in these unsettling thoughts, Holly gave her baby a bath in the en suite bathroom, then dried him off with a thick cotton towel. As she nuzzled his dark hair, breathing in his sweet newborn smell, she suddenly wished she'd never left Switzerland. All she wanted to do was be safe.

And nothing about Stavros Minos was safe. Not to her body. Not to her heart.

She shivered, remembering how his dark eyes had burned when he'd said he intended to marry her. Every moment she spent with him, every look, every innocent touch, reminded her of the night they'd conceived their child. Every moment close to him caused new sparks of need to crackle through her body.

She took a deep breath, looking out at the balcony where the sun was setting brilliantly over the Aegean Sea, past the palm trees. Oh, what she was doing on this remote Greek island, in a place that seemed expressly made for seduction?

Grabbing Freddie's old, clean footie pajamas from her overnight bag, she dressed him on the changing table and then carried him to the rocking chair near the window, overlooking the sea where the sun was falling into the water. Twenty minutes later, she tucked him into the crib, drowsy with a full belly.

Going to the en suite bathroom, Holly took a quick shower, avoiding her own eyes in the mirror. Wrapping herself in the thick white robe from the door, she went back into the closet and looked in her overnight bag. The thick hoodie, turtleneck and jeans she'd packed seemed all wrong for Greece. Snowy Switzerland seemed a million miles away.

Biting her lip, Holly slowly looked around the enormous closet. New clothes, in both her size and the baby's, had been neatly folded on the shelves and were hanging from the racks. Rising to her feet, she touched a white cotton sundress. For a moment, she was lost in a sudden dream, imagining soft fabric sliding over her skin as Stavros kissed her, his naked, powerful body hard against hers—

Electricity burned through her, making her breasts tighten and her body tremble.

No!

Holly couldn't allow herself to let down her guard. The last time she had, she'd ended up pregnant and alone.

And the stakes were far too high now. If she ever gave herself to Stavros again, either her body or her heart, he'd have the power to destroy her…and Freddie. She couldn't let that happen.

Holly lifted her chin. She was no longer an innocent girl who could be easily swayed by passionate kisses or sweet lies. She'd learned about consequences. She had a baby to think of.

This time, there was nothing Stavros could do to seduce her. If he truly wanted to help her raise their son, if his only intention was to be a good father, she would try to let him, for Freddie's sake.

She would have good manners. She would be courteous.

But Holly would never let Stavros back into her bed, or her heart. Never. Never ever!

Stavros stood out on the terrace, leaning against the white balustrade overlooking the cliff. He was still dressed in a tailored black button-down shirt and trousers that fit snugly against his body. He'd thought of changing to casual clothes, but there was no point in pretending to be casual, when the truth was, he felt anything but.

A table had been set up on the terrace, with three place settings. But he knew his father would not come.

His jaw tightened, and he looked behind him at the house of his childhood. He felt his back break out in a cold sweat. How unhappy he'd been here. He still remembered his mother's wretchedness and heartbreak. His father hadn't just been selfish. He'd been cruel to her, flaunting his affairs, just to prove his power over her.

Now, the sprawling white villa glowed gold, orange and red, illuminated like King Midas's palace by the sun setting over the Aegean to the west.

It had been a shock to return here. He wondered how long he'd been frozen when he'd arrived in the convertible, staring up at the house. He'd been stunned to see Eleni. Like Vassilis, the guard, she'd grown much older. Even the villa, which had loomed so large in his youth, had grown much smaller. Or maybe, like Eleni had said, it was just Stavros who'd grown larger.

He'd lived here until he was eight. He had strong memories of his father's violent arguments with his mother, that had left Aristides shouting insults, and Rowena weeping.

When, after years of emotional abuse, his mother could stand no more, she'd announced she was divorcing him and moving back to Boston.

In response, Aristides had coldly informed Stavros he could either remain in Greece as a rich man's son, or go to Boston to be a "nobody" and a "pitiful mama's boy."

Stavros had made his choice, and his father had been livid. He'd spoken with Aristides only once since then, when Stavros was seventeen. After months of ignoring his son's increasingly frantic phone messages, his father finally answered the phone on the day Stavros called to tell him Rowena had died.

"Why would I care about that?" Aristides had responded.

Now, every time Stavros thought of his mother's heartbreak, how hard she'd tried to love her husband through his betrayals, how hard she'd worked to try to support her child when the divorce had left her with nothing but custody of him…he was furious. His mother had died from overwork and grief, as much as the cancer that had claimed her life.

No wonder, when Stavros had gotten his own diagnosis, he'd been so sure he would obviously die. How could he live, when his mother—so much better and kinder than he—had not?

Setting his jaw, he stared out bleakly at the sea. The sun was setting, leaving a red trail against the dark water that looked almost like a trail of blood.

It was a strange irony that he had lived. And now he had a son of his own. He would not abandon Freddie. He wouldn't leave Holly to raise their son alone.

But how could he convince her to let him into their lives?

When Stavros had decided to bring her here from Switzerland, he'd been sure all he needed to do was spend a little time with her to make her see things his way.

But she'd shot him down every time he'd tried to speak with her on the jet. He didn't blame her. He was totally off his game. Being back in his childhood home had thrown him in ways he hadn't expected. Now, just when he most needed to be confident and powerful to win her, he was instead feeling uncomfortably vulnerable.

He hated it.

So how could he convince Holly? What could he do or say?

Sex wouldn't be enough. He'd felt the way she shivered when he "accidentally" touched her, seen the way she licked the corners of her mouth when he looked deeply into her eyes, as if waiting for his kiss. She wanted him.

But she didn't trust him. She refused to share a bedroom with him. Bedroom? Hell, she wouldn't even let him hold his son.

No mere charm, no regular seduction, would win her now. So what would?

Leaning against the balustrade, staring out at the sea, Stavros took a deep breath. Hearing a noise, he looked behind him.

And gasped.

Holly had come out on the terrace looking like a goddess of beauty, Aphrodite rising from the sea. She was wearing a simple white sundress, exposing her bare shoulders and legs to the pink light of the setting sun. Brilliant red hair tumbled over her shoulders like fire as she walked toward him in her sandals.

His heart lifted to his throat.

Coming close, she looked up at him, her green eyes big, her dark lashes trembling with emotion. "Good evening."

"Kaló apógevma," he replied. He held out his arm.

Ignoring it, she went straight to the table, without touching him.

Following her, he pulled out the chair. She sat down, her lovely face expressionless. As he politely pushed the chair forward beneath the table, his fingers briefly brushed the soft bare skin of her back. He felt her tremble, which he'd expected.

But he trembled, too, which he hadn't.

Going to his own seat on the other side of the small table, he opened a waiting bottle. He paused. "Wine?"

"Just a taste."

He poured the white wine into two glasses, then passed one to her. His fingertips brushed hers, and again he felt her shiver. Again he held his breath.

Then she leaned back in her chair, looking away as she took a single sip of the wine, then placed it back quietly on the table.

No. Desire would not lure her this time.

Stavros lifted the silver lids off their china plates, and saw lamb and rosemary and potatoes. Sitting in the seat across from her, he sliced the lamb cleanly with his knife and chewed slowly. "You should try this. It's delicious." He smiled. "My favorite dinner from childhood. I can't believe Eleni remembered."

"She seems to think a lot of you."

"I think the same of her."

Holly ate almost mechanically, sipping mostly water, not meeting his eyes. He wondered what she was thinking about. Strange—he'd never had to wonder that about any woman before. Usually they couldn't wait to tell him. But Holly was different. Holly mattered—

Just that thought caused ice down his spine.

She mattered only because of his son. That was it. She'd never be more than the mother of his child to him. He'd never give her his heart. He couldn't, because he didn't have one.

The thought made him able to breathe again.

Biting her lip, Holly suddenly leaned forward. "I'm sorry about what you went through."

How did she know about his father's abandonment? Who had told her? He said stiffly, "What do you mean?"

Taking a deep breath, she said in a low voice, "I can't even imagine what you went through last year. Being sick. All alone."

"Oh." His shoulders relaxed. He was touched that she suddenly seemed to care. It gave him hope. "It's all right."

"No. It's not." Looking down at her hands, she said, "I just remember how I felt in the doctor's office when I found out I was pregnant." She looked up, her eyes glistening. "And that was happy news. I can't imagine going through what you did all alone. With no one at your side to help you through. To hold your hand."

A strange emotion rose inside him. Ruthlessly, he pushed it away. It was in the past. He'd battled through. He hadn't needed anyone then, and he didn't now. He was too strong for that. But he wanted to protect his child—and his child's mother.

Reaching over the table, he put his hand over her smaller one. His lips curved. "Does this mean you don't want me dead?"

An answering ghost of a smile touched her lips. "I never wanted you dead. I just…"

Her voice trailed off as she looked away.

The sun had disappeared, and the moon was rising in the darkening night. Stavros polished off his glass of wine, watching her. Wishing he could take her in his arms.

Looking up at the dark sky, Holly pulled her hand away. "The stars are bright here." She tilted back her head. "My dad and I used to look at the constellations together. He taught me a bunch of them. Orion." She pointed. "The Big Dipper, Gemini."

"He was an astronomer?"

She smiled. "A bus driver. Astronomy was his hobby. A hobby he shared with my mother." Her smile lifted to a grin.

"That made him want to learn even more about the stars to impress her. They used to go out driving at night, going outside the city to get away from the city lights. Until—"

Her expression changed and she looked down at her own still full wineglass.

"Until?"

"They went out on their twentieth wedding anniversary, and a drunk driver plowed into their car on the interstate."

"I'm sorry" was all he said, which seemed the wiser choice than "love always ends with tragedy."

"Don't be." She looked up, her eyes glistening. "My parents were happy, chasing their stars. My father always said loving my mother changed his life. She made him a husband. A father. More than he ever imagined he could be." She wiped her cheek with her shoulder. "He always said she changed his stars."

Her voice trembled with pride and love. And Stavros suddenly envied the man.

He poured another glass and took a gulp of wine. "You were lucky to have a father who loved you."

"You aren't close to yours."

Stavros barked a short laugh. "I despise him."

"You told me in Switzerland he was a good man."

"No, I said he was honest. It is not the same. He is honest about who he is. A greedy, selfish monster."

She stared at him, her face shocked.

"But perhaps you think the same about me." His lips twisted as he swished the wine in his glass. "That I am as selfish and coldhearted as every other man in my family." He looked up at the beautiful, tranquil villa. "I hate this place."

"This?" Holly looked up in bewilderment at the magnificent Greek villa, overlooking the dark Aegean Sea. She shook her head wryly. "You should have seen the house I grew up in. A two-bedroom apartment, with peeling wallpaper and a heater that broke down in winter."

"After my parents' divorce, my mother and I briefly lived in a homeless shelter in Boston."

He'd never shared that little tidbit with anyone. She looked shocked.

"How is that possible?" She pointed toward the villa. "There's no way you could be homeless. Not with a father as rich as that!"

"He cut my mother off without a penny in the divorce."

"How could he?"

"He found a way." A humorless smile traced his lips. "When my mother got tired of all his blatant cheating, he was too spiteful to even pay her the paltry amount guaranteed by the prenup. So he gave her a choice—if she voluntarily gave up that income, she could have full custody of me. He knew she'd agree." He took a drink. "The last thing she wanted was to leave me here with him."

"He cheated on your mother?"

Stavros snorted. "You think my cousin Oliver is bad? My father was worse. And my grandfather worse still. He impregnated every willing woman for miles around. My grandmother just gritted her teeth and pretended it wasn't happening." He shook his head. "I don't even know all my cousins. Oliver's mother was the result of a fling between my grandfather and one of the maids."

"Oh," she said lamely.

Looking toward the sea, he said softly, "But my mother grew up in a different generation. She couldn't put up with it forever. Seeing her suffer broke my heart. I vowed I'd never be on either side of it."

"Never love anyone?"

"Or let them love me. Love always has a winner and a loser. A conqueror and a conquered." He gave a smile that didn't meet his eyes. "I decided long ago I never wanted to be either."

Holly looked past the villa's whitewashed terrace, illuminated by light from the villa behind them, to the black moon-swept sea beyond.

"But you still hurt me," she whispered. "In spite of that."

"I know." He took another slow, deliberate sip of wine. "No wonder when you found out you were pregnant, you decided I was a cruel bastard who didn't deserve either of you."

"Was I wrong?"

Her words seemed to echo in the soft Greek night. In the distance, he could hear the roar of waves pounding the beach.

"I was selfish when I seduced you," he said slowly. He lifted his gaze to hers. "But not when I let you go. I pushed you away because I was no good to anyone, least of all you."

"Like I said, you could have told me—"

"Holly, if I'd told you I was dying, it would have only bound you to me more. You would have given me everything, all your heart and your life, until I died—and even after. It would have destroyed you."

Her lovely face looked stricken, then angry.

"You really think I'm pathetic, don't you?" She raised her chin. "You're so sure I would have fallen in love with you?"

"Yes."

"Because you think you're irresistible." Her tone was a sneer that seemed like an ill-fitting costume on her.

Stavros took a deep breath. "Because you're the most loving person I've ever known. And I couldn't ruin your life like that." He gave a small smile. "Not even me."

Her eyes were huge and limpid in the moonlight.

"I expected to die," he continued in a low voice. "But to my surprise, I lived. And now we have a child. Surely you must see that my life can never be the same."

"It doesn't have to change for you..."

"You're wrong," he said simply. Reaching out, he took her hand across the table. "I want us to be a family."

He heard her breath catch. Her hand was suddenly trembling. Nervously, she tried to pull it away, turning toward the villa. "I should check on the baby..."

"Eleni will listen for him." He was close, so close, to achieving his objective. Leaning forward, holding her hand, he urged, "Give me a chance."

Silence fell. Then she said in a small voice, "It would take time for me to trust you again."

Joy rushed through him. "Whatever time you need—"

"I want separate bedrooms tonight."

Silence fell.

Separate bedrooms? That was not at all what he wanted. What he wanted was to make love to her tonight. Right now. But since he'd just promised her time, what else could he do?

"Very well," he said stiffly.

Exhaling, Holly looked out at the sea. "It's beautiful here. Like a dream." She tried to smile. "The white puffs of cloud look like ships in the moonlight."

Stavros watched her. "I like the joy you take in life. Most people forget that when they leave their childhoods behind. If they ever even knew."

She snorted, her expression incredulous. "You think I'm a child?"

"Far from it," he said quietly. "You're the most intensely desirable woman I've ever known."

Her eyes widened. Then her lips curled in a brief, humorless smile. She clearly didn't believe a word. "That's quite the compliment, considering how many you've known."

"None hold a candle to you." He looked at her across the table. "There's been no other woman for me, Holly. Not since we were together."

She blinked, then slowly looked at him. "What?"

"I don't want anyone else," he said simply.

For a moment, their eyes locked in the moonlight. He saw yearning in her lovely face. Then, as if on cue, the lights in the villa's windows behind them went dark, and she seemed to catch herself. Biting her lip, she rose with an awkward laugh. "It's late. I should go to bed."

Polishing off his glass of wine, he rose to his feet. "Of course."

"Should we bring in the plates?"

"It's not necessary."

"I don't want someone else cleaning up my mess." Picking up her plate and glass, she paused. "What about your father's plate?"

"Leave it." He added with irony, "He doesn't have your same concerns."

Stavros picked up his own plate and glass, and the bottle of wine. As they walked back across the terrace, he felt the chill of the deepening night. A cool sea breeze blew against his skin. He looked up at the sprawling white villa.

Getting her into bed was going to take longer than he'd thought. And marrying her would be even longer.

But he didn't know how much more of his past he could share with her. Every small story was like pulling his soul through a meat slicer. He would have far preferred to seduce her.

But he'd seen the change in her. He saw it now, as they took the dishes back to the enormous, modern kitchen. The anger in her eyes when she looked at him had changed to bewilderment, even wistfulness. His plan was working.

So he'd just have to endure it.

Stavros walked her back to their large guest bedroom. Passing her without a word, he quickly grabbed his leather overnight bag. He paused only to look down at his baby, sleeping in the crib. He didn't touch him, out of fear he might wake.

"Good night, my son," he whispered.

Freddie yawned, his eyes closed as he continued to sleep, flinging his chubby arms back over his head.

Stavros turned, lifted his bag over his shoulder and started down the hall. Turning back to say good-night, he stopped when he saw Holly standing in the doorway. Her heart-shaped face was haunted.

"Do you really care about Freddie?" she said hoarsely. "You're not just doing it out of pride, or to hurt me? You really want to be his father?"

"Yes," he said in a low voice. He dropped the bag to the floor and moved close to her. "And I want you."

She looked up, her expression stricken. "You…"

"I want you. I want to hold you in my arms. I want you in my bed. I've tried to forget that night. I can't. I've thought of it for the last year."

She trembled, searching his gaze.

"You're trying to seduce me," she whispered.

"Yes. I am." Cupping her face, he lowered his head toward hers. "I want you forever…"

And in the shadowy hall outside the bedroom, he lowered his lips toward hers and kissed her, soft and slow.

For a moment, she froze beneath his embrace, and he thought she'd push him away.

Then slowly, tremblingly, her lips parted. And it was the sweetest, purest kiss Stavros had ever known. It took every ounce of his willpower to finally pull away, when all he wanted to do was take her back into the bedroom and make love to her.

But he didn't want her for just one night. He wanted her as his wife. And if he'd learned anything from nearly twenty years in mergers and acquisitions, it was to always leave the other side wanting more.

"Good night," he said huskily, cupping her cheek as he looked deeply into her eyes. And he left her.

CHAPTER EIGHT

HOLLY HAD TOSSED and turned all night in the big bed.

She couldn't stop thinking of Stavros's voice last night.

Holly, if I'd told you I was dying it would have only bound you to me more. You would have given me everything, all your heart and your life, until I died—and even after. It would have destroyed you.

Put that way, she could almost forgive him for what he'd done. Because he was right. If, last Christmas, he'd taken her in his arms and told her the truth, she would have immediately done anything, given anything, to help him.

You're the most loving person I've ever known.

He'd made it sound like a character flaw.

Maybe it was. She thought of how she'd spent all her adult life caring for others over herself. She didn't mean Freddie. He was a helpless baby.

But Oliver wasn't helpless. Neither was her sister. And for years, Holly had sacrificed herself for their needs, for no good reason. She thought of how Nicole had blamed Holly on the phone for their marriage problems.

You should be here taking care of things for him. And for me!

Maybe Stavros was right. Maybe, in some ways, Holly's need to always put other people first had been wrong. It certainly hadn't done anything good for Nicole or Oliver, who only seemed more helpless and resentful after her years of sacrifice.

And if Holly had let herself fall in love with Stavros last year, she suddenly knew she would have given him everything, too—whether he wanted it or not.

Instead, when he'd rejected her, she'd been forced to do everything on her own. She'd gained strength, and confidence she'd never had before. Both important qualities for a good mother.

And for a good father?

She shivered. She was starting to believe that Stavros really cared about Freddie, and wanted to be a family. He seemed determined to marry Holly.

Could they actually be happy together?

The idea was growing harder to resist. It would be too easy to love a man like Stavros, when he poured on the charm. She fell a little every time he spoke to her. And when he'd kissed her—

All night afterward, she'd lain awake, wondering what would have happened if she hadn't insisted on separate bedrooms. If she'd let him share her bed. Wondering, and knowing. And wishing…

Now, as Holly looked at Stavros across the breakfast table, with the morning sun shining gold from the double-story window and the sea outside a brilliant blue, her heart was in her throat.

They barely said a word to each other as they ate breakfast. She was dressed simply, in a T-shirt and jeans, while he was in his usual tailored shirt, jacket and trousers. He'd just looked at her, then kissed her on the cheek. But that had been enough to make her pulse pound.

"I know what you're thinking," Stavros said now as his eyes met hers over the table. She broke out in a hot sweat.

"Oh?" she said, praying he didn't.

He tilted his head. "You're wondering how long we have to wait. I say we don't."

"Really?" she croaked, still filled with images of him naked in her bed.

He gave her a crooked grin. "Honestly, I'm glad my father never showed up last night. I only brought you here because I couldn't think of any other way to convince you to give me a chance. I knew with your loving heart, you would feel like you had no choice but to let him meet his grandson."

Her *loving heart* really was starting to sound ridiculous. As if Holly was determined to see only the best in people, even when her positive image of them was totally untethered to reality. What she'd learned last night about Stavros's father didn't make her particularly keen to get to know him better, either.

As Freddie started fussing in her arms, she reached for a prepared bottle on the table. "You want to leave after breakfast? Without seeing him?"

"It would feel like dodging a bullet." Leaning forward, he suddenly asked, "Could I hold the baby, Holly?"

His darkly handsome face was vulnerable, his deep voice uncertain, as if he wasn't just asking her permission, but her opinion.

He still hadn't held their son yet. Because Holly hadn't let him.

Suddenly, she hated herself for that. Who did she think she was, keeping Freddie from Stavros—a man who'd made it clear that he only wanted good things for their baby?

"Of course you can," she said. "You're his father."

His dark eyes lit up. "Yes?"

"Definitely." Gently, she lifted the two-month-old into his father's strong arms, where Stavros sat on the other side of the breakfast table in the morning room. She handed him a warmed bottle. "You'll need this."

"Like this?" he asked, angling the bottle. His boyish uncertainty made her heart twist inside her.

"Tilt your elbow a little more," she suggested, touching his bare forearm. He looked up at her, and for a moment, electricity crackled between them. She saw him start to rise, as if he intended to take her in his arms.

Then he looked back down at the baby, and didn't move from his chair. Freddie wrapped his hands around the bottle, drinking with greedy gulps, his black eyes looking up at his father trustingly.

Holly watched them with a lump in her throat. The baby's sucking noises gradually slowed, then stopped altogether, as his eyes grew drowsy as he drifted off to sleep, held tenderly in his father's powerful arms.

Stavros looked up with obvious pride, his dark eyes shining.

"Look," he whispered. "He's sleeping!"

And something broke inside Holly's heart.

Stavros seemed so different now—

"So you finally came crawling back."

Holly looked up to see a wiry, elderly man standing in the doorway with two young women on his arm. The man had brightly colored, youthful clothes that did little to disguise his potbelly and skinny legs. His hair was pitch-black, except for half an inch near the roots that was white. Even from this distance, he reeked of alcohol, cigarettes and expensive cologne.

Stavros's face turned briefly pale. As if by instinct, he turned his body in the chair, as if protecting the sleeping baby. Then, as if a wall came clanging down, his expression became totally flat.

"Hello, Father." His bored gaze glanced dismissively at the two young women, both of whom looked younger than Holly, perhaps even younger than her little sister. "Friends of yours?"

"From the club." He waved toward them airily. "We

stopped to change clothes. Or at least—" he gave a sly grin "—take them off."

Holly looked with dismay at the girls, who both looked, if possible, even more bored than Stavros. They had to be a third of Aristides's age. One of them was already giving Stavros a frankly flirtatious smile that made Holly, who'd never considered herself prone to violence, want to give her a hard smack across the jaw.

The older man stepped forward, then looked down at the sleeping baby with a sniff. "Is that the baby Eleni was going on about?"

"This is my son, yes," Stavros said stiffly.

"Looks tiny. Runt of the litter."

"He's two months old."

Aristides winked back at the young women. "I'm sure you girls can hardly believe I'm old enough to be a grandfather."

"Uh, yeah," the blonde replied with an American accent, turning so that her friend could see her roll her eyes. "Look, Aristi, if we're not going out shopping like you promised then we've got to go."

"Things to see, people to do," her brunette friend agreed, giving Stavros another flirtatious smile.

"No, wait—I have gifts for you girls upstairs. Go up and wait."

"Where?"

"Up the top of the stairs. The big purple bedroom all the way at the back," he called jovially, then ran his hands slickly through his hair. After they were gone, he turned on Stavros with a scowl. "So why did you come here?"

"No reason."

"You want money, right?"

Stavros stiffened. "No."

Aristides stared at him, then shrugged. "All right, fine,

I saw the kid. Now get the hell out of here. You're nothing to me. I have no desire to be a grandfather."

Holly could hardly believe it. She tried to imagine a world in which she'd ever ignore family, or tell a son or grandson that he wasn't wanted. The thought was like an ice pick in her heart.

"Are you serious?" she blurted out. "After we came all this way?"

Aristides's rheumy, drunken eyes focused on her. "Who are you? The wife?"

"She's my son's mother." Stavros's voice was low. Holly felt, in her bones, how much he would have liked to claim her as his wife.

"Ha! So not your wife. She had your kid, but you still didn't marry her?" The man snorted a laugh. "Maybe you learned from my mistakes after all. You're more like me than I thought, boy."

"I'm nothing like you," Stavros growled, his hands tightening around his sleeping baby son.

"No?" His father stroked his chin. "You were so high and mighty when you called me after your mother's funeral. I was a monster, you said. You'd never whore around like me, you said. Now look at you."

Stavros looked speechless with rage.

Turning to Holly with a crafty expression, Aristides purred, "You're smart not to marry him. What did you say your name was?" Without waiting for her to answer, he continued flirtatiously, "A beauty like you can do far better."

With a sly glance toward his son, Aristides Minos lifted a calculating eyebrow, as if plotting what to say next; for an appalling instant Holly wondered if he was considering inviting her to join the other girls in his bedroom. Suddenly, she couldn't stand it.

"I didn't want to have a wedding while I was pregnant.

But Stavros and I are getting married soon," Holly said, meeting the older man's gaze steadily. "In a few days."

She felt, rather than heard, Stavros's intake of breath.

"Your loss," Aristides said, sounding bored. "All right. Thanks for the visit." He looked down at his son scornfully. "But don't think that this means I'll put you back in my will."

"Are you kidding?" Holly said, outraged. "Do you actually think he needs your money?"

"Shh, Holly. It doesn't matter." Holding his sleeping baby carefully, Stavros rose to his feet. He was taller than his father, and his expression was utterly cold. "Keep your money, you cheap bastard."

"Cheap!" The older man's eyes blazed. "Just because I wasn't willing to hand off my family fortune to some little waitress I met in a bar, who convinced me to marry her when she got pregnant." He scowled at Stavros. "I'm still not sure you're even mine."

"I wish to hell I wasn't," he said quietly.

"Gotten full of yourself with that company of yours? Just because you think you're richer than me now?" His father drew himself up, slicking his hand back through his skunk-striped hair. "You'd never have built that company without me."

Stavros's eyes went wide. "You say that, after what you did to Mom—"

"If I hadn't cut her off without a penny, you'd never have had the drive to make something of yourself. You should thank me." Aristides tilted his head, in the exact same gesture she'd seen Stavros use. "I should own half your stock, purely as an issue of fairness."

Stavros's fists tightened, then he looked at his baby sleeping nestled in the crook of one arm, and he exhaled.

"You're not worth another minute of my time," he said, and he turned to Holly. "Are you ready?"

"Definitely."

"Good. Go!" His father's black eyes narrowed as his voice built in rage. "Get out of my house!"

Holly looked for one last moment at the rich, horrible old man. "Goodbye. Sorry you've made such bad choices in life."

Aristides looked shocked.

Without another word, Holly turned and followed Stavros out of the villa's morning room.

"I'm sorry, too!" he screamed after her. "Sorry I wasted my time talking to you! You're not even that pretty!"

She expected Stavros to head upstairs to get their overnight bags, but instead he went straight for the front door, pausing only to talk to Eleni, the housekeeper.

Following him outside, Holly said quietly, "What about our things?"

"We'll get new ones. I'm done here."

"I understand."

"Eleni's gone to pack. She heard everything and says she can't work for him anymore." Stavros lifted a phone to his ear and spoke to his pilot. She saw how his hand trembled as he ended the call. Turning to her, he said quietly, "Did you mean what you said?"

Holly couldn't pretend not to know what he meant.

"Yes." She looked down at their precious sleeping baby cradled against his chest. "I want us to be a family." She lifted her gaze to his and whispered, "I'll marry you."

His dark gaze filled with light. "You'll come to New York?"

With a deep breath, she nodded. He cupped her cheek, running his thumb along her tender bottom lip, causing electricity to pulse through her body.

"You won't be sorry," he promised.

Shivering, Holly prayed he was right.

* * *

New York City was a winter wonderland, decorated with fresh snow and all the lights and decorations of Christmas. To Stavros, the city had never looked so beautiful. It was as if all the world had decided to celebrate.

Today was his wedding day.

His wife. Holly was going to be his wife…

Since their arrival from Greece, their wedding plans had been rushed through in only two days. Stavros wished to marry her as quickly as possible, before she had the chance for second thoughts.

Also, he had a major upcoming business deal, the acquisition of a local technology business-management firm for nearly two billion dollars, which he knew would keep him busy the last weeks before Christmas.

And as in all acquisitions, Stavros had learned from experience that speed was key. Once a man knew what he wanted, there was nothing to be gained from waiting. Better to strike fast, and possess what he wanted, before anyone else could take it. That was true in business—and marriage.

Holly had agreed to be married as soon as they could get the license. Her only request was that they invite her sister to the wedding. Apparently when she'd phoned Nicole with the news, her little sister had begged to bring Oliver to the ceremony, too. Stavros was none too pleased. He cynically expected his cousin, who'd been unemployed for months, to ask him for money. But having her sister there seemed important to Holly's happiness, and her happiness was important to his.

When Holly had said she'd marry him, Stavros thought he would explode with joy.

No, not joy, he told himself. Triumph. He'd achieved his objective. His son was secure. Or he would be, as soon as they were married today. They'd be a family. And Holly would be in his bed.

Stavros pictured how she'd looked in the moonlight, so unabashedly emotional. She didn't seem to realize how foolish it could be, to show feelings, to even have them at all: it left you vulnerable. He felt uncomfortable remembering everything he'd shared with her in Greece. He'd never been that open with anyone.

He'd only done it to achieve his objective, he reassured himself. There was no danger of him giving his heart to Holly, no matter how tempted any other man would be. Stavros's heart had been charred to ash long ago.

He'd meant it when he'd told her she'd never regret marrying him. But he'd have to walk a careful line. He wanted to make her happy, but not so happy she fell in love with him. He couldn't be that cruel, when he'd never be able to return her love. And he couldn't bear the thought of hurting her. Dread went through Stavros at the thought.

He remembered how she'd spoken so dreamily about how her parents had loved each other.

My father always said loving my mother changed his life. She made him a husband. A father. More than he ever imagined he could be. He always said she changed his stars.

Holly knew that love wasn't something that Stavros—or any Minos man—was capable of, he told himself firmly. She'd still chosen to marry him. Therefore, she'd accepted him as he was.

He might not be able to experience love, or give it, but damn it, he'd be faithful to her. He'd be a solid husband and father. He'd always provide for her and the baby.

He'd made sure of that in their prenuptial agreement, much to the dismay of his lawyers. His terms had been far more generous than needed. But he wanted Holly to know she'd never be left penniless by a divorce, as his own mother had.

If he couldn't love Holly, he'd make damn sure she was always cared for.

Stavros could hardly wait to make her his wife and make love to her. It was all he'd been able to think of on the flight from Greece. He would have taken Holly back to the jet's bedroom while the baby slept, if it hadn't been for the presence of Eleni. Nothing like a sharp-eyed, grandmotherly former nanny aboard to keep one's basest desires in check.

A judge would be arriving later today to marry them at his penthouse, which was already decorated with candles, flowers and Christmas holly and ivy. The rings had been bought, the wedding dress and tuxedo secured and the food arranged by the wedding planner.

Somewhat to his shock, Holly had let the planner sort out everything.

"You don't even want to pick out your dress?" Stavros had grinned. "You are the most easygoing bride in the world."

She'd shrugged. "It doesn't really matter."

He'd sobered. "Are you sure? If a big wedding is important to you, Holly, we can be married in a cathedral and invite the whole damn city."

She shook her head. "I had my dream wedding last year, for Nicole. And I'm not sure it made any difference for them." She lifted her gaze to his and said, "Our marriage is what I care about, not the ceremony."

Cradling her head in his hands, he gently kissed her. "But you deserve a party…"

She'd looked at him for a long moment. "I'd rather have this day just be about us. But if you really want to throw me a party, you know what I'd really like? A birthday party on the twenty-third of December, with all my friends."

"The twenty-third?" He was ambushed by the memory of that date last year, when he'd gotten his fatal diagnosis.

She'd smiled. "It's why my parents named me Holly, because my birthday's so close to Christmas." She tilted her head. "For just one time, I'd love to have a real birthday party, without Christmas taking over..."

Then she happily told him a story he barely heard, something about everyone always wrapping her birthday gifts in Christmas paper, or giving her a single gift for a combined Christmas/birthday present, or forgetting her birthday entirely. But he was distracted by memories of the shock and weakness and vulnerability he'd felt last year. He never wanted to feel like that again.

Especially now. As a father, soon to be a husband, he couldn't afford to ever feel weak or vulnerable again. He wasn't afraid of the cancer returning. His recent checkup had placed him in full remission. But emotionally, he'd have to be strong to make sure he never totally let down his walls. He didn't want to hurt Holly. Or be hurt himself...

"Of course." As she finished her story, Stavros gave her a charming smile. "The best birthday party you've ever seen."

Then they went to city hall, where a very bored-looking city employee gave them a marriage license, and an excited paparazzo took their picture as they left.

Within twenty minutes of the photo getting posted online, he'd started getting phone calls from shocked acquaintances and ex-girlfriends around the world, demanding to know if it was true and the uncatchable playboy was actually getting married. He'd ignored the messages. Why explain? Silence was strength.

But now that Stavros was about to speak his wedding vows, he felt oddly nervous. He'd told himself that he was different from the other Minos men. He was determined to be an excellent husband and father. But what if he was wrong? What if he broke Holly's heart?

He'd make sure it didn't happen. If he cared for her, respected her, honored and provided for her, how could it matter if he loved her or not? How would she even know the difference?

Stavros was distracted by a hard knock at his penthouse bedroom door. Turning, he saw his cousin, who'd arrived with Nicole an hour before, looking shifty-eyed in his well-cut tuxedo.

"I say, old man," Oliver said with an artificially bright smile. "Before you speak vows and all that, I wonder if I could have a word?"

Stavros checked his expensive platinum watch.

"I have five minutes," he said shortly.

He'd regretfully agreed to Holly's suggestion that his cousin could be best man, as Nicole had begged her to be matron of honor. It made sense, the two of them returning the favor after Stavros and Holly had done it for them the previous year.

But Stavros and his cousin had never been particularly close, and Oliver had been a very unsatisfying employee at his company. And since the other couple's awkward arrival at the penthouse, Oliver had seemed to be working up to something. Stavros had a good idea what it was. He set his jaw.

"You might have heard," Oliver began, "that I've rather had trouble finding work…"

"Because your employers actually expect you to work?"

His cousin gave a crooked grin. "Turns out I'm not good at it."

"Or interested in it." Checking that he had the wedding ring in his pocket, Stavros looked at himself one last time in the full-length mirror and adjusted his tuxedo tie. "So?"

"I never thought you'd get married, Stavros. I always figured I'd be your heir."

"Sorry to disappoint you." Since he was only a few years older than Oliver, it was a little disconcerting to realize his cousin had counted on his death as a retirement plan.

Oliver paused. "It's funny to see you in love. I never thought you'd fall so hard for any woman."

Stavros didn't bother to disabuse him of the notion he was in love with his bride. It seemed like bad form on their wedding day. "What did you want to ask me?"

"Right. Well. Since it's obvious how much Holly's happiness means to you..." Oliver gave his most charming grin. "I wonder if you'd be willing to pay me ten million dollars to stay married to Holly's sister."

CHAPTER NINE

"COME ON, HOLLY. Please! You have to help me!"

Her little sister's insistent, whining voice hurt Holly's ears as she sat in the chair of the penthouse's guest bedroom, waiting for the stylists to finish doing her hair and makeup for her wedding.

When Nicole had begged to be her matron of honor, Holly had actually hoped it was because she wanted them to be close again. Instead, she'd spent the last twenty minutes blaming Holly for her marriage problems and asking for money.

"I'm sorry, Nicole. I can't just tell Stavros to hire Oliver back." She hesitated. "We both know he wasn't a very good employee..."

"Oh, so you don't care if my marriage is ruined? If we both starve? How can you be so unfeeling? You're my sister!"

Holly's cheeks were hot as she glanced at the two stylists, who were pretending not to listen. "Fine," she sighed. "I have five thousand dollars in my retirement account. It will be a little hard to get it out but if you really need it—"

"Five thousand dollars? Are you out of your mind?" Nicole cried. "That's nothing! My handbags cost more than that!"

The two stylists glanced at each other. Holly's cheeks burned even hotter. She asked the makeup artist, "Am I done?"

"Yes." The woman put final touches on her lips. "Now you are."

"Thank you." She looked around for her bag. "I'll get my wallet—"

"We've already been paid by your husband," the stylist said, smiling at her. "And lavishly tipped, I might add."

"Congratulations, Mrs. Minos," the other stylist said warmly. "I hope you will be very happy."

Mrs. Minos. Just the name caused a flutter inside Holly's belly. As the stylists gathered their equipment and disappeared, she looked at herself. She hardly recognized the glamorous bride in the mirror, with her glamorous makeup and unruly red hair tamed into an elegant chignon beneath a veil.

She was wearing expensive lingerie, a strapless bustier and white panties, and a white garter holding up old-fashioned white stockings. The long, translucent veil stretched behind her. For a moment, she was lost in a dream, picturing a lifetime as Stavros's wife, the two of them in love forever—

In love? Where had that idea come from?

"It's easy for you to be happy," Nicole said resentfully. "With all your money." Lifting Freddie, who was whining in a similar tone, from his nearby crib, she said to the baby, "You're the luckiest kid in the world."

Lifting her simple white wedding dress from where it was spread over the bedspread of the guest bed, Holly said distractedly, "You don't believe that, Nicole. You know it's not money that makes a happy home, but love. And your money problems will work themselves out. You have a college degree. You could always look for a job yourself..."

"It's not just money." Cuddling her nephew close, Nicole closed her eyes. She took a deep breath. "Oliver's cheating on me, Holly."

Holly stiffened as she held her simple strapless white dress over her undergarments. "Oh, no!"

"He only married me because I threatened to break up with him if he didn't. But that was when he had an easy job and plenty of money. Now, he regrets he ever married me. I'm not good enough."

"That's ridiculous!" Scowling, she whirled to face her little sister. "He's the one who's not remotely good enough—"

"He's going to leave me for someone rich," she choked out, wiping her eyes. "I just know it. And I'll be all alone."

When she saw Nicole's woebegone face, Holly's heart broke for her.

"It'll be all right, Nicky," she whispered, using her old childhood nickname as she reached out to touch her shoulder. "Everything's going to be all right."

"I'm so sorry." Trying to smile, Nicole choked back her tears. "I'm wrecking your wedding day. We can talk about this all later."

But as Holly left the guest bedroom a few minutes later, and went into the grand salon of the penthouse, she still felt troubled. And not just by what she'd learned from her sister, who was dressed in a pink bridesmaid's dress, following her with yawning Freddie, resplendent in a baby tuxedo.

Holly's teeth chattered nervously as she thought of the irrevocable vows she was about to take. Just this time last year, she'd been planning Nicole's wedding. She'd never expected she'd so soon be a bride herself. Now, as she walked down the short hallway, she clutched her simple bouquet of pink peonies as if her life depended on it.

She was getting married.

To him.

Stavros stood waiting near the Christmas tree, imposing and breathtakingly handsome in front of the floor-to-ceiling windows with all of New York City at his feet. Next to him stood Oliver, blond and debonair. On his other side was the jocular, white-haired judge who would marry them, smiling broadly in his black robes, and lastly Eleni, in an old-fashioned, formal dress, beaming as if she herself were mother of the groom.

But Holly had eyes only for Stavros.

He was wearing a sleek tuxedo that clung to his powerful, muscular body. Her eyes moved up from his black tie to his powerful neck, his square jaw, his gorgeous face. His dark eyes burned through her.

Their wedding ceremony was simple, lasting only a few minutes. It seemed like a dream.

She couldn't look away from his face.

"And do you, Holly Ann Marlowe, take this man to be your lawfully wedded husband...?"

"I do," she breathed, trembling as he slid the huge diamond ring over her finger.

"And do you, Stavros Minos, take this woman to be your lawfully wedded wife?"

"I do," he growled in his low, sexy voice, looking at her in a way that made her toes curl in her high-heeled shoes. And suddenly, all her nervousness about the permanency of their wedding vows melted away.

"Then by the power vested in me by the State of New York, I now pronounce you husband and wife." The judge beamed between them. "You may now kiss the bride."

Stavros's dark, hooded eyes held the red spark of desire as he took her in his arms. As he lowered his lips to hers, her breasts felt heavy, her nipples taut beneath the sweetheart neckline of the silk wedding dress. Tension coiled low and deep in her belly.

For days, he'd been teasing her with butterfly kisses and little touches. Now, his kiss made her forget all her doubts and regrets. It made her forget her own name.

Then she remembered: her name had changed. From this moment forward, she was Mrs. Holly Minos.

She watched the judge sign the marriage license, followed by Nicole and Oliver, as witnesses. She saw Nicole look at her husband nervously, with pleading in her eyes. Oliver gave his wife a warm smile, put his arm around her and kissed her forehead. Nicole looked as if she was about to cry with relief.

Holly exhaled. Her sister must have been wrong. Oliver couldn't be cheating on her, not if he kissed her like that. Everything would be fine…

"Congratulations, you two," the judge said, smiling at Holly and Stavros. "Now I'll leave you—" he winked "—to your private celebrations."

Holly's eyes went wide. *Private celebrations.* She looked up at the handsome, powerful man beside her. *Her husband.*

She'd only had one lover her whole life, and for only one night. She'd never forgotten the way Stavros had made her feel so alive, or the ecstasy of his touch. The night she'd spent with him last Christmas Eve had been the most magical of her life, before it had all come crashing down the next morning.

But there would be no more rejection. They were married now. For better, for worse. For the rest of their lives…

"We'll head downstairs," Eleni said happily, holding Freddie, who looked very sleepy in his baby tuxedo. Stavros had hired Eleni as their highly paid part-time housekeeper. Holly wasn't sure it was necessary, but how could she object to Stavros giving a job to the woman who'd taken care of him in childhood?

Besides, she liked and trusted Eleni, and was grateful the other woman would be watching Freddie tonight in her new suite downstairs, giving them privacy for their wedding night.

Holly shivered. *Their wedding night.*

"We'll go now, too," Nicole said, leaning back against her husband, who cuddled her close.

"Talk later?" Holly said to her anxiously, thinking of their earlier discussion. Her little sister smiled.

"Stop worrying," she said cheerfully, patting her on the shoulder. "You need to be more selfish. You're a bride."

And everyone left at once. For the first time since Freddie had been born, Holly was alone.

Alone with her husband…

"Mrs. Minos," Stavros murmured. He slowly looked her over, making her shiver inside. Then, without a word, he lifted her up in his arms, against his chest. He looked down at her. "I've waited a long time for this night."

"Days," she sighed, thinking of the anticipation she'd felt since they'd left Greece.

Stavros looked at her seriously. "A year."

He carried her down the penthouse hall, then set her down gently beside the same enormous bed where, last Christmas Eve, they'd conceived their son. She glanced down at it, thinking how much had changed since then.

They had a future. They were a family.

Gently, he pulled off the headband of white silk flowers that held her long veil in place. He dropped it on the nightstand.

The gas fire caused flickers of white light to move against the dark shadows of his face. The room was black, gray and white. The Christmas tree lights. Through the windows, New York City at night.

Taking off his tuxedo jacket, he dropped it silently to the floor, along with his black tie. He unbuttoned the cuffs of his shirt. Never taking his gaze off hers, he reached his powerful arms around her and unzipped her strapless wedding gown. It slid down her body to the floor, revealing her white bustier bra, tiny white lace panties and white garter.

She heard the low shudder of his breath, felt the tremble of his hands as he stepped back to look at her.

"You're magnificent," he whispered.

The heat in his gaze melted her. All she could think about was that she wanted to make him hers. *Forever.*

Reaching forward, Holly yanked on his white shirt, popping off buttons that scattered to the floor. She could hardly believe her own boldness as she reached inside his open shirt to slowly stroke down his hard-muscled bare chest, lightly dusted with dark hair.

With a low growl, he grabbed her wrists. For a moment, he just looked down at her, his black eyes searing her. Then without a word, he pushed her back on the bed.

Never taking his gaze off her, her husband took off his shirt, dropping it the floor. She had the sharp image of his powerful bare chest, all shadows and hollows in the flickering firelight. She reached toward him. She couldn't wait. She had to feel his body, his weight. She had to feel him against her. *Now.*

"Stavros," she whispered, arms extended.

He moved instantly, climbing over her on the bed in a single athletic movement. She exhaled as she felt his body over hers, his heavy weight pushing her into the mattress, felt the bare skin of his chest and arms against hers. Lifting himself up on one powerful arm, he cupped her cheek, looking down at her intently.

"You're mine now," he whispered. "And I'm never going to let you go…"

He lowered his lips to hers, softly at first. Then his embrace deepened, turning hungry, almost savage. Her nipples tightened beneath her white silk bustier as his powerful muscles moved against her. As he kissed her, he stroked down her cheek, her neck, her shoulder. He cupped her breast over the silk, then reached beneath it to caress her taut nipple, making her gasp.

Pulling away, he looked down at her, his eyes dark. Sitting up, he pulled the silk off her body as if it was nothing more than a thought. Lowering his head between her full breasts, he kissed down the valley between them, all the way to the soft curve of her belly. He ran his hands over the edge of her hips, where her white lace panties clung, digging into her skin. He kissed her belly button, flicking his tongue inside it, as he unbuckled her garters. His large hands caressed each cheek of her bottom before he slowly moved down her body. Sensually, he rolled down each white stocking, soft as a whisper and elusive as a dream.

As the silk slid slowly down her skin, he followed it with kisses down one leg, then the other, down her thighs to the curve beneath her knees, all the way to the hollows of her feet. She shivered on the bed, feeling vulnerable, wearing only her tiny thong panties. After tossing the stockings aside, he pushed her legs apart. She looked up at him in the silver-white firelight, which left dancing patterns across his powerful naked chest.

She looked at his trousers, then met his eyes as she whispered like a fearless wanton woman, "Take them off."

He moved so rapidly he was almost a blur, ripping off his trousers and the dark boxers beneath. In half a second, they were on the floor, and he was on her.

Then her flimsy lace panties were gone, disintegrated beneath the force of his powerful hands. Cupping her breasts, he positioned himself between her legs. As he lowered his head, possessing her lips with his own, she felt the hard thickness of him pressing between her thighs. Her hips moved of their own volition, swaying against him, as her hands raked down his back, settling against his hard-muscled backside.

She felt his powerful body shiver. Lifting his head, he looked down at her face. For a moment, she thought he would say something, something that could either annihilate her or make her soul explode with joy—one or the other. Instead, he just lowered his head and kissed her fiercely. Pulling his hips back, he thrust inside her in a single smooth movement, making her gasp as he filled her, all the way to the hilt.

Her fingernails dug into his skin as she looked up at his handsome face. His eyes were closed, his expression one of ecstasy.

Drawing back, he pushed inside her a second time, this time very slowly, so she could feel him, inch by inch. She closed her own eyes, surrendering to the pleasure building inside her, spiraling rapidly out of control.

She gasped as he suddenly moved, rolling her on top of him. Her eyes flew open. She looked down at him.

He reached up and tenderly caressed her cheek.

"I want to watch you," he whispered. His hands moved down the edge of her throat, lazily cupping her full breast, stroking his thumb against her taut, aching nipple. "I want to see what your face is like when you're the one in control."

Stavros looked up at his bride, naked astride him on the enormous bed in his penthouse bedroom.

He was telling her the truth. But not all of it. He watched the play of lights and shadows on her beautiful face. Across the room, the artificial Christmas tree sparkled in front of floor-to-ceiling windows revealing Manhattan at their feet.

He did want to see her in control. But only because, being inside her, he'd been about to lose his own.

She felt too good. She felt too tight. After a year of rampant hunger, of repressed longing, he'd nearly lost his mind pushing inside her once. For the second thrust, he'd applied the brakes, going as slowly as possible. But that hadn't helped. He'd known, if he thrust a third time, that he would have exploded inside her.

Hardly the wedding night he wanted, or the one Holly deserved. And so he'd rolled on his back, thinking to give his willpower some respite. If she controlled the rhythm, surely he could make it last.

Instead, as he looked up now into her glowing emerald eyes, he saw the red blush on her cheeks as she bit down harder on her swollen lower lip, and his shaft, already so hard he groaned with need, flexed instinctively. She hesitated, glancing down at his naked body, now spread beneath her. She said uncertainly, "What do I do?"

"As you want, *agape mou*," he said huskily.

Her face was uncertain. Then as she looked down at him, her expression changed. Lowering her head, she whispered, "Don't move a muscle."

She kissed him, entwining his tongue with hers. A shiver went through him and he started to lift his arms around him. Punishingly, she ripped her lips away. "No." Grabbing his wrists, she pushed his arms down firmly into the mattress. "Don't move. And don't say a word!"

He started to reply, then saw her glare.

When she saw his surrender, she gave a satisfied nod and then kissed him again, lowering her lips to his. She was careful to let no other part of their bodies touch, teasing him.

It was hard not to move or speak, when all he wanted to do was wrap his arms around her. She kissed his rough, bristly chin, then down his neck, flicking her tongue over his Adam's apple, caressing down his collarbone to his muscular chest. He felt the delicious warmth of her breath on each nipple. He held his breath as she lowered her head, swirling her tongue around him, drawing him further into her warm, sensual mouth as she suckled him.

And all the while, she was careful not to touch any other part of his body. His shaft was hard, bucking and swaying toward her desperately. Glancing down at him, she smiled: a very smug feminine smile. As if she not only accepted her total power over him in this moment, but she also relished it.

"Holly," he breathed, reaching for her.

"No," she said sharply, pressing down his wrists against the pillow. "If you move again..."

"If I do?"

A strange look came over her face, and she looked him straight in the eye. "You won't feel what you're about to feel."

With an intake of breath, he blinked, then gave her a slow nod, keeping his wrists against the pillow, where she'd pressed them. Her intent gaze burned through him as she slowly lowered her head, sucking on his earlobes, then down the edge of his throat, nibbling on the sensitive corner between his neck and shoulder. She watched how his body reacted, and he saw her triumph. As she kissed her way down his body, he vowed that soon, very soon—

Then all rational thought disappeared as, never taking her eyes from his, she slowly lowered her head between his legs.

He couldn't look away from the sight of her beautiful, angelic face as her full, swollen, ruby-red lips lowered to take in his hard, throbbing shaft. Her pink tongue snaked out to lick the drop of opalescent liquid at the tip. Then she licked her lips, and murmured, "Mmm..."

He sucked in his breath, staring at her in shock. What had happened to the shy virgin of last Christmas Eve? This woman seemed sure of herself, and ready and able to torture him with his own desire for her.

He held his breath as he watched her take the tip of him into her wet, soft mouth, swirling him with her tongue. Then she took him in deeper, and deeper still. He felt her small hand run exploratively beneath the shaft, juggling him as she sucked him more deeply into the sweet heaven of her mouth. She peeked up at him, and he felt, rather than saw, her satisfied smile.

He could take no more. With a strangled groan, he reached for her, ignoring her weak protest, "I told you not to move!"

He picked her up by the hips as if she weighed nothing, lifted her over his shaft, then slowly lowered her, impaling her inch by delicious inch. With a gasp, she swayed against him, and the sensuality of even that simple movement pounded through his veins. He released her hips, to give her freedom of movement, praying she wouldn't move, praying that she would.

She answered both his prayers when she leaned forward, gripping his shoulders. She closed her eyes, holding still. But just as he started to exhale, she began to move, sliding over him, riding him slowly at first, but then with increasing rhythm. Watching her generous breasts sway over him as she moved, with their tight, deep pink nipples, was too much for him. He closed his eyes, tilting back his head, fighting to keep control. But the image remained. He was lost in the incredible sensation, in pleasure such as he'd never felt before, pleasure he'd never imagined.

She rode him harder and faster, pounding him, until he filled not just her hot wet core, but the universe itself, which began to spin all around him. Finally, gripping his shoulders, she gasped his name.

That pushed him off the edge, and catapulted him into the sky. He thrust one last time, then exploded inside her. He heard a low voice, rising to a ragged shout, crying out her name…and realized to his shock that it was his own.

She collapsed over him, their naked, sweaty, slick bodies intertwined and tangled on the bed. He held her, kissing her temple, and cradled her close. He was lost, he thought. He was found.

His eyes flew open in the darkness. As he held his wife,

who'd fallen asleep cradled in his arms, all he could think was that he'd tasted the sweetest drug of his life. But if he consumed too much of it, it would destroy him. There was another name for something like that.

Poison.

CHAPTER TEN

MARRIAGE TO STAVROS was wonderful. Incredible. Better than Holly had ever dreamed.

At first.

After their wedding, they spent a few honeymoon days touring the city with their baby. They'd visited the big Christmas tree at Rockefeller Center, drunk hot cocoa, seen all the festive lights. Stavros had insisted on taking them shopping. When she'd told him they wouldn't need any winter clothes, since her former employer in London had promised to arrange for her possessions to be boxed and sent from Switzerland, Stavros had shrugged. "It's my duty to provide for my wife and child. Not just my duty—my pleasure."

He'd looked so serious and determined, it would have been churlish to refuse.

But instead of just buying her and the baby a few things, as Holly had expected, Stavros had gone as crazy as a contestant in a game show trying to throw as many items in his shopping cart as possible before the timer sounded. Only in this case, he wasn't shopping in a discount mart, but the most expensive boutiques and department stores in the city, and there were endless supplies of carts with no buzzer to stop them.

Finally, after they had more clothes than they'd need in a lifetime of New York winters, he'd taken them back to the chauffeured Rolls-Royce. Even then, instead of returning to the penthouse, her husband had told the driver to take them to the biggest toy store in Manhattan, where, like some darkly sexy Santa, he bought cartloads of toys for Freddie—baseball gear, books, games, an expensive train set, a teddy bear bigger than Stavros himself.

"Freddie's just a baby," Holly had protested, laughing. "He can't play with any of that stuff!"

"Not yet. But soon," he'd replied, kissing her. As his driver arranged for the toys to be delivered to the penthouse, Stavros looked at Holly, his black eyes suddenly hungry. Leaning forward, he stroked through Holly's long red hair beneath her pink knit cap and whispered in her ear, "Let's also get some things we can play with now."

Their exhausted baby had fallen asleep in his car seat by the time they'd arrived at a ridiculously expensive lingerie boutique. Holly had stared at the mannequins in the windows in shocked fascination, before ducking her head, blushing at the image of all the demi bras, garter belts, and crotchless panties that she might have called cheap, except they obviously were not. Aside from her wedding lingerie, which had been procured by the wedding planner, Holly had always purchased simple, sensible cotton bras and panties from places like Wal-Mart or Target.

Reluctantly walking into the French lingerie boutique with Stavros pushing a baby stroller, she'd felt nervous and out of place. When she'd looked at a price tag, she'd gasped and turned around, intending to walk straight back out again.

"Where are you going?" her husband had said, grinning as he grabbed the stroller handle.

She'd looked at him incredulously. "It's two hundred dollars!"

"So?"

"For a *pair of panties*!"

"I would pay far more than that," Stavros had said huskily, running his hand along the sleeve of her long, sleek black coat he'd just bought her at Dior, "to see you in them."

Her blush had felt like a raging fire, and she'd glanced right and left, hoping the salesgirls, all as glamorous as French supermodels, hadn't heard. Then her husband leaned forward and whispered what he planned to do to her later that night, and she was relieved that Freddie was still sleeping in the stroller so his innocent ears wouldn't hear.

"And," Stavros had said when he finally pulled away, "jewelry."

"What could I possibly need more than this?" she'd blurted out, lifting her left hand, with its huge, bulky, platinum-set diamond on her ring finger.

Her husband had given a low laugh. "Oh, my sweet wife," he'd said, cupping her cheek. He ran his thumb lightly along her lower lip, which was still swollen from their lovemaking the previous night. That simple touch made her tingle from her mouth to her breasts and lower still. "You will have rubies as red as your lips. Emeralds bright as your eyes." He'd looked at her with sensual, heavy-lidded eyes. "I will see you naked in my bed, wearing only diamonds that sparkle like Christmas morning..."

And he had.

Holly shivered now, remembering.

For the last three weeks, since their marriage, he'd made love to her every night. Somehow, each night was more spectacular than the last. She didn't understand how it was possible.

Perhaps it helped that she was no longer so exhausted from waking up multiple times with their baby throughout the night. As if even Freddie felt the new stability and security of their lives, he'd started sleeping better and longer at night than he had before. And she also had Eleni's help now.

So, almost against her will, Holly had found herself spending the holiday season as a princess in a New York penthouse, draped in jewels and expensive designer clothes, a lady of leisure whose only job was to cuddle her baby by day and be seduced by her husband at night. A life so wonderful it made her feel guilty, wondering what she'd done to deserve so much, when other people she knew had so much less.

So she'd asked Stavros if, instead of giving each other gifts for Christmas this year, they could donate money to charitable causes. He'd grudgingly agreed, seeing how important it was to her.

Holly was happy to make homemade Christmas gifts—knitted booties for Freddie, and a red felt star for Stavros, in the Marlowe family tradition. Whenever her former employer got around to sending her old Christmas decorations from Switzerland, Holly couldn't wait to add her husband's star to her family's heirloom garland.

Wrapping his red felt star in homemade wrapping paper, Holly had hidden it amid the branches of the brightly lit white Christmas tree in their bedroom, and waited for the right moment to surprise him.

But after the first delicious week of their honeymoon, things seemed to change between them. Stavros went back to work. Instead of spending all day with him, she saw him only in the middle of the night, when he would wake her up to make passionate love to her. By dawn, when Holly woke, Stavros was gone again.

Finally, out of desperation, Holly had put the baby in his stroller and gone to the offices of Minos International, hoping to see him, maybe take him to lunch. But Stavros had been deep in a conference meeting and barely spoke two words to her, seeming only annoyed by the interruption. Rejected, she'd gone to talk to her old coworkers. She'd relished the other secretaries' excited congratulations and demands to see Holly's spectacular diamond ring. They'd invited her to lunch, and she'd accepted happily.

But seated at their usual delicatessen, the conversation had dwindled. The other secretaries, who'd once been her colleagues, didn't really know how to act now she was the CEO's wife. A few were clearly trying to repress burning jealousy, while others seemed merely uncertain what to say.

Holly yearned to show them that she hadn't changed since her marriage, and was still the same person. But how?

As she ate her favorite Reuben sandwich with dill pickle, she listened to the other women talk about their problems. One had an ex not paying child support, another was falling behind on medical bills, another couldn't find good day care. Then their eyes inevitably fell on Holly's huge diamond ring, and baby Freddie, sleeping in his expensive, top-of-the-line stroller. Holly could see what they were thinking: lucky Holly and her baby were set for life.

Cheeks burning, Holly had said quickly, "If there's anything I can do to help—"

"No, no," her former friends had said, waving her off. "We'll be fine."

"Perhaps my husband could give you a raise…" But before Holly even finished her sentence, she knew she'd made a mistake. Her friends had stared at her, quietly offended.

"We're fine, Holly."

"We don't need your charity," another had muttered, sucking down the last of her soda noisily through a straw as she glared at the floor.

The lunch had gone downhill after that. When it was finally over, Holly had suggested they make plans soon. But none of her old friends seemed particularly keen to set a date.

"Don't worry," Audrey, her closest office friend, had whispered as they left. "They'll get used to it. Just give them a little time."

Holly hoped she was right. She still felt a lump in her throat, remembering that awkward lunch.

But at least she and her sister were friends again. Though Nicole hadn't told her much, apparently Oliver's financial situation had improved. Either they'd learned to live on less, or Oliver must have found a job. Either way, she was happy to have her sister back. Nicole now answered all her texts, and had even visited Holly last week at the penthouse.

But when Holly asked how things were going, Nicole had given a wan smile. "You know how marriage is. Or at least," she'd sighed, "you will."

And maybe Nicole had had a point.

Because Holly felt like something had already changed in her marriage. She and Stavros had started in such bliss, with such joyful days together. It hadn't been just shopping. She'd gotten lots of his time and attention. She'd watched him play with their baby. They'd spent hours talking, hours just kissing—in front of the fire, on the sidewalk as they pushed the stroller…he kissed her anywhere—but somewhere along the line, something shocking had happened.

She'd fallen in love with him.

It was the purest bad luck, a horrible coincidence, that the very day she realized she loved him, and started trying to find the words to tell him, Stavros had become utterly distracted at work by the acquisition of some billion-dollar tech company.

He wasn't avoiding her deliberately, she told herself. Of course not. Why would he? True, he'd told her he had some issues about fearing love and commitment, but that was all in the past. He'd married her, hadn't he? He'd promised to be faithful forever. That proved he was more than ready to open up his heart!

But Stavros had run his company for nearly twenty years. That mattered to him, too. He'd tried to explain the new technology to her, and why Minos International needed to acquire it, but Holly's eyes had crossed with boredom halfway through the first sentence.

Or maybe she just hadn't wanted to understand it. What she wanted was for him to finish the deal, so he could stop spending eighteen-hour days at the office and spend time with her and Freddie again.

Like tonight. For the umpteenth time, Holly glanced at the clock over the mantel in the great room of the penthouse. It was nearly ten now, and Stavros had been at the office since dawn. He hadn't seen his son before he left; and now, Freddie had been asleep for hours.

"Is that all, Mrs. Holly?"

Looking up from the chair where she was reading a magazine, Holly saw Eleni. The white-haired Greek woman, who'd by now become part of their family, still insisted on calling her by that formal name. "Yes, Eleni. Thank you."

She nodded. "*Kalinixta*, Mrs. Holly."

"Good night. Thank you." After the older woman headed to her suite downstairs, Holly tried to read, watching the clock, waiting always to hear Stavros at the door.

Finally, she yawned and stretched. Letting the magazine drop against her chest, she looked out at the nighttime city through the wide windows.

She just had to be patient, she told herself. After his business deal was done, their marriage would return to the way it had been during their honeymoon. He would have time for their family again.

And Holly would finally tell him she loved him.

She closed her eyes, hope rising in her heart as she pictured the scene. And then—and then…he'd tell her he loved her, too.

She hoped.

What if he didn't?

Nervousness roiled through her. She set down the magazine on the end table, then rose to her feet and paced in front of the windows. She stopped. There was nothing to be gained by being afraid, she told herself. She'd just have to be brave, and trust everything would be all right. Her husband would love her back. Of course he would.

Holly pushed away her fear. Glancing at the clock over the mantel, she saw that it was just past midnight. It was December twenty-third. Just a few minutes into her twenty-eighth birthday. She brightened.

At least she'd finally get time with him at the surprise party he'd promised her. Could it be called a surprise party when she was counting on it, longing for it? She smiled. He hadn't said a word about what he'd planned, but Holly knew it would be wonderful.

Turning off the lamp, she looked around the quiet, lonely penthouse. It was dark, except for the lights of the Christmas tree shining in the great room.

She wished she didn't have to go to bed alone. But she comforted herself with thoughts of tomorrow. As she brushed her teeth in the enormous, gleaming master bathroom, she closed her eyes in anticipation, imagining her friends and family celebrating together. They'd talk and laugh and eat birthday cake, and all awkwardness with her former colleagues would be smoothed over. Nicole and Oliver would be there. And best of all, she'd finally have time with her husband.

Looking at herself in the mirror, she came to a sudden decision.

Tomorrow at the party, she'd tell Stavros she loved him.

Yes. Tomorrow. Smiling, she peeked into the nursery to check on her sleeping baby, then padded softly back to climb into bed. Glancing at the empty bed on Stavros's side, she looked out the window and made a birthday wish that he'd finish the deal tonight, and starting tomorrow, he'd never be gone so much again. And why shouldn't it happen? Her smile became dreamy. When she woke up, they'd celebrate her birthday, and the day after that would be Christmas Eve. And sometime in the middle of the night tonight, Stavros would wake her with a kiss, and make passionate love to her.

She fell asleep when her head hit the pillow, and spent the night dreaming of her husband's hot kisses.

When she woke up the morning of her birthday, she saw the sky was blue outside, and the sun was bright and gold. She looked over at Stavros's side of the bed, and saw it hadn't been slept in. Stavros had never come home last night at all.

Holly heard echoes of Oliver's laughing voice. *Minos men are selfish to the bone. We do what we like, and everyone else be damned.*

And worse, Stavros's words. *Love always has a winner and a loser. A conqueror and a conquered.*

If she loved him, and he didn't love her back, which would she be?

With a chill, Holly knew the heartbreaking answer.

When his eyes opened, Stavros sat up straight from the sofa.

Seeing the full morning sunlight coming from the window, he gave a low curse, then stood up so fast he almost felt dizzy. His muscles were cramped from a long night spent hunched over the conference-room table, and a few hours of unsettling sleep on his office sofa had left his spine and joints out of place.

He stretched painfully, blinking with exhaustion as he looked around his spacious private office. Piles of papers covered his large, usually pristine black desk, along with empty takeout cartons, the remnants of the kung pao shrimp and broccoli beef his support staff had arranged to be delivered for the negotiating team's dinner at midnight. Stavros had brought the cartons in here to eat privately as he read through the other company's last-minute counter-offer, striking out lines with his red pen before he returned to the conference room to compare notes with his lawyers.

Sometime around 4:00 a.m., he'd realized his brain was in a fog. So he'd stretched out on his sofa. He'd only meant to rest his eyes for a moment, but now it was—looking at his smartwatch, Stavros cursed aloud—nearly eight o'clock. He was supposed to meet back with his team in ten minutes.

Stavros should have texted Holly to let her know he wouldn't be coming home. He should have—

He should do nothing. The cold voice spoke calmly in his soul. Keep his distance. Let her know that their marriage could never be more than a domestic and sexual partnership. Romantic love would never—could never—be a part of it. He wanted Holly to realize this without him having to tell her. The last thing he wanted to do was hurt her.

The first week of their marriage had been the best week of his life. Pleasure, enjoyment, friendship…and mind-blowing sex. He'd been happy with her. He'd forgotten to be so guarded. He'd spent hours with her, not just in bed, but talking about his past. About his feelings. About everything.

And he'd caught Holly looking at him with wistful longing in her beautiful emerald eyes. Something more than admiration. Something far more than his dark soul deserved.

It had shaken him to the core. He'd crossed a line he shouldn't have crossed. He couldn't let Holly fall in love with him. He couldn't. And not just because he'd never love her back.

Love was tragedy. There were only two ways love could end—betrayal, or death.

It was a thought made all the sharper today, Stavros thought now. The one-year anniversary of when he'd gotten his fatal diagnosis last year. He'd lived, against all odds. But the miracle could so easily have not happened. And though his last medical scan had showed him in complete remission, one never knew. He could die of something else. Or Holly could.

How could anyone think of loving each other, knowing it could only end in tragedy?

So he'd forced himself to turn away from all the joy and light his wife had brought to his days. He'd grimly reassembled the walls that guarded his soul. He couldn't let her love him. He had to hold the line. He couldn't be so cruel as to lure her into loving him when he knew it would only bring her pain. He had to fight it.

He couldn't bear the thought of ever seeing Holly suffer. He had to protect her—even from himself.

But how could he pull away, without making her feel the sting of rejection?

He'd grabbed onto the negotiations for this business deal with force. It was an amazing excuse to create some distance from his wife.

Although spending an entire night apart was a little *too* much distance. Going into the private bathroom of his office, he brushed his teeth, then spat out the toothpaste. He looked bleakly in the mirror.

There were dark circles under his eyes from stress and lack of sleep. He missed Holly. He missed his son. He wanted to be home.

He had to remind himself, again and again, that he was staying away for their sakes. Because if Holly fell in love with him, sooner or later she'd demand he love her back. When he couldn't, she'd ask for a divorce. And just like that, their family would be destroyed.

Or maybe she wouldn't ask for a divorce. Maybe it would be even worse. Maybe she'd stay in their marriage, trapped forever in silent desperation.

Last year, when Stavros had thought he was dying, he'd feared leaving Holly behind as a brokenhearted widow. How much worse would it be if instead, she loved him without hope for the rest of her life, making their marriage a sort of living death?

Stavros's shoulders ached as he took a quick, hot shower, trying to wash his churning feelings away. Getting out, he toweled off and pulled on the spare suit that he kept cleaned and pressed in his closet.

Quickly shaving, he avoided his own eyes in the mirror. He hurried out of his private bathroom, already late, trying to focus his mind only on the upcoming conference call—

Stavros stopped flat when he saw his wife waiting in the middle of his private office.

"Hello," Holly said, gripping the handle of the baby stroller.

"Hello," he replied, shocked. The one time she'd visited the Minos building since their marriage, he'd made sure he was too busy to talk to her.

Now, against his will, his eyes drank her in hungrily. Gone were the beige, baggy suits she'd worn as a secretary, and the casual jeans and sweater she'd worn in the Swiss chalet. Now she dressed like the wife of a billionaire CEO. She wore a sleek black cashmere jacket over a white button-down shirt, fitted black pants and knee-high black leather boots. Diamond studs sparkled in her ears. "What are you doing here, Holly?"

She ducked her head. "I was in the area. Nicole asked me out for coffee." She gave a shy smile. "For obvious reasons."

Obvious? How obvious? Then he remembered. "To thank you? So Oliver got the paperwork."

"Paperwork?"

"For the ten million."

Holly's expression was blank. "What are you talking about?"

Stavros frowned. If his financial gift to his cousin wasn't the obvious reason, what was? "The annuity I arranged."

Her lips parted. "You're giving Oliver money?"

"Don't worry," he assured her. "The contract is airtight. He just gets a million up front, and each year they remain married, he'll get another. But only if Nicole signs a statement each year that he's keeping her happy."

Instead of looking reassured, she looked shocked. "You're *paying* Oliver to stay married to my sister?"

"Just for the first ten years," he said, confused. Why did Holly seem so upset? "I know you can't be happy unless the people you love are happy, too. The money is a pittance. So I took care of it."

Her face was incredulous. "And you think paying that—that *gigolo* to stay married to my sister will make her happy?"

"Doesn't it?"

"Love is what makes a marriage! Not money!"

Stavros didn't like where this conversation was going. His fear about making Holly love him, about breaking her heart and ruining her life, started pressing against him as heavily as an anvil. Folding his arms, he said tightly, "Fine. I'll tell my lawyer to cancel the annuity. Is that all?"

"No, it's not all!" Her lovely heart-shaped face was pale as she lifted her chin. "Why didn't you come home last night?"

Her lips were pink and chapped, as if she'd chewed them for hours. Her green eyes were vulnerable, troubled with shadows. Had he put those shadows there?

The thought of hurting her made him sick inside. It made him angry. He glared at her. "I've been closing an important deal. As you know. Which is what I need to be doing now. So if you'll excuse me..."

But she blocked him with the stroller, where their baby was babbling and waving his pudgy arms. "And that's all you have to say to me? After you were gone all night? Without a single message?"

A low Greek curse rose to his throat. It was all he could

do to choke it back. "Holly, I'm working. I'm sorry I didn't call. Now please let me go."

She took a deep breath. "Stavros, we need to talk."

But the last thing he wanted to do right now was talk to her. She was blocking him from where he needed to be. And if he stayed, he'd only be forced to say things that might hurt her.

Why couldn't she take the hint that he didn't want or deserve her love? Did he have to spell it out for her?

Stavros nodded scornfully toward the sofa where he'd slept a few uncomfortable hours. "What is it? Do you think I was here all night with some other woman, making hot, sweet love to her? You think I'm like all the other Minos men—after just a few weeks, I'm already bored of my wife?"

Her beautiful face went white, then red. She whispered, "You don't have to be cruel."

Grinding his teeth, Stavros clawed back his dark hair. "Look, if you don't trust me, why are we even married?"

Folding her arms, she glared at him in turn. "Yes, why, when Freddie and I barely see you anymore?"

Exhaling with a flare of nostrils, Stavros glanced at his watch, imagining the conference call had already started. If he didn't hurry, it might cost his company millions of dollars. But that wasn't the reason he had to get away from her, from the bewildered suffering he saw in her expressive green eyes.

"Fine," he growled. "We'll talk. Tonight."

"All right." Biting her lip, she lowered her arms and said uncertainly, "I just remembered. Today is the anniversary of your diagnosis last year. How are you feeling?"

"Never better," he said shortly. "I got a clean bill of health last month. Still in complete remission."

A warm smile lit up her face. "I'm so glad. I wish you'd told me you—"

"Look, Holly, I don't mean to be rude, but can this wait? I have a conference room full of lawyers waiting."

"Yes. Yes, of course." She blushed a little, looking sweetly shy. "I'm looking forward to tonight. Will you be home early?"

"Unlikely," he said shortly, wondering why she'd be excited for him to come home tonight so they could argue, and he could tell her, to her face, what she should have already known—that he'd never love her. "I've got to go."

"All right." She came closer, her eyes glowing, her expression caught between hope and fear. "There's something I want to tell you. Something important. I—"

But as she looked at him, something made her expression change. Something made her back away.

"Never mind," she choked out, shaking her head. "It doesn't matter. I'll see you later—"

And she turned, and fled his office with the baby.

Stavros exhaled, relieved. Maybe he'd been wrong. Holly wasn't falling for him. She was too smart to give her love to a man who didn't deserve it. And what could a man like Stavros ever do to truly deserve her love and light?

He couldn't. So there was no point in trying. It would only lead to loss and darkness—

Pushing away the twist in his gut—it felt like being punched—he clenched his hands into fists. Striding out of his office, he barked at one of his assistants, "Call my lawyer. I want the deal with my cousin canceled at once."

He didn't slow down to hear the reply. Because if there was anything his illness had taught him, it was that life was short. You had to do the important things now, because you never knew if there would be a tomorrow. You had to know what was really, truly important.

And blocking out all emotion from his soul, Stavros hurried to the conference room, where a billion-dollar deal waited.

CHAPTER ELEVEN

SHE'D ALMOST MADE a horrible mistake.

Holly was still shaking as she pushed the stroller down the long city block toward the small café where she was supposed to meet her sister for coffee.

She'd been heartbroken when she'd woken up to discover Stavros had never come home last night. When her sister had invited her out for her birthday, she'd chosen a café near his office. She'd gone there with her heart on fire, half longing for him, half hurt.

And she'd nearly blurted out that she loved him. Surely, once he knew that, once he understood that he held her heart in his hands, he would treat her with greater care?

But looking at his coldly handsome face in his office, Holly had suddenly realized that he wouldn't. Because he already knew.

He knew she loved him. But he didn't want her to speak the words aloud.

Because then he'd be forced to admit he didn't love her back.

Now, hurt and grief threatened to overwhelm her as she maneuvered the stroller down the Midtown sidewalk, crowded with last-minute holiday shoppers. The windows were full of brightly decorated Christmas scenes. But in her current mood, as her eyes fell on the vestiges of melted snow in the shadowed places on the sidewalk, the city seemed gray and dirty. Just like her dreams.

Her baby gave a little plaintive cry from the stroller, snapping Holly back to reality. Stopping on the corner to wait for the crosswalk light, she caressed Freddie, even as she fiercely blinked back tears. Reaching into his blankets, she found his pacifier and popped it back into his mouth, causing him to settle back into the stroller.

Straightening, Holly took a deep breath. As the light changed, she crossed the street surrounded by happy, smiling crowds laden with holiday gifts. Looking down at Freddie in the stroller, she felt her heart in her throat as Stavros's words came back to her.

Love always has a winner, and a loser. A conqueror and a conquered. I decided long ago I never wanted to be either.

She'd thought, when Stavros married her, he'd changed his mind. But he hadn't. He just wanted them to be a family.

So did she.

Holly took a deep breath. Maybe she could love him enough for both of them, she tried to tell herself. If Stavros treated her well, if he cherished her, couldn't that be enough? As long as he was a good father, and a good husband? As long as he spent time with them? Which she was sure he would, as soon as this business deal was over.

Stavros might not be in love with her, but he cared about her. After all, he'd arranged a big birthday party for her tonight. A sort of surprise party, their first social event as a married couple. All their friends and family would be there.

She just had to focus on the positive. She was twenty-eight now, a married lady with a baby. It was time to grow up.

She could live without her husband's love.

Lifting her mouth into a smile as she reached the café, she pushed the stroller inside. She saw her little sister sitting at a nearby table, her face in her hands. Next to her on the table, there was a small birthday gift beside a large coffee mug.

Holly parked the stroller beside the small table. "Nicole?"

Her sister looked up. Tears were streaking her face.

"What is it?" Holly cried, horrified.

"I just got a call from Oliver," she whispered. "Stavros canceled the annuity. So he's leaving me."

"Oh, no!"

"He's moving in with someone else." Her voice choked. "A rich older woman who can give him the lifestyle he deserves."

Sitting in a nearby chair, Holly pulled Nicole into her arms as her baby sister cried against her shoulder.

"I'm so sorry, Nicole," she whispered, rubbing her back. "This is my fault. I told Stavros he shouldn't pay Oliver to be married to you. You deserve more. Marriage should be about love, not money." But as her sister's crying only increased, Holly blurted out, "I'm sorry."

Nicole pulled away, wiping her eyes. "This *is* your fault, Holly. Your fault for trying to take care of me, even when I didn't deserve it. You fault for always thinking I was wonderful, even when I was a total jerk. Even when I stole the man you wanted."

"Stole…" Nicole had tried to steal Stavros? Holly stared at her, confused. Then she understood and exhaled in relief. "Oh, you mean Oliver."

"I knew you had a huge crush on him as his secretary," Nicole sniffed. "But I still took him. And now the universe is punishing me as I deserve."

"You're wrong," Holly said. "Oliver was never mine. The romantic dream kept me company, that was all. It was never real. You didn't take anything from me, Nicole. You don't deserve anything but love!"

"That's what I mean," her little sister said, shaking her head as she gave a tremulous smile. "Even when I've been horrible to you, you find a way to see me in the best possible light." She wiped her tears. "When Mom and Dad died, you gave up everything to raise me. I never appreciated that. It's only now I realize how selfish I've been."

"Oh, Nicole..."

Her sister took a deep breath, leaning back into her own chair. "It's time for me to strike out on my own. The fact that Oliver has left makes it easier."

"You don't have to be alone. Come stay with us for Christmas. There's plenty of room!"

Nicole shook her head. "I'm going to visit my old roommate up in Vermont. Her family has a ski resort, you know, a little one, which they operate on a shoestring. I need some time away, to figure out what to do with my life." She paused. "Besides. You have your own problems."

"What are you talking about?"

"Like I said. You always see the best in people, Holly. Even when they don't deserve it. You see what you want to see with those rose-colored glasses. Oliver. Me." She tilted her head. "Stavros."

"You think I don't see him how he really is?" she said slowly.

Her sister's eyes challenged her. "Do you love him?"

Holly took a deep breath. The truth forced itself from her lips. "Yes."

"Does he love you?"

In spite of Holly's efforts to convince herself she didn't need her husband's love, a lump rose to her throat. She looked away.

"That's what I thought," Nicole said quietly. Putting her hand on her shoulder, she repeated the same words Holly had just said to her. "You deserve more."

Suddenly, Holly was the one who was crying. Angry at herself, she wiped her eyes. "We can still be happy. Stavros just loves me differently, that's all. He cares for me. He shows it through his actions. Like the party tonight..."

Nicole frowned. "What party?"

She smiled through her tears. "You don't need to pretend. I know he's throwing me a birthday party. He insisted on doing it, since I didn't want a wedding reception. There's no way he wouldn't invite you." Holly's lower lip trembled. She desperately needed to feel some hope. "So you can tell me about it. It's not a surprise."

"I'm not trying to keep anything a surprise. There's no party, Holly."

She stared at her sister. As a waiter came and asked if they needed anything, Nicole shook her head. Holly didn't even look at him.

"No party?" she said numbly.

"I'm sorry. Maybe he's doing something else to surprise you?" Her sister tried to smile as she pushed the small, brightly wrapped present toward her. "Here. Wrapped in birthday paper, like you always wanted." She smiled ruefully. "Not Christmas paper, which you've always had to put up with from me."

Holly looked down at the present. It was beautifully wrapped, in pink and emerald, her two favorite colors.

"What's inside is even better. Something I know you've always wanted but were never selfish enough to admit it. Open it."

Slowly, Holly obeyed. And gasped.

Inside the box, nestled in white tissue paper, was the precious gold-star necklace that had once belonged to their mother.

"Told you I'd find it," Nicole said smugly. "It was tucked in my old high-school sweatshirt buried at the bottom of my keepsake box."

A lump rose in Holly's throat as she lifted the necklace. Their mother had worn it every day. It had been a gift from their father, who'd always called Louisa his north star.

"I know you wanted me to have it, so I'd never lose my

way," her sister said in a low voice. "But I think you need it more than I do now."

Nicole's husband had left her, they'd soon be going through a divorce, but she still thought Holly needed it more? Her hand tightened around the necklace as she said hoarsely, "Why?"

"You told me love makes a marriage, not money." Nicole shook her head. "Are you really going to spend your life waiting for Stavros to love you—waiting hopelessly, until you die?"

Holly stared at her little sister in the small New York café. As customers and waiters bustled around them, the smell of coffee and peppermint mochas in the air, the heat of the café made her feel sweaty and hot, then clammy and cold.

Then she realized it wasn't the café, but her heart.

She'd spent her whole life taking care of others, imagining herself in love with unobtainable men—first Oliver, then Stavros. Even now, she'd been ready to settle for a dream to keep her warm, so she didn't feel so hopeless and alone, rather than be brave enough to hold out for the real thing.

Her gaze fell on Freddie, wrapped in blankets, sucking his pacifier in the stroller. Was this the example she wanted to set for her son? That marriage meant one person martyred by love, and the other a tyrant over it?

Love always has a winner and a loser. A conqueror and a conquered.

Which one was she?

Closing her eyes, Holly took a deep breath.

Then she slowly opened them.

No. She wouldn't settle. Not anymore. Not when her and Freddie's whole lives were at stake.

And Stavros's, too.

He'd never wanted to hurt her. He'd said from the beginning that he had no desire to be a conqueror. And yet her love for him would make him one.

Holly reached up to clasp her mother's necklace around her neck. She touched the gold star gently at her collarbone. No. She wanted love, real love. She wanted what her parents had had.

Love made a marriage. Not money. Not sex. Not even friendship. Only love.

And she wouldn't, couldn't, spend the rest of her life without it.

It was nearly midnight when Stavros arrived home.

For a moment, he leaned his head against the door, exhausted. He'd only slept three hours in the last forty-eight. But the deal was struck at last. He was done.

At least until the next deal. He was already considering a potential acquisition of a company in Pittsburgh that had developed an AI-based sales networking platform. He would call his lawyers about it tomorrow. With any luck, they could strike first, while his competitors were still lazing over Christmas presents and turkey dinners.

Entering the dark, silent penthouse, he turned on a light in the foyer. He nearly jumped when he saw his wife sitting on the sofa of the great room, staring into the pale flames of the gas fireplace. Beside her, the lights of the Christmas tree sparkled wanly.

"What are you doing up so late?" he said uneasily. It couldn't be anything good.

Slowly, she rose to face him. She wasn't in pajamas, as one might expect, but was fully dressed, and not in the sleek designer clothes he'd bought her, but the simple sweater and jeans she'd worn when they'd left Switzerland last month.

"We need to talk."

"So you said. But it's been a long day. Can we do it tomorrow?" *Or never.* He raked a hand through his dark hair, setting down his laptop bag as he gave her a small smile. "The deal is signed."

"Oh?" She came toward him. "So you're done?"

"Yes."

She paused. "So you'll be home more—"

"There's always another deal, Holly." He hung up his black Italian cashmere coat. "There's a new potential acquisition brewing. I'll need to leave for the office early tomorrow."

Her lips parted. "But tomorrow's Christmas Eve. And you just got home. We haven't seen you for weeks—"

"I'm CEO of a major corporation, Holly." His voice was more harsh than he intended, but he was tired. He didn't want to hear her complaints. He didn't want to feel guilty right now—or feel anything at all. "This is how we pay for this lifestyle. For all your jewels and fine clothes."

Holly lifted her chin. "I never asked for any of that."

She was right, which left him no room to negotiate or blame her. It irritated him. "Look, I'm exhausted. Our talk is just going to have to wait."

"Until when?"

He shrugged. "Until I have time." Which, with luck, he never would. All he needed to do was line up endless mergers and acquisitions, endless reams of work, and he'd have an excellent excuse never to have to tell her out loud that he didn't love her, or see her beautiful face break into a million pieces.

But as he turned away, he was stopped by her voice.

"Do you know what today is?"

Scowling, he glanced back. She'd better not bring up last year's fatal diagnosis again. "The day I signed a new billion-dollar deal?"

She gave him a thin smile. "My birthday."

He blinked, then a savage curse went through his mind. Of course. December twenty-third. Her birthday.

Now he felt guiltier than ever, which only made him angrier. He'd totally forgotten her birthday, and his promise to throw her a party. He was the one who'd first insisted on throwing her one, like a big shot. Now he looked like a flake. Now he'd let her down.

Stavros hated the disappointment in her green eyes—the hollow accusation there. It was the same way his mother had looked at his father when Aristides failed her, time and time again. As a boy, Stavros had always wondered why his mother put up with such treatment.

Now, he was somehow in his father's place. He hadn't cheated, but he'd accidentally lied. There was no party. He wouldn't, couldn't, bear to think of himself as the villain in this equation.

"I'm sorry," he said tightly. Admitting a mistake was difficult for him. He resisted the temptation to make excuses, to blame her for expecting too much when he'd been swamped with the business deal. Setting his jaw, he said only, "I forgot about the party. I will have my secretary arrange it as soon as possible."

"Your secretary?"

His jaw tightened further. "Would you rather have a gift? Jewels? A trip?"

She took a deep breath. He saw tears in her eyes. "What I wanted was your time."

Seeing her tears hurt him so badly, he couldn't help lashing out. "Then you had unrealistic expectations. Did you really think our honeymoon could last forever?"

"Yes," she whispered. She looked down at the big diamond ring sparkling on her left hand. It glittered like the tears in her eyes. "I love you, Stavros. Can you ever love me?"

It had finally come. The moment he'd dreaded. He wanted to avoid the question.

But looking at her miserable face, he had to tell her the truth.

"No," he said quietly. "I'm sorry, Holly. It's nothing personal. I told you. I'm just not made that way."

Her shoulders sagged. Then she looked up with a tremulous smile. "I'm sorry, too. This is what you meant, isn't it? About the conqueror and the conquered."

"Yes." His heart felt radioactive. Grimly, he buried it in lead, beneath ten feet of ice. "I never wanted you to love me."

"I know. And I was so mad when you told me this would happen." Her expression was wistful. "That I wouldn't be able to resist falling in love with you."

His shoulders felt painfully tight. "You're a good person, Holly. I don't want you to suffer." He pleaded, "Can't you be happy with the life we have? Can't you just take your love back?"

Holly stared at him for a long moment, then slowly shook her head.

"I can't. I can't pretend not to love you. I can't wish it away. I'm sorry. I know I'm putting you in a position you never wanted to be." Blinking fast, she tried to smile through her tears. "It'll be all right."

Stavros frowned, coming closer. He yearned to wrap his arms around her, to comfort her. But how could he, when he himself was the reason she was crying? "It will?"

Holly nodded. "It's time for me to grow up. To see things as they really are." She looked at him. "Not as I wish they could be."

He felt her words like an ice pick through his frozen heart. And it was then that he saw her old overnight bag, sitting by the front door.

"You're leaving me," he whispered, hardly able to believe it.

Looking away, Holly nodded. Tears were streaking her

face. "I knew what you were going to say. But I… I guess I just had to hear it aloud. To know there was absolutely no hope."

Reaching forward, he grabbed her shoulders and searched her gaze. "You don't have to leave. I want you to stay…"

She shook her head. "I saw Nicole today. Oliver's left her for another woman. In the past, I would have been scrambling to try to fix her life, to smooth her path. But she doesn't need that anymore. She's stronger than I thought. And you know what? So am I." Lifting her gaze to his, she said simply, "I've been on my own before. I can do it again."

Stavros dropped his hands. "On your own?"

"I once thought the only way I'd be loved was if I sacrificed myself for others. It's taken all this—" she looked around the elegant, sparsely decorated penthouse "—for me to realize that's not how love works. You can't earn someone's love by giving them your soul. They either love you, or they don't." She gave him a tremulous smile. "It's all right, Stavros. Truly. You'll be better off this way, too. You have nothing to feel bad about."

"Holly, damn it—"

"It's no one's fault." She tried to smile. "Thank you for telling me the truth."

"And this is my reward?" A lump was in his throat. "To have you leave?"

"No one will be surprised when we break up. You gave your baby your name. That's enough." Wiping her eyes, she gave a wry grin. "I mean, come on, a secretary and a billionaire tycoon? No one would ever think *that* marriage could last."

"And Freddie?" he said hoarsely.

A wave of emotion went over Holly's face. But he saw her control it, saw her accept it and master it.

"We'll share custody," she said quietly. "You'll always be

in his life." She allowed herself a rueful smile. "Although let's be honest. Working eighteen-hour days, Christmas included, you weren't exactly going to see him much, anyway, were you? Even if we all lived in the same house."

Stavros's heart twisted at the thought of no longer living in the same house as his baby son. But how could he argue with her?

Everything she'd said was true. Just like with her birthday party, he'd made grand promises he hadn't kept. He'd sworn he'd be an amazing father. Then he'd disappeared to the office.

He yearned to reach for her, to drag her into his arms, to kiss her senseless until she agreed to forget this love idea and stay with him forever.

But he was backed into a corner. Holly was leaving him, and there was nothing he could do about it. He couldn't lure or romance her into staying, knowing he'd be stealing her soul and giving nothing back in return. He couldn't be such a monster, allowing her to remain and look at him each day with heartbreaking hope in her eyes, yearning for love he couldn't give.

Nor could he be the spiteful, selfish man his father had been, trying to hold her against her will, by threatening to take custody of Freddie or withholding the five million dollars guaranteed by their prenuptial agreement, in a malicious attempt to punish her, or keep her down.

No.

"Where will you go?" he asked in a small voice.

"Switzerland."

"Tonight? So late?"

"I wasn't sure when you'd get home tonight." She gave a brief smile. "Or even *if* you'd come home."

His eyes tightened. "I explained why I was late."

"It doesn't matter anymore." Her smile was sad. "Freddie and I are booked on the first plane to Zurich tomorrow. It leaves at five. It seemed easier to stay overnight at a hotel by the airport. Eleni's already there with him."

He wouldn't even get to say goodbye to his son? He felt a lump in his throat, a coldness spreading to his chest. He wanted to argue, to demand more time.

Then he looked at Holly. She'd already decided. Once a woman knew what she wanted, what was to be gained from waiting?

He'd never admired her more than he did in this moment.

All he could try to do was accept her decision better than his own father had. He forced himself to ask the question. "When can I see him again?"

"Anytime you come to Switzerland."

His voice was hoarse as he said, "Take my jet."

Holly looked surprised at his offer, then gave a crooked half grin. "We don't need anything so fancy. Commercial is fine. Just a seat in economy class with my baby in my lap."

Stavros imagined his wife crammed into an uncomfortable middle seat, with four-hundred-pound men on each side of her, and their baby squirming and crying in her lap for nine hours straight. "If you don't want to take my jet, at least fly first class. You don't need to economize. Your prenuptial agreement guarantees—"

"No." She cut him off harshly. "That's Freddie's money."

"I'll always provide for Freddie. The five million is yours."

"I don't want it." Her green eyes were hard. Then she added lightly, "Anyway, first class is no place for a baby. The executives and supermodels up there would smash their champagne flutes and attack us if Freddie started crying. Which he will. His ears always hurt during takeoff. You remember how it was when we flew to Greece. And New York."

Their eyes met, and he felt a stab in his chest.

"My jet will take you." He was proud of his matter-of-fact tone.

"It's not necessary—"

"Stop arguing." His voice was flat, brooking no opposition. "You don't need to sleep in a motel 'til morning. You can leave at once. Freddie will be more comfortable. You know it's true."

She sighed. "Thanks," she said slowly. Pulling the huge diamond ring off her finger, she held it out. "This belongs to you."

Reluctantly, he took it. The ten-carat, platinum-set diamond that had been the symbol of forever was now just a cold rock in his hand. He gripped it in his palm.

"I'll have a lawyer contact you after Christmas." She tried to smile. "We'll be civilized."

He'd never felt this wretched, even when his mother had died. As Holly turned to go, he choked out unwillingly, "How can you do this? If you love me, how can you leave?"

She turned back, her eyes full of tears. "If I'm not strong now, I never will be. And we'll both have lifetimes of regret. I know what your childhood did to you. I won't let our son believe all the wrong things about what a marriage is supposed to be. I won't let him grow up crippled like…"

"Like I am?" Stavros said in a low voice.

Coming forward, she kissed his cheek. He felt her warmth, breathed in the scent of vanilla and orange blossoms.

"Be happy," she whispered.

And, picking up her overnight bag, Holly left.

CHAPTER TWELVE

THE NEXT MORNING Stavros woke up to the blaring sound of an alarm on his phone. Without opening his eyes, he reached out for Holly's warmth.

Her side of the bed was cold. And he remembered. Slowly, he opened his eyes.

She was gone.

With a hollow breath, he looked down at his rumpled clothes. He'd fallen into bed last night in his white shirt and black trousers. He hadn't had the energy to change his clothes. He hadn't wanted to think. It was either fall into bed, or into a bottle of whiskey, and the bed had been closer.

But he'd dreamed all night, strange dreams where he was smiling and happy. Beautiful, vibrant dreams in which he'd held his wife's hand, and they'd been together in a wintry valley, making a snowman with their son. Stavros hadn't been afraid to love her. In his dream, he'd fearlessly given her all his heart.

The cobwebs of those dreams taunted him as he stiffly sat up in the cold light. It was Christmas Eve morning. Everything looked gray. His empty bedroom. The city outside. The sky. Gray. All gray.

Except—

His eyes narrowed when he saw a strange flash of color. Something red. Getting out of bed, he padded softly across the marble floor as he reached for something in the branches of the artificial tree. A small Christmas present, wrapped in red homemade paper with a red bow.

To my husband.

His heart twisted. For a moment, he stared at it, like he'd discovered a poisonous snake amid the branches. Then, grimly, he lifted the small box in his hand. It weighed almost nothing. He wondered if she'd gotten him the gift before she'd decided to leave him, or after. He hoped it was after. He couldn't bear to open a gift filled with all the awful hope of her romantic dreams.

He didn't want it. He'd have to be a masochist to even look. He dropped the gift back into the tree, then went to take a shower. Taking off his wrinkled clothes, he let the scalding hot water burn down his skin. He scrubbed his hair until his scalp ached.

Perhaps it was better their marriage had ended this way. Swiftly. Cleanly. Before anyone got seriously hurt. Before they realized how little he deserved their love, when he was incapable of giving himself in return.

He remembered Holly's haunted, heartbroken face.

I love you. Can you ever love me?

And his cool, factual response as he'd told her he'd never love her. Told her it was nothing personal.

Shutting off the hot water, he stood still in the shower, remembering. His heart was pounding strangely.

Going to his walk-in closet, he tried not to look at all the designer clothes Holly had left behind, many of them still unworn, wrapped in garment bags from the boutiques. Feeling hollow, he turned away, pulling on black silk boxers and black trousers. He would call his acquisition team to tell them they needed to come in tonight. Christmas Eve be damned. Business was what mattered. Building his empire for his son to inherit—

What was in Holly's gift?

Turning on his heel, he almost ran across the bedroom to the Christmas tree. Grabbing Holly's present, he ripped off the wrapping paper and yanked open the tiny cardboard box.

Inside, tucked into white tissue paper, he saw a homemade Christmas ornament, a red felt star. He heard her sweet voice like a whisper through his heart.

My parents were happy, chasing their stars.

A lump rose in his throat. Not everyone was so lucky. Not everyone could—

"You are a fool, Stavi."

The words, spoken in Greek, were more mournful than accusing. Turning, he saw Eleni standing in the doorway.

"She chose to go. I could not stop her," he replied in the same language. The elderly Greek woman shook her head.

"She loves you. The last thing she wanted was to go."

"Her quick departure proves otherwise," he said flatly. He looked out the window at the gray morning above the gray city. He knew the stars existed above the clouds, even now. But he couldn't see them. Just like his wife and child.

He wondered if his private jet had landed yet. If the sky in Switzerland right now was bright and blue above the sparkling Alpine snow. He imagined them decorating a Christmas tree. Drinking cocoa. He saw Holly, so beautiful and loving and warm, wearing flannel pajamas tonight as she put stockings on the hearth of the old cabin's stone fireplace. She believed in love. She probably believed in Santa, too.

"Oh, Stavi." Eleni sighed, making clucking noises with her tongue. "Why did you not just tell her the truth?"

Anger went through him.

"I did," he growled. "I can never love her."

The older woman's dark eyes looked back at him, and she sighed again.

"Men," she chided, shaking her head slightly. "The truth is, you already do."

Stavros stared at her.

"Love Holly?" Ridiculous. He wouldn't love anyone. Love was a tragedy that made victims out of at least one, if not two people. He scoffed rudely, "You're out of your mind, old woman."

But she didn't let his insult stop her. "Of course you love her. Why else would you send her away?"

"Now I know you're crazy." He looked at her incredulously. "Sending Holly away proves I love her?"

Eleni looked at him steadily. "You think you're not worthy of her. So you won't let her waste years of her life, like your mother did, loving someone who obviously doesn't deserve it."

Stavros stared at her in shock. His eyes narrowed.

"I'm nothing like my father."

The white-haired Greek woman tilted her head, her dark eyes glinting in the shadowy dawn. "No? It's true you don't sleep with other women. But do you ignore? Do you abandon and neglect?"

His hands tightened at his sides. "I've been nothing but good to them."

"You forget I've been living here lately." She lifted her chin. "While you have not."

Stavros opened his mouth to argue. Then he closed it again. Yes, all right, he hadn't been around much for the last few weeks. He'd barely seen either his new wife or his child. But he'd been trying to protect them. From loving him. Because he didn't want them hurt.

He'd tried his best. He'd given Holly his name. His money. They'd wanted for nothing.

Except his attention and love.

Because they deserved more. They deserved better.

Because he wasn't worthy.

Swallowing hard, Stavros stared out the floor-to-ceiling windows at the city.

"Go to her," Eleni said softly behind him. "If you do not, if you are not brave enough to fight for her, brave enough to give her everything, you will regret it all your life."

Silence fell.

He whirled around, but she was gone.

Pacing the room, he stopped, staring down at the red felt star his wife had made for him. He'd brought her to New York with great fanfare, promising he'd be a good husband, promising he'd be a good father, promising her she'd never regret it. Insisting he wanted to throw a party for her birthday.

Then he'd done none of it, and ghosted her.

Eleni was right. He'd abandoned his family. Not because of some business deal. And not even because he was trying to protect them.

He'd deliberately avoided his wife because he was afraid.

Afraid if she ever really got to know him, she would finally realize that she was the conqueror, not him.

My father always said loving my mother changed his life. She made him a husband. A father. More than he ever imagined he could be. He always said she changed his stars.

Slowly, Stavros held up the red felt star.

He wasn't worthy of her. That was true. He didn't know if he ever could be.

But he'd never let fear stop him before. It hadn't stopped him from building a billion-dollar company out of nothing. It hadn't stopped him from marrying Holly, though he'd somehow always known this was how it would end.

Could he change?

Could he be brave enough to give her everything?

Could he win her heart?

Tears filled his eyes as he looked out over New York City.

He couldn't see the stars above the clouds, but they were there. Waiting for him to see them. Waiting to guide him.

Stavros gripped the red felt star in his hand. It was as soft as her red hair. As tender as her heart.

Blinking fast, he took a deep breath.

Maybe, just maybe…it wasn't too late to change his stars.

The Swiss valley was dark and silent, late on Christmas Eve.

Outside, the stars were bright as diamonds in the cold, black night. In the distance, Holly could hear church bells ringing for midnight mass. The road in front of her cabin was empty. Her neighbors had all gone to spend time with friends and family—those who hadn't gone to sunny climes for a holiday.

She was glad she'd taken Stavros's jet, as he'd insisted. Freddie's ears had hurt, and he'd cried the whole way. So had she. Exhausted from crying for hours, her baby had finally gone to sleep an hour before. Now, she was alone in the quiet.

Holly wondered what her husband was doing right now, back in New York. She looked out the cabin's window, but all she saw was the reflection of a young red-haired woman, lonely and sad.

No. She couldn't feel sorry for herself. She was lucky to have this cabin for herself and her child. Lucky to have time and space to figure out how to start over.

Opening the front door, Holly looked out at the quiet, wintry valley. Moonlight swept the snow, and she could see the sharp Alps high above. Her breath was white smoke dancing in the air, the icy cold a shock against her lungs. From a distance, she could see a car's lights winding down the valley road toward her tiny chalet. Someone was traveling to be with family for Christmas, she thought, and her heart felt a pang.

Shivering in her thin white T-shirt and tiny knit shorts, she closed the door, turning back inside. She had family, she told herself. Her sister had just texted her from Vermont, to tell her that the ski slopes were snowy and beautiful. Yuna's family was already stuffing Nicole with Christmas cookies and eggnog.

I think I'm going to be all right. It might take a while. But the New Year is just around the corner.

Holly smiled wistfully. Her little sister had truly grown up.

Then with a shake of her head, she started tidying up the small interior of the rustic chalet. The Christmas decorations were still up from last month. Nothing had been changed. She blessed her former employer's frantic schedule for keeping him too busy to arrange for her possessions to be packed and sent to New York.

Picking up her grandmother's old quilt from the back of the tattered sofa, Holly wrapped it around her shoulders. Taking a freshly baked sugar cookie from her chipped ceramic Santa cookie jar, she bit into it and sat down, staring at the fire.

Even the fire was different here. At Stavros's penthouse in New York, the flames had been white and without heat, fueled by cold gas, over elegant stones. Here, the fire was hot enough to warm up the cabin, fueled by split logs she kept on her porch.

When her neighbors had heard of Holly's return, they'd rushed to welcome her. Elderly Horst, bright-eyed and spry, had brought her a small Christmas tree, which he'd hewn from the nearby forest. Kindly, plump Elke had brought sugar cookies, decorated by her grandchildren.

So Holly wasn't alone. Not really. And she'd tried her best to make Freddie's first Christmas special. Her eyes lifted from the roaring fire to the two homemade knit stockings hanging over it. Before she went to bed tonight, she'd fill them with the oranges and peppermints that Gertrud had brought her, and the bag of homemade candies from Eleni. Not that Freddie could eat them yet, but at least he'd know he was loved…

The car lights outside grew brighter. Holly wondered if someone was visiting one of her neighbors. Elke's son from Germany, perhaps. Horst's brother from Geneva.

Her gaze trailed to her Christmas tree, now sparkling between the stone fireplace and the small, frosted-over window. She'd decorated it with big colorful lights and the precious vintage ornaments from her childhood. The only thing she'd left untouched in her family's old Christmas box was the garland of red felt stars. The tree seemed sparse without it. But she just couldn't.

When she'd made Stavros his homemade red felt star, she'd hoped it would start a new tradition for their marriage—blending his sophisticated Christmas tree with her own family's homespun style.

She'd only remembered her gift on the plane, when it was too late to take it back. She wondered if Stavros would even notice it, tucked amid the branches of his artificial tree, or if Eleni would toss it out with his other unwanted things.

Like Holly.

A lump rose in her throat. No, that wasn't fair. Stavros had been clear all along that he would never love her. She was the one who'd tried to change the rules. She was the one who, in spite of all his warnings, had given him her heart.

She heard the sudden slam of a car door outside, followed by the crunch of heavy footsteps in the snow. Had another neighbor decided to visit, this late on Christmas

Eve? It had to be. Who else could it be—Santa Claus delivering toys for Freddie from his sleigh?

She set down the barely tasted cookie on the saucer next to her cold cocoa. Rising to her feet in her fuzzy bootie slippers, she glanced down worriedly past her mother's gold-star necklace to her old white T-shirt, so thin it was almost translucent, showing not just the outline of her breasts, but the pink of her nipples beneath. Her knit sleep shorts were so high on her thighs that they were barely better than panties. She'd dressed for solitary sobbing and brokenhearted cookie-snarfing, not to entertain guests.

A knock rattled the door, reminding her of Marley's ghost in *A Christmas Carol*. Pulling her grandmother's quilt more tightly over her shoulders, she came close to the wooden door. Quietly, so as not to wake the tired baby sleeping in the next room, she called, "Who is it?"

For a moment, there was no answer. She wondered if she'd somehow imagined the knock, by a trick of a passing car's lights and rattle of the icy winter wind. Then she heard her husband's low, urgent voice.

"Holly..."

Now she really knew she was dreaming. She ran a trembling hand over her forehead and looked back at the sofa, half expecting to see herself still sleeping there.

"Holly, please let me in. Please."

It couldn't be Stavros, she thought. Because he never talked like that. He didn't plead for her attention. *Please* was a foreign word to him.

Frowning, she opened the door.

Stavros stood there, but a different Stavros than she'd ever seen.

Instead of his sharply tailored power suit and black Italian cashmere coat, he was dressed simply, in jeans, a puffy coat and knit beanie cap. And somehow—it didn't seem fair—his casual clothes made him more handsome than ever. He looked rugged, strong. The vulnerability in his dark eyes, shining in the moonlight, made her heart lift to her throat.

"What are you doing here?" she breathed.

"May I come in?" he asked humbly. "Please."

With a shocked nod, she stepped back, allowing him entrance to the cabin. Her knees felt so weak, she fell back against the door, closing it heavily behind her.

He slowly looked around the room, at the homespun ornaments on the Christmas tree and two stockings above the roaring fire.

"It's Christmas here," he said softly. He looked at her, and his black eyes glowed above his sharp jawline, dark with five-o'clock shadow. "The Christmas I always dreamed about."

She said hoarsely, "What do you want?"

With a tentative, boyish smile, he said almost shyly, "I want you, Holly."

Her heart twisted. Had he come all this way just to hurt her? To taunt her with what she'd never have? "You came all this way for a booty call?"

Slowly, he shook his head.

"I came to give you this." Pulling his hand out of his jacket pocket, he opened it. The red felt star she'd made him as a gift rested on his wide palm.

Looking down at it, she felt like crying. Why had he come all this way? To reject her homemade gift? To throw it callously in her face? "Do you really hate me so much?"

"Hate you?" Shaking his head ruefully, he lifted her chin gently with his hand. "Holly, you had no reason to love me. I made my position clear. I was scarred for life. I had no heart to give you. All I could offer was my name, my protection, my fortune. That should have been enough."

Holly couldn't move. She was mesmerized by his dark, molten eyes.

"But it wasn't." His lips curved at the edges. "Not for you, my beautiful, strong, fearless wife." He ran the tips of his thumbs lightly along the edges of her cheekbones and jaw. "You wanted to love me, anyway," he whispered. "Even if it cost you everything, heart and soul."

Holly shuddered beneath his touch, unable to speak.

"And now…" Stavros paused, and to her shock she saw tears sparkling in his dark eyes, illuminated by the fire-light and the lights of the Christmas tree. "There's only one thing left to say."

She held her breath.

His dark gaze fell to the tiny gold necklace at her throat. Taking her hand in his larger one, he pressed something into her palm. Looking down, she saw the red felt star.

"You've changed my stars," he whispered.

She looked up. His handsome face was blurry from the tears in her eyes. She saw tears in his gaze that matched her own.

"I love you, Holly." Stavros put his hand against her cheek. "So much. And when you and Freddie left me, it was like I'd lost the sun and moon and Christmas, all at once."

She searched his gaze. "You…" Licking her lips, she said uncertainly, "You love me?"

He gave a low, rueful laugh. "I think I loved you since last Christmas Eve, when I first saw you in that red dress, standing in the candlelight of the old stone church."

With a snort, she shook her head. "You didn't act like it…"

"I hid my feelings, even from myself. I was afraid."

"You didn't want to be a conqueror," she murmured.

"I didn't want to be conquered."

"Conquered?" She choked out a laugh. "As if I could!"

He didn't laugh. "When I met you, for the first time in my life, I wanted marriage, children. I thought it was just because I wanted a legacy. Because I believed I was dying. But it wasn't."

"It wasn't?"

Stavros shook his head. "It was because of you. You made me feel things I'd never felt before. And after we slept together, I knew you could crush me if you chose." He took a deep breath. "So I pushed you away. I was afraid of hurting you. But more. I was afraid you could destroy me." Cupping her cheek, he looked down at her intently. "But I'm not afraid anymore."

"You're not?" she whispered.

"My heart is yours, Holly," Stavros said humbly. "My heart, my life, are both in your hands." His voice became low as he looked down at her hands, clasped in his own. "Can you ever love me again?"

For a moment, Holly stared at him.

Then her heart exploded, going supernova, big enough to light up the entire world. Gripping his hand, she led him to the tree and gave him the red felt star. "Put it on our tree."

With an intake of breath, Stavros searched her face. What he saw there made joy lift to his eyes. Tenderly, he placed the homemade star on a branch of the fresh-cut tree. Reaching into her family's Christmas box, she pulled out her mother's garland of red felt stars, which she wrapped beside it, around the tree.

"Now," she whispered, facing her husband with tears in her eyes, "it's really Christmas."

Love glowed from Stavros's handsome face. Then his expression suddenly changed. His dark gaze lowered to her breasts.

Holly realized that when she'd bent to get the garland, the quilt had slid off her shoulders to the floor. Her husband's eyes trailed slowly over her thin, see-through white T-shirt and the tiny knit shorts. Her body felt his gaze like a hot physical touch.

"Stavros," she breathed.

Pulling her into his arms, he kissed her, his lips hungry and hard. His jacket flew off, followed by his knit hat.

And as they sank together to the quilt on the floor, bodies entwined, Holly felt not just passion this time, but true love and commitment. The cabin was fragrant with pine and sugar cookies and a crackling fire. She'd never known joy could be like this.

And as her husband made love to her that night, on the quilt beneath the sparkling tree, Holly knew that even with the ups and downs of marriage, they'd always be happy. For there was nothing more pure than true love begun on Christmas Eve, when all the world was hushed and quiet, as two people spoke private vows, holding each other in the silent, holy night.

Three babies crying, all at once.

Stavros looked helplessly at his wife, who looked helplessly back. Then Holly's lips suddenly lifted, and they both laughed. Because what else could you do?

"I'm sorry," Eleni sighed, standing on the snowy sidewalk as she held the hand of Freddie, now fourteen months old, wailing with his chubby face pink with heat and lined with pillow marks. She continued apologetically, "I shouldn't have woken him from his nap. But I was sure he'd want to meet his new brother and sister."

Holly and Stavros looked at each other, then at their hours-old babies behind them in the third row. Stella and Nicolas had both seemed to agree, with telepathic twin powers, that they hated their car seats. They'd screamed the whole ride home from the hospital. After one particularly ear-blasting screech, Stavros had seen Colton, his longtime, normally unflappable driver, flinch beneath his uniformed cap. As if they hadn't already shocked the poor man enough by trading in the Rolls-Royce for the biggest luxury SUV on the market.

And that wasn't even the biggest change. Six months before, when they'd discovered Holly was pregnant with twins, they'd decided to move to Brooklyn, of all places.

"Our kids will need friends to play with," Holly had wheedled. "And I want to live near the other secretaries from work."

"You're friends again?"

"Most of them were finally able to forgive me for marrying a billionaire." She flashed a wicked grin. "In fact, when you're grumpy at the office, they even feel a little sorry for me..."

"Hey!"

"The point is, I don't want to raise our kids in a lonely penthouse. They need a real neighborhood to play in. Like Nicole and I had when we were young."

Eventually, Stavros had agreed. Now, he shook his head. If his father could only see him now, living in Brooklyn, surrendering to domestic bliss—and liking it! Aristides would swear Stavros wasn't his son!

His father had replaced him with a son more to his liking, anyway. After Nicole and Oliver's divorce was settled last summer, his cousin had soon found himself dumped by his wealthy lover. Facing the daunting prospect of finding a job, he'd gone to visit his Uncle Aristides in Greece, and never come back.

Now Oliver would never have to work, and Aristides had the perfect wingman to help pick up girls in bars. It was a perfect solution for them both, Stavros thought wryly.

Luckily, his wife's family wasn't as embarrassing as his own. Nicole was apparently settling in nicely to her new life in Vermont, working as a schoolteacher and dating a policeman. The relationship didn't sound serious yet, but he was sure he'd hear all the details when Nicole arrived tomorrow morning for Christmas breakfast. Whether he wanted to or not.

"Oh, dear," Eleni said, pulling him from his thoughts as she peered into the SUV's back seat with worried eyes. Freddie continued to noisily cry in harmonic counterpoint to his younger siblings. "Do you need help, Stavi?"

"May I help with the babies, Mr. Minos?" Colton offered. For Eleni to offer help wasn't unusual, but for his grizzled driver to offer to provide baby care was unprecedented. The crying must be even louder than Stavros thought.

"Yes. Thank you." In a command decision, Stavros snapped Stella's portable car seat out of the base first, then Nicolas's. He handed the first handle to Eleni, who capably slung it over one arm, and the second to his driver.

"We can manage," Holly protested beside him.

"I have someone else to worry about."

"Who could be more important than our babies?"

Stavros looked at his wife. "You."

She blushed, and protested, "I'm fine."

Fine. Stavros shook his head in wonder. Holly had spent most of yesterday, her twenty-ninth birthday, in labor at the hospital, then given birth to twins at two that morning. She should have remained in the hospital for another week, relaxing and ordering food as nurses cared for the newborns. But it was Christmas Eve, and she'd wanted to come home.

"We have to be with Freddie for Christmas, Stavros," she'd insisted. "I want to be in our new home, waking up together on Christmas morning!"

Even though mother and babies were healthy, Stavros had been doubtful they'd be allowed to leave the hospital just twelve hours after delivery. But Holly had been adamant. The instant she'd gotten her doctor's slightly bemused approval, she'd insisted on coming home.

That was his wife, he thought, shaking his head in admiration. Determined their family would be happy, and letting nothing stand in her way.

"Wait," Holly called as Eleni and Colton and Freddie started up the steps of their brownstone. "I can help—"

Now it was Stavros's turn to be adamant. "No, Holly. Be careful!"

"Wait," she cried after her children, pushing herself up from the seat before he saw her flinch and grimace with pain.

Setting his jaw, he lifted her from the SUV in his powerful arms, cradling her against his chest.

"What are you doing?" she gasped.

"Taking care of you."

"It's not necessary—"

"It is," he said firmly. "You look after everyone else. My job—" he looked down at her tenderly "—is looking after you."

And he carried her up the stoop, into their five-story brownstone.

The hardwood floors creaked, gleaming warmly as the fire crackled in the hundred-year-old fireplace. Holly had decorated the house for Christmas with her family's homemade decorations. They hadn't expected the babies to arrive early. They weren't due until January. Although when, he thought ruefully, did any Minoses let other people's expectations stand in their way?

When Holly had gone into labor yesterday, she'd stared at the three stockings on the fireplace with their embroidered names, and cried, "The twins can't be born before Christmas. I haven't made them stockings!"

Now, as Stavros carried his wife past the five stockings hanging on the fireplace, he smiled with pride when he heard her gasp.

"Nicolas… Stella—you got them Christmas stockings!"

Holly looked up at him in shock. "Their names are even embroidered!"

His smile widened to a grin. "Merry Christmas, *agape mou*."

"But—" She looked at him helplessly. "How? You were with me at the hospital the whole time!"

Stavros looked down at her. "I have my ways."

"Santa? Elves?"

Lifting a dark eyebrow, he said loftily, "Call it a Christmas miracle."

She gave him a slow-rising grin. "Oh, was it now?"

"What else could it be?" He gently lowered her to her feet, then looked down at her seriously. "But not as much a miracle as this."

And putting his arms around her, he lowered his head to give his wife a tender kiss, full of love and magic, of sugarplums and sparkling stars.

After a lifetime of being frozen, it had taken a fatal diagnosis to make Stavros open his heart the tiniest crack. In that moment, Holly had gotten inside him, warming his soul with her golden light.

Once, he'd been grimly ready to die. In an unexpected miracle, he hadn't.

But Holly was the one who'd truly brought him to life.

He'd been wrong about love all along, Stavros realized in amazement. Love hadn't conquered him. It had saved him. It had set him free to live a dream greater than any he'd ever imagined. His children. His home. His wife. Especially his wife.

Being loved by Holly was the greatest Christmas miracle of all.

* * * * *